BOUND BY TRADITION,
TEMPTED BY LOVE ...

Where his strong hands clasped her shoulders, it was as if the sun scorched her skin, burning away the layers of clothing. The heady scent of him filled her senses with forbidden thoughts. The broad expanse of his white-clad chest beckoned. She wanted to pillow herself there, to be held tightly in his arms. But from the beginning, this man had been an unwelcome thorn in her side, telling her what to do, challenging her ownership of the land. Rather than wanting to be held in his arms, she should run from him, as fast as her legs could carry her. . . .

BOOK YOUR PLACE ON OUR WEBSITE AND MAKE THE READING CONNECTION!

We've created a customized website just for our very special readers, where you can get the inside scoop on everything that's going on with Zebra, Pinnacle and Kensington books.

When you come online, you'll have the exciting opportunity to:

- View covers of upcoming books
- Read sample chapters
- Learn about our future publishing schedule (listed by publication month *and author*)
- Find out when your favorite authors will be visiting a city near you
- Search for and order backlist books from our online catalog
- Check out author bios and background information
- Send e-mail to your favorite authors
- Meet the Kensington staff online
- Join us in weekly chats with authors, readers and other guests
- Get writing guidelines
- AND MUCH MORE!

**Visit our website at
http://www.zebrabooks.com**

TEMPT FORTUNE

Hebby Roman

Zebra Books
Kensington Publishing Corp.
http://www.zebrabooks.com

ZEBRA BOOKS are published by

Kensington Publishing Corp.
850 Third Avenue
New York, NY 10022

Copyright © 2000 by Hebby Roman

Zebra and the Z logo Reg. U.S. Pat. & TM Off.

First Printing: March, 2000
10 9 8 7 6 5 4 3 2 1

Printed in the United States of America

For my writing buddy and good friend,
Laurie Vanzura,
if it hadn't been for you
I would have given up
and given in!
You're a wonderful writer
and an inspiration
to me.

Chapter One

Key West, Florida
1868

"Three hundred."

"Three hundred and fifty."

Rafael Estava narrowed his eyes and studied the last bidder. Three hundred and fifty was high, even for a barrelful of fine Wedgewood china. Could there be something else hidden in the bottom of the barrel?

"Señor auctioneer." Rafael raised his voice above the buzz of the crowd. "May I have your leave to examine the contents before the bidding continues?"

The florid-faced auctioneer paused in mid-arc, his gavel raised high. Impatience clipped his words when he directed the assistants, "Unload the barrel for Mr. Estava. But have a care! Broken china isn't worth a twopenny."

Stepping forward, Rafael watched as the barrel emptied. The murmur of the crowd grew louder. Like the auctioneer, they were impatient to get on with it.

But as an underwriter's agent, he possessed certain rights, and one of them was the license to examine each item in the wreckers' auction from ships his company had insured. And that particular right had proven effective to further his cause.

Surrounded by heaps of plates and teapots, the two assistants stopped unpacking the barrel when, one third of the way from the bottom, they found a tarpaulin covering the remainder of the contents. Pushing the men aside, Rafael reached into the barrel and jerked the tarp back. Boxes of percussion caps and fuses lay nestled in sawdust at the bottom of the barrel.

Pivoting quickly, he searched the crowd for the last bidder, another Cuban whom he knew only as Cortez. But Cortez was gone, melted into the crowd.

Not surprised, he directed the assistants to upend the barrel. The deadly cargo plopped softly onto the floor of the warehouse. Turning to face the auctioneer, Rafael indicated the secret contents with a sweep of his arm.

The auctioneer's face flushed a deeper shade of red. Scowling, he carried out his duty, instructing the assistants, "Get that contraband out of here. Lock it up until I can advise the magistrate." Turning back to Rafael, he inquired, "Would Mr. Estava care to examine the remainder of the cargo? It seems you have a bloodhound's nose for contraband."

His observation acknowledged Rafael's success at uncovering and stopping contraband armaments from being sold off with the cargo from wreckers' salvage. Rafael realized his success didn't make him popular in Key West. Not with his fellow countrymen or the Americans.

Other Cubans despised him because he interfered with their filibustering activities supporting the revolution at home. The Americans didn't like him meddling with commerce. Seized goods didn't pay taxes or make profits.

Glancing at the remaining crates and barrels heaped beneath the auctioneer's stand, he didn't find anything of interest, neither as an underwriter's agent nor in his other, private capacity.

"Nothing more today, Señor auctioneer. Thank you." He

lifted his wide-brimmed Panama hat. A collective gasp swept the crowd before he replaced it, shadowing his face again. Pushing a path through the throng, he heard the ugly whispers that followed him.

"Look! Did you see his face?"

The promise of freedom had failed her. Instead of giddy excitement, Angelina felt as nervous as a young girl at her first ball. As she glanced around the bustling dock, the ninety miles to Havana stretched into a thousand.

What had she gotten herself into? The people appeared ruddy-faced and impatient, their English-speaking voices strident and shrill to her ears.

The soft lilt of her native Spanish wafted to her on the breeze. When she turned toward the sound, the porter she'd hired bumped into her. Burly and with long mustaches drooping to his chin, he moved with barely controlled ferocity, pushing past her and knocking her baggage against a post.

"Portero, portero, por favor." Stopping herself, she remembered to speak English. "Porter, please, have a care. My mynah bird is—"

But her warning came too late. The cage door sprang open, and a streak of ebony cleaved the brilliant blue sky. Squinting her eyes against the sun, she managed to follow his zigzag path until he disappeared among the flaming blossoms of a mimosa tree.

Dropping her parcels and facing the porter, she controlled her frustration long enough to direct, "Wait for me *here*. Watch my baggage."

The porter called after her, but she'd already sprinted away. Dodging sailors and piles of freight heaped on the wharf, she trained her gaze on the tree ahead, searching for the telltale flash of black against the luxuriant greens and reds.

Heart pounding, she reached the tree and looked up, desperate to find her mynah bird among its feathery-tipped branches. Her tall mantilla snagged on a limb. Yanking it from her head, she muttered, *"¡Madre de Dios!"*

Her pet must have heard her voice because she glimpsed a sudden movement in the tree overhead. He hopped from one limb to the next, clinging precariously with his head tipped to the side. Realizing she'd caught his attention, she knew she must calm him or he would fly away again. The ship's rolling had unsettled her bird, making him cranky and agitated.

Taking a deep breath, she willed her heart to slow. Moving carefully, she tugged open her reticule while murmuring, "Sweet Malvado, beauteous bird. My pet, *mi niño."* Scooping a handful of birdseed, she held out the offering, stretching on tiptoe.

Malvado cocked his head, studying her. His garnet-red eyes sparkled with interest. Or was it with mischief? With Malvado, she couldn't be certain.

Wiggling her fingers, she extended her hand higher, straining upward. Something hit her from behind, upsetting her precarious balance. She landed with an unceremonious thud on her backside. A ball of gray fur hurtled past, hissing and spitting, clawing its way up the tree. Malvado must have realized he was the cat's target because he squawked and flew to a higher branch.

Spanish oaths followed the gray cat, turning the air blue and threatening to singe the fur of the attacker. Jumping to her feet but keeping a string of vituperative words directed upward, Angelina grabbed for the first limb to go after the interfering feline.

"I wouldn't try that in skirts if I were you," a soft drawl declared.

Whirling around, she faced the voice's owner—a red-haired, green-eyed young woman of approximately her same age.

Before she could form a proper answer in English, the green-eyed woman called out, "Tabby, here, kitty. Kitty, kitty, come down." Lifting her arms, she coaxed, "Come to Mommy. Here kitty, kitty."

The gray tabby swiveled her head from side to side, scanning the top of the tree where Malvado had retreated. Either heeding her owner's call or deciding the tasty bird was out of reach, Tabby executed an about-face and daintily picked her way down the tree. When she reached the lowest branch, she stopped and lifted one paw to her mouth. Oblivious to the havoc she'd wrought, the cat began to groom her whiskers.

With an exasperated sigh, the red-haired woman stretched up and gathered Tabby into her arms, stroking the cat's long, smoky-hued fur. "Naughty kitty, knocking over this lady. What were you doing?"

With uncommon forwardness, Angelina placed her hand on the young woman's arm, pleading, "*Señorita*—ah, miss, I need your help. Could you remove the cat and possibly bring a net? Your pet knocked me over to get at my bird, Malvado. He's up there." She pointed to the top of the tree but didn't see the mynah.

Panic froze the blood in her veins as her gaze darted from empty branch to empty branch. Where was Malvado? He was all she had. The only breathing creature who had accompanied her from home.

The red-haired woman lifted her freckled face, inquiring innocently, "Is that your bird, Miss, uh . . ."

Angelina followed her glance and found Malvado perched just above their heads, eyeing them intently. With his yellow bill stretched into a grin, he managed to keep a wary eye on the cat, now curled in her owner's arms and purring like a steamship at full throttle. Afraid to utter a word, Angelina merely nodded and moved away, edging closer to her pet while distancing herself from the furry predator.

Within moments, Angelina had coaxed Malvado into her open hand, and he pecked industriously at the birdseed. Placing her other hand over his back, she grasped him firmly under his wings and breathed a sigh of relief. And she prayed that the fool who had loosed him was waiting on the dock with the cage.

When she started to retrace her steps, she found the cat's owner approaching. The cat was gone, replaced by a fine-meshed net. Offering it, she said, "I thought you might need this."

"Thank you, I have him now. My luggage and his cage are on the dock. You've been very kind, but I think I can manage." Even as she said the words to dismiss her, Angelina was touched by the stranger's concern. She almost wished the cat's owner would stay and acquaint her with the town, although that would be an imposition.

"You have just arrived? From Cuba?" The young woman asked, showing no sign of leaving.

"How did you know?"

Bending to retrieve Angelina's forgotten mantilla, she replied, "From this and your accent. Quite a lot of Cubans are coming to Key West. I believe the revolution is to blame."

The information both reassured and alarmed Angelina. Reassured her that she wouldn't be alone in this strange land. Alarmed her that she might be recognized.

"My name is Destiny Favor." The cat's owner extended her hand in greeting.

Angelina accepted her hand and shook it while her mind raced. Should she offer her real name or change it to avoid recognition? Changing her name might not be such a bad idea. She hated being dishonest, but she didn't want to be recognized, either.

"My name is Angelina Herrera," she said, substituting her mother's maiden name for her surname of Ximenes. Recalling Miss Favor's earlier comment about her accent, she asked, "Do you understand me? Is my English adequate?"

"More than adequate." Miss Favor was quick to offer the compliment. "Your English is perfect, and your accent is so beautiful, Señorita Herrera."

"Thank you, you're very kind. Please call me Angelina." Normally, she wouldn't be so forward as to place them on a first-name basis, but she was uncommonly drawn to this friendly

American. "May I call you by your first name? What did you say it was?"

"It's Destiny."

"Destiny Favor." She tested it, mentally translating the words into Spanish and back again. "A most unusual name. If you take the English meaning for 'destiny' and the meaning for 'favor' and put them together, they mean—"

"Destiny's Favor."

"Yes, that's it. A propitious name, to say the least."

"My father was very superstitious . . . or so I've been told."

Catching the hesitation in Destiny's voice, she felt compelled to inquire, "Your father is—?"

"Yes, he died when I was a baby."

"My sincerest sympathies," she offered, wondering how different her life would have been if her father had died when she was a baby.

Tossing her head as if dismissing the loss, Destiny murmured, "It's all right. I miss having a father, but I never knew him."

Angelina detected a trace of pain in her new friend's voice and guessed there was more to the story than her brave words. Before she could probe further, Destiny pointed. "Are those your things?"

"*Sí.* Yes, those are mine. And that's the fool who crashed open Malvado's cage."

The burly, surly porter awaited them, arms crossed over his ample chest, leaning against the pier piling that had done the damage. As soon as he caught sight of her, he started forward, declaring insolently, "This waiting will cost you. You'll have to pay extra."

She drew herself up to her fullest height and faced the man. Never again would she allow herself to be intimidated by a man . . . any man.

"I refuse to pay. It was your careless incompetence that caused the trouble in the first place. If you hadn't bumped the cage against the pier—"

Destiny interrupted by tugging at her sleeve and whispering,

"Don't. It's not worth the trouble." She reached into her reticule and drew forth some coins. "Let me pay. After all, it was my cat who compounded your problem."

"I can't allow you."

"I insist."

Their gazes locked.

Sensing that her will was stronger than Destiny's and feeling honor bound not to pay the awful porter one extra *centavo,* she silently battled with her newfound friend. To her amazement, she was the one who dropped her eyes and shrugged. Destiny might not be as strong-willed as she was, but her openhearted kindness was disarming.

After Destiny paid the porter, they secured Malvado in his cage. Arm in arm, with the porter trailing behind, they started for town.

"Do you have lodgings?" Destiny inquired.

"No. I would appreciate it if you would show me the best boardinghouse in town."

"Nonsense, you'll stay with us."

"I couldn't impose."

"But I want you to stay with us. Gramps's house is big and lonely. He won't mind. You'll see."

What a generous invitation. Never had she met such openness and honesty. In her country, words were used as tools or weapons. Insincere flattery was the custom, the sly innuendo second nature. Her new friend intrigued her; she was so guileless and naive.

"Perhaps for tonight," she acquiesced, "until I become acquainted with the town. I appreciate the offer. It's most kind of you."

"It's nothing." Destiny waved her hand. "I like you. You're easy to talk to. But I want you to stay longer than one night."

Angelina noticed that Destiny hadn't mentioned a mother, either, only someone named "Gramps," probably her grandfather. No wonder she had said it was lonely at home. To

Angelina, who had been raised in a large, extended family, such a home life was almost impossible to imagine.

"I'm curious about your bird's name," Destiny interrupted her thoughts. "I know some Spanish, and I was wondering if there is an English translation for Malvado?"

Unable to suppress a smile, she nodded. "Oh, yes, there's a translation. Malvado means Wicked One."

"¡Maldita sea! ¡Coño! ¡Perdición!"

Destiny's eyes popped open at the raucous clamor. She didn't know much Spanish, but she knew enough to recognize that the words coming from the balcony weren't ones to drop at the next tea party she attended. Throwing the covers back, she grabbed her wrapper and thrust her arms through the sleeves, belting it as she ran.

What could be the trouble?

When she reached the balcony, she found the awful sounds emanating from the draped cage of Malvado. No cats threatened, and there was no one around. It was early-morning peaceful, except for Malvado's indecent shrieking.

Jerking back the cover, she peered at the bird.

His garnet eyes glistened back. His yellow bill snapped shut. After a moment, he crooned, *"Mujer preciosa, mujer preciosa."*

"He's thanking you for taking his cover off."

She turned to find Angelina standing behind her, rubbing sleepy eyes with her knuckles. "I usually rise at dawn and uncover him." She yawned. "The voyage must have tired me more than I realized. Thank you for attending to him."

"What was he saying?"

Angelina smiled. "Before or after you uncovered him?"

"Both, although I don't think I want a literal translation of the 'before.' "

"You understand more Spanish than you think," Angelina

observed wryly, shaking her finger at her pet. "Naughty bird, to scare Destiny awake.

"That's why I named him Malvado, the wicked one," she explained. "The 'before' was . . . how would you say . . . not nice words. The 'after' was his way of thanking you. He called you a beautiful lady. It's all he knows to say, words not so nice and 'beautiful lady.' " She shrugged. "I've tried to teach him other words, but he refuses to repeat them. He must have learned the 'before' words from the servants."

Amazed at Angelina's ingenious answer, Destiny couldn't help but remember the "before" words that had sprayed the air yesterday when Tabby had taken after Malvado. Was her newfound friend completely oblivious to her own verbal indiscretions? It was on the tip of her tongue to remind Angelina of the incident, but wisdom prevailed. She didn't want to ruin their budding friendship.

She was often indiscreet, too, not with improper language, but with saying the wrong things at the wrong times. Even the fancy finishing school in Charleston, where Gramps had sent her, hadn't completely tamed her tongue. But she continued to work on that flaw and her general deportment. It was important to cultivate genteel manners if she wanted to realize her dream.

Her stomach growled, recalling her wandering thoughts. From the balcony, she judged the ascent of the morning sun in the eastern sky. Gramps's house stood on the corner of Caroline and Elizabeth Streets, facing west to the harbor. Her bedroom was at the back of the house, and based on the sun's position, Tilly should already have brought their breakfast.

As if in answer to her thoughts, there was a knock on the door and Tilly entered the room, carrying a large tray. "Ah sees y'all is up. I fetched your breckfus'," she offered without preamble. "Sit y'selves right 'ere on the balcony and Ah serves you."

"Thank you, Tilly. I'm famished. Are you hungry, Angelina?"

"Yes, thank you."

"Dat's 'cause y'all din't eat 'ardly nuffin' las' night."

"We were too tired and excited. You know I love your conch stew, but last night we were busy getting acquainted," Destiny apologized in her most placating voice.

Tilly merely muttered, "Hummph," and continued setting the table.

"Has Gramps returned from the wreck?"

"Not yet, but I 'spects 'im back soon and roarin' for 'is breckfus'."

Destiny smiled at Tilly's prediction. Gramps, who styled himself a "retired" wrecker, still kept a ready schooner and full crew. As opposed to "active" wreckers, he didn't send his crew scouring the Florida coast for salvageable wrecks, but kept close to home. Yesterday, there had been a wreck off Alligator Reef, and her grandfather had answered the siren call of "Wreck Ashore!"

At first, she'd been disappointed that he wasn't home to meet Angelina. Upon further reflection, she realized his absence made things easier.

Gramps, who possessed a heart as big as Lake Okeechobee, could be a trifle irascible about strangers. He kept mostly to himself, seldom socializing in the close-knit society of Key West. Her grandfather had become reclusive when his only child, Destiny's mother, had died. And with the passing of his wife, Destiny's grandmother, he'd all but embraced the life of a hermit.

She sighed, wishing for the thousandth time that she had a proper family who held social gatherings. It would make her plans so much easier.

Seating herself across from Angelina, she unfolded her napkin and surveyed the table. As usual, Tilly had forgotten nothing, from crusty biscuits to a steaming pot of coffee.

She smiled at Tilly, inquiring, "Have you eaten? Are you going to join us?" From the corner of her eye, she glimpsed Angelina's startled reaction to her unconventional invitation. If Angelina was going to stay with them, as she hoped she would, it would be better if her new friend understood her unusual family.

"Laws, chile, I 'ad mah breckfus' hours ago." Tilly folded her arms across her chest. "You knows Ah'm an early riser. An' Ah gots lots to do. Do y'all 'ave eve'ythin' y'all needs?"

"Angelina, do you require anything else? Some cocoa or tea? Or will coffee do?"

"No, this will be fine." Angelina smiled at the servant. "Thank you, Tilly. I hope you don't mind if I feed some of this fruit to Malvado. I didn't bring anything but birdseed. He loves fruit."

Tilly cast a wary eye at Malvado and muttered something under her breath that sounded suspiciously like "bird of doom." Aloud she offered, "You's Miz Destiny's guest. Y'all's welcome to what we's got, you and your bird." Nodding her turbaned head, she said, "Ah wishes y'all a good mornin'."

"Thank you, Tilly," Destiny echoed Angelina.

The bedroom door had barely shut before Angelina asked, "Your Tilly is more than a servant?"

"My mother died when I was three years old. Tilly raised me as if I were her own. I love her like a mother."

"She is free now—your civil war freed the slaves?"

"Tilly was free from the day she came here, before I was born. It's true Gramps bought her at auction, but then he freed her, asking only that she stay as a servant for one year. He did the same thing for Rufus, our manservant."

"That's unusual. I thought southern Americans clung to slavery."

"Not all southern Americans. Gramps's family is from South Carolina, but they weren't planters. His family followed the sea. When he saw, firsthand, the cruelty on slave ships, he learned to abhor slavery. He refused to own slaves long before the Civil War."

"I don't approve of slavery, either," Angelina declared while buttering a biscuit. "It's one of the issues in my country's rebellion against Spain. Forward-thinking Cubanos want to free the slaves, but the Spanish won't allow it.''

Destiny nodded and cut a slice of smoked ham, chewing it slowly, waiting for Angelina to continue about her country, curious to learn more. But Angelina veered from the subject, inquiring instead, ''Have you thought about that boarding-house? If you don't mind, I would like to find lodgings after breakfast.''

Reaching across the table, Destiny placed her hand on Angelina's arm, coaxing, ''Please, stay with us. You've seen the house. We've plenty of room.''

Hesitant to pry into her new friend's private affairs, but possessed by an overpowering curiosity, she ventured, ''I know it's none of my business, but isn't it unusual for a young lady to arrive in a new country without a companion? Won't it ruin your reputation to stay at a boardinghouse alone? Will someone be joining you from home?''

Angelina lifted her head and regarded Destiny, hesitating as if weighing her answer. Destiny feared she might have offended her, but then Angelina lowered her eyes and patted her hand.

''You're so kind and hospitable, Destiny, but also very curious. I wonder.'' She paused and pursed her lips. Shaking her head as if deciding against her first inclination, she admitted, ''It *is* scandalous to travel alone. My maid was to have accompanied me, but she panicked at the last minute and refused to leave Cuba.''

Lifting her shoulders, she said, ''There was no going back for me. I had to come, so I came alone. As for scandal . . .'' She waved her long, slender fingers in airy dismissal. ''I don't give a fig for scandal.''

Destiny gasped.

She doesn't care about scandal? The thought shocked and amazed her at the same time. All properly bred young ladies cared about scandal, and Angelina was obviously well bred. The Cuban ladies she knew were even more careful of their reputations than their American counterparts.

"But you'll never marry if you don't care about scandal!" She couldn't stop from blurting. As soon as the words had left her mouth, she wanted to bite her tongue.

Again, her new friend didn't take offense, answering calmly, "I don't want to marry. Not now or ever."

"What? Not marry!"

"Don't be so shocked. Not all women marry."

"Yes, but . . ." She didn't know what to say. She'd never met a single woman who didn't yearn for marriage.

"I refuse to give a man control over my life," Angelina declared. "I will live my own life as I see fit. It is my own private rebellion." Her tone of voice was determined.

But Destiny thought she detected a note of rancor, as if Angelina had been hurt. What man in his right mind would harm a hair on her beautiful head? Gazing at her Cuban friend across the breakfast table, she found it hard to believe that a woman so lovely would eschew men and marriage.

Her own red-haired, freckled looks faded against the dramatic backdrop of Angelina's dark beauty. With long black hair that flowed past her waist and exotic, violet-colored eyes, she was an open invitation to love. Not many men Destiny knew could resist such enticements.

"I bet you wed before I do, Angelina. And I'm *looking* for a husband," she added wistfully.

The Cuban beauty arched an eyebrow, countering in confident tones, "And I wager you marry before I. What's the prize to be?"

Surprised that Angelina had taken her words seriously, she couldn't help but think how unconventional their behavior was. Proper young ladies didn't place wagers or bets. Such activities were reserved for men only. Weren't they?

"Why do you hesitate? Afraid you'll lose?" Angelina taunted.

"It's not that. It's just . . ." But the more she thought about it, the more the idea appealed to her. It might be fun. It certainly carried the taint of the illicit, and she wasn't one to back down from a dare.

A wager . . . a wedding wager. She searched her mind for an appropriate prize. Snapping her fingers, she had it. The perfect prize.

"A bolt of the finest Brussels lace to be used for a wedding veil."

"Done." Angelina reached her hand across the table.

Destiny clasped her hand, sealing their wager. "Done."

Chapter Two

After breakfast, instead of seeking lodgings, they'd gone to see Angelina's land. Destiny had convinced her to stay, at least until Angelina met her grandfather. For Angelina, it was only common courtesy; she'd availed herself of the man's hospitality, so the least she could do was be introduced to him.

"Your aunt left you this land?" Destiny inquired. They stood on Frances Street, and behind the indicated site stretched a low, muddy swamp.

"Yes, it was hers from an old grant of her father's. I was her favorite niece." She didn't bother to mention that she was her aunt's *only* niece. What did it matter? She owned the land, and it offered her freedom. "I know it doesn't look like much," she admitted. She strode forward, testing the solidness of the plot with each step. "But it will do for my purposes."

"You'll die of fever in the summer here. The malodorous airs come from the swamps, you know."

"Then I'll be in Europe when the fever time comes."

"What?"

Halting her exploration, Angelina faced Destiny. "I don't plan on living here. I plan on building my factory here."

"Your what?"

Angelina found herself savoring each new shock she sent her friend. Destiny was even more conventional than she'd been while growing up. And Destiny wasn't that much younger than she was, possibly a year or two. But she felt a thousand years older than her friend.

At the same time, she experienced a twinge of conscience at shocking Destiny. Why didn't she explain herself? Because she was distrustful by nature or because her family had shattered her trust forever? Even if she did explain, could she trust Destiny with her secret? Destiny of the open nature and quick tongue?

Civility bade her to quit leading her new friend on. *Either explain or concoct some story,* she silently chided herself. To hurt Destiny was inconceivable.

But something held her back. She wasn't ready to open herself. Wanting to postpone the inevitable, she changed the subject, observing, "It's getting awfully hot, and I feel as if we ate breakfast yesterday. Could we talk at your home over luncheon? I hope to meet your grandfather too."

Destiny smiled. "I'll go to the corner of Fleming Street and fetch a carriage. I'll just be a minute." Turning, she crossed to the street, leaving Angelina before she could protest.

Her sense of guilt deepened at Destiny's accommodating nature. She had been the one who had dismissed the hired carriage, saying she wanted to spend time looking over the property.

She'd been surprised to learn that Destiny and her grandfather walked to most places on the island. They didn't own a carriage or horses. And despite the numerous rooms and lavish appointments of their home, they kept only two servants, living quite frugally. It was very different from her own home with its numerous servants and large family.

There would be more surprises in store for her, she realized. Key West and its American inhabitants were proving to be quite an experience. Even the food was different, although Tilly's flaky biscuits were a culinary delight she hadn't minded discovering.

"I've had my eye on this land for some time. I didn't know there was another interested buyer." A deep male voice rumbled from behind her.

Surprised by the unexpected intrusion, she turned to find a man standing on the rough planking bordering the street. He wore a white linen suit, a cream-colored shirt, and an unusually large Panama hat, pulled low. With the hat shading his face against the brilliance of the midday sun, his features were hidden from her.

He stood with his legs spread and hands on his hips, and she found something strangely familiar in his stance. At the same time, he alarmed her, appearing so precipitously from nowhere. And the soft lilt to his voice? Could she have mistaken it?

"*Yo soy Cubana,*" she ventured.

"I'm Cuban also," he answered in English.

She found his answer odd. Expecting to meet other Cubans in Key West, she had anticipated lapsing into her native tongue. If he was Cuban, why was he speaking English?

Uncomfortable in the stranger's presence, she glanced down the street, hoping to see Destiny returning with a hired carriage, but the street was empty.

"English is the native tongue here. You need to speak it, if you want to survive." He seemed to have read her thoughts.

Drawing herself up to her fullest height, she belatedly wished she'd worn her mantilla for today's outing; her customary headdress made her appear taller and more unapproachable.

"I speak beautiful English and am staying with an American family," she defended herself.

"That's good. If you come here, you must adapt."

Who was he? Better still, who did he *think* he was, to tell her how to behave? Another man trying to order her life? She wouldn't stand for it.

Itching to take him down a notch or two, she went on the offensive. "You mentioned you're interested in this land. Don't be. It belongs to me."

"Really," he drawled. Slowly, he removed his gloves, finger by finger. "The authorities told me title to this land is in dispute."

"No longer. It's mine," she trumpeted.

"Really," he repeated insouciantly.

She stared at him, purposely looking down her nose, hoping to intimidate him with a haughty attitude. But when he shifted his booted feet, she glimpsed the bunching of his thigh muscles beneath the white linen. The width of his shoulders seemed to fill the horizon. The sight made her feel weak inside.

Despising herself for responding to his obvious masculine attributes, she countered, "The authorities told you the title was in dispute because it's an original Spanish grant, and no one has laid claim to it."

"Or the back taxes," he shot back.

"I will pay the taxes."

"And do what?"

"I don't think that's any of your business."

A clattering filled the street. Lifting her gaze from the annoying stranger, she found Destiny hurtling toward them in an open carriage. Relieved, she gathered her skirts and swept past him, purposely murmuring, *"Con permiso,"* hoping to pique him by speaking the Spanish he'd so officiously banned.

He ignored her sortie, stepping forward and stopping the hired carriage with an uplifted hand. When the vehicle drew to a halt in a swirl of dust, he moved to her side and offered his assistance.

She didn't want his help, and his nearness disconcerted her. He smelled of sandalwood with an underlying earthy aroma that hinted of the man himself. She could feel the heat from his body radiating through his clothes. The breadth of his chest blocked her access to the carriage, calling further attention to his magnificent physique.

Dropping her eyes, she avoided looking at him and concentrated on his outstretched hand. It was the hand of a gentleman, with long, tapering fingers ending in clean, square-cut nails. Wanting to refuse his offer but not knowing how, she placed her gloved hand in his bare one. His hand closed over hers with surprising strength.

The moment of their touching lengthened and grew. It was as if the sun had stopped in the sky, and the world had stilled. Something stirred within her, a feeling both new and wonderful, like a baby being born. Suddenly, instead of wanting to avoid him, she wanted the moment to last forever. But it was he who broke the spell by boosting her up and releasing her as soon as she found her seat in the carriage.

Disturbed by her reaction to him, she nodded her thanks in his general direction. Perched upon the carriage seat, she leaned forward, urging, "Please, drive on."

Destiny thwarted her escape by contradicting, "Wait, driver."

Nudging Angelina, she whispered, "Who is he? You're not going to introduce us?" Beneath the slow drawl of her friend's voice, she detected a hint of offended impropriety.

"I don't know his name. He didn't introduce himself," she whispered back from between clenched teeth.

Despite their lowered voices, he must have overheard because he said, "Please excuse me. My manners have been sorely lacking. I should introduce myself. My name is Rafael Estava." Moving closer, he inquired, "To whom do I have the pleasure of addressing myself?"

"I'm Destiny Favor, and this is my friend, Angelina Herrera." Destiny's natural friendliness surfaced, relieving Angelina from answering. "We're pleased to meet you."

"Not as pleased as I am to make the acquaintance of two such lovely ladies." He bowed low and swept the wide-brimmed hat from his head, straightening slowly.

Destiny gasped. Angelina gulped and stared, managing to hold her breath.

The right side of his face was distorted, twisted and criss-crossed by hideous scars. His right eye dipped low in his face, tugged downward by the disfiguration. But his full lips were perfect, rugged and sculpted, as if by a master's touch. With his square chin framed by long dark-brown curls, he could have been a very handsome man.

Angelina's gaze met his. His cinnamon-colored eyes appeared to stare straight through her, filled with a strange kind of knowing, almost anticipation. Knowing what? What her startled reaction to his face might be? Or was it something else? Could he have recognized her? Did he know her? But she would have remembered him, if they'd ever met. Who could forget him?

A small shudder shook her, thinking of the awful burden his disfigurement must be. Even as she pitied him, she couldn't help but notice that, like the way he stood, there was something vaguely familiar about the curvature of his lips. The hazy recognition bothered her, and she wondered if she were doomed to spend her life fearing discovery. Suddenly, the ninety miles to Havana wasn't nearly far enough.

She had known another Rafael, but that was a long time ago. His surname hadn't been Estava—not even his mother's maiden name had been Estava, she thought wryly, remembering her own duplicity.

The taut silence hummed with unspoken thoughts. Even her talkative friend appeared to be at a loss for words. After all, what more was there to say?

Gathering her inbred courtesy like a cloak, she managed, *"Buenas tardes,* Señor Estava."

"Yes, good afternoon, pleased to meet you, Señor Estava," Destiny echoed.

As if on cue, the driver whipped the horse, and they drove away. But something made Angelina look back. Something indefinable and haunting.

He stood in the middle of the rutted street. The wide-brimmed hat shaded his scarred face again, and the perfectly fitted white suit displayed his strong, male body.

A feeling of premonition pricked her, raising the hairs on the back of her neck. She knew him. She couldn't say where or how, but she knew him.

Skirting the waterfront in the hired hack, Destiny spied the square-rigged masts of her grandfather's schooner. With the gangplank lowered, sailors and dockhands scurried like ants up and down the ramp, unloading a variety of crates and barrels. Destiny glanced at the sun. It was well past noon. The wreck must have proven difficult to salvage.

Her heart skipped a beat and tripped faster. Where was Gramps? Each time he went to sea, she worried. The sea was dangerous; it had taken her father's life. Scanning the dock, relief washed over her when she spotted his battered, blue sailor's cap bobbing among the milling crowd.

"There's Gramps," she told Angelina.

Leaning forward, she ordered, "Driver, stop." Turning to her companion, she said, "I'll just be a minute. Let me get Gramps. I can't wait for him to meet you."

Angelina murmured something about not bothering her grandfather right now because he looked busy. But Destiny was too excited to wait. Jumping from the carriage, she fixed her attention on his cap and made steady progress toward it. Grabbing him from behind, she cried, "Oh, Gramps, I'm so glad you're back! I was worried about you."

Her grandfather chuckled and twisted around to face her. Sweeping her up in a tight hug, she felt the power in his short arms. Descended from hearty Scottish stock, he boasted broad shoulders and a barrel chest. His mane of white hair fell to the threadbare collar of his captain's coat.

His voice still held the faintest Scottish burr. "Ye shouldna worried, lass. Don't I always come home to ye?"

"Yes, you do, but . . ."

She knew he was an accomplished sailor, having been raised on the sea. But she couldn't shake the image of her mother waiting for her father, who never returned. It was the only enduring image she had of her mother—pacing the widow's walk on top of Gramps's house.

"Ye canna get rid of me so easily." Winking, he added, "We made a good haul too."

"You were gone longer than usual."

"Aye, it was a difficult wreck, one of those crackerbox steamships." Her grandfather had nothing but contempt for steamships, declaring them, despite their speed and efficiency, unnatural beasts, belching smoke and fire.

"She was built from cheap wood, and she broke up on the reef like a rotten egg. We had to dive for most of the cargo. That's what took so long."

Nodding, Destiny knew she should stop him before he got started on the wreck. Wrecking was his only passion these days, and when he returned from a successful salvage, he could talk for hours about it.

"Gramps, I have a surprise. I've invited someone to stay with us. She spent last night at our home. I want you to meet her."

Her grandfather checked his rolling sailor's gait and stared at her as if she'd gone mad. "Lass, ye know I don't like guests. I'm too old—"

"Not too old to go wrecking," she interrupted pointedly.

"Aye, but that's different. That's a living."

"Gramps, you can't fool me. I know you don't need the money."

His weathered blue eyes searched her face, as if he were surprised she knew so much about their finances. Finally, he puffed out his cheeks and loosed a long breath. "Aye, that's true. But I'm not partial to guests. Ye know that."

"I know, Gramps, but it's so lonely in the big house. She's close to my age and I like her."

"Do I know her? Do I know her family?"

"Of course not. She just arrived in Key West yesterday. She's from Cuba, but she speaks the most beautiful English. Her name is Angelina Herrera."

"Ye've brought a stranger to live with us?" he reproved her, his voice uncommonly harsh.

"I had to. She was all alone, and Tabby chased Malvado up the tree, causing Angelina the worst distress. It was the only decent thing—"

He held up his hand to stop her disjointed outpouring, his brow creased in bewilderment. She realized her tongue had gotten away with her again and that her explanation sounded like the driveling of a crackpot. Taking a deep breath, she decided to start at the beginning.

Before she could explain, he said, "I don't mind her being foreign, but I don't hold with Papists. She's a Papist, isn't she?"

"I guess so," she sputtered, surprised by his question. She'd never heard Gramps utter a prejudiced word before—against anyone. "I didn't realize her religion was important." Her grandfather had raised her to be a strict Presbyterian, like all of his family, but she'd never known him to be impassioned about his faith.

"It's not about religion. It's their unholy allegiance to the Pope," he muttered darkly. "It's not natural."

She knew her mouth was open and ripe for catching flies, but she couldn't help herself. This was a side of her grandfather she hadn't seen before.

"Quit gaping at me, lass. It's not becoming."

Snapping her mouth shut, she coaxed, "Gramps, I *want* Angelina to stay with us. It would mean so much to me. What does her religion matter if she's a good person?" Her eyes stung, but she managed to hold back the tears. She didn't want her grandfather to think she would use tears to soften him.

He met her gaze and shook his head. "It shouldna matter. Forgive me." His eyes, although staring directly into her own, appeared to be looking at something far away, as if beholding a distant horizon.

Dropping his hand, he relented. "Since it means so much to ye, I'll welcome her to our home. She may stay as long as she likes."

"Oh, thank you, Gramps." Throwing her arms around his neck, she hugged him again and swallowed the lump in her throat. She was surprised by her emotional reaction, surprised to realize that Angelina meant so much to her after such a short acquaintance. But it had been a long time since she'd had a friend close to her own age.

"There, there, lass," he intoned softly, patting her back before releasing her. "Let's not keep the lady waiting. I want to be properly introduced to your new friend."

Rafael made his way to the waterfront, knowing a new cargo of goods had arrived. Old Man McEwen had gone out the day before and now his schooner had returned.

It was Rafael's custom to inspect the cargo before it was logged by the officials and stored away for future auction. He'd found a casual survey, before the officials got hold of it, often lent him clues about possible contraband. But the excitement of uncovering contraband deserted him when he spied Angelina again, sitting alone in the hired hack.

Little Angelita Ximenes in Key West. Who would have expected it? He'd been shocked to find her pacing the empty lot on Frances Street, recognizing her instantly, even after all the time that had passed since he'd seen her last.

He'd kept the recognition to himself, wondering if she would remember him. But it had been obvious that she didn't recognize him. He'd been confounded when her friend had introduced her as Angelina Herrera.

What was she doing in Key West, laying claim to land? And why was she using her mother's maiden name? The double mystery intrigued him.

She'd mentioned she was staying with an American family, and he'd met her friend, Miss Favor, but that connection only puzzled him further. Knowing her father the way he did, he would have wagered that Señor Ximenes would die of apoplexy before allowing his only daughter to stay with an American family.

He hadn't seen her in over twelve years, not since he went away to school in Spain. She'd been but a child then. Upon his return to Cuba, he'd gone to her home and asked for her, but her father had refused him admittance. Señor Ximenes had his sights set higher than his own merchant class, the same class as Rafael's family. Rumor had it that he was saving his beautiful daughter for an important marriage into the sugar aristocracy of the island.

Stepping into the shadow of the schooner, he paused to observe her. She'd surpassed the promise of her childhood beauty. Her masses of midnight hair, swept up in an elaborate coiffure, begged to be unleashed. He closed his eyes, imagining the feel of it tumbling down her back in long, silky waves. The thought made his groin tighten, an unusual occurrence. He'd believed himself beyond the passions of the flesh, that they'd been purged from him, burned into cinders . . . like his face.

His eyes opened slowly. Angelina's head swiveled from side to side, taking in the bustling dock. She'd always had a lively mind and a quick wit. Curiosity shone in her eyes, eyes the color of a sultry summer twilight.

High cheekbones and a patrician brow provided the perfect frame for her exotic eyes. But if they were the window to her soul, reflecting her intelligence, her mouth was purely erotic, an invitation to her body. Full and enticing, with a bottom lip that almost pouted in its abundance, it made him want—

Sharp-toothed reality intruded, shredding his daydreams. He laughed out loud, a hoarse bark laced with self-loathing. The beautiful woman Angelina had become would never allow him to kiss her. She would turn away in disgust. If he revealed who he was, he had no doubt that Angelita, the friend of his youth, would welcome him with open arms. But her embrace would be filled with pity.

He didn't want her or her pity. He didn't want anyone. That was the secret to life, he'd discovered. Don't care about anyone, and you can't be hurt. His philosophy had served him well, and he didn't intend to tempt fate again.

But he couldn't help being drawn to her. She reminded him of happier times, bittersweet memories of laughter and innocent play.

She pulled at him, like a magnet tugging north. He gave in to that need, telling himself it might be amusing to confirm his suspicion that she'd run away from the constricting confines of her family.

With that thought in mind, he sauntered forward, greeting her with, ''Señorita Herrera, we meet again and so soon. How fortunate.''

When she realized who was speaking to her, she flinched and retreated to the far side of the carriage. Despite the iron self-control he exercised over himself, her reaction knifed his guts, making him want to run and hide in the shadows. But he forced himself to remain.

''Señor Estava, I'm honored.'' Her words belied her physical reaction.

''I was thinking about home after meeting you,'' he remarked. ''Are you from Havana? I know several Herreras there. I might know your family.'' He was gratified to see her start at his question. Her brow creased. She was obviously searching for some way to deflect him.

''I'm not from Havana,'' she replied haughtily. ''I come from Santo Esteban in the interior. I doubt you know my family.''

Clever. He had to give her that. She was clever to come up with such a quick response.

''Still, you're familiar to me. You must have relatives in the capital. I feel that we've met before. Herrera is your surname, not your mother's name. Isn't it?''

Her violet eyes went wide, and her face paled. Was his

pointed question too direct? Had he revealed knowledge that was too intimate, leading her to guess who he was? Or was she merely afraid of having her identity revealed?

She shook her head and turned her face away, ending their conversation. It was strangely reassuring to him that she'd been unable to bring herself to *say* the lie.

Suddenly, the game didn't amuse him. He could find no pleasure in frightening her or forcing her to lie. He didn't want her to uncover his identity, just as she didn't want hers revealed. He'd made a foolish mistake, allowing his emotions to take over, wanting to talk with her. He should have left well enough alone. The past was dead, buried, and best forgotten.

Both he and Angelina were fugitives, hiding their identities, attempting a new life. If he valued her as an old friend, the least he could do was honor her privacy.

"I apologize if I've offended you with my forwardness. I realize I must have been mistaken. Good afternoon, Señorita Herrera." He bowed.

Before he could withdraw, he heard voices behind him and found Captain McEwen and Angelina's American companion, Miss Favor, barring his escape.

Tipping his hat, he continued on his way, but Miss Favor caught his arm, offering, "Señor Estava, please allow me to introduce my grandfather, Captain McEwen."

Now he understood what had kept Angelina on the dock. He knew McEwen by reputation, but he'd never been introduced to him. The captain was Miss Favor's grandfather. He hadn't realized the connection before.

Captain McEwen enfolded his hand in a hearty shake, declaring, "Pleased to make your acquaintance, Señor Estava."

"And this is Señorita Herrera, Grandfather."

Angelina extended her gloved hand, clasping the captain's broad paw. "I've looked forward to meeting you, *señor*. I would be honored if you would call me Angelina."

"Miss Herrera—ah, Miss Angelina, forgive an old salt, but

it might take some time for me to address ye by yer given name.''

''I understand, *capitán.* I am a stranger to you. I have tried to explain to your granddaughter that it might be better if I found other lodgings, but she—''

''I wouldna hear of it, Miss Angelina,'' he interrupted. ''No, ma'am, ye must stay with us.''

Rafael felt like an eavesdropper to their conversation. But what he'd heard only confirmed his suspicion that Angelina had escaped to Key West in a desperate attempt to free herself from her family.

Bowing low, he tried to withdraw again. ''Miss Favor, Señorita Herrera, and Capitán McEwen, if you'll excuse me, I have business to attend—''

Both Destiny and Angelina inclined their heads in polite acceptance, but Captain McEwen stopped him with, ''Wait a minute, Señor Estava.''

Gripping his arm, the captain led him a few paces away, admitting, ''I've heard about ye. Ye've built quite a reputation for yerself. I've wanted to talk to ye for some time.''

Intrigued by McEwen's reference to his reputation, Rafael allowed himself to be drawn aside before asking, ''Yes? How can I be of service?''

The captain countered with his own question, indicating the cargo he'd salvaged with a broad sweep of his arm. ''A fair haul, wouldna ye say? As an underwriter, I mean.''

Dutifully, Rafael followed his gesture, confirming, ''Yes, a good salvage.''

''And an honest one.'' Captain McEwen's blue eyes glittered in his face.

''Pardon me, *señor,* what do you mean by that?''

''No Cortez at the site. No cry of misleading lights in the night. Do ye get my drift, lad?''

''Yes, I understand.''

''Good. I thought ye might want to know.''

* * *

Captain Nathan Rodgers, commander of the Navy's revenue cutter *Columbia,* leapt ashore as soon as the gangplank touched the dock. If he hurried, he might catch Captain McEwen still unloading his salvage. McEwen, being semi-retired, didn't often bring in a wreck, and this was a golden opportunity to question him.

Captain McEwen's reputation was impeccable. He was known as a gentleman of the "old order," honest and upright to a flaw. If there had been anything suspicious about this wreck, McEwen would tell him.

Spotting the captain talking to a man in a wide-brimmed Panama hat, he pushed his way through the throng on the dock. When he reached the two men, he stood a few paces to one side, waiting for them to finish their conversation.

McEwen must have noticed him because he hailed him with, "Captain Rodgers, glad to see ye. I would have been looking for ye shortly. As fates would have it, ye found me. And I've someone I want ye to meet, too."

Nathan started forward, his hand outstretched, first shaking McEwen's hand and greeting him. "Glad to see you, captain." Turning to the stranger and taking his hand, he offered, "I'm Captain Rodgers. Honored to meet you, sir."

"Rafael Estava," the stranger replied, grasping his hand in a steely grip.

"I've heard of you, sir. It's a pleasure to finally meet you, Señor Estava," Nathan declared. And he *had* heard a great deal about Estava, none of which added up, to his way of thinking.

Estava was a mystery, and Nathan didn't care for mysteries, particularly in his jurisdiction. As a Cuban who wasn't caught up in the filibustering fever, Estava was unpopular with both Cubans and Americans alike. Most Americans in Key West were sympathetic to the revolutionary cause of the Cubans.

Unfortunately, most of the revolutionary activities, while

tolerated by the locals, weren't strictly legal. As a captain in the United States Navy, Nathan was bound to uphold the law, popular or not. Even though Estava's efforts helped to make his job easier, he didn't trust the Cuban.

Flashing perfect teeth, Estava smiled. "I've also wanted to meet you, *capitán.*"

It took all of Nathan's force of will to not stare at Estava. Along with his reputation for finding smuggled armaments, he'd heard about the man's scarred face. He managed to keep his attention on Estava's dazzling smile because he sensed the man would scorn pity. And he hated to admit it, even to himself, but confronting Estava's disfigurement made him feel silly and vain, concerned as he was about his own thinning hairline.

Dismissing Estava with a nod, he faced McEwen. "I'd like to have a few words with you, if I may."

"Go ahead, lad."

"Privately, sir." He cast a sidelong glance at the Cuban.

Regarding him with a reproachful look, Captain McEwen countered, "Come to my house later then."

McEwen's quiet rebuke made him feel like an awkward youth, but he refused to discuss confidential naval business in front of an unknown quantity like Estava. He was a blunt man of few words. Parlor manners weren't his forte.

"Gentlemen, glad to have met you both," Estava interjected, tipping his hat. "If you'll excuse me, I have an appointment."

Captain McEwen nodded and shook Estava's hand. Nathan snapped his heels together and bowed. "My compliments, Señor Estava."

"There goes a gentleman," McEwen observed.

"Yes, it was good of him to pick up the hint and—"

"Hint? A sledgehammer is more delicate than ye, sir."

Embarrassed, Nathan shuffled his feet, not knowing what to say.

"Ye might not trust him, but I do. What's this pressing private business?"

"It's about the wreck you salvaged. Was it a good haul?"

"Aye, a bit difficult to retrieve but well worth it."

"Anything unusual about this wreck?"

"No, Alligator Reef got her. If ye've any pull with the government, ye might want to remind them of their promise to put a lighthouse on that reef. The currents are treacherous there."

"It's not common knowledge, sir, but I can confide in you. The next lighthouse to be built *will* be on Alligator Reef."

"That's fine. Not that I don't like a good wreck now and then, to keep me hand in, but the government should safeguard the shipping lanes."

"I agree." Nathan paused, wondering how to continue. McEwen hadn't risen to the bait of his first probe. Now it was time to get specific. He was a straightforward man, and he didn't like beating about the bush.

"The crew of the wreck—did they mention anything unusual, such as lights that led them astray onto the reef? Did you notice anything amiss? Anything that might smell of foul play?"

He would be questioning the steamer's captain shortly, but he trusted few men. The stories about captains of vessels purposely wrecking their own ships in a conspiracy with others for gain were legion in Key West. But he knew McEwen to be above reproach, and he valued the older man's knowledge of ships and the sea.

"Nay. As I was telling Señor Estava earlier, it was a clean wreck. A joy to salvage, despite the diving. I don't like dirty tricks, either. If there had been any, ye'd be the first to know. I was coming to tell ye just that."

"Thank you, sir, I appreciate your opinion. You've helped me immensely. I'm in your debt, captain."

"Glad to be of service."

A female voice called out, "Gramps, we're getting tired of waiting!"

"Ah, my granddaughter beckons," McEwen declared. "I've left her and her friend for too long."

"Forgive me, sir, I'll excuse myself. Thank you again for—"

"Nonsense, lad," he cut him off. "Ye must meet the ladies. Come with me."

"Delighted, sir. Thank you for the invitation."

Nathan followed McEwen to an open carriage a few yards away. Glancing up, he felt the breath leave his body. Never before had he beheld such beauty. The lady with black hair was lovely, exotic and regal-looking, but the red-haired one made his heart stop.

Her complexion was radiant. Creamy and dusted with light freckles, it reminded him of spiced milk punch. Good enough to eat. Wavy, titian locks framed her face, shining like burnished copper. Her blue-green eyes sparkled like the sun-kissed waters of the Caribbean.

Married to the sea, Nathan had believed himself a confirmed bachelor, past his prime for settling down and taking a wife. Pinching himself, he stayed his wayward thoughts. Marriage, indeed. A few seconds gazing at this flame-haired beauty, and he was already thinking of marriage. He must have been out in the sun too long.

The introductions went forward in a haze. It took all of his self-discipline to attend to Captain McEwen's words.

When McEwen offered the red-haired beauty as his grand-daughter, Destiny Favor, and she extended her hand to him, he accepted it, holding it tightly in his own and gazing into her eyes like a moonstruck calf. Despite the covering of her glove, her touch traveled through him, making his knees quake. Her small hand was warm in his. The holding of it, pure pleasure. He could die now and feel that he'd already gone to heaven.

He realized something was expected of him. He should speak. His tongue felt thick in his throat. He wasn't an experienced suitor, and the language of love was foreign to him.

But this was the chance of a lifetime, and he refused to let it slip away. For the first time he could remember, he forgot his position and how he might appear. He misplaced his natural shyness, letting go of it without a backward glance.

As if he courted women every day of his life, he raised her gloved hand to his lips, murmuring, "I'm most honored and gratified to make your acquaintance, Miss Favor."

Chapter Three

"I've deceived you."

Recoiling from Angelina's bald statement, Destiny wanted to believe that she hadn't heard her friend correctly. Curled up in bed and cocooned beneath a layer of mosquito netting, Destiny had looked forward to their late-night talk.

With her grandfather retired to his own bedroom and Malvado's cage covered for the night, it was just the two of them. She had often dreamed of sharing secrets with a friend into the wee hours of the morning, but she'd never had any close girlfriends before.

Unwilling to relinquish the growing friendship with Angelina, she refused to allow the deception, whatever it might be, to come between them. If Angelina had deceived her, she was more than willing to forgive.

"Aren't you going to say something? Haven't I shocked your propriety again?" Angelina prompted.

Covering Angelina's hand with her own, Destiny replied, "I trust you. If you deceived me, it must have been for a good reason."

"Madre de Dios, you are *too* trusting, Destiny. Has life always been sweet and gentle for you, so that trust comes so easily?" There was a harsh edge to Angelina's voice, almost as if she envied Destiny.

"No, life hasn't been sweet or gentle . . . at least, not all of the time. Gramps has been good to me, but . . ." She swallowed the lump in her throat. "It's not like having your own parents. When I was younger, I used to think losing my parents wasn't real. I believed one day I would wake up and they would be there, waiting for me. Like I was a princess in a fairy tale."

Angelina clucked her tongue. "Forgive me, I didn't think. To be orphaned must be cruel. Although I've wished it at times," she murmured, almost to herself.

"No, you couldn't have wished that!"

"So, I finally shocked you?"

"You haven't shocked me, it's just that I don't understand—"

"Ah. But that's how I've deceived you," Angelina interrupted, "by *not* explaining, while you've been so honest with me." Shaking her head, she admitted, "I was frightened at first. I don't trust as easily as you do."

"Tell me."

"I have aroused your curiosity?"

"Yes, please, Angelina."

"First, my name is Angelina Ximenes, not Herrera, although Herrera is my mother's maiden name. I'm ashamed to have lied to you."

Destiny released her hand, waving her own in a dismissive gesture. "I don't care about your name. I can't pronounce Him . . . that other name, anyway. But I am curious *why* you lied."

"Because I ran away from home, and I don't want to chance being discovered if I use my father's name. I wouldn't put it past him to offer a reward for me."

"Is . . . is your father so horrible?"

"Horrible, no," Angelina corrected. "He's not horrible, just stubborn and proud and accustomed to having his own way.

In Cuba, a father's word is law, particularly for his daughters. I was his only daughter, the youngest child. I have seven brothers who are older than me.''

"Oh, Angelina, how could you leave such a family? You don't know how many times I've prayed for brothers and sisters of my own.''

"I wish it were that simple.'' She sighed. "It's true I love my family, but I couldn't bring myself to sacrifice my life for their plans.'' She paused, as if gathering her thoughts.

"When I was young, I did everything to please them, as a dutiful daughter should. I even attended an awful convent school for years. That's where I learned to speak English,'' she added. "As I grew older and saw my brothers leading the lives they desired while I was shackled by convention, I began to envy my brothers' freedom and long for my own.''

"It's not the same for women, Angelina, you must realize that.''

"I don't see the difference. If a woman is wise and circumspect, she is perfectly capable of being free. After all, we are human beings too. But my family, led by my father, treated me as less than human. They treated me as a *thing*—a pawn to be auctioned off.'' She tossed her head. "Even my childhood friend, a sweet boy, was barred from seeing me because my father considered him unworthy.''

"Surely your father simply thought he was protecting you from—''

"Pah,'' she spat. "My father kept me locked away like a prisoner to further his ambitions. I was to be perfect and whole, untouched by human hands. But I fooled him! I ran away! If Cuba can rebel against Spain, then I can rebel, too.''

"But what are you rebelling against? I'm certain your father only wanted the best—''

"No!'' Angelina cut her off, her voice rising to a shriek. Leaping from the bed, she swept aside the mosquito netting. Pacing furiously, she declared, "He did *not* want what was best for me. He only wanted to further his family, to realize his ambitions through me. Not for one moment did he consider my feelings. I wasn't expected to have feelings.''

Destiny shifted on the bed, amazed by the vehemence of her friend's reaction. Not knowing what to say, she waited for Angelina to continue.

''My father wanted to marry me to a sugar planter. Cuban aristocracy, rich as Croesus, but three times my age,'' she explained, plucking at her skirts and twisting the fabric in agitation. ''To bear him children, one after another, like a broodmare. Becoming old before my time, just as my mother has done.''

She stopped and covered her face with her hands. ''I miss my mother, Destiny. I love her so. Why wouldn't she stand up to my father?'' Her voice throbbed with pain and bewilderment. ''She is a woman like me, but she refused to listen to my feelings, saying I must acquiesce and be an obedient daughter. I begged her to intercede on my behalf, but she refused.''

Uncovering her face, she demanded, ''Why, Destiny? Doesn't she love me enough?''

Vaulting from the bed, Destiny gathered Angelina in her arms. Holding her tightly, she felt her friend's pain as her own. Something indefinable had drawn her to Angelina. Could it be she'd sensed the same turmoil in her friend that she'd felt all her life? She'd often asked herself the same tortured question: Had her mother loved her enough?

Remembering the half-whispered innuendos of her youth, she relived the pain of believing that her mother had deserted her. But Angelina needed her comfort now; she mustn't think about herself.

''Your mother loves you.'' She spoke the words as if she believed them, because she knew it was necessary for her friend to believe them. ''I know she does, and she thinks she's doing the right thing by you. Every woman must marry. Your mother believed your marriage would provide a secure life for you.''

Twisting in her arms, Angelina hissed, ''A secure life with

an—an—old goat! Allowing his palsied hands to touch me in the most intimate—''

''Angelina!'' Destiny cried out, aghast at her friend's bluntness.

''Shocked you again, didn't I?'' She tossed her head. ''Not every woman must marry. Not if she can support herself.''

''What do you mean?''

''The land we saw today. I plan on building a cigar factory there and running it. My father manufactured cigars, and I followed him around for years, learning his business.''

Pulling loose from Destiny's arms, her features hardened and her violet eyes glittered with conviction. ''I shall never marry, only grow richer with each passing year. If I want a man, it will be on *my* terms, not his. I will take lovers,'' she declared haughtily, ''but only if they amuse me.''

Destiny stared at her, her mouth hanging open, shock reverberating through her. Of all the times Angelina had scandalized her before, they didn't compare with this time.

Angelina had discouraged Destiny from accompanying her to the magistrate. If she was to become a businesswoman in Key West, she must learn to stand on her own two feet. With the Spanish land grant and the coins she'd brought from home in her reticule, she approached the official who could clear her title.

Thankfully, he only seemed interested in her money and paying off the back taxes. He peered briefly at the spidery scrawl of Spanish words on the old grant but didn't ask her to prove her identity. Obviously, he couldn't read Spanish, and she guessed that his lack of knowledge facilitated the transaction.

After instructions to his clerk and a short wait, she found herself the proud possessor of a new deed. This time, the deed was written in English, and it verified her as the owner of her aunt's land. Triumphant, she folded the document and placed it in her reticule.

With her first objective behind her, she turned her thoughts to the next step: converting her jewelry into hard currency so she could build the factory. The back taxes had all but exhausted the reserve of money she'd brought from home. But she possessed numerous pieces of jewelry, that she felt would bring a good price. She decided to approach Captain McEwen, thinking he might know who could make the best offer.

Deep in thought about her plans, she wasn't looking where she was going when she left the courtroom. When she bumped into his starched shirt, she was brought up short to find herself face-to-face with the disturbing countenance of Rafael Estava.

Flustered, she flung out her arms to regain her balance. His hands caught her, steadying her. Righting herself with as much dignity as she could muster, she couldn't decide if his help was a blessing or a curse.

Where his strong hands clasped her shoulders, it was as if the sun scorched her skin, burning away the layers of clothing. The heady scent of him, sandalwood and musk, filled her senses with forbidden thoughts, erotic thoughts. The broad expanse of his white-clad chest invited. She wanted to pillow herself there, to be held tightly in his arms.

What was wrong with her?

From the beginning, this man had been an unwelcome thorn in her side. Telling her what to do, challenging her ownership of the land, and probing her identity. Why would such a man's mere touch turn her to jelly?

And she worried that he knew her from Cuba and would reveal her masquerade. Rather than wanting to be held in his arms, she should run from him as fast as her legs could carry her.

Drawing herself up, she took a wobbly step backward. He released her.

She murmured, "*Gracias,* Señor Estava," without thinking before amending, "Thank you."

"*De nada,*" he responded in the Spanish he'd banned before.

The sound of her native tongue was music to her ears, and she replied in kind, "You don't mind speaking Spanish?"

White teeth shone in his dark face. "That was very forward of me, telling you what to do. I must have been in an exceptionally foul mood. *Por favor, perdóneme.*" He paused, and his eyes raked her form. "Speaking Spanish is one pleasure we can freely indulge without consequences."

Heat surged through her as the meaning of his words and his gaze registered. She'd been admired by many men, especially when her parents had spent a fortune having her presented to society in Cuba. But no one had affected her like this.

Ignoring his double meaning, she replied, "I'm glad you don't mind. I miss speaking Spanish."

"Getting homesick already?"

How did he know?

Upon awakening this morning, she'd felt alone, isolated and cut adrift from familiar moorings. Her conversation with Destiny the night before had laid open old wounds. She longed for her mother, and at the same time she felt guilty, too, for admitting to Destiny that she doubted her mother's love. Upset and yearning for her family, she'd decided to press ahead with business, hoping that if she kept busy, the ache would go away.

A man pushed past them, doffing his hat and excusing himself. Another man and then a woman followed.

Rafael took her elbow, drawing her aside. "I think we're in the way. Would you care to sit over there?" He indicated a bench outside the door, under the sheltering branches of a huge banyan tree.

"I don't want to keep you from your business," she protested. "You were going into court."

"And you were coming out." He ignored her protest and led her to the bench.

"*Sí*, I paid the back taxes. The land is mine." She couldn't keep the hint of triumph from her voice.

Expecting him to be disappointed, she was surprised when

he said, *"Muy bien.* I'm glad your title is cleared." He seated himself at the other end of the bench.

"You don't want the land?"

He shook his head. "I decided it didn't suit my purpose."

"And what is that?"

"To build a warehouse for salvaged goods."

"Are you a wrecker like Captain McEwen?"

"No, nothing quite so exciting. I'm an insurance underwriter for the Medrano Company of Cuba. I represent their interests in Key West. In my business, I often discover goods that I think would fetch a profit if sold to the appropriate buyer. I want to build a warehouse to store them."

Another connection between them. Her father's cigar factory was insured by the Medrano Company, the largest insurance firm in Cuba. She had thought Rafael was familiar to her. Could she have met him at her father's factory?

But she couldn't cower and hide forever. If he were to say he recognized her, she would tell him he was mistaken. And if he was the gentleman he purported to be, he wouldn't dare challenge her.

Dismissing her fear of recognition, she realized that she enjoyed having a man discuss business with her, as an equal, granting her a taste of the freedom and autonomy she sought. It was a rare pleasure, indeed.

"So, you will work for yourself as well as the Medrano Company?" she asked, hoping to draw him out, to hear more about his plans.

"For a time. If my hunches are correct, I'll be working for myself in a year or two."

"As will I. I plan on building a factory on my land."

His cinnamon-colored eyes widened, and she recognized the surprise in his face. Removing the broad hat that hid his scarred features, he combed his fingers through his hair.

"That's quite a goal for a *woman.*"

She stiffened at his emphasis on the word "woman." Why had she thought, just because he'd shared his business plans with her, that he would be any different from other Cuban men? In her culture, women weren't deemed capable of taking care of themselves. A woman running a business was out of the question.

Purposely, she stared at his scarred face, hoping the sight would repulse her even more than his words. But repulsion didn't come. Instead, an overwhelming tenderness welled in her breast. She wanted to stroke the ugly scars with her fingertips and absorb his accumulated pain.

He didn't need her reassurance, she reminded herself. No matter how disfigured he might be, he was still a man. That one fact overshadowed any limitations he might have, making him more powerful than any woman.

Anger surged in her, blotting out the tenderness. She wanted to raise her arms and rail at the sky, but she restrained herself, affirming softly, "It's *my* goal."

Leaning forward, he surprised her by taking her hands in his. His touch ... his touch again. It was her undoing, his touch. Streaking through her like the lightning of a summer storm, leaving her breathless. His calloused fingers entwined with hers, and she closed her eyes, imagining his hands caressing her body.

What was this new weakness within her? She must find a way to root it out. Power accrued to those who took and didn't give. She had learned that lesson at her father's knee. Needing someone else was the quickest route to dependency. It was a luxury she could ill afford.

"I hope you attain your goal, but it will be difficult. A woman in a strange land is at a disadvantage."

His words caught her off guard. She had expected him to be appalled by her ambition. She'd thought he would deride her at best and forbid her at worst. But he hadn't. He'd merely warned her of the difficulties.

Lifting her head, she stared into his eyes, afraid he might be mocking her. But his gaze was guileless, open and filled with concern.

She didn't know how to react. His acceptance stole away her ingrained resentment, leaving her strangely empty, like a rag doll without stuffing. She needed her bitterness, needed her resentment to succeed. If she lost that, the obstacles would overwhelm her.

Withdrawing her hands from his, she replied brusquely, "I know there are formidable problems to overcome, but I enjoy a challenge." Rising from the bench, she acted on instinct, wanting to distance herself from him, both physically and emotionally.

His touch drove her crazy, making her forget her ultimate objective: to be free. His disfigured face called forth every nurturing nerve in her body. Far from being distasteful to her, she wanted to soothe away his hurt.

But the most dangerous part of him was his mind. That he could accept what she was trying to do was incomprehensible. Never before had she met such a man—one who was willing to meet her on equal ground, only concerned for her welfare.

"Thank you for your words of caution, Señor Estava. I enjoyed talking with you. I hope we'll meet again, but I've—"

"I understand," he interrupted and rose to his feet. Bowing, he said, *"Buenas tardes. Por favor,* give my regards to Miss Favor and Capitán McEwen."

"Miz Destiny, they's a gen'lman 'ere to sees you," Tilly called from the bedroom.

Destiny dropped the piece of fruit she'd been bribing Malvado with, trying to teach him some new words. It landed with a small plunk on the bottom of the cage. Triumphant, Malvado swooped from his perch to claim the prize while she secured the cage door.

Her mind tumbled. What gentleman would be calling on her? She never had gentleman callers. Could it be . . . ? No, that was too much to hope for. Entering the bedroom from the balcony, she found Tilly holding a silver tray with a card on it.

"Who is it, Tilly?" she asked, barely able to contain her excitement.

Hurrying to her dressing table, she picked up an abalone-backed brush and pulled it through her hair. Then she pinched her cheeks for color, studying her freckles with disapproval and wishing her grandfather would allow her to wear face powder. Once she'd tried using flour from the kitchen, but it had made her look like a sick ghost.

"It's a Cap'n Rodgers, so 'e says. I brung you 'is card," Tilly offered, extending the tray.

Her stomach plummeted with the demise of her hope. It wasn't James Whitman or any of Key West society, merely the naval captain her grandfather had introduced the day before. Taking the card from the tray, she perused it briefly. It did, indeed, identify her caller as Captain Rodgers. Disappointed, she replaced the card.

" 'E's waitin' for you in the parlor, Missy," Tilly prompted. "Ah's gots work to do."

Destiny frowned, calling Tilly back and demanding, "Where's Rufus? Why didn't he answer the door?"

Tilly shrugged. "You'm knows 'ow Rufus is. Always off doin' what 'e wants, not tendin' to bidness."

"Well, it's not proper. He's the butler. I'll have a word with him." Irritated by the informality and lack of protocol in her home, she continued, "And I noticed the card tray is a bit tarnished. Do you think you could polish it?"

Swiveling around, Tilly planted fists on her wide hips. "Missy, we don' git many callers, an' Ah's gots so much to do in dis big 'ouse. But iffen it'll make you—"

"No, forget I mentioned it." She rushed to withdraw her request, realizing she was frustrated and being petty. "I'll polish it myself. I know you're busy."

"Tha's mah baby." Tilly patted her cheek before leaving.

Alone again, Destiny stared at the tray. Its blackened surface symbolized what was wrong with her grandfather's household. Tilly was right. They seldom received callers. What was the use of keeping the tray polished?

How she wished things were different. How she longed for a normal family, who had callers and entertained visitors. She had a caller now, she reminded herself.

Returning to her vanity mirror, she made a face at herself, pulling her mouth wide and crossing her eyes. Not exactly the caller she'd dreamed of, but Captain Rodgers had seemed nice enough, even if his hair was a trifle thin on top.

With her initial disappointment giving way to a guarded excitement, she worried about receiving him. What refreshments should she offer? It was early afternoon, too late for lunch and too early for tea. Perhaps she should suggest some dry sherry, which her grandfather kept in the parlor. She hoped that offering sherry would be the sophisticated thing to do.

What would they talk about?

If only Angelina were here and not seeing the magistrate about her deed, Destiny felt certain her friend would know what to do with a gentleman caller, despite her professed disregard for men. But Angelina hadn't returned, and it was up to her to entertain the captain.

When she entered the parlor, Captain Rodgers stood at the far window, gazing out, with his back turned to her. Pausing on the threshold, she studied him. She hadn't remembered his shoulders being so broad, but from the back, his form filled the window. His brown hair, from this vantage point, was thick and glossy, gathered neatly at the nape of his neck in a sailor's queue.

He appeared at ease, standing casually with one foot thrust forward, his captain's cap tossed upon the horsehair settee. She wished she shared his nonchalance, but butterflies were square-dancing in her stomach.

Extending her hand, she announced herself with, "Captain Rodgers, what a pleasant surprise."

Turning from the window, he met her halfway and raised

her hand to his lips again, as he'd done the day before, this time with a subtle difference. Her hand was bare, and the gesture took on a strange form of intimacy, the touch of skin against skin.

His lips felt warm and firm, with a trace of moisture. His beard rubbed across her sensitive skin. She'd never been kissed by a gentleman before, not even on her hand.

Suddenly, she wanted to know what it felt like to be kissed on the lips. To have him press his mouth against hers. Did one pucker one's lips? Should she hold her mouth open or closed? Would his beard tickle her? What was the proper way to receive a gentleman's kisses? She would bet Angelina had been kissed. She made a mental note to ask her friend what to do.

"I'm glad I found you at home and that you would receive me," he said.

"Of course. You're a friend of grandfather's. He's not at home, but I could send someone to fetch him."

His wide smile melted, and she observed the stiffening of his body. He released her hand and moved a few steps away. He stood there, looking thoughtful and stroking his beard. Had she said something to offend him?

The silence in the room was deafening. Falling back on her earlier plan, she offered, "Would you care for some sherry?"

"No. No sherry, thank you." He paused, his high forehead bracketed with lines. "I didn't come to see your grandfather, Miss Favor, although I asked his permission. I came to see *you.*"

With his admission, a flush spread across his face, darkening the skin above his beard. Destiny was surprised to see a man blush. She had thought that was a female trait. Gramps never blushed.

Her heart softened, realizing their encounter was as awkward for him as it was for her. He'd said that he'd come to see her. A shiver of pleasure trickled down her spine. She felt wholly female, triumphantly female. Even as she savored her triumph, she wondered what to do next. Should she acknowledge his announcement or gloss over it?

Choosing the latter course, she murmured, "It was kind of you to come. If you don't care for sherry, at least let me offer you a seat. Please." She moved to the settee and seated herself at one end.

"Thank you." Captain Rodgers snatched up his cap and settled on the other end of the sofa.

He cleared his throat and ran an index finger between the starched collar of his uniform and neck. "Awfully hot for early spring," he observed.

"Yes, Gramps would say there's a storm brewing. It's so still and hot." She managed a small laugh and added, "But you would know that, Captain Rodgers. You're a sailor, too."

"Your grandfather is much more experienced than I. I defer to his wisdom," he offered modestly and hesitated. "I wish you would call me Nathan, not Captain Rodgers. Do you mind?"

She liked this game. If only she'd known how delicious it was to have a man paying court to her, she would have … What would she have done? What *could* she have done? She was seldom invited to parties or other social occasions. Her grandfather didn't entertain, so no one thought to include her.

Gazing into Captain—Nathan's blue-gray eyes, she wondered if his comment about her grandfather had merely been polite conversation or was he hinting at something else? Had he been emphasizing the difference in his and Gramps's ages?

She studied him from beneath her eyelashes and decided he was probably not as old as she'd originally thought. Somewhere in his mid-thirties, she guessed. Young for being the commander of a revenue cutter but older than any suitor she might have imagined for herself.

"I would be honored to use your given name, Nathan. Please, call me Destiny."

His earlier smile returned, making him appear even younger. He scooted forward a few inches on the settee and captured her hands in his. Her eyes drifted shut, thinking he was going to kiss her hand again.

The rumble of his deep male voice tugged her eyes open. "I'm not very good at small talk, Miss—uh, Destiny. I hope you won't hold that against me. When we know each other better, well, then . . ." His words trailed away. He cleared his throat again.

"What I came for . . . why I called on you, with your grandfather's permission, that is," he reminded her, "is to ask you to a ball next Saturday night. The Browns are giving it for their daughter's eighteenth birthday. I hope you don't think I'm too forward, considering our brief acquaintance."

If there had been butterflies dancing in her stomach before, they'd metamorphosed into galloping horses. Her mind whirled, somersaulting with a thousand thoughts. She didn't have an appropriate gown to wear. Could she find one on such short notice? And what about Angelina? She couldn't go to a ball and leave her at home.

Charlotte Brown's ball.

Destiny Favor was being invited to uppity Charlotte's ball— Charlotte, who had never invited her to anything, not even birthday parties when they'd been children. In the social hierarchy of Key West, the Browns and Whitmans were on equal footing, being the two most distinguished families on the island. She was certain James Whitman would attend. It was the perfect opportunity for him to notice her.

But that wasn't fair, was it? a voice inside her head remonstrated. *To go to a ball with one man to be noticed by another.*

Pushing the nagging voice aside, she returned her thoughts to Angelina. Her friend must go, too, or she wouldn't. Feeling noble, she decided to practice her newfound feminine wiles.

"I would love to go with you, but . . ." She purposely hesitated.

He squeezed her hands. She found she liked his touch. His hands were rough, the hardened hands of a man of the sea, like her grandfather's. In some strange way, that was comforting.

"It would mean a great deal to me if you would consent to go." His hazel eyes shone with anticipation.

She wanted to go with him. He wasn't the practiced suitor she'd imagined, but his honesty and guileless infatuation gave him his own particular charm.

"I've a house guest, Nathan. You met her, Señorita Herrera. I couldn't leave her at home. You must understand my dilemma."

Releasing her hands, he stood and paced. Although she knew little about courting, she assumed that most men would have agreed readily to bring her friend along. Because he hesitated, she sensed that he wanted them to go to the ball alone, that he wanted her for himself. The thought was very flattering.

He stopped pacing and agreed, "Bring her along. I'm certain the Browns won't mind an extra guest."

"That's very gracious of you. Are you sure you don't mind?"

"I would do anything to make you happy."

Destiny paced the widow walk, perched atop the highest peak of her grandfather's house. Back and forth, turn right and then right again, with the sea on two sides and a view of the lush green island from the remaining vantage point. The widow walk circled three sides of the house, with the fourth side containing a large window to the attic, giving access to the walk.

The widow walk, aptly named by seafaring families, was fashioned so wives could watch for their men coming home from the sea. Too often, the men never returned, and the women were widowed, thus earning the walk its name.

When she was troubled, Destiny liked to come up here. She came to feel closer to her mother, almost as if she could ask her mother questions and have the sea whisper the answers. Destiny's only memories of her mother were on this walk, waiting for her husband, who never returned. Based on what Tilly had told her, Destiny's father had died at sea when she was a baby, but her mother didn't learn of his death until two years later. Her mother died shortly after hearing the news.

Gramps refused to talk about it, saying that Tilly had already told her everything.

Sometimes, Destiny felt as if her mother had deserted her in favor of joining her father. She tried not to think that way. It hurt too much.

Shading her eyes with her hand, she looked out to sea, toward the harbor. The ocean was calm, glassy, and clear, a blue-gray color under the brassy afternoon sun . . . like Nathan's eyes.

Since she was ten years old, she'd wanted James Whitman for her husband. As a child, he'd embodied everything she desired, social acceptance and the respect of her peers. When she grew older, she became infatuated with his easy charm and handsome face. She'd endured two long years in Charleston at Miss Prentiss's finishing school before the War Between the States, in order to acquire the proper accomplishments of a young lady and catch his attention.

But he'd never noticed her.

Now, someone else had noticed her . . . Nathan. And he was taking her to a ball where she would see James. Would James notice her? The thought made her feel guilty. Nathan was such a nice man, older and with a thinning hairline, but very nice.

It was at times like this that she wished she could talk to her mother, woman-to-woman, and ask for advice. Gazing out to sea, she realized no answers were forthcoming. She tried to remember her mother, tried to imagine what her mother would say. It was no use, she realized. She'd been too young when her mother died.

The wind freshened, blowing her bell-shaped skirts flat and making her shiver. The air was warm, she knew. There was no reason to feel cold. No reason at all, except for the bone-deep loneliness that haunted her life.

Chapter Four

Destiny's bedroom door thudded open and Angelina came rushing in, waving a piece of paper. "I've got it!" her voice trumpeted. "I've got the deed, Destiny. It was easier than I thought."

Ecstatic that her friend had returned at last, just when she needed her the most, Destiny launched herself at Angelina. Caught off guard, Angelina staggered back before returning the hug. After a moment, she disentangled herself and held Destiny at arm's length.

"What's this? I knew you would be happy for me but . . ." Her voice trailed away. Seizing Destiny's chin, she lifted her face toward the waning western light spilling from the open balcony doors. "But you're not happy. Something is worrying you." Her voice was almost accusing. "What's wrong *amiga mía?*"

Destiny didn't understand much Spanish, but she understood Angelina's kind words: she'd called her "my friend." Warmth spread through her, ameliorating her loneliness and sense of vulnerability.

Grasping Angelina's hands, she admitted, "It's probably silly of me. You'll laugh when I tell you." Releasing her friend's hands, she backed away and seated herself on the edge of the four-poster bed. "I've had such a strange afternoon that—" She stopped, realizing she was being selfish, thinking of only herself. "I'm so happy you got the deed, Angelina."

"Forget about the deed." Angelina dropped the paper on the dressing vanity. "I'm dying of—how do you say it?—the curiosity. *Madre de Dios,* what happened while I was gone?"

Taking a deep breath, Destiny made an effort to marshal her thoughts. "I received a gentleman caller, Captain Rodgers. He called to ask me to a ball. The Browns are giving a ball for Charlotte, their daughter, for her eighteenth birthday."

Angelina tossed her head. "This is a reason to be worried and upset? For a ball? If you don't want to go, don't go. Your grandfather won't force you, will he? He doesn't seem like my father, forcing society upon you. Or is it Capitán Rodgers who upsets you? He's a nice-looking man, although his hair is—"

"It's not that I don't want to go to the ball," she interrupted. "I want to go very much. And I like Captain Rodgers. He's not my idea of Prince Charming, but he's very nice." She covered her face with her hands. "Unfortunately, you're not the only one who is prone to deception."

"You? Are you saying you deceived me? But why?"

"Not exactly deceived, I guess." Destiny uncovered her face. "Omitted some things." She sighed and her shoulders drooped. "I didn't want you to despise me. You're so sophisticated and at ease with yourself. You said you 'came out' in Cuba. I can only imagine the balls and parties you must have attended. I've led a very sheltered life," she confessed. "I've never even been to a ball before."

"You are not telling me what I hadn't already guessed." Angelina's voice was soft, comforting. Crossing the room, she seated herself beside Destiny. "Why would I despise you for not going to parties? I don't care."

"You don't care?"

"No. Should it be important?"

"Nobody likes an outcast. I haven't gone to parties because no one has invited me," she admitted.

"Because your grandfather doesn't entertain. Am I right?"

"That's a part of it."

"You make too much of this, Destiny. Your future is beginning now. You'll see. This first invitation will lead to another and yet another."

"But I'll have to reciprocate. Won't I? And Gramps doesn't entertain."

"One bridge at a time, *amiga mía.* Let's cross one bridge at a time. I'll help you."

"Will you?"

Destiny couldn't believe her good fortune. Angelina was going to help her. Smart and sophisticated Angelina, beautiful and refined Angelina. But a dark shadow fell over her heart. She'd heard the whispers since she'd been old enough to understand. There was a scandal attached to her parents. Had people forgotten about it? Would Key West society accept her? Gramps refused to tell her what the scandal had been about.

She shook her head. It wasn't important. She wanted to put it behind her. Wanted to be accepted. All that mattered was that she'd been invited to a ball, and James Whitman would be there.

"There's more, Angelina."

"*Sí.*"

"I'm in love, but not with Captain Rodgers. I love James Whitman. He'll be at the ball."

"Does he know how you feel about him? Does he return your feelings?"

She laughed, a short bark of irony. "He doesn't know I'm alive, much less that I have feelings."

Angelina clucked her tongue. Encircling Destiny's shoulder with her arm, she pulled her close, reassuring her. "Then we'll make certain he notices you, won't we?"

"Oh, Angelina, I knew you would help. But I haven't a gown to wear and I don't—"

"Don't worry about the gown." Angelina cut her off and rose to her feet. "I've brought several dresses that might suit you." Cocking her head, she studied Destiny's figure. "Stand up and turn around," she instructed. "I think we're about the same size. Does Tilly know how to sew? We might have to make some minor alterations."

Rising and pivoting slowly as Angelina had bid her do, she replied, "Yes, Tilly sews. But there's so little time."

"Don't worry. There's time enough. I also sew. The sisters at the convent taught me." Holding out her hand, she directed, "Come to my room. Let's look at the gowns and see which one will flatter you."

Linking hands, Destiny trailed after Angelina, crossing the balcony, passing Malvado's cage. The bird squawked and hurled imprecations at them. She was becoming accustomed to hearing Spanish curse words. The words might come in handy, some day, she mused to herself.

Angelina glared at Malvado. "Stupid bird."

Malvado responded by crooning, *"Mujer preciosa."*

Sniffing, she promised, "I'll deal with you later."

They entered Angelina's bedroom. Gowns, cosmetics, bottles of scent, and frilly undergarments cluttered every surface, strewn haphazardly over the room's furniture.

Angelina stopped and surveyed the scene, explaining with a shrug, "I'm accustomed to having a personal maid. I'll need to become more self-reliant until I can afford one." She paused. "Which reminds me, does your grandfather know a jeweler in town? I need to raise some money, and I want to get a good price."

"Adolph Weingarten," Destiny replied. "He's a friend of Gramps. He handles precious items from wrecks. My grandfather says he's honest and reliable and knows his business. He could help you. I'll have Gramps mention that you'll be coming in."

Angelina rushed forward, plucking a rose-colored gown from a loveseat. Holding it up, she shook her head. "The color's not right for you." Dropping the gown, she resumed their conversation. "You must thank your grandfather for his recommendation."

"It's nothing. I know Gramps won't mind." She hesitated before asking, "You're not trying to raise money to move to a boardinghouse, are you?"

"Of course not. I wouldn't leave you now. We must make you the most desirable woman at the ball." She faced Destiny. "No, it's just that after paying the back taxes on my land, I realized I was low on funds. I'll need to sell my jewelry to start building the factory."

"Then you're going ahead with it?"

"Of course. It's why I came to Key West. As kind as you and your grandfather have been, I can't live on your generosity forever. I want to be self-supporting. Then no man can tell me what to do."

Destiny slowly lowered herself into the one uncluttered chair in the room. "I guess it's a good thing the ball will be next Saturday. Once Key West society learns what you're doing, you'll be an outcast, too, Angelina."

Her friend laughed and crossed the room with a vibrant green satin dress in hand. Holding it up to Destiny, she swiveled her head from side to side with her eyes narrowed. "The color is almost right but a touch too flamboyant. It makes your complexion pale and competes with the green in your eyes."

"Angelina, I want society to accept you," she insisted.

"Why? I don't give a fig about society. I've had enough of society to last me for a lifetime."

"But you'll go to the ball with me," she almost pleaded. "I didn't explain . . . I thought you would understand. I told Captain Rodgers that you were my guest, and I couldn't go without you."

Tossing the green gown on a chair, Angelina grasped one of the posts at the foot of the bed. She smoothed her hands absent-mindedly over the carved pineapple ornamenting the post. The look in her eyes was far away.

Destiny held her breath, waiting. Her first impulse was to beg, but she restrained herself, knowing she often said too much.

"I'd rather not," Angelina finally answered. "It could be dangerous. Someone might recognize me."

"Oh, Angelina, someone might recognize you in the street." Destiny rose. "You can't go into hiding." She stopped herself. She was being selfish again, she realized.

Angelina lifted her head and met her gaze. She had the strangest look in her eyes. As if what Destiny had said had found its mark.

"Why is it so important to you?" Angelina broke the silence.

"Because . . . because I'm not sure of myself. I'm afraid I'll make a mess of things, that I'll talk too much and say the wrong things and . . . But with you by my side, I know that—"

"Won't Capitán Rodgers take exception?" her friend interjected. "After all, it is he who should be by your side."

"You're right," she admitted, adding, "I don't think he was excited about your coming along. But I can't do without you."

"Pah!" Angelina released the bedpost and cast her a disapproving look. "What kind of talk is that? You must believe in yourself, *amiga mía.* Even if no one else does. That's the key to getting what you want." She crossed the room and began searching through the piles of clothing again.

"So you won't come with me?" Destiny asked, trying to modulate her voice so as to not sound desperate. But desperation and panic intermingled inside of her, squeezing her heart in an icy fist, making her shiver despite the balmy breeze from the balcony.

"I will think about it. *Por favor,* give me time to consider." Pulling a gold-bronze gown from beneath a pile of undergarments, she declared, "This is it. This is the gown for you. It will be perfect with your coloring." Rushing across the room, she held it up, exclaiming, "I knew it! Perfect! Come and look at yourself."

Reluctantly, Destiny crossed the room to join Angelina in front of the full-length pier glass. Angelina held the gown by its sleeves, pressing it against her torso.

It was beautiful, Destiny had to admit to herself, gazing at her reflection. Made of a stiff, bronze-colored taffeta shot through with golden threads, the fabric appeared to give off sparks. The gown's rich hues heightened the roses in her cheeks and made her eyes glow like emeralds. And its effect on her hair was nothing short of magic, transforming her carrot-hued mane into a bright flame, shining with auburn and blond highlights.

"Take off your gown. You must try it on," her friend urged.

In awe of the beautiful gown, she obediently allowed Angelina to unhook her day dress. Then Angelina handed her several more petticoats to put on. The golden gown possessed a huge bell-shaped skirt. She stepped into the dress and her friend fastened the hooks. Angelina circled her, stopping to fuss with the puff sleeves and neckline. When she stepped back, Destiny darted a quick look at herself.

She gasped. The neckline was so plunging, it barely covered her breasts. She wailed, "I can't wear this. It's too daring. Gramps will have a fit."

"Not if you cover yourself with a shawl until you arrive at the ball."

"I'll need to cover my red face too."

Angelina laughed again, a deep, throaty growl. Ignoring Destiny's discomfort, she pulled and tugged at the waist, observing, "Possibly a stitch or two here. You're smaller in the waist than I am." Her voice betrayed an uncharacteristic hint of envy.

"I think I need a whole new bodice, one that covers my chest."

"You want this . . . this man. I don't remember his name."

"James Whitman," she supplied.

"You want this James Whitman to notice you. Don't you?"

"Yesss." She drew out the one-syllable reply. "But I'm not certain if I'm prepared for that kind of attention."

"You better be prepared," her friend countered. "That's what men notice."

"Not all men, Angelina. I don't think Captain Rodgers is like—"

The French doors banged against the wall with a loud crack, drowning out her words. The balmy evening breeze had suddenly become a howling wind, sweeping through the room, sending frilly undergarments sailing to the floor. The mynah bird, out on the balcony, squawked in protest.

"I'll get Malvado," Angelina said, abandoning her and rushing to the balcony. Returning with the birdcage in hand, she placed it on a table and faced Destiny again, regarding her with a critical look. "I think a few tucks at the waist will do it. Except the gown's a little long. I'm taller than you. Do you have high-heeled slippers? I'm afraid your feet are larger than mine."

"No, I don't have high-heeled slippers."

"Then we'll go shopping tomorrow and find you some."

Trembling inside, Destiny gazed at herself in the mirror. She wanted to attribute her sudden chill to the rising wind, but she knew better. It was hard to believe that she was going through with this: going to her first ball and wearing such a daring gown. She didn't even look like herself.

Straightening her shoulders, she pushed her doubts away. Remembering her friend's advice, she tried to think positively. As Angelina had said, if she didn't believe in herself, no one else would.

"The jewels are paste, Señorita Herrera. I'm sorry," Adolph Weingarten intoned solemnly.

"The jewels are paste," Angelina echoed, too stunned to absorb the full meaning of his words.

She took a deep breath, gulping air as if she were a fish

thrown upon a beach. Grasping the strap of her reticule, she twisted it around and around until it bit into her fingers.

Slowly and with an insidious cruelty, reality dawned upon her. She was in Key West, a stranger in a foreign country with no funds. The thought raced through her mind, sucking the breath from her lungs again, leaving her gasping.

"Señorita Herrera, I'm sorry to have distressed you. Is there anything I can do? Perhaps you have other valuables? Paintings, decorative items, tortoise-shell combs?"

"No, no other valuables." She shook her head. "Except the clothes on my back," she remarked bitterly. There hadn't been time to take anything else when she fled. And she'd thought her jewels were real. Remembering the decadent opulence of her "coming out," she cringed. It had all been a sham, a carefully orchestrated sham by her father.

"You're a friend of Captain McEwen. I could lend you some money on his word."

The thought horrified her. Before, when she believed she had money of her own, it was one thing to stay with Destiny and her grandfather because Destiny wanted her to stay. Now, it was quite another. Her inbred sense of pride surfaced. Now she was at their mercy, quite literally. She had barely enough funds to feed and house herself for a week. To accept their generous hospitality and use Captain McEwen's good name for a loan as well was too awful to contemplate.

"No, I don't want a loan," she managed to croak.

"What about the pearl choker and earbobs you're wearing. They look real enough. Might I examine them?"

Lifting her hand, she fingered the pearl choker at her neck. The necklace and earbobs had been her mother's. On her sixteenth birthday, amid tears and smiles, her mother had given them to her. Of course, they were real. Her only real jewels, a legacy from her mother.

Why didn't Mami stand up for me? she asked herself again, an endless litany that had no answer. She couldn't give up the pearls, she told herself. They were all she had left of her mother.

Adolph Weingarten extended his hand. "They look to be very fine Majorca pearls. They'll fetch a good price," he urged.

Nodding, she unfastened the choker and pulled the earbobs from her ears. She reacted automatically, feeling like a Haitian zombie, doing his bidding. Now wasn't the time for sentiment. She'd needed her mother in Cuba, and her mother had failed her, caving into her father's demands.

The pearls, no matter how fine they might be, wouldn't fetch enough to build her factory. But she couldn't go without funds, either, reliant on Destiny for her every need.

"Yes, they're Majorca pearls. Very fine." The jeweler stroked the choker, indicating, "See how they shine. Notice the rose tints. I can give you—"

"I'll take it," she purposely interrupted, not wanting to haggle, feeling unable to negotiate. She would rely upon Captain McEwen's recommendation that he was a fair man.

Appearing mildly surprised at her easy capitulation, Mr. Weingarten smiled, revealing a gold tooth. "I understand. Discretion is one of the underrated virtues."

With those words, he retrieved his strongbox and counted out a small pile of American double-eagle gold pieces. Rummaging through a drawer, he found a velvet pouch and poured the gold into it, handing it to her with a flourish.

She placed the pouch in her reticule. Then she gathered her "fake" jewels and put them there, too. At least they would serve to ornament her if she decided to go into society again. The thought reminded her of Destiny's ball. She'd promised to take her friend shopping this afternoon for high-heeled slippers.

"Thank you for your business, Señorita Herrera." The jeweler bowed from the waist. "It's been a pleasure serving you."

"The pleasure was mine, Señor Weingarten," she responded with irony.

With a will of their own, her fingers drifted to her throat. Her skin felt feverish to the touch. Aching and feverish, and so very bare.

*   *   *

They stood outside a shoemaker's shop on Duval Street, peering at the rows of shoes inside the glass case. Duval Street was the main artery of Key West, where most of the shops were located. Three doors down stood Weingarten's jewelry shop.

Angelina shuddered, remembering the terrible news she'd received this morning. Feeling vulnerable and alone, she linked her arm with Destiny's. Destiny half-turned and smiled, patting her hand.

"See anything you like?" Angelina prompted.

"I'm not sure. What do you think?"

Pushing her own problems to the back of her mind, she concentrated on the task at hand: get Destiny ready for the ball. They'd already set Tilly to altering the waist of the gown. Her friend needed a pair of high-heeled slippers to complete the ensemble.

Perusing the ready-made slippers through the glass, Angelina studied each pair, discarded it, and went on to another. She hoped this wasn't the only shoemaker in town. Compared to Havana, the selection was rather limited. And there wasn't time to have a pair specially made. Her gaze fell on a black pair with gold toes. They looked to be about the right size.

Pulling Destiny forward, she pointed through the glass. "How do you like that pair?"

"They're beautiful, but so elegant. Do you think—?"

"Of course they're elegant," she agreed. "I think they would be perfect with your gown."

"I think so too." The sound of a male voice, tinged with a Latin accent, came from behind them.

Surprised, they turned together to face Rafael Estava, wearing his trademark Panama hat, pulled low. Removing the hat, he swept it in a wide arc and executed a low bow.

"Shopping, ladies?" he inquired. "For the Browns' ball?"

At the sight of his marred face, Destiny gasped. The sound

made Angelina wince. *What a burden it must be to carry one's disfigurement for all the world to see,* she thought. Destiny's involuntary reaction irritated Angelina.

Far from repelling her, Rafael's scarred face evoked a powerful maternal protectiveness in her. She wanted to reach out her hand and touch him, smoothing the scars away with her fingertips. If only she possessed such magic.

"Yes, we have been trying to find a pair of slippers for Destiny," Angelina replied, bridging the awkward moment. "And you're well informed, Señor Estava, to know about the ball," she added. "Destiny plans to attend with Capitán Rodgers."

Destiny had her head down, embarrassment coloring her face red. She was obviously uncomfortable having Angelina discuss her plans. Angelina shook her head. Destiny really was an innocent. But if she wanted to win this Whitman's notice, she'd have to overcome her shyness.

Uncommonly irritated again, she pinched Destiny's arm. Her friend's head shot up. Angelina gave her a sharp look.

As if awakening from a dream, Destiny blinked, managing, "Señor Estava, it's good to see you again." She glanced at Angelina. "If you'll be so kind as to excuse us, I want to try on the slippers." Destiny tugged on her arm.

"Of course, I understand," Rafael murmured. Replacing his hat, he turned to go.

But something made Angelina stop him. Pulling free from Destiny, she touched his linen-clad arm. Then she faced her friend, directing, "Go inside and see if the slippers fit. I'll be along shortly."

Destiny opened her mouth as if to argue. Angelina shook her head. Her friend closed her mouth, nodded to Rafael, and obediently entered the shop.

"That wasn't necessary, you know," he said. "I merely stopped to say hello. And you needn't pity me, either." He reached up, touching his marred cheek. "I've grown accustomed to people's reactions. They don't bother me."

Was she that transparent? Angelina wondered. During her debutante season in Cuba, she'd learned to hide her emotions behind a carefully constructed mask. She mustn't lose the ability to dissemble. It gave her an advantage.

"I don't know what you're talking about," she replied coolly.

"Don't you?" He smiled, a mocking smile. "And I thought we agreed you would call me Rafael. I have every intention of calling you Angelina."

Hearing her given name on his lips, her heart raced. *"Claro que sí,"* she managed. "Forgive my ingrained formality."

"If you'll forgive my forwardness. You'll be going to the ball, too, I assume."

"Destiny wants me to go. I haven't decided yet."

"You can't hide in Key West. It's too close to Cuba."

His flat statement echoed her friend's argument. How had he guessed that she was afraid of being recognized? At first, she could have sworn he'd recognized her. Now she wasn't so sure.

Her first impression remained, nagging at her, teasing the corners of her mind. She could swear that she knew him from home. But she couldn't allow him to know her suspicions or that he'd correctly guessed her fear.

"No, I won't forgive your forwardness, Señor—ah, Rafael. What a terrible accusation you make." She tossed her head. "And for your information, I'm not in hiding." Shrugging, she added, "I've merely retired from society."

"You're too young and beautiful, Angelina Herrera, to retire from society."

His compliment thrilled her, sending tiny waves of pure pleasure through her. She'd heard many compliments from men's lips before. Most of them she ignored or discounted. But there was something about this man, an almost indefinable force that drew her to him.

"After your terrible accusation, you're wise to flatter me," she threw back, smiling and trying to make light of their conversation.

"It's not flattery. It's the truth, and what's more, you know it."

She felt the hot flush start in her bosom and rise to her neck. When was the last time she'd blushed? She couldn't remember. If she didn't watch herself, he'd think her as naive and innocent as Destiny. And maybe that wouldn't be such a bad thing. Her sophisticated wiles paled before his brutal honesty and his almost eerie ability to see through her.

"I'll bid you *buenas tardes,* Rafael."

This time, he reached out and stopped her. His hand fell on the bare skin of her forearm. When his flesh touched hers, it was as if lightning cleaved the sky. Electricity flowed between them, sending shock waves along her nerves, raising gooseflesh on her arms. After the briefest moment, he removed his hand. Without thinking, she rubbed the place where he'd touched her.

"Don't go yet," he requested. "I've something to ask you. Would you do me the honor of accompanying me to the ball?"

"I told you I haven't decided if I'm going."

"But Destiny wants you to go."

"*Sí.*"

"What's the old saying—three's a crowd?"

"It won't be a problem if I don't go," she shot back.

"Are you still planning on building your cigar factory?"

"Of course."

"Then you'll need to be introduced to Key West society. You'll need business contacts. Haven't you thought of that? While Captain McEwen is a pillar of the community, he doesn't go out much. I wouldn't rely upon him." He paused, as if giving her time to consider. "This is the perfect opportunity for you to make contacts. That's why I'm asking you to go. Think of your business interests, if nothing else."

His words created a welter of emotions in her, a confused muddle of feelings that coalesced in her chest. That he should be concerned about her future business was a pleasant surprise. She remembered yesterday morning outside the court house when they'd talked about business together, as one colleague to another. She'd hoped that he believed in her, but she'd had her doubts. Here was concrete evidence that he wanted her to succeed.

At the same time, she wanted him to ask her to the ball because he wanted to take her, for purely personal reasons. But wanting him to desire her as a woman was both surprising and bewildering to her. She hadn't wanted a man to ask her out for a very long time.

She should count her blessings that he wanted to help. Keeping Rafael as a friend and business colleague would be a wise move on her part. He was obviously attuned to what was happening on the island, and his knowledge could only help her.

But as a potential lover . . . that was another story. Despite her brave words about taking lovers, she didn't know if she were capable of flouting society. Raised strictly in the Roman Catholic faith, she would find it difficult to abandon her upbringing. Besides, she wasn't ready. Her feelings were still too tender, her vulnerabilities too fresh.

Having Rafael as a confidant and friend was perfect.

He was right about another thing, too—she needed business contacts. She needed a loan to start her cigar factory. In order to get a loan, she needed to meet people and gain their confidence. Thinking about obtaining a loan when she knew how difficult it was for a woman to own a business filled her with dread.

She mustn't allow her fears to deter her. She would find a way. She was dedicated to making a free life for herself.

Proudly, she lifted her head. "You convinced me, Rafael. I would be more than pleased to accompany you to the ball."

Chapter Five

Arm in arm with Captain Rodgers, Destiny stepped over the threshold into the Browns' house and the world of Key West society. Waiting in line to be received, she glimpsed a glittering assembly of men and ladies.

The huge foyer stretched before her, filled with people greeting their host and hostess along with their daughter, Charlotte Brown, the guest of honor. Rafael and Angelina stood behind them, waiting, too.

Angelina leaned forward, whispering in her ear, "Relax, Destiny. You'll do fine. Just be yourself."

Nathan turned to her and winked, squeezing her hand. With so much encouragement, she relaxed a fraction and allowed her gaze to wander over the house. She'd passed this house thousands of times before but had never been invited inside.

Looking around, she realized that it wasn't so different from her own home. The rooms were larger and the ceilings higher. She glimpsed the ballroom at the end of the foyer and noted its proportions. Gramps's house had a ballroom, too, though smaller than this one and unused since she could remember.

When she was a child, she'd often played there, sliding over the polished hardwood floors in her stocking feet, pretending she was ice-skating. Growing up in Key West, she'd never known snow or ice, but she'd seen pictures in books.

Feeling more at home, she studied her surroundings. The house, although built along the same lines as her grandfather's, was different. More elaborate, perhaps, she thought to herself, trying to analyze the difference. The Browns' house, unlike her spartan home, seemed filled to bursting, like a fat man about to split the seams of his trousers.

Instead of nautical etchings on the walls, there were large oil paintings in gilt frames. The chandeliers overhead, unlike the functional ones at home, sported elaborate designs and a wealth of crystal prisms. Vases, flowers, lace doilies, and knickknacks covered every available surface. Huge potted palms and other hothouse plants crowded, cheek by jowl, among the heavy, lavishly carved furniture. Where clear glass graced her windows, here stained glass reflected the light, bathing the rooms in an array of colors. Underfoot, thick Aubusson carpets covered the hardwood floors, compared to the threadbare Oriental rugs in her home.

If she had to put a name to it, she would say the Browns' home had the unmistakable stamp of "a woman's touch." With that thought came a stab of pure, undiluted grief, grief for the mother she'd lost so young.

Nathan glanced at her, a question in his blue-gray eyes. She shook her head and tried to relax again. The line inched forward, moving at a tortoise's pace.

Having regained her composure, she focused her attention on the guests. Gazing into their faces, she found that she recognized most of them. How strange, she thought to herself. She'd seen these people every day of her life, even greeted them on the streets. But she'd never seen them in their evening clothes. The women wore low-cut evening gowns, sporting feathers in their hair and jewels at their throats. The men were garbed in their best frock coats or dress uniforms, their hair tonsured with oil and their beards carefully trimmed, smelling strongly of bay rum.

They finally reached the Browns. Nathan bowed and murmured greetings to Colonel Brown before introducing her. He shook Destiny's hand quickly and offered a perfunctory greeting, not commenting on the fact that he'd known her all his life. They moved to his wife and repeated the ritual.

When Destiny took her hand, she said, "I'm so happy to see you, Mistress Brown. Thank you for having me to your home."

She returned Destiny's handshake, looking her up and down before replying, "Quite so."

Feeling uncommonly miffed by the elder Browns' reception, she watched as Charlotte Brown greeted Nathan with effusive enthusiasm—too much enthusiasm, to her way of thinking. Watching them together, their hands clasped and Charlotte smothering him in charm, her heart contracted painfully. Jealousy, like some malevolent poison, poured through her veins, making her pulses pound.

Charlotte Brown could have any man in this house or in all of Key West, for that matter. Why would she want Nathan? As soon as the thought entered her mind, she chided herself. Glancing at her escort, she saw him in a new light. With his hair carefully arranged, his handsome features were compelling. Fitted out in his best dress uniform, she had to admit he possessed a male physique that would make any maiden swoon.

Realizing how lucky she was, she squeezed his arm. He reacted instantly, dropping Charlotte's hands. Bowing low, he began a formal introduction.

But Charlotte cut him short, reaching for Destiny, and squealing, "No introductions are necessary, Captain Rodgers. Destiny and I have been friends since childhood." Giving Destiny a smothering hug, she said, "I'm so happy you've come to help me celebrate my eighteenth birthday."

Destiny wanted to return the hug, but her body went stiff, unyielding. She remembered Charlotte's other birthday parties, from which she'd been excluded. She particularly remembered the one when Charlotte turned twelve. Colonel Brown had brought in a circus for the celebration, and it had been chronicled in the Key West newspaper. Destiny hadn't been invited.

Feeling the old wounds reopen, she pulled free from Charlotte's embrace. Hurting, she couldn't bring herself to dissemble. Instead, she mimicked Charlotte's mother, responding, "Quite so."

Charlotte glared at her, indignation burning in her light blue eyes. Destiny turned from her and asked, "Nathan, shall we go in to the ball?"

Nathan looked at Charlotte and then at Destiny. He leaned toward Charlotte. "Thank you for—"

Destiny purposely cut him off, complaining, "Please, Nathan, I'm feeling faint. Waiting in this stuffy foyer for so long and . . ." She allowed her voice to trail away.

She couldn't believe how she was acting. She'd waited for this opportunity all of her life, and now she was purposely trying to irritate Charlotte. There would be no more society invitations for her, she realized. At this particular moment, she didn't care.

The old rebuffs, along with her reception tonight, hurt too much.

Nathan, considerate of her welfare, made their excuses, tucking her hand into his arm. Guiding her along, he offered, "Let's step outside on the terrace where you can get some fresh air."

Obediently, she followed him through the crush in the ballroom. Her thoughts and feelings in turmoil, she barely noticed the dancers or the music or the throng of people. They appeared as if far off, as if she were seeing them from the wrong end of her grandfather's spyglass.

They'd almost cleared the ballroom when she glimpsed him. James Whitman stood before the French doors opening to the terrace, bent low, kissing Frances Brown's hand. Digging her heels in, Destiny stopped in her tracks. James and Frances exchanged glances and murmured words. Then he swept Frances into his arms and they entered the ring of dancers, whirling to a Viennese waltz.

Frances Brown, Charlotte's elder sister, at age twenty-one was practically a spinster. What did James see in her? she wondered. Unlike Charlotte, who was renowned as the prettiest girl in town, Frances possessed a very long nose and thin lips. Her hair was a mousy brown color. And her figure suggested spinsterhood. Garbed in a beautiful blue satin gown, even the dressmaker's art couldn't disguise her bony figure.

Ignoring Frances and concentrating on James, she felt the breath leave her body. He was so handsome. His fair hair fell forward on a wide forehead. His gray eyes sparkled with humor and sophistication. And his full lips beckoned her. She'd dreamed of his lips touching hers.

Lost in her reverie, she was surprised when Nathan gently tugged at her arm. "Destiny, are you all right? Come, let's go to the terrace."

They were held up in line. Angelina was incensed when some dignitaries cut in front of them. Destiny and Nathan had already advanced to the head of the receiving line and entered the ballroom, when they reached Colonel Brown.

Luckily, Rafael had a steadying effect on her. He was cordial and jovial, despite the waiting. Taking her cue from him, she put a huge smile on her face and suffered through the ignominy.

It was worth the suffering, she soon realized. Although she was eager to find Destiny, Rafael held her back, introducing her to people. She met the mayor of Key West, along with the Browns, who controlled much of the area's shipping. Rafael introduced her to the Whitmans, another family involved in shipping. She recognized the name, knowing Destiny was in love with one of their sons, James. She also met the most successful merchant in town, a Mr. Greene, as well as the harbormaster. More merchants and a banker or two followed.

Exhausted with introductions, she turned to Rafael, inquiring,

"Might I have some refreshment? Fruit punch, if they have it."

He held out his arms. "Let's dance first. Then refreshments."

She started to argue but remembered all the help he'd already given her tonight. Inclining her head, she agreed. "One waltz and then I want some fruit punch."

"One waltz." With those words, he took her into his arms.

Tucked into his embrace, spinning around the floor, proved to be a heady experience. His touch gave her shivers, making her feel hot and then cold, as if she'd been taken with the ague. Her pulses pounded and her heart raced, one beat ahead of the music. His hand on her back seemed to burn a hole through the fabric of her gown.

Closing her eyes, she fought the disturbing tremors coursing through her body. Fought the almost mesmerizing effect his closeness evoked. Fought the dizzy feeling that had nothing to do with their dancing.

With her eyes closed, she tried to concentrate on the music, but her other senses intervened. She smelled his own particular scent, sandalwood and musk. It curled into her nostrils, both familiar and exotic, hinting at sultry nights filled with passion. His strong arms enfolded her, and she could feel the primitive strength of his male body beneath the genteel covering of his evening clothes. His steps were strong and sure. He was a marvelous dancer, she realized, guiding her effortlessly around the floor.

Gazing up at him, she found his face in profile. This side of his face was untouched, as perfect as the day he'd been born. He had been a very handsome man. And he was still a very handsome man, she told herself.

His features were classic, reminding her of profiles found on old coins or etchings of Greek gods. He possessed a wide forehead, high cheekbones, hawklike nose, full lips, and a square jaw.

"Did anyone look promising for backing your venture?" he asked, breaking their self-imposed silence.

"Too soon to tell. But thank you for introducing me. Is there anyone else I should meet?"

"Señor Warner, he's a banker and known for liking risky investments."

"There's nothing risky about my cigar factory," she retorted. "I learned the business from my father. He was very successful." As soon as the words left her mouth, she could have bitten her tongue in two. She'd just given him another clue to her identity.

He didn't capitalize on her lapse of judgment. Instead, he murmured, "Concentrate on Warner, anyway. He's not married."

"What do you mean by that?" She bristled.

"Angelina, let's be realistic. Most men don't believe women should engage in commerce. If they're married, they can't help but think about their own wives running a business. The mere thought, for most of them, is enough to frighten them to death. You're more likely to convince an unmarried man to help you."

"With a little added incentive, Rafael? Is that what you're trying to say?"

His body stiffened and his cinnamon-colored eyes flashed a warning. Rather than pulling away, he crushed her to him. His breath was harsh against her ear. "I wouldn't be helping you if I thought that, Angelina. You're well-bred and beautiful and intelligent. There's no need for you to play the harlot. That is, unless you want to."

Recoiling from his words, she pushed against his chest. "Let go of me! How dare you say such a thing to me!"

"*¡Silencio!*" he hissed in her ear, switching to Spanish. "Don't make a scene. You need these people and their good opinion. Remember?"

Realizing that what he said was true, she allowed his arms to encircle her again. Plastering a wide smile on her mouth, she dazzled their fellow dancers and onlookers with her brilliant smile as they swept by.

"*Mucho mejor,*" he said.

"Bastardo."

He laughed, throwing back his head. "You better keep your tongue sheathed, if you know what's good for you."

She glared at him.

The waltz ended and he took her arm, leading her to one side.

"Where's this Warner? I want to meet him immediately," she demanded.

"What about refreshments?" Lifting his head, his gaze swept the room. "Besides, I don't see him yet. He usually arrives late at these dress functions. Arrives late and leaves early." He winked at her. "It's rumored he keeps a very beautiful quadroon as his particular . . . companion."

"It would seem your mind is in the gutter tonight, Señor Estava."

"You said you wanted fruit punch?"

"That's what I said earlier. Now I've changed my mind. Do they have anything stronger?"

"I'll see what I can find. Try to keep out of trouble."

"Shouldn't be difficult with you gone," she muttered, half to herself.

"¿Qué?"

"My refreshments, *por favor.*"

"Claro que sí." He clicked his heels together and bowed over her hand.

"If you see Destiny, tell her where I am," she added.

"Your word is my command." Facing about, he headed for the end of the ballroom, where white-coated servants presided over tables laden with food and drink.

She watched him saunter away, admiring his jaunty walk from the back. His evening clothes fit him like a second skin, unlike his loose-fitting white linen suits. Each line of his muscular body was outlined in detail, straining against the expensive fabric. She wondered if his body had been disfigured when his face had been scarred. She hoped not. It was such a beautiful male body.

A vision of what he would look like unclothed rose in her mind. Even though she'd led a sheltered life, growing up with seven brothers she possessed a fair idea of the male physique. Her brothers had all been good-looking men, but they couldn't compare with Rafael.

Envisioning him in the nude, heat flooded her. Opening her reticule, she retrieved her fan. The ballroom felt suddenly hot and close. Remembering their conversation, her temperature rose a notch or two.

Thinking about him and what the proximity of his body did to her, she realized that her plan to keep him as a friend and confidante was ludicrous. Tonight, his conversation had hinted at something more as well. Why else would he have talked to her in such a manner? Could he have been testing her?

She looked around the ballroom, recognizing some of the people he'd introduced her to earlier. She wished Warner would show up. Rafael seemed to think he would be the most likely to help. The sooner she met Warner, the sooner she could leave. And the sooner she could rid herself of the disturbing presence of Rafael Estava.

Nathan guided Destiny to a stone bench on the terrace, directing, "Please, sit down. Do you have a fan with you? Can I get you anything? Are you feeling better, Destiny?"

She lifted her head and gazed up at his kind face. Solicitude was evident in every line of his body. He hovered over her like a mother hen, his concern obvious in the features of his face.

And he made her feel like a complete fraud.

He was her escort for the evening. A handsome man, a successful man, accustomed to being a leader. Liked and respected by the community of Key West, he was every maiden's dream. And he cared about her, really cared about her. Even she, as naive as she was in the ways of men, knew it instinctively. But all she could think of was James Whitman, dancing and laughing with Frances Brown.

She lowered her head, murmuring, "Thank you. I don't need anything. I'm feeling better now. The night air has restored me."

"Wonderful. Marvelous." He smiled. "May I join you?"

"Yes, please." She scooted over on the bench, indicating the opposite end.

He didn't take the hint. Instead, he seated himself beside her, so close they almost touched. Reaching up, he ran his finger between his neck and the collar of his uniform. Then he cleared his throat. "May I hold your hand, Destiny?"

Should she allow him the liberty? It seemed little enough to ask. And she *was* feeling guilty. Unable to look at him, she lifted her right hand, the one closest to him, offering it.

He accepted her offering, engulfing her hand in his large paw without a word. They sat together for several minutes in total silence with her hand cradled in his. Strange thoughts coursed through her. What if James Whitman came on the terrace and saw her holding hands with Nathan? Would he believe her betrothed? Would it make him jealous? Would he care?

Closing her eyes, she willed the disturbing questions away. Slowly, she relaxed. Nathan's calloused hand was warm but dry, comforting in its masculine contours. His skin felt good next to hers. She wondered again what it would feel like if he kissed her. Would his lips, pressed against hers, feel as good as his hand did?

Thinking about kissing Nathan, her blood heated. Her heart thumped in her chest, like a rabbit caught in a snare.

Alarmed at her reaction, she pulled her hand free, exclaiming, "It's so hot here on the terrace!" Dropping her shawl, she fanned herself with her hand, complaining, "I can't find my fan."

Nathan turned to her, new solicitude stamped on his features. Then he glimpsed her bared bosom. His eyes widened and he gulped. His gaze snagged hers for one brief instant and then returned to her chest.

Realizing she had shed her concealing shawl, she hastened to retrieve and replace it. But his hand on her wrist stopped her.

"Don't," he almost groaned, going down on one knee.

Astonished by his reaction, she sat very still, wondering what he would do next. She didn't have long to wait. He brought her captive hand to his mouth and kissed it, feathering light kisses over her sensitive skin.

Her eyes drifted shut as she gave herself over to the pleasure of his lips on her flesh. Soft and wet, his mouth caressed her, sending tiny shivers of shimmering sensations through her body. Her blood turning molten, it spread like sweet honey through her veins.

Reaching up, he cupped her chin in his hand. His mouth found hers. His lips were warm and firm. If kissing her hand had fired her blood, this was so much more, beyond her wildest imaginings. She felt both slack and warm, as if the bones had melted in her body, leaving her without support. At the same time, every nerve in her body seemed to leap alive, straining toward him, demanding more . . .

More of what, she didn't know.

Gasping against his mouth, he took her cue, deepening his kiss. His mouth pressed down, claiming her, adjusting to the contours of her lips. Heated and supple, his lips moved over hers, exploring and molding, sending shivers of ecstasy down her spine.

Crushed to him, she responded feverishly, raking her finger-nails down the soft wool of his uniform. She felt hot all over, as if someone had started a fire deep inside her. And at the same time, she shivered in anticipation, savoring every scintillating moment. She was spinning out of control, she realized foggily. He shifted, trailing kisses across her cheeks and chin and down her throat.

His beard grated against her face, abrading her tender skin.

She started at the unexpected sensation, retreating a little, recovering her senses. Her earlier questions had been answered. It was both wonderful and terrifying to be kissed on the mouth. The sensations were marvelous, making her feel attuned, for the first time in her life, with her body. But the feeling of losing control was too new, too frightening in its intensity.

Gently pushing at his chest, she protested, "Your beard scratches me, Nathan. Please."

Releasing her, he vowed, "I'll shave my beard. Anything to make you happy." Grasping her hands, he stammered, "I know . . . that is . . . I mean you haven't known me for very long. I realize this is sudden and probably unexpected." He ducked his head and cleared his throat. "But you're so very beautiful, Destiny. The most beautiful woman in the world. I wouldn't have taken the liberty of kissing you if . . . if I hadn't . . ."

Obviously at a loss for words, he raised her hands to his mouth and showered kisses over them. Lifting his head, he clasped her hands tighter and placed them on his chest. "Feel my heart. It beats for you, only you. I thought I was married to the sea, but when I first saw you, I knew. I love you, Destiny. Will you be my wife?"

She stared at him in stunned silence. Her mouth dropped open. Remembering her grandfather's admonishments, she closed it. She could feel his heart beneath her hands, pounding like the surf hitting the rocky shore. Had she heard him right? He thought she was the most beautiful woman in the world. He loved her. And he'd asked her to marry him.

Destiny Favor, the girl whom everyone shunned, the girl with carrot-colored hair and a scandal surrounding her heritage, was loved? A handsome and successful man thought she was beautiful and wanted to marry her. It was almost too much to contemplate, too bizarre to believe.

And she'd used no feminine wiles on him, executed no dazzling maneuvers to win his regard. He loved her as she was:

naive to the ways of the world, unsure of her conversation, and innocent of pleasing a man.

Her heart somersaulted and then expanded. Warmth filled her, a dizzy yet comforting warmth. A feeling of belonging, of coming home, of being wanted. Like his kisses, the feeling was both marvelous and terrifying at the same time.

How could she answer him? She, who knew nothing of men and less of love, except for her secret desire. She wished she could talk to someone . . . Angelina or her mother. Although Angelina was a wonderful friend, it was her mother she really wanted. What advice would her mother have given?

According to Tilly, her mother had worshipped her father. She'd thought the sun rose and set on her father's countenance. Destiny's most lasting memory of her mother was watching her pace the widow walk, waiting for her husband to come home from the sea.

Gazing down at Nathan's kind face, she tried to imagine that kind of dedication and encompassing love. He'd said he loved her. Did she return the sentiment? If something were to happen to Nathan at sea, as it had to her father, would she pine away for him, as her mother had?

Turning her face away from the expectant look in his eyes, she tried to gather her thoughts. It was very flattering to have a man fall in love with you, to think you were beautiful and desirable, to want to marry you. Would it be enough to sustain a life together? she wondered.

She liked Nathan's touch, his lips on hers, his gentle caresses. But she was an innocent. No other man, besides Gramps, had ever touched her. No man had kissed her lips. If she found Nathan's kisses pleasing, what if she found another man's kisses even more pleasing?

And then there was James Whitman. She'd loved him since she could remember. How could she dismiss years of secretly longing for him? Gramps always said a bird in the hand was worth two in the bush. Was that true? Was her love for James so shallow that she could forget him at the first proposal from another man?

Did she love Nathan as her mother had loved her father?

"Nathan," she began tentatively. "I'm honored by your proposal." Gathering courage with each word, she continued, "But you admitted this was sudden. And I don't know how Gramps feels. Give me time to consider your proposal. Please."

"Of course. Take all the time you want. My feelings won't change. I'll love you tomorrow and the next day and the one after that." He raised his head. "If you want me to speak to your grandfather, I will," he offered.

"No, not just yet." She smiled at him, dissembling for the first time, using her feminine wiles.

Clutching two champagne glasses, Rafael returned to the spot where he'd left Angelina. Searching the crowd for her rose-colored gown, he didn't find her. Pivoting right and then left, he scanned the crowd on this side of the ballroom. She wasn't there.

Knowing without having to look, but drawn to look anyway, he shifted his attention to the whirling dancers. Across the wide ballroom, near the French doors leading to the terrace, he caught a glimpse of rose-colored satin. He followed her as she spun around. Seeing her in the arms of another man, one of the merchants he'd introduced to her earlier, his muscles tensed. Blood poured through his veins in a hot rush. He had a sudden splitting headache, as if demons were pounding his temples with tiny hammers.

It was as if he were preparing to fight. He knew the symptoms well. But he wasn't prepared to fight. Not over Angelina. Shaking his head, he wondered at his response. Could it be a protective reaction on his part? After all, he'd taken on the role of her protector and guide in Key West.

Lifting one champagne glass and then the other, he downed the wine in two gulps. He wasn't a drinking man, and he felt the flush of the champagne almost immediately. It invaded his body, relaxing his taut muscles, slowing his pounding heart. That was better. He mustn't allow Angelina or her actions to affect him. He would help her get started, for old times' sake. Nothing more. That part of him had died, long ago, devoured by the flames that had scarred his face.

There was a time, years past, when he'd fancied himself in love with her. He'd held fast to that dream during the long years in Spain, where he'd been sent to complete his education. He'd even brought her a token of his affection: a raucous, saucy mynah bird. He wondered what had happened to the bird.

Angelina flashed by and he inclined his head toward her, raising one empty champagne glass in a mock salute. She acknowledged his gesture with a tight smile before focusing her attention on her dancing partner.

When the music ended, he expected her to return. But she didn't. Instead, she stopped across the room and was immediately surrounded by a coterie of young and old men, fawning over her.

Cocking his head, he tried to study her objectively. She was beautiful, always beautiful, but he didn't think the rose-colored gown suited her. It made her appear pale, almost wan. She should wear deep, rich hues, to offset her midnight hair and violet eyes, like crimson or emerald green or gold. He shrugged to himself. Probably she'd chosen the gown to appear demure, wanting to be accepted by Key West society. He approved of her foresight, if that was what had influenced her choice.

When the first strains of a quadrille started, she was swept away again, this time by a young swain he didn't recognize. The boy looked barely old enough to be shaving. He shrugged again and stuffed his hands in his pockets. Wanting something to do, he walked around the ballroom, searching for Destiny and Nathan. But he didn't find them.

The quadrille ended, and he found himself on the same side of the ballroom as Angelina. Expecting her to come back, at least for the sake of appearances, he was surprised when the band began a furious polka and she flew by in the arms of yet another man. It was one of the bankers he'd presented her to, a much older man with fierce mutton-chop whiskers.

Young and old alike, Angelina charms them all, he thought, feeling used and abandoned. It was true that he'd brought her to the ball to make contacts, but he hadn't expected her to take him so literally. As soon as he was out of her sight, she'd abandoned him without a word, capitalizing on his earlier introductions.

Indignant over her self-centered behavior, he cast around the ballroom for something to do. He knew most of the people. He could always strike up a conversation about business. But he also realized his activities in Key West weren't looked upon with favor. Most businessmen resented him for uncovering armaments, believing his actions stifled trade.

Gazing around, he searched for Warner, only to be disappointed. The man might not even show tonight. He preferred other pursuits to society parties. He couldn't rely upon Warner coming. So where were Nathan and Destiny? Had they disappeared for the night? If he could find them, at least he would have someone to talk with.

Was that the real reason he wanted to find them? Or was the real reason that he wanted to use them to lure Angelina back?

With that thought in mind, he shifted uncomfortably on his feet. He was suddenly conscious of the scars on his face and wished for his wide Panama hat. Flicking a piece of lint from his lapel, he snorted. He didn't need to lure Angelina. He didn't need anyone or anything. His life was quite complete as it was. *Gracias a Dios.*

With nothing better to do, he wandered toward the tables at the end of the ballroom. Once there, he requested a brandy. Champagne wasn't his drink of choice. He preferred brandy when he chose to drink. He drank one glass, allowing the liquid to trail its fiery tendrils down his throat. Armed with a second glass, he moved around the ballroom.

Several acquaintances tried to draw him into a conversation, but he wasn't interested. Drinking the brandy had fomented a certain restlessness, making him desirous of idle chatter. He wanted to relax tonight. He'd done his part, introducing Angelina. Each time he paced the room, she had acquired a new dancing partner. He wondered if she were charming them to invest in her cigar factory.

After swallowing the last of his second brandy, he felt strange. His head felt light and his body heavy. A little fresh air might clear his head, he decided. Moving to the French doors, he stepped onto the terrace. He overheard a muted conversation a few paces away. Gazing into the darkness, he was mildly surprised at his discovery.

He'd finally found Nathan and Destiny. Nathan was on his knees in front of Destiny, kissing her hands. Glimpsing the tender scene, he felt like an intruder. Reversing his steps, he reentered the ballroom.

Once inside, his head felt better. In fact, he felt much better. He decided to get another brandy. The band had stopped, taking an intermission. He glanced around, trying to find Angelina. People stood in tight circles, gossiping. He didn't see her.

Fetching another brandy, he twirled the snifter in his hand and wondered where she was and who she was with. The tender scene he'd glimpsed on the terrace haunted him. What if it had been Angelina there, with a man kissing her hands on bended knee? How would he have reacted?

He heard a loud clatter across the ballroom, silence, and then a collective gasp. He couldn't see what had aroused the crowd. There were too many people huddled on the fringes of the ballroom. He searched for a rose-colored gown but didn't find Angelina. Shrugging, he sauntered toward the deserted foyer. If the terrace was occupied, he'd step outside the front door and get some air.

The butler, standing at attention at the end of the hall, bowed and opened the door for him. Once outside, he fished inside his vest pocket for a cigar and one of the newly invented safety matches. Finding both, he lit his cigar and puffed, trailing a stream of smoke. Gazing out at the quiet night, savoring his cigar, he regained a modicum of composure.

Angelina could lead her life without his help, he decided, feeling mellow from the brandy and cigar. He needn't interfere. If she wanted to dance the night away and ignore him, he shouldn't concern himself.

The night sounds soothed him: crickets chirping, frogs croaking, the call of nightjars. It was refreshing to be away from the crush inside.

Why stay? The thought surfaced in his mind. Angelina obviously didn't need him. He would alert Nathan and Destiny and ensure that they would accompany her home. Then he would make his farewells to the host and hostess.

With that thought in mind, he ground out his cigar and tossed it aside. Reentering the house, he pushed past the butler, intent upon finding Nathan and Destiny. Upon entering the ballroom, he realized the orchestra had resumed playing, another waltz, this time.

And then he saw her.

She'd changed partners again. The dark countenance of this partner swam into view. It was Cortez, Rafael's enemy, a dangerous man. What was he doing at the ball, dancing with Angelina?

Chapter Six

Destiny readied herself to enter the ballroom, carefully draping the shawl across her shoulders, not wanting to detract from the daring cut of her gown. For once in her life, she felt flushed with triumph and uncommonly brazen. Nathan's words of love and marriage had buoyed her, lifting her to an incredible height, as if she floated on a soap bubble, far above mere humans.

She'd seen Nathan's gaze, hot and full of desire, fall upon her bared bosom. She wondered what effect the gown would have on James Whitman. Would it make him forget bony Frances Brown? Would he finally notice her?

Nathan escorted her into the ballroom, but no one was dancing. The guests stood in tight knots around the perimeter of the room. The orchestra had ceased, taking an intermission. She had thought to be swept into Nathan's arms and spun around the room, entering seamlessly into the festivities.

Instead, she was confronted with a room full of people, their heads close together, talking and whispering. The bubble burst inside of her, bringing her abruptly to earth. Her old insecurities flooded back. She fumbled with her reticule, hunting for the fan she thought she'd lost. At the bottom of the bag, she found the elusive fan. As she grasped it, her shawl slipped. She reached for the shawl, and the ivory-backed fan fell to the hardwood floor, making a horrible clattering sound.

In the hushed ballroom, all eyes turned to her. The talking and low conversations ceased, as if everyone took a collective breath and held it. Like a ship caught in the beacon of a lighthouse, she felt illuminated, trapped in the glare.

She didn't know if it was her imagination or not, but she thought she heard gasps from the corner where the matrons were gathering. Glancing down, she realized again how much of her bosom was exposed. Covertly, she stole a quick peek at the other women's gowns. With a sinking feeling, she wilted inside, shriveling up, wanting to cover herself.

Nathan came to her rescue.

He cleared his throat, inquiring, "Would you care for refreshment?"

Wetting her lips with the tip of her tongue, she responded, "Yes, please."

"Some fruit punch?"

"That would be wonderful."

"Would you care to accompany me?"

She flinched, understanding his solicitous request. She was a social pariah, outside the pale. There was no one for her to talk with while he fetched the punch. Lifting her head, she looked around the ballroom, trying to find Angelina, but she didn't see her.

Squaring her shoulders, she refused to succumb to the social norms. If she had to stand alone, so be it. She would wait for Nathan here.

"No, thank you. I'll be fine." She smiled at him. "Maybe I'll see Angelina and Rafael."

"I won't be but a moment." He bowed over her hand.

Before the crowd had swallowed him up, Henry Greene, a prominent merchant, approached her. Following in his wake were several other men, whom she'd seen on the streets of Key

West. Some of them were young, scant years older than she; more were middle-aged, like Henry. A few were bachelors, but most were married men.

Gazing at the ring of faces, she remembered the matrons' gasps. Her brave front evaporated and panic streaked through her. Had the women sent a contingent of men to publicly condemn her manner of dress?

At the thought, she became frantic. Rising on tiptoe, she searched the ballroom, desperate to find Nathan or Angelina. But Nathan had disappeared into the crowd around the refreshment tables, and Angelina remained conspicuously absent.

The next thing she knew, Henry Greene had bowed over her hand and said something. Unfortunately, the buzzing in her head obliterated his words. She didn't want to hear what he had to say, anyway. Like a treed squirrel, she glanced around, looking for an escape route. But the men pressed closer, all talking at once.

Terrified, she took a step back and then another. Bumping against the man behind her, a shriek rose to her throat. Off-balance, she swayed and stumbled. Henry reached out and caught her elbow.

Gazing into her face with a curious expression, he asked, "Miss Favor, are you all right? Didn't you hear what I said? Would you do me the honor of the next dance?"

"I can't do that," she managed. The buzzing inside her head had subsided. "I promised my escort, Captain Rodgers, the next dance."

Was that all Henry Greene wanted from her, just a dance? With the knowledge came a relief so profound, she felt as if an anchor had been lifted from her shoulders.

"Captain Rodgers can't keep you to himself all night." Henry indicated the assembly of men with a sweep of his arm. "We're all old friends, aren't we? Where's your program, Miss Favor? You must promise us all a dance."

Had she heard him correctly? She glanced at the other men, who bowed and nodded, murmuring their agreement.

Astonished by her sudden popularity, she fumbled for the reticule at her wrist. The discarded dance program, like the elusive fan, must lie somewhere at the bottom. While she searched for it, she wondered again at their sudden interest. They'd never done more than smile and tip their hats when she passed them on the street. Now they all wanted to dance with her.

Holding the program and its tiny attached pencil, she lifted her head. The men waited, expectant looks on their faces and an avid gleam in their eyes. She was grateful for their interest, but at the same time, her stomach felt suddenly queasy, the way it had the time she'd eaten too many raw oysters.

Then everything seemed to happen at once. The orchestra started playing again, a waltz. Henry leaned forward and took the program from her hands. He scratched his name on a line and handed it to the man behind him. The next instant, she was in his arms, being whirled away on the dance floor.

Clinging to Henry's shoulders, she saw Nathan from the corner of her eye. His startled face swam into view for a second. Then Henry spun her around and she found herself on the opposite side of the ballroom amidst the crush of dancers.

Nathan stood stock still, almost at military attention, except for the two cups of fruit punch gingerly held at arm's length. He watched as Destiny twirled away in the arms of one of the local merchants. He'd only left her alone for a few minutes. He hadn't expected to find her dancing with another man.

But he should have expected it. Destiny was a very beautiful woman. A very beautiful and desirable woman, he amended. One dance wouldn't hurt. Besides, Henry Greene, a middle-aged, married businessman, wasn't really a threat. There was no cause for concern.

Craning his neck, he watched Destiny dance until she disappeared on the other side of the ballroom. Realizing he was probably making a spectacle of himself, he turned his face away. The stiff wool of his uniform rubbed against his skin, making his neck itch. He wished his hands weren't full. Casting about for some place to put the punch cups, he noticed a knot of men precisely where he'd left Destiny.

They were mostly local businessmen, standing together, chatting and gesturing. Bewildered by their sudden intrusion where no one had been before, he approached them.

Major Beale, an army officer whom he knew slightly better than the others, detached himself from the crowd and took one of the punches. "Here, Rodgers, let me help you."

"Thank you, Beale. I was getting tired of balancing them."

Gesturing toward a sideboard a few feet away, the major said, "Why don't we put the refreshments down." Then he withdrew a dance program from his breast pocket, explaining, "I believe this belongs to your beautiful companion. Since you're her escort, you should keep it."

Wondering how Beale had gotten hold of Destiny's program, he kept the question to himself, accepting the cardboard square with the dangling pencil. When he happened to glance down at it, he was astonished to find it completely filled with men's names. A different one for each dance. And as hard as he stared, he couldn't find his name there.

"She's a popular lady, your companion," Beale commented, almost as if he'd read his thoughts. Then he winked and nudged Nathan with his elbow. "You sly old dog."

Nathan bridled at his effrontery, taking a step back and clearing his throat. He searched for a properly scathing retort but found himself at a loss for words.

"I've never seen Miss Favor at a ball before. I had no idea . . ." Beale mused, half to himself. "Been keeping her a secret? I can understand why."

Finally, Nathan found his voice, managing to grate out, "How did you get her dance program? I went to get some fruit punch and—"

"Oh, that." Beale snorted. "You can blame Henry Greene for that. He practically snatched it from her hands and then passed it around. We all wanted a dance with her. I guess we took advantage.'' He shrugged. ''As one military man to another, I'll gladly give you my dance, especially since you're her escort.'' Beale clapped him on the shoulder, emphasizing their comradeship.

Nathan cringed under the hearty gesture. Was there a trace of mockery in Beale's voice? Was Beale insinuating that he hadn't done his proper duty as her escort, leaving her unattended and easy prey? He felt both furious and foolish at the same time.

Shaking his head, he remembered he was no good at this. No good at social games and courting women. Less than an hour ago, he'd been on bended knee before her, baring his soul and offering himself as her husband. Now, he was left to cool his heels with her refreshments and a pack of vultures, Beale included, waiting to get their hands on her.

Greene couldn't have taken the dance program without her consent. She'd put it in her reticule earlier, he recalled. She must have wanted to dance with these men. The thought both infuriated and frightened him, making his hands shake.

He needed something stronger than fruit punch, he realized. The thought of strong drink made him glance back at the refreshment table. He longed to fetch himself a whiskey, but he didn't dare leave. When the dance finished, Destiny would return and he would . . .

What would he do? Storm up to her and demand she change the program, giving him all her dances? He couldn't do that. He'd never done anything so impetuous in his life. It wasn't his style, allowing unbridled emotions to rule him. Except where Destiny was concerned.

Lifting his head, he caught Major Beale's curious stare. The major had spoken several moments before, and he hadn't responded, being lost in his thoughts. He smiled tightly and nodded, realizing he must look like a fool. Did he seem a fool to Destiny? he wondered, remembering the scene on the terrace.

Major Beale returned his smile and bowed. Then he rejoined the circle of men waiting for their dances with Destiny.

Watching them, he knew he wasn't a proper suitor. He'd married the sea and been content until he gazed into Destiny's turquoise eyes, losing himself. Could he play this game? This courting game?

There were many men more handsome than he, and Destiny hadn't accepted his proposal. Instead, she'd put him off, asking for more time. If she didn't reciprocate his love, could he wait, as he said he would? More to the point, could he compete with the other young swains? Did he want to compete, making a silly ass of himself again and again, undermining his respectability?

The dance ended, and he saw Destiny approaching, her arm linked with Greene. The sight made him physically sick to his stomach, and he wished even harder for a whiskey to end his pain and humiliation.

Acting on impulse, he half-turned, intent upon seeking the refreshment table. But from the corner of his eye, he glimpsed Destiny. She surprised him by detaching herself from Greene. Lifting her skirts, she began to run to him from halfway across the ballroom.

Beholding her flushed face, he fell in love all over again. Her excitement added color to her perfect milk-punch complexion and made her sea-green eyes sparkle. Watching her run to him, he felt his heart expand and swell, threatening to burst from his chest.

She was so lovely and young and innocent. Innocent, like he, to the ways of courting. After all, this was her first ball, he reminded himself, excusing her. If Beale said that Greene had taken advantage of her, it was probably true. He mustn't allow self-doubts to overwhelm him. She was a prize worthy of his patience and understanding.

Catching her in mid-stride, he drew her to him, claiming her for all of Key West to see. Breathless, she collapsed against him, her arms clinging tightly to his waist, anchoring them together, as if they'd both come to safe harbor.

* * *

Angelina danced without thinking, silently following her partner's lead. There had been a string of partners, one after another. She couldn't remember most of their names, and they hadn't been interested in discussing business. When her sorties about commerce fell on deaf ears, she'd exhausted her small talk. And she was tired of dancing. Her feet ached, and her throat felt like a desert. She longed for the fruit punch she'd sent Rafael to fetch.

She'd been surprised that Rafael hadn't reclaimed her, but after further reflection, she decided it was for the best. Rafael was too dangerous. She thought she knew him from home but couldn't remember where or when they'd met. That was dangerous, in and of itself. But the way he looked at her and the way her body responded and what his simple touch did to her heightened the peril.

All she wanted was financial support for her cigar factory. With her factory built and running, she'd be her own woman, dependent upon no one, capable of charting her own course. As it was, until she received financial backing, she was vulnerable. Being around Rafael only made her feel doubly vulnerable.

Lifting her head, she gazed over her partner's shoulder, wishing she knew what Warner looked like. Wishing he would show himself. Even as she wondered if he would appear tonight, she realized she was relying on Rafael's judgment that Warner had the propensity to take on "risky" ventures. She didn't like relying on Rafael's judgment. It made her feel uncomfortable.

Someone tapped her partner's shoulder, cutting in on their dance. This time, though, it didn't startle her, as it had before. In Cuba, no one usurped dances. Here, even though there was a dance program to be filled, it was meaningless. Men cut in with ease and partners relinquished her with equal ease. It was a strange custom, she thought to herself.

Sliding into the new man's arms, she glanced at him. He was swarthy and short, just above her height. She hadn't noticed him before, but she recognized the racial imprint of his features. He must be Cuban. When she opened her mouth to confirm her suspicions, he silenced her by placing one finger across her lips.

Offended by his gesture but also intrigued, she kept quiet. He spun her around and around, very quickly, until they were close to the entry hall. Then, without warning, he grasped her hand and pulled her after him. Halfway down the deserted foyer, he opened a door and thrust her inside.

The door shut behind them and he said, *"Yo soy Cubano. ¿Y tú?"*

She nodded, not certain if she liked his treatment. On one hand, it was good to meet another Cuban, other than Rafael. On the other hand, his abrupt and secretive manner left much to be desired.

"Me llamo Cortez," he continued in Spanish. "To whom do I have the pleasure of addressing myself?"

"Angelina Herrera."

"Ah, Señorita Herrera, you are Cuban?"

"Sí, yo soy Cubana. And I'm delighted to meet you, Señor Cortez, although I don't understand the secrecy."

"As a fellow Cuban patriot, you must understand that enemy eyes are watching us."

"I'm afraid I don't share in the political upheaval of my country, although I sympathize." Taking a deep breath, she added, "I came to Key West for business, not politics."

"Business," he softly chided, "you came for business. One so lovely as you, Señorita Herrera, doesn't need to bother with business. It is superfluous." He waved his arm, incongruously sweeping the empty room. "Others might be concerned with business, but not you. It is beneath you, far beneath your beauty and poise."

Here it was again, the age-old argument of her culture. Women were too beautiful and fragile to talk of business, much less engage in it. As dangerous as Rafael was, at this moment she wished he were here. He, at least, of all her countrymen, believed in her. Or he acted as if he did.

Drawing herself up, she squared her shoulders and gathered her skirts in one hand. She tried to push past Señor Cortez, dismissing him with, "It's been very pleasant, but I must return to the ballroom."

"Patience, patience," he counseled, placing himself between her and the door. "Have a Madeira with me? This is Colonel Brown's study, where he keeps his finest Madeira."

"I don't care for a Madeira, *señor*. Perhaps another time. And you are blocking my way," she added pointedly.

"Perdóneme, señorita." Bowing low, he moved to one side. "I had so wanted to talk with a fellow Cuban that I must have forgotten my manners. I would never dream of detaining you against your will."

His need to speak with another Cuban struck an answering chord within her. Being in Key West and accustoming herself to an alien culture could be very trying. It was what had probably driven her to form an attachment with Rafael. She longed to meet other Cubans, particularly Cuban ladies, but hadn't been afforded the opportunity. As far as she'd been able to discern, Rafael and Cortez were the only other Cubans at the ball.

"Perhaps a small Madeira then," she capitulated. "You must miss home as much as I do."

"Sí, sí," he agreed readily, "I miss home and speaking Spanish." He rubbed his hands together and appeared delighted she'd decided to stay. Indicating the settee, he offered, *"Por favor,* take a seat, make yourself comfortable."

"This is Colonel Brown's study, you said." She remembered meeting the stern-faced, white-haired man in the entry hall. "He won't mind us being here and drinking his special Madeira?"

Cortez had moved to a sideboard, where a cut-glass decanter held a ruby-red liquid, presumably the Madeira, and a set of small crystal glasses. Glancing up, he smiled, admitting, "I wouldn't rush to tell the colonel that we're here. Still, I don't think his Southern hospitality would allow him to deny his guests.''

His oblique answer did little to alleviate her unease, and when he smiled, she noticed his teeth were black. Despite her misgivings, she sat down, perching on the edge of the sofa. Watching Cortez from the corner of her eye as he poured the Madeira, she realized he wasn't very good looking. And his stature, half a head taller than she, was short by most men's standards.

Covertly studying him, she realized that if they'd been introduced in Cuba, she wouldn't have spoken more than three words to him. But in Key West, removed from her familiar surroundings and the support of her family, she had allowed herself to be maneuvered into a closed room with this man, where they were probably unwelcome by their host. If she'd done such a thing in Havana, her father and brothers would have demanded satisfaction from Cortez and locked her up for weeks to do penance.

She should feel thrilled by her audacity. Wasn't it why she'd come to Key West, so she could behave as she wanted, with whomever she wanted? Even if that person might appear a bit unsavory? Unfortunately, she didn't feel thrilled. Instead, she felt uneasy in the presence of this small, ugly man, even though he was a fellow countryman. She decided to drink her Madeira as quickly as possible and leave.

He crossed the room with two glasses. Remembering her wishes, he offered her the half-full glass and bowed. Pulling a leather chair up, he seated himself across from her, not beside her on the sofa, as she had feared. At least his manners were acceptable, she thought, relaxing a fraction and sipping the wine.

Leaning over, he clinked his glass with hers, toasting, ''To our beautiful island home, Cuba.''

Acknowledging the toast, she nodded and took another sip of Madeira. It was on the tip of her tongue to ask him what part of Cuba was his home and how long he'd been in Key West.

But he forestalled her by commenting, "You mentioned earlier you were interested in business. I find I'm intrigued. Most beautiful young—"

"I'm not just a pretty face with an empty head, Señor Cortez," she interrupted sharply.

"Ah." He released his breath and leaned back in the chair. As if the shoe were on the other foot, she found him studying her. Unlike her, he was quite open about his scrutiny and despite her best intentions, she found herself squirming beneath his gaze.

"I plan on building and operating a cigar factory in Key West."

There. She'd said it. If he wanted to denigrate her ambition, let him. She didn't care. If she had to beg in the streets, she would find the money to build her factory.

"That's quite an ambition," he remarked.

"Especially for a woman. Isn't that what you meant?"

"*Por favor,* Señorita Herrera." He held one hand up, palm out. "If I've given offense, I didn't mean to. If you have the requisite knowledge to run a cigar factory, who am I to say you shouldn't?"

"You don't mean that."

"*Claro que sí.* In this country, women take an active interest in commerce. All the boardinghouses are run by women, as are several mercantile establishments. There are, of course, dress shops and laundries operated by women, too."

"But those businesses are the traditional provinces of women. What surprises you is my intention to operate a cigar factory."

"Do you have the knowledge to make fine cigars?" he challenged.

"I do. I was taught by the best, my father."

"Pardon my ignorance, but I've never heard of Herrera cigars. Is your father going to back you in this venture?"

She recoiled from his blunt question. Here it was again, the need to fabricate her past. But she'd brought it upon herself. In her rush to convince him of her sincerity and capability, she'd made reference to her family. Now, she would need to lie and dissemble again as she had with Rafael. If someone had warned her about the constant lying before she ran away, she might never have left home.

No, that wasn't right. If she'd bowed to her father's wishes and married that ancient planter, her entire life would have been a lie. That was worse. And her homesickness was at fault, too. It made her seek out fellow Cubans, but it was with her countrymen that she was forced to deceit. From now on, she'd banish homesickness and concentrate on accustoming herself to her new country. With the natives of Key West, there was no need to practice deceit.

He took a sip of wine and crossed his legs, patiently awaiting her answer. She'd already been silent too long, she realized. Anything she said now would be suspect, especially if he was as intelligent as he seemed.

Again, she decided to stick as close to the truth as possible without giving herself away. "My father's cigars aren't well known. His factory was a small venture, but the quality was the best." She paused purposely, as if reluctant to admit the rest. "To answer your other question, no, my father won't be backing my venture. He would have preferred me to marry." She lowered her head, continuing, "After his unexpected death, his debts . . . his debts swallowed up my inheritance. All I had left was a parcel of land in Key West. There was nothing to keep me in Cuba, so I came to make a fresh start."

Having told the lie, she silently prayed to the Virgin Mary to forgive her mendacity and speaking of her father as if he were dead.

"What a sad story, Señorita Herrera. My profound sympathies in this time of your sorrow." His gaze swept her, and his eyes narrowed. She knew what he was thinking. In Cuba, a dutiful daughter wore black for at least one year of mourning. Her rose-colored gown didn't fit with the story.

She lifted her head and met his eyes. Let him think what he wanted. She wasn't in Cuba now, and she was starting a new life.

"There was no other family, no relatives to help?" he asked.

"There were relatives, but I didn't want to burden them. Another spinster to feed without a proper dowry wasn't . . ." She allowed her words to taper off. She was tired of lying and disgusted with herself, despite the necessity of it. He could finish the rest.

"If you have no dowry," he started and then stopped himself. His voice softened, became almost coaxing. *"Perdóneme* for my forwardness and interest in your personal affairs. But without funds," he began again, "how do you propose to build this factory?"

"I plan on getting a loan."

Incredulity suffused his features and then he must have caught himself because he looked away. When he faced her again, his swarthy face was wiped clean of emotion. "I'll wish you good fortune then." His voice was carefully neutral. He finished the remainder of his Madeira and placed the glass on a table.

His casual dismissal of her plan rankled. He'd been outwardly polite, not saying what he was thinking: that she had no chance of obtaining a loan. At least, Rafael believed she had a chance. She shook her head; she must quit thinking about Rafael. He wasn't her savior, and the sooner she realized it, the sooner she would be able to face the obstacles awaiting her.

Swallowing the last of her wine, she placed the empty glass on the table. Silence stretched heavily between them, but she didn't want to be the one to break it. The silence extended even beyond the room. The orchestra had quit playing. They must have declared an intermission, she guessed. She found the sudden quiet unnerving, almost oppressive.

And she felt very weary. Exhausted, really. The weight of

her dilemma pressed upon her. Without money, she was a fool to think she could build a factory. And she couldn't continue living off Destiny's charity, either. She wondered where Destiny was and if she were dancing and having a good time. She hoped so.

Her last chance might be Warner. Maybe he would have arrived by now. Gathering her skirts in one hand, she rose to her feet.

"*Un momento,* Señorita Herrera. There might be a way for you to get your loan." He got to his feet and smiled at her.

Careful to avoid looking at his teeth, she responded shortly, "*¿Sí?*"

"I also came to Key West to make my fortune. So far, I've done rather well." His pigeon's chest puffed up. "I'm always looking for new ventures, new ways to make money. If you have the land and the expertise, I might be interested in helping you. Not strictly as a lender, though—more as a silent partner."

It was her turn to hide her astonishment. Not even Rafael had offered to back her. *Stop thinking about Rafael!* she commanded herself. *Pay attention to the business at hand.*

Cortez was offering her a glimmer of hope. But the thought of him as her partner, or any man as her partner, dampened her enthusiasm. She had a decision to make, and it wouldn't be easy.

In the past, she'd learned to follow her instincts, and her instincts had seldom proven wrong. Her mother called it her sixth sense. Intuitively, she knew better than to take a man as her partner. It would defeat her plan for independence.

"Thank you for your kind offer. I'm flattered you would consider going into business with me. But I'm afraid I must insist upon a loan. I don't believe in partnerships. The unfortunate choice of a partner is what ruined my father's estate," she supplied adroitly, hating how easily the lie slipped from her lips.

"I see." He rocked back and forth on the balls of his feet and steepled his hands together. "That is unfortunate. I prefer a partnership because if you're successful, I would share in the profits. A loan's rate is fixed.''

"Yo entiendo, Señor Cortez, and if I didn't feel so strongly, I would—''

"Don't apologize," he interjected. As if to soothe her, he reached out and placed his hand on her arm.

She stared at his hand in horror. Was this the way of it? Was this why he'd offered to back her? Would this be the only way she'd obtain financial help, as Rafael had insinuated? By whoring herself? At the thought, she recoiled, flinching away from him.

He hastily withdrew. *"Por favor,* I didn't mean to . . . to . . . I was merely trying to . . .'' he stammered. Pulling a silk handkerchief from his vest pocket, he mopped his brow and looked utterly stricken. "A thousand apologies, Señorita Herrera. I've offended you and rightly so. *Por favor,* take the loan. I will make you a loan and at a good rate, too. It is the least I can do, especially with you orphaned and having no protector.'' His chest swelled again. "We Cubanos take care of our own. We are an honorable people. Let me help you, Señorita Herrera.''

She weighed the sincerity in his voice. From the corner of her eye, she stole a glimpse at him. She could detect no hidden lust lurking in the depths of his muddy brown eyes. He appeared to be sincere in his apologies, that he hadn't meant anything improper when he touched her. That he didn't expect "other favors'' for his financial backing.

Closing her eyes, she searched her heart, allowing her instincts to take over. What did her inner voice tell her? Try as she might, she received no strong impulses, one way or the other. She felt neither trepidation nor enthusiasm. It was strange, this sudden lack of emotion, this stillness of her inner voice.

But she'd suffered a surfeit of emotions already. Maybe she didn't feel strongly because this would be, as he'd protested, an honorable proposition. A business proposition, nothing more. Thinking of it that way, she felt her hopes lift. Her dream was within reach. After the disappointments of the past few days, it was almost too good to be true.

"I accept your apology, Señor Cortez, and your kind offer to help me. But I must insist that it be handled as you would any other business transaction. I expect to pay a fair rate of interest to cover your risk. We'll need to work out the details and put them on paper."

"*Gracias,* Señorita Herrera, for your forgiveness. We will, as you say, make this a fair business proposition."

"*Muy bien.*" Feeling powerful and a little closer to her dream of independence, she thrust her hand out, wanting to seal their bargain with a handshake, as the Americans did.

He stared at her hand for a long time before tentatively taking it and giving it the briefest squeeze.

"Shall we discuss the details?" she asked.

"*Sí.* But first, I think we deserve a celebratory dance. Don't you?"

Thinking of the bright future ahead, her heart raced, pounding in her chest. A celebratory dance sounded good. Suddenly, she wasn't tired anymore. In fact, she could dance all night, the way she was feeling. Nodding agreement, she linked her arm with his and they exited the study.

Chapter Seven

"Oh, Nathan, I'm so sorry. I had intended to wait for you," Destiny rushed to explain. It felt good to be held in Nathan's strong arms after being leered at by the middle-aged, married Henry Greene. "I didn't want to dance, but Mister Greene—"

"Don't worry, I understand," he stopped her. "Major Beale explained what happened and gave me your dance program." He drew it from his breast pocket. "They took it from you, didn't they?"

She nodded, feeling callow and naive. What must Nathan think of her, allowing those men to take her program and usurp her dances? Glancing at his face, she found his features had turned to stone and his eyes glittered with suppressed fury. He drew himself up and his body went rigid. Surely, his anger and displeasure weren't for her?

"Do you want to honor any of these dances?" He thrust the program at her.

Reluctantly, she took it from him and looked at the names scrawled there. Not knowing what to do, she stared at it until the names blurred, running together. Another dance had started and Rudolph Phillips moved toward her, avid interest gleaming in his eyes. Seeing his look and remembering the way Henry had looked at her, she recoiled, sheltering in the crook of Nathan's arm.

She'd wanted to appear attractive and desirable tonight. She'd wanted men to seek her out to dance, especially one man. But she'd gotten far more than she bargained for. It was one thing when Nathan looked at her and offered his undying love and the honorable institution of marriage. It was another thing when her neighbors, who had barely acknowledged her existence before, stared at her as if they wanted to undress her and . . . and . . .

"No, I don't want to honor any of the dances. They were taken without my permission." Gazing up at him, she breathed, "I only want to dance with you."

He smiled at her, his features relaxing for a moment. "I thought so." Taking the program from her, he declared, "I'll take care of this."

Leaving her side, he strode forward. His wide shoulders blocked most of her view, and she rose on tiptoe, straining to see, wondering what he would do.

She didn't have long to wait. Without breaking stride, he grasped Rudolph Phillips's arm and steered him back to the ring of men. Rudolph appeared to take offense at Nathan's action, wresting his arm free and rebuking him.

But Nathan merely ignored his protests and faced the group with her dance program in one hand. Lifting the program high, he slowly tore it into tiny pieces, allowing the flimsy cardboard bits to drift to the floor.

"Gentlemen, and I use that term lightly after what happened tonight, Miss Destiny Favor has declined to dance with you." Rudolph Phillips started forward again, arguing. Nathan reached out, placing his hand on Rudolph's chest, pushing him back. "She's declined to dance with *any* of you." He leaned into Rudolph's face. "Do I make myself clear?"

The ring of men fell back, murmuring and gesturing. Nathan

and Rudolph, frozen together in a tableau of simmering animosity, glared at each other, eyeball to eyeball.

Destiny gasped, afraid of what might happen. Placing her hand over her heart, she tried to slow its painful galloping.

Nathan's voice, strong and clear but deceptively soft, drifted to her. "If anyone objects to Miss Favor's decision, I'll gladly give him satisfaction."

Raising his head, he glanced at Major Beale, who had been standing apart from the proceedings and watching with a wry smile. The two men exchanged the briefest of nods before Nathan continued, "Major Beale will stand as my second. Any arrangements can be made with him." Carefully lifting his hand from Rudolph's chest, he paused, staring hard at the men before bowing to them. "I bid you good evening, gentlemen."

Gasping again and unable to draw breath into her lungs, Destiny thought she would faint. Nathan had just offered his life for her honor. She could scarcely believe what had happened. He was so brave and noble! Tears stung the corners of her eyes, threatening to spill down her cheeks.

She drew her shoulders back, pride suddenly filling her, making her feel like the most cherished woman alive. But then she glimpsed the men's faces as they turned away, especially Rudolph's. His face was purple, looking for all the world like a ripe eggplant, and his features were twisted with rage.

Half-forgotten childhood memories of Rudolph rose to her mind. He'd been a mean boy with a streak of cruelty, she remembered, recalling how he liked to catch spotted geckos and dismember them, limb by limb. Shuddering at the memory, she feared for Nathan. What if Rudolph challenged him to a duel? She would never forgive herself.

Nathan rejoined her, taking her trembling form in his strong and capable arms. Murmuring into her hair, he soothed, "Forget it ever happened, Destiny. It shouldn't have happened. I'll speak to Colonel Brown when we leave."

"No, please, don't do that," she replied without thinking. What had made her say that? After everything that had happened tonight, she didn't care what Key West thought of her. If tonight was any indication, Key West society, to which she'd aspired, was composed of leering men and sneering women. Maybe Gramps had been right all this time, to keep her from so-called "polite society."

Lifting her head proudly, she glanced around the ballroom, dismissing its occupants with a haughty stare. She didn't need them, not any of them. She had Nathan—strong and capable, comforting and reassuring Nathan. He loved her and was willing to sacrifice his life for her. What more could she possibly want?

"Let's dance," he said, taking her into his arms.

She followed him willingly, reveling in his strength and gentleness, and the love she saw shining in his eyes.

Acting on instinct, Rafael moved purposefully across the crowded dance floor, angling to cut off Angelina and Cortez. The three of them arrived together in front of the orchestra. Rafael leaned over and tapped Cortez's shoulder. *"Con su permiso,* I believe Señorita Herrera promised this dance to me."

Cortez spun to a halt but kept his arm around Angelina's waist. Lifting his face to Rafael, he smiled, revealing blackened teeth. Rafael suddenly realized they'd never been this close before. Their struggle was a hidden one, played at arm's length, like a chess match with both opponents blindfolded but each intuitively aware of the other's strategy.

"Señor Estava, what a pleasant surprise." Cortez dripped oily, false cordiality. "This is certainly a special occasion with the three of us, the only Cubanos in the room, coming together. It's a night for celebration." He glanced at Angelina, giving her a knowing look.

Rafael thought he saw some kind of recognition in her deep violet eyes. A flicker and then it was gone. What had Cortez meant by that? That he and Angelina were sharing more than a dance together was too hideous to contemplate. Then Rafael remembered Angelina's absence from the ballroom. Where had she been? Not closeted with his enemy.

The ballroom started spinning, even though he was standing quite still. His earlier headache returned with sudden ferocity. The images of Angelina's and Cortez's faces blurred and wavered, stained with a delicate crimson to match the blood thundering in his veins. Clenching and unclenching his hands, he needed every shred of self-control to resist grabbing Cortez's throat and squeezing until the man's beady eyes popped from their sockets.

He held out his arm, prompting, "Angelina."

Her violet eyes bore into his, and she pursed her lips. He could see her chin trembling with the effort to bring herself under control. For a brief second, he thought she would refuse him.

Finally, she said to Cortez, "I must apologize for my escort's discourteous manner. *Por favor,* accept my apologies, as I'm certain it's my fault. He *did* bring me to the ball, and I've ignored him disgracefully. You must understand his displeasure. We'll talk more later."

Stiffly, she took Rafael's arm and riveted her gaze upon him, twin fires of fury burning in the depths of her eyes.

"Claro que sí, Señorita Herrera. I accept your apology and can quite understand your escort's displeasure," Cortez replied. "It must be painful to lose such a beautiful and charming lady as yourself to other admirers." Bending from the waist, he took her hand and slobbered over it. Rafael averted his eyes in disgust.

Releasing her hand, he bowed low to Rafael, offering, "And I forgive you, too, Señor Estava, as one Cubano patriot to another."

"I'm not a fellow patriot, not the way you mean it," Rafael contradicted him. "And I don't need a woman to apologize for my behavior either." He glared at Angelina. "If you demand further satisfaction, Señor Cortez, you know where to find me."

Taking Angelina's arm, he started to pull her away. But

Cortez forestalled them by interjecting, "Señorita Herrera, it will be my pleasure to call for you tomorrow morning after breakfast. You can show me the property then, and we'll finish discussing our terms. Will that be convenient?"

"Perfectly convenient. I'll look forward to it," she responded, smiling like the cat that had just swallowed the canary. With a forceful shake, she wrenched her arm from Rafael's grasp and started across the ballroom floor.

Gazing after her stiff-necked form, he cursed her headstrong ways under his breath. It was beneath his dignity to trail after her, but she had a great deal of explaining to do. Then he glimpsed the smirking face of Cortez from the corner of his eye. To stay where he was, was even more distasteful.

Muttering, *"Maldita sea,"* he went after her.

Destiny retrieved her ivory-backed fan and set it into motion, fanning her flushed face. She and Nathan had just danced the last four dances, and the ballroom felt stifling after their exertions. And her new slippers pinched her toes. She was glad they'd stopped to rest.

"What about that fruit punch you never had?" Nathan asked, as if he could read her mind. Pulling a silk handkerchief from his pocket, he mopped his brow, admitting, "I could use some refreshment, too."

Obviously not wanting to tempt fate again, he tucked her arm in his and led her toward the refreshment table. Halfway there, the crowd shifted and moved away, leaving them isolated among a sea of faces. Whispered snatches of conversation reached Destiny's ears, heating her flushed face even hotter.

Lifting her head, she came face-to-face with the clear gray eyes of James Whitman. The breath left her body, and her mouth dropped open. He was making straight for them. What could he want? After what had happened earlier, she was in no rush to find out. In fact, she had the strongest urge to bury her face against Nathan's broad chest, like pictures she'd seen of ostriches burying their heads in sand.

She'd come to the ball to snag James's attention and charm him. Unfortunately, the Destiny that had been naive enough to believe she could accomplish that goal with no repercussions was gone forever.

He stopped before Nathan, his hand outstretched. "Captain Rodgers, your servant, sir."

Nathan clasped his hand, returning the handshake. "You have the advantage, sir. I've seen you in town, but I confess I don't know your name."

"James Whitman of Key West." He bowed.

"Pleased to make your acquaintance, Mr. Whitman." Turning to her, Nathan offered, "And this is Destiny Favor."

Recovering from her initial astonishment, Destiny realized she'd gone and done it again. Left her mouth hanging open. Covering her face with the fan, she closed her mouth, berating herself under her breath.

"I know Destiny, Captain Rodgers. She and I are old school chums. Aren't we, Destiny?"

If adoring James Whitman from afar had set her pulses racing, being this close to him and having his considerable charm directed at her was something else entirely.

"Yes, I mean, I guess we are," she agreed.

He smiled at her, making her stomach somersault. Then he directed his attention to Nathan, lowering his voice, "I heard about your earlier trouble. The colonel sent me to apologize for the lack of manners among his guests. Unfortunate business."

"Yes, indeed, unfortunate." Nathan glanced at Destiny.

It was obvious from his look that he didn't like James bringing up the subject in front of her. She bridled at his subtle criticism of James. After all, the incident had involved her. James was only trying to reassure her.

"Under the circumstances, I know it's very forward of me to ask . . ." James paused and looked at Destiny. His steel-gray eyes gave her shivers, while at the same time, she felt her insides liquefying into mush.

"Would you mind if Destiny and I shared this next dance?" he continued. "For old times' sake, of course. The ball's almost over, and I wanted to ask her earlier but feared to intrude."

Nathan hesitated, glancing at her again. Destiny met his gaze, trying to appear calm and unruffled, but inside, she quaked with barely suppressed excitement.

It was the moment she'd been waiting for!

James Whitman had noticed her and asked her to dance. Her earlier problems receded, faded away, disappearing as if they'd never happened. And more important, James didn't seem offended by the unfortunate scene. He'd even come to offer the colonel's apologies, which must mean he sided with her and thought the other guests were in the wrong. Her hopes took wing and flew.

"Ask Destiny if she wants to dance. It's her choice," Nathan responded gruffly.

"Destiny?" James addressed her.

Gazing into his handsome face, inches from her own, she almost swooned. This was *her* moment, the moment she'd dreamed about for years. But she must appear cool and sophisticated, even if the effort killed her.

"For old times' sake," she accepted with a laugh and toss of her head. Offering her hand to James, he took it. Almost as an afterthought, she said, "Thank you, Nathan. I'll be back before you know it."

Then James drew her into his embrace, and the everyday world faded away. Whirling around the dance floor, she savored each second of their contact. So intent was she upon memorizing every detail of his handsome face, the smell of him, and the feel of him, that she completely lost track of time.

"A penny for your thoughts." His deep voice shocked her back to reality.

Realizing she'd been dancing, mute and probably with a stupid look on her face, she tried to cover her feelings by admitting part of the truth. "I was thinking how handsome you look in formal attire. I don't believe I've ever seen you in evening clothes before."

As soon as the words left her mouth, she was astonished by her own audacity. What she'd just said amounted to nothing less than a thinly veiled admission that she'd never been invited to a Key West society function before tonight. Did the exclusion so rankle her that she had to remind James of her nonexistent social status?

Despite her internal precautions, her careless tongue had already done its damage. She could have bitten it in two.

But James didn't make the connection or he chose to ignore it because he played along, drawling, "What a coincidence. I was thinking I'd never seen you in a ball gown and couldn't believe how stunning you look. You've grown up, Destiny Favor, into a very beautiful young woman."

For once in her life, she was speechless. She hadn't conquered her tongue, not exactly, it was just that neither her brain nor her tongue seemed to be in working order. All she could think about was that he'd said she was beautiful. James Whitman, the man of her dreams, thought she was beautiful. There were no words to say.

Her lack of response didn't seem to deter him, though. He leaned closer and brushed his lips against her neck. It was the lightest of touches, a gossamer kiss.

With his lips close to her ear, he murmured, "I feel that I've discovered hidden treasure tonight, right here in Key West. And one dance isn't enough to savor that discovery, not nearly enough. May I call upon you tomorrow after supper?"

Taking several long strides, Rafael caught up with Angelina. With his blood boiling and his pride in tatters, he didn't bother with social amenities. Grabbing her elbow, he jerked her around and brought her up hard against his chest.

The feel of her body pressed tightly against his only added

fuel to the fire simmering in his veins. It had been one thing to hold her in his arms, observing the social proprieties and spinning around the dance floor. He'd felt his passion rise then, and to deflect it, he'd taunted her. But when he pulled her to him in anger, the sensation was altogether different. Passion, he knew, even the most tender kind, held an element of danger and suppressed violence, a sense of losing oneself in sensations of the flesh.

He'd thought that part of him was dead. But he'd been wrong, so very wrong.

With her breasts crushed against his chest, he felt his body come alive, alive after all these years. His manhood rose, throbbing and turgid, straining against the placket of his pants. He wanted to bury himself in her, bury himself and his painful past, forgetting everything that had happened. Returning to a youth they'd never been allowed to share, a younger and more carefree time.

"Rafael," she hissed, struggling in his arms.

A portion of his sanity returned. He remembered where he was, where they both were, in a crowded ballroom with plenty of wagging tongues around them.

In an effort to cover his impropriety, he tightened his hold and moved into the dizzying stream of dancers. With Angelina resisting every step of the way, he half-led, half-carried her across the dance floor, spinning her around and around until they reached the French doors leading to the terrace.

Despite her continued resistance, he pulled her through the open doors, praying the terrace would be deserted this time. Glancing about, he found his prayers had been answered. Urging her forward like a recalcitrant mule, he pushed her toward a stone bench. Taking both her shoulders in his hands, he gently forced her down upon it.

But she didn't stay there. Instead, like a demented jack-in-the-box, she rose again before he could stop her. Toe-to-toe, she confronted him. Even in the semi-darkness he could discern the flash of fury in her eyes, could sense the rigidity of her body.

"How dare you manhandle me," she spat.

"How dare you consort with the likes of Cortez," he countered. "The man's a viper."

"Oh, really, and I suppose you're an angel sent from heaven." She rolled her eyes, the whites gleaming in the spilled light from the ballroom.

"I'm no angel," he admitted, remembering his response to her body. And feeling the burning need of it still. "But I do possess a modicum of honor. Cortez has none. He will do anything to line his pockets, including killing people."

"What do you mean by that?"

He hesitated, calculating how much he should tell her. She was adept at deception and quite capable of keeping a secret, he knew that much about her. But he must be careful what he told her, lest she piece together his past and uncover his identity.

"Do you know what filibustering means?"

"No, should I?" she huffed. "And if this is going to take all night, I'm not interested." She tried to move past him, but he blocked her way.

"You're going to hear this, whether you want to or not."

"Then I might as well make myself comfortable," she muttered with an exasperated sigh. Turning, she flounced down on the bench and stared at him, an explicit challenge in her eyes.

"Make yourself comfortable, *por favor,*" he agreed with irony. It was one thing when he'd tried to seat her on the bench, another when she decided to seat herself.

"Tell me, I'm all ears," she mocked. "What is this filibustering?"

"Filibustering is a way of raising arms for the Cuban revolution from a safe distance, here in Key West."

"So? It sounds like a good plan to me. Aren't you in favor of freeing our homeland?"

"*Sí,* I am. But not by armed conflict. There are other ways."

Her eyes narrowed. "Not by armed conflict," she repeated,

her voice making a mockery of his words. "This, from a man who just challenged another man to a duel."

"Don't use that against me, Angelina," he managed to grate out.

"*¿Por qué?* What is so awful about this filibustering if it will set Cuba free?"

"Many innocent people have been killed, Angelina. That's why it's so awful." He felt his stomach clench, remembering. And he didn't want to remember. It was as close as he dared to come to the truth. "Besides, Cortez, despite his protestations, doesn't filibuster out of patriotic fervor. He does it to make money. He doesn't *give* the armaments to the rebels, he *sells* them."

She didn't answer. Instead, she sat, as still as if she'd become a part of the stone bench. Finally, she muttered, "And?"

"Isn't that enough, Angelina?"

"No, it merely means he's hungry for money. Many men are hungry for money. And the revolution in Cuba will continue, whether people give or sell the arms. You must know that, Rafael."

Did she really feel that way? So cynical and jaded about human behavior, believing there was nothing one could do to stop the devastation of human life? If she did, then she was far more scarred than he.

"What if I told you he caused wrecks, like the one Destiny's grandfather salvaged? That he sent innocent men to the bottom of the sea for his own gain?"

Her head lifted and she searched his face. "Do you have proof of this? And if you have proof, why haven't you gone to the authorities?"

He expelled his breath. Her logic was irrefutable. She'd seen to the heart of the matter without really trying. He remembered her as a young girl, quick and intelligent, grasping complex concepts readily. Angelina was no fool to be easily led.

Dipping his head, he admitted, "No, I don't have proof. There are only rumors. Rumors, I might add, which Destiny's grandfather believes.'' He paused, lowering his voice to a whisper, "Proof will be forthcoming, you can count on that."

She rose to her feet. "Are you finished?"

"*Sí.*"

He lifted his hand to his scarred cheek and wearily brushed the deep grooves there, thinking he hadn't accomplished anything. Angelina was headstrong and determined. She'd always been that way. Her seven brothers, taken collectively, didn't possess half of her iron will.

"Then I'll find Destiny and Nathan," she declared. "The ball is coming to an end. I'll go home with them. You needn't bother."

But he couldn't let her go like this. He'd exhausted all of his arguments and not convinced her to stay away from the man. He had to know what she planned to do.

"What does Cortez mean to you?" he challenged. "What has he promised you? Why is he taking you to see your land? What are you going to discuss?"

She laughed. Laughed in his face, her laughter taunting him, daring him. "I thought you brought me to the ball to find financial backing. Well, I found it. Cortez is willing to lend me the money for my factory."

"You can't be serious."

"I'm serious. More than serious. And your attempt to blacken his reputation only shows petty jealousy on your part. You're not my keeper, Señor Estava." She tossed her head. "No man is."

"It's not jealousy, Angelina. And his reputation doesn't need to be blackened by me; it's already as black as his teeth."

Her head snapped back, and he knew he'd scored a hit, bringing up Cortez's unsavory personal hygiene. But she was furious with him as well, he realized.

"*¡Basta!*" she spat, gathering her skirts in one hand.

For the second time, she tried to brush past him. Her haughty dismissal and hardheadedness infuriated him. To join herself to Cortez was tantamount to throwing herself to the lions. But he'd failed to convince her about Cortez, and recognizing his failure, he felt his temper flare and his passion rise in direct proportion.

Reaching out, he grabbed her shoulders and roughly pulled her to him. She struggled in protest, just as she'd done in the ballroom. But he didn't care, as long as she didn't scream out. He'd waited a lifetime for this. A lifetime of pain and hurt and unfulfilled desire. Glancing down at her violet eyes, he read the condemnation there.

When she opened her mouth, he knew she was about to scream, but before the breath could leave her body, he covered her mouth with his.

His lips met stony resistance. Her body was rigid in his arms. She elbowed him hard in the stomach, and he almost released her. But he was stronger than she and more determined.

Enfolding her in his embrace, he ignored her struggles and concentrated on taking what he wanted. What he'd wanted for the better part of his life. He'd dreamed of holding Angelina and kissing her. Of making love to her. *Dios* help him, he'd dreamed of it when he'd honeymooned with his young wife . . . And for this, he was damned. Damned and guilty for all eternity.

His mind grasped the implications, but his flesh held him prisoner.

And now his dreams were reality. He was holding Angelina in his arms and kissing her. She probably hated him. Or at least, hated his forceful approach. Hate was a strong emotion, closely akin to love. Did he want her to love him?

There was no time to consider.

The sensation of kissing Angelina was too bittersweet, too piquant to ignore. His mouth moved over hers, lavishing tiny kisses over her closed lips. His tongue explored the corners of her mouth, licking and nipping. Slowly, bit by bit, he felt her unfold, like a delicate blossom loosing its petals to the sun.

He felt her body melt into his embrace, flowing, like molten lava, from stony indifference into liquid heat. She pressed closer, twining her fingers into his hair and moaning against his mouth.

Her lips opened to him, wet and sweet, clinging and tantalizing, welcoming him. Accepting her unspoken invitation, he insinuated his tongue within, plunging into the hot honeypot of her mouth. Touching her intimately, he almost recoiled from shock. Every nerve in his body stretched taut, thin as wire, strumming with need. His blood heated, moving thickly through his veins.

His hands came up and he cupped her breasts through the rose satin fabric of her gown. Her nipples strained against the gown, rising into stone-hard points. Finding the pebble-points, he stroked them, setting up a delicious friction between his fingertips and the fabric of her bodice.

Leaning against him for support, she moaned into his open mouth and returned his kiss, meeting his tongue with her own. Twirling the soft nap of it around his, she explored the recesses of his mouth with her own feverish need.

With her mouth clinging to his, she devoured him with a ferocity to match his own. Reaching up, he encircled her neck with his hand. Her flesh was hot and moist to the touch, lightly scented with lavender. At the base of her throat, he felt her pulse, pounding like a bass drum against his fingertips. Realizing that his touch and kisses had affected her strongly, he groaned and moved, grinding his hips against her until he flattened her thick petticoats and could feel the outline of her slender legs beneath her satin skirts.

Her body yielded to his invasion, going taut and then supple in his arms. Recognizing her sweet surrender to his brutal invasion, the fever raged in his blood. When it came to Angelina, he realized darkly, he was an animal. A rutting animal, desperate to have her.

Slowly, he circled his fingertips over her heated throat, slipping lower and lower, delving past the lace at her neckline, careful lest his enthusiastic passion tear its fragile scallop. Sliding lower, he found the full, round swell of her silken breast.

Touching her petal-soft skin, he caught his breath, reveling in the rich reward of her. His hand caressed her fullness, slipping lower until he found the budded point of her nipple and the delicately puckered aureola surrounding it.

Constrained by the tightness of her bodice, he managed to splay his fingers over her nipple, stroking and caressing, wanting to give her pleasure, as the feel of her gave him pleasure. A pleasure so pure, so profound that he wanted to scream her name at the top of his lungs. Wanted to bend her to his will and strip the clothes from her. Wanted to drop her to the fragrant grass and thrust into her with all the savage force of his desire.

Thinking of having her, he went wild with need. Forgetting the fragile fabric of her bodice, he flexed his hand, straining to touch her other breast, to claim all of her for his own. A loud, tearing sound ruptured the silence.

Angelina reared back, wrenching her mouth from his. Clasping her torn bodice to her bosom, her breath came in pants, slow and thick. Light from the ballroom caught in her wide eyes, striking sparks in their midnight-purple depths. Unfulfilled passion burned there, mixed with indignation and fury.

Intuitively recoiling from the strange mixture in her eyes, he took a step back and opened his mouth. He wanted to apologize for his impetuosity and for spoiling her gown. For allowing his unbridled lust to overcome his common sense. For being a fool.

Her hand lashed out before he could speak, striking his scarred cheek with a resounding blow, making his ears ring.

Sweeping her shawl up, she covered her ripped gown, warning him, "Don't ever come near me again, Señor Estava."

Then she ran from the terrace, as if all the hounds of hell pursued her. He watched her go, knowing it was he, not her, that the hounds pursued.

Chapter Eight

"I plan on building my factory there." Angelina pointed to a barely perceptible rise of land on her lot. "It's approximately at the center and slightly higher than the rest."

"*Sí,* that seems to be a good choice," Cortez responded while prodding the soft ground with the tip of his walking cane.

She sighed, guessing what he was thinking. "I know my land is marshy and not ideal for structures. I had thought to build a simple structure, open to the air, with a thatched roof overhead. It will provide a cool place to work while being economical to build."

"Economical maybe, but hardly practical. You'll need, at the least, an enclosed storage place." He glanced at her. "That is, unless you intend upon curing your own tobacco. Then you'll need—"

"No, Señor Cortez, I won't be curing tobacco. I plan on purchasing the filler, binders, and wrappers from Cuba. But you're right, I'll need enclosed storage space to protect against thieves."

He relaxed a fraction. She could sense his relief. It was odd, his intense interest in her plans, down to the smallest detail. She hadn't expected him to be so interested. But then, she hadn't known what to expect. This was her first foray into the business world.

"You'll need an enclosed office, too. You can't expect to keep records and transact business in the open like a common peddler."

She glanced at him from the corner of her eye. Gone was the courteous cavalier of last night's ball, to be replaced by a hard-headed businessman. She couldn't fault him for his attention to detail. But this was the first open criticism he'd voiced. His censure stung. Not because her "delicate" sensibilities were offended, but because what he said was right.

Silently cursing herself for not thinking ahead, she agreed, "You're right. I'll need a large enclosed storage space as well as a secure office."

"Made of brick," he added.

"Brick would be serviceable, but wood is more economical."

"*Sí,* more economical, but easy prey to fire. You must build for the future, Señorita Herrera, rather than worrying about finances. I will worry about the finances, and I want you to build a factory that will last. Only through longevity, profitable longevity, will I recoup my loan and interest."

So he wanted to protect his investment. That made sense to her. Remembering Rafael's condemnation of the man, she wondered how much truth there was to his accusations. Truth or petty jealousy, it was hard to tell. She pushed away her doubts, not wanting anything to interfere with building her factory. And she didn't want to think about Rafael.

What he'd done last night had been monstrous. She'd fled Cuba to rid herself of domineering men. Rafael had forced himself upon her, kissing and fondling her as if she were a backstreet harlot.

And the most monstrous part was that she'd wanted him to do exactly what he'd done. Every fiber of her being had strained toward him, welcoming his touch. He'd awakened a fire in her that she didn't know she possessed. He'd commanded her flesh and her flesh had answered, craving more.

It was too horrible to contemplate, the power he held over her. She'd thought she would be her own woman in Key West, capable of making her own decisions. She hadn't counted on becoming a willing slave to her body. If he hadn't torn her bodice and inadvertently brought her to her senses, she didn't know what would have happened.

Shuddering, she pulled her shawl tighter around her shoulders, despite the morning heat, and tried to forget what had happened.

They'd paced the boundaries of her land and arrived back at their starting place on Frances Street. She was eager to discuss the terms of the loan and when she would get the money to start.

Unfortunately, Cortez wasn't done with probing her plans. Next, he asked, "How large will the structure be, Señorita Herrera? Have you thought of the dimensions? How many workers will you employ?"

He was shrewder than she'd given him credit for. He was willing to lend her the money and not stint on the fundamentals. But it was obvious he wanted an accounting of every *centavo*. For the first time, she felt over her head and wondered if she were suited to the world of business. She was accustomed to doing things on a whim without considering the details. Her mother had often chided her for her frivolous attitude.

Taking a deep breath, she realized that if she wanted to succeed in business, she must pay more attention to details. It would take an effort of concentration. Maybe she should start making notes so as to not forget anything. She wished she'd brought a piece of paper and pencil.

"I had hoped to start with ten workers and grow to twenty," she finally answered after considering.

"Twenty might give you a good living, any number below that will provide mere subsistence." He flashed a smile at her, and she automatically recoiled from his rotting teeth before she could stop herself. His gaze fastened on her best day dress, an exquisitely tailored, midnight-blue serge, finished with antique lace. "You are accustomed to a certain style of living, are you not?" He smiled again, but this time she was prepared and didn't flinch.

Instead, it was his comment that caught her off guard. Realizing the hidden meaning behind his words, she felt her neck grow hot. She'd worn her best dress to impress him. Unfortunately, the expensive dress didn't mesh with the story of her father's financial ruin. And last night, he'd appeared skeptical because she wasn't wearing mourning. Did he doubt her story? And if he doubted it, why was he willing to lend her money?

Because, as Rafael had said, Cortez was willing to do anything for a profit. If that was the case, rather than make her uneasy, the realization buoyed her. Here was a shrewd businessman, who believed in her venture and its capability to make money. That thought gave her added hope for success.

Still, she didn't want to give away her real story, whether Cortez cared or not about her background. Her sixth sense told her not to take him into her confidence, to keep their dealings centered upon business.

"I'm accustomed to very little, Señor Cortez. My father possessed limited funds, and I grew up in a provincial town. I didn't even have the money to buy a proper mourning wardrobe, beyond two or three dresses for church." She found herself elaborating, hoping to deflect him. "I'll consider your recommendation."

He nodded, almost absentmindedly. Rising on the balls of his feet, he rocked back and forth. "With twenty workers, you'll need a foreman," he remarked.

"Señor Cortez, I want to run the factory myself. I really don't need the added expense of hiring a—"

"I know of an excellent man," he interrupted smoothly, "and he can be had very cheaply. He's currently working for the Silva's cigar factory but isn't happy there." He held up one hand, palm out, to stop her from protesting again. "I don't think you realize how much work it takes to properly supervise twenty workers. And you'll be busy with other duties, I assume. Such as procuring the best tobacco and wrappers, as well as overseeing the blending process. Let someone else take over the tedious task of watching the workers."

"You don't think I'm capable of running the factory because I'm a woman. That's it, isn't it?" Her old insecurities found voice, despite her best efforts to appear confident and self-assured.

The more he talked and urged his ideas upon her, the more she felt control slipping away. At first, she'd been grateful to him for making her think about the future. She'd been living in a dream world, expecting the cigar factory to spring forth with little or no effort on her part. He'd opened her eyes to her impetuous approach, and now she was trying to give every aspect her utmost consideration.

But he wanted to usurp every decision, forcing her to accept his point of view. Why would he want to do that? If she'd acceded to a partnership with him, it would make sense. As a lender, it didn't. She could only believe he didn't trust her because she was a woman.

He didn't answer. Instead, he turned away and withdrew a snuff box from his sleeve. Delicately, he inhaled the powdered tobacco and sneezed. Pulling a handkerchief from his pocket, he dabbed at his nose.

Watching his slow and deliberate actions, her frustration mounted. She twisted the strings of her reticule, tighter and tighter, until they made a red mark on her wrist. Exasperated, she untangled the strings and waited.

Had she offended him? Probably she had. It was unfortunate, but she wanted this factory to be hers, not his. She should have the final say. Realizing she had probably ruined their deal, she thought ahead. Would another lender, if she were to find one, be so demanding? And if they were, what would she do then?

Silently, she cursed her frantic departure from Cuba. Not

one to look back, she was beginning to recognize her past mistakes. If only she'd taken the time to have her jewelry appraised. If only she'd cajoled her brothers into lending her some extra spending money. If only she'd stolen the necessary funds from her father's strongbox. But a thousand regrets and recriminations wouldn't change her present situation.

Sneezing again, Cortez pinched his nostrils. Facing her once more, he said, "I thought we had settled your capabilities last night. I apologize if I've given offense, but I'm merely trying to help you, my dear. The final decision is yours." He gazed at her. "Might I inquire how large an operation your father ran? How many workers did he have?"

Angelina sucked in her breath. More lies, he needed to hear more lies from her. She hated lying. If only she'd brought enough money, she thought again. But to keep looking back would only lead to failure. She must keep her wits about her and answer as honestly as she could.

Her father had run a large factory, employing fifty workers. The operation had kept her father and four of her brothers occupied. With her father and four brothers, that was one supervisor for each ten workers. Maybe Cortez wasn't far from wrong, but she couldn't tell him the truth.

"My father's factory was small, employing ten workers," she fabricated. "That was why I wanted to start with ten."

He snorted. Whether in reaction to her statement or to clear his nostrils, she didn't know. Frustrated and half angry at how their meeting was going, she was beginning not to care.

"There, you see, Señorita Herrera. Your father's operation was small enough to be easily controlled by one person. You haven't had any experience with a larger operation?"

She shook her head.

"Then please consider my arguments." He pulled his gloves from his coat pocket and carefully replaced them, finger by finger. She thought she would scream, watching him. "I think we should reconsider, Señorita Herrera."

Here it was. The crushing end to her dream. She drew inward, preparing herself for the blow.

"You should do some research and decide exactly what you want. I can only suggest. The decision must come from you because you are the one who will make this venture succeed, not I." He paused before adding, "You might want to visit the Silva factory and the other cigar factories in Key West, Señorita Herrera. For comparison purposes only, of course. When you've decided and put your plans into writing, please contact me."

He was dismissing her because her plan was vague and because she couldn't effectively argue her position. She felt totally deflated and lost, like a ship at sea without a rudder. She'd been so sure of herself, so certain of her capabilities when she'd started her self-proclaimed quest for freedom.

Now she was certain of nothing. Cortez, with a few carefully chosen inquiries had revealed the shallowness of her vision. He'd unmasked her ill-preparedness, her complete lack of business sense. Confidence and courage were important, and she felt she possessed both. But those traits rang hollow when struck against the unforgiving forge of knowledge. She thought the experience in her father's cigar factory would carry her through, but she was learning it wasn't that simple. Far from that simple, if she wanted to convince an investor to lend her money.

"How will I find you when I've made my decisions?" she asked.

"I have a modest office by the wharf. Ask anyone, they'll direct you." He offered his gloved hand. "The sun grows hot, don't you think? May I escort you home?"

Angelina chewed the stub of her pencil, her mind grinding. So many details and plans to organize. As she stared at the figures, they started to dance in her head, twirling and spinning before her eyes as if mocking her.

Furious, she grabbed up the papers and tore them to shreds, flinging the pieces to the four corners of her bedroom. For good measure, she tossed the pencil into the dustbin. Muttering to herself, she realized it was no good. Before she could make a plan, she must visit other cigar factories, as Cortez had suggested.

Without warning, Destiny burst into her room, dancing on the balls of her feet, arms outstretched as if she were embracing an invisible partner. Seeing her blatant joy, Angelina winced and sank into an even darker mood.

"Buenas noches, Angelina,'' Destiny greeted her. Beaming, she declared, ''I've been practicing my Spanish. Aren't you proud of me?''

"Muy bien, amiga mía,'' she saluted in return. ''And to what do I owe this honor?''

''Oh, Angelina, don't scowl so! Be happy for me, *amiga mía.''* Destiny's Southern drawl obliterated the accent of the Spanish words, rendering them almost unintelligible.

Wanting to grasp Destiny's shoulders and shake the happiness from her face, Angelina was appalled by her reaction. Forcing herself to return her friend's smile, she tried to put aside her depression. But it was difficult for her to forget her dilemma.

Away from the shelter of her father's home and his overbearing demands, she was beset by another unpalatable set of circumstances. Bleakly, she wondered if this was what it felt like to grow up, as her mother had so often suggested.

Destiny danced on, spinning around the desk where Angelina sat, moving to the music in her mind. Without stopping, she inquired, ''How many kinds of kisses are there, Angelina? I know you know.''

''How should I know?'' she countered, feeling uncommonly miffed at Destiny's reference to her unlimited experience in matters of the heart. True, she was more experienced than her friend, but if she had to bet again, she'd wager Destiny's experience was fast approaching her own.

Except with regard to Rafael. She'd never been so affected by a man before. His mere touch turned her to water. She shook her head. *Forget him,* she commanded herself.

Reaching out, she placed her hand on Destiny's arm. "If you would stop spinning around like a demented dervish, I might answer. You're making me dizzy."

Destiny laughed and stopped, pulling a chair up to the desk. Flouncing into it, she put her elbows on the desk and rested her face in her hands, a silly smile wreathing her face.

"Angelina, I just had the most wonderful evening of my life." She sighed and closed her eyes.

"With James Whitman?"

"Yes, with James. He's so wonderful."

"Seems everything is wonderful tonight," she remarked caustically.

"Oh, it is, it is." Destiny's eyes flew open. "Just think, *amiga mía,* my dreams are finally coming true."

Angelina felt a twinge of envy. She wished her dreams were coming true; instead, they were fast becoming dust. "That's wonderful," she observed halfheartedly, keeping the game going.

"Yes, wonderful," Destiny breathed again. "James took me walking and we talked and we watched the sunset and . . ."

"And kissed?"

"Yesss," her friend drew out the word, sighing again.

"So you want to know about kisses?"

"Please—ah, *por favor,*" Destiny replied.

"Let's skip the Spanish lesson tonight. Shall we?"

Destiny frowned. "You don't want me to learn your native tongue?"

"I'm honored that you want to do so." And if she put aside her own frustration and envy, she had to admit she was touched by her friend's gesture. "But you asked about kisses. That's serious business. I'll work on your Spanish later."

"That's fine. Just tell me about kisses."

"All right, I'll try. Of course, there's the chaste kind of kiss. Such as Gramps gives you on your forehead, but—"

Waving her hand, Destiny interrupted, "I know about chaste kisses. What about the other kind?"

"You want to know about a lover's kiss?"

"Yes, that's what I want to know about."

Angelina had guessed what she wanted to hear, but she was loath to discuss the subject. Unfortunately, she doubted that her friend would be dissuaded from the topic.

Taking a deep breath, she began, "There are two kinds of kisses a lover gives: one with his mouth closed and the other with his mouth open."

"And does the one with his mouth open involve tongues?" Destiny asked candidly.

Here it was. The question she'd been dreading. Feeling her eyes roll to the back of her head, she realized Destiny had been raised without a mother. And without a mother to discuss certain delicate matters, she doubted her friend knew the first thing about lovemaking. To put the matter bluntly, it was up to her to explain the facts of life to her friend.

When her own mother had thought she would be marrying that ancient planter, she'd explained, in detail, the conjugal duties of a wife. Angelina shuddered, remembering how ugly the instruction had been, especially considering her intended. Unfortunately, the details didn't repulse her when she thought of Rafael fulfilling them.

She stopped herself again. *Quit thinking of Rafael.*

Taking another deep breath, she wondered if she were equipped to properly act the part of a surrogate mother. But if she didn't do it, who would?

Destiny straightened her back, dreading the confrontation. She'd asked Tilly to say she wasn't at home, but Tilly had refused, claiming she wouldn't lie for anyone, especially not Destiny. For good measure, Tilly had told her that if she was so bent on lying, Destiny could go down herself and inform Nathan that she wasn't at home. She smiled to herself and shook her head at Tilly's ironic sense of moralizing.

The parlor door loomed before her. Stopping, she smoothed her skirts and pinched her cheeks for color. Throwing her shoulders back, she told herself there was no sense in waiting. Better to get it over with. Placing her hand on the brass knob, she pushed the door open slowly.

Nathan was standing in front of the window at the end of the parlor with his back to her, just as he had been that first day. Remembering, her heart executed a funny little leap in her chest.

She couldn't help but notice his broad back and wide shoulders. He stood with his hands laced behind his back, balancing on the balls of his feet, looking for all the world as if he were on the bridge of his ship, sailing into dangerous and uncharted waters. The thought gave her a funny thrill, as if an electric shock had passed through her body, leaving her breathless.

"Captain Rodgers—ah, Nathan, it's good to see you," she greeted him.

He spun around, surprise etched on his features. She'd thought he'd heard her come in and had chosen to wait until she spoke to him. But it was obvious he hadn't; she'd taken him unawares.

He lifted his hand and tugged at his collar while clearing his throat. She recognized his familiar gestures as nervous ones. Somehow, realizing he was as nervous as she made her feel more sure of herself.

"Good afternoon, Destiny," he finally returned her greeting. "You're looking very beautiful today," he offered and then averted his eyes.

His gesture struck her. Before, having no experience with men, she'd been a poor judge. After spending one evening with an imminently self-assured James, she recognized the signs. Nathan was an innocent like herself, at least in the ways of courting a woman. Nathan was shy!

The realization touched her, making her feel uncommonly warm and tender, as if her insides had turned to jelly. She found herself drawn to his full, expressive lips, remembering what they felt like, brushing over the skin of her hands, as soft as a butterfly's wings. And against her mouth, worshipping her as if she were a goddess.

Angelina had explained about the two kinds of lover's kisses and more. Much more. She felt her cheeks burning at the thought, recalling their discussion. Then another realization struck her, and she clapped her hands to her flushed cheeks, blurting, "You shaved your beard!"

His hazel eyes met hers for one brief second before focusing upon some point above her head. He rubbed the palm of his hand over his naked chin as if he wasn't quite accustomed to his bare skin, either. His newly shaven skin was much lighter than the tanned and weathered skin of his forehead.

"Yes, I shaved. I promised you I would. Remember?"

Heat suffused her, rising from her toes and fanning through her body, scorching her already flushed cheeks. How could she not remember? He'd offered to shave his beard when he'd kissed her because she'd protested that his beard scratched.

Looking for all the world like a cornered but determined animal, Nathan closed the gap between them in two swift strides. Clasping her shoulders, he murmured, "I've been dreaming of this."

His mouth descended, his full lips molding to hers, moving over her mouth with tender reverence. His fresh, baby-smooth flesh brushed against her, as soft as down and smelling of bay rum. Reveling in the sensation of kissing him, she raised her arms and twined them behind his neck. Standing on tiptoe, she found herself straining into his embrace.

Responding to her eagerness, he deepened the kiss, drawing her closer. Her breasts, crushed against the wall of his chest, tingled with a newfound awareness. Half-formed, forbidden images played through her mind, fueled by the titillating knowledge she'd learned from Angelina. Her blood heated, feeling like warm molasses flowing slowly through her veins. A strange languor stole over her, but at the same time, parts of her body felt more alive than ever before, aching with a bursting fullness of need.

Feeling wanton, she opened her mouth, wanting to draw him in, wanting him to invade her, to steal the very breath from her mouth. He reacted slowly, tentatively, brushing the tip of his tongue at the corners of her mouth, searching and soothing at the same time.

Her open mouth clung to his with feverish need, velvet flesh against velvet flesh. She stretched her tongue forward, meeting his. Their fine-grained, intimate flesh twined together, sending a jolt of indescribable desire flashing through her. The aftershock stole her reason, sapping the will from her, leaving her gasping and holding tight to his comforting strength.

Without warning, he broke off their kiss and pulled away, holding her at arm's length. She felt the abandonment keenly, wanting to cuddle in the reassuring strength of his arms, wanting to trace her tongue and lips over other parts of his sensitive skin. Wanting to explore . . .

Her reason returned with the swiftness of a lightning strike, and she felt her face flame hotter. What was she thinking? Had Angelina's discussion of the intimacies between a man and a woman affected her so that she couldn't wait to experience the forbidden pleasures?

But this was Nathan, not James, not her beloved. What had made her react so strongly to him? she wondered.

"I—I must know something, Destiny." He released her and lifted his hand to where his beard had been. Discovering its absence, he dropped his hand. "I can't just go on kissing and making love to you, although, as Jehovah is my witness, it's what I would like to do." He shook his head, as if to clear his thoughts. "But it's not right, I must know where I stand. Have you thought about what I asked at the ball?"

What had he asked at the ball?

Her passion-fogged mind strove to focus. The ball seemed

a million years ago; she'd learned so much, discovered a whole new world since then. Gone was the naive and trusting Destiny Favor who had attended that ball, gone forever, for better or for worse.

Realization dawned, painful and brittle-clear. He wanted to know where she stood with regard to his offer of marriage. Now that she knew everything marriage entailed and where children came from, she should feel repulsed. Shouldn't she?

Angelina had intimated that most women were repelled by intimacies with men they didn't love. But she didn't feel that way at all. She welcomed Nathan's kisses and caresses with a feverish abandonment, despite the fact that her heart was firmly with James.

Did that make her like the other kind of women Angelina had talked about? Women of the night, who for a sum of money, pleasured men as if they were wives? But she couldn't be like that. Could she? The very thought alarmed her, filling her with disgust.

"I don't know what to say, Nathan." She forced her lips to move. Her swollen lips, swollen with his kisses.

His gaze snagged hers, old and weary and sad, and she glimpsed the pain buried in the depths of his eyes. "Then you've answered me." He turned from her and walked across the room, appearing to study a portrait of her mother hanging over the mantelpiece.

"Your mother was very beautiful. It's easy to see where you inherited your looks," he observed.

"Thank you," was all she managed.

She wished there were words to ease his hurt. She couldn't help but remember how he'd championed her at the ball, standing up for her and sending her unwanted suitors packing. Risking his life to face down Rudolph Phillips, cruel and mean Rudolph Phillips. Thinking about it, she closed her eyes, feeling unworthy of his devotion.

But her heart belonged to another. Didn't it?

"You haven't . . . that is . . . Rudolph Phillips didn't call you out. Did he?" She held her breath, dreading the answer.

"No, I haven't received any summons. Nothing so dramatic." His voice sounded wounded and almost bitter. Rounding on her, he demanded, "Is that what it will take to secure your affections? A show of arms, proof positive that I would die for you?"

Reaching out suddenly, he grabbed her shoulders, but not to pull her into his embrace. Instead, he gave her a little shake before releasing her, muttering, "Forgive me, Destiny. I shouldn't have said that—or grabbed you." His blue-gray eyes found hers, and she read the suffering there. Pity lanced through her, piercing her heart.

"No, Nathan, I don't want you to fight for me," she replied. "It's the last thing I want."

"Because you don't want me on any terms, especially not marriage, especially not with me. That's it. Isn't it?"

"Nathan, I . . ."

"I understand, Destiny. You needn't explain. I understand," he repeated. "I just need to be patient." Moving to the settee, he retrieved his hat. "If you'll excuse me, I'll be taking my leave."

She approached him slowly and touched his arm. In her heart she knew she should let him go. It would be simpler than allowing him to hope. Patience, she knew, wouldn't be enough to change her mind.

"I wish you wouldn't leave so quickly," she soothed. "Please, have a seat and we'll sit and talk."

If she were honest with herself, talking was the last thing on her mind. The imprint of his lips were still on hers, and she'd responded to his kisses. How could she let him go like this? But if she were true to her heart, how could she *not* let him go? After all, it was James whom she wanted to share her kisses with. Today, tomorrow, and forever.

He shook his head. "I'd rather not stay, but I want to see you again. Will you accompany me to a church social? The

Methodists are giving a picnic by the seashore after church on Sunday. Would you like to go with me?''

Hesitating, he turned his hat over and over in his hands. After clearing his throat, he continued, ''I know you need time to get used to me and the idea of marrying, Destiny. Marriage is a big step, and you'll want to be sure.'' Stopping, he glanced at her, admitting, ''It's just that when I kiss you, I seem to lose all control. Begging your pardon, but kissing you makes me wish the wedding was already over and the honeymoon beginning.''

With those revealing words, he clapped his captain's hat on his head but not before she saw the tell-tale crimson spreading across his face. She'd never known another man to blush except Nathan. And it touched something inside of her, something deep inside, making her feel warm and wanted, making her feel as if she were the most special person in the world . . . at least to Nathan.

Did James make her feel that way? she asked herself. She didn't know. Couldn't be certain . . . yet.

But Nathan had asked her a question. Hadn't he? Something about a church social next Sunday. Her first inclination was to say yes, although why she wanted to encourage him further, she couldn't say. She should put a stop to his hopes. Shouldn't she?

It was on the tip of her tongue to refuse him but when she opened her mouth, she couldn't bring herself to dismiss him so coldly. Try as she might, she couldn't get the words out. What if James asked her to the social? He'd said he would take her walking again this evening.

She found herself not declining but putting him off. ''I don't know if I can go to the social with you. Gramps may have something planned after church,'' she evaded. ''Can I let you know tomorrow?''

As soon as she said the words, she felt like the biggest liar in the world, as well as the biggest coward. Now, if James asked her, she would feel guilty accepting him. And if he didn't ask her, she didn't know what she would do.

"Of course, ask your grandfather for permission. I'll stop by at the same time tomorrow for your answer." Bowing low, he caught her hand in his. Turning her hand over, he rained kisses over her palm until she giggled and tried to pull away.

But he caught her to him and kissed her mouth again with all the fierce, heart-stopping passion they'd shared before. When he lifted his mouth from hers, he asked, "How do you like kissing me without my beard?"

Nestling her cheek against his clean-shaven one, she didn't lie when she said, "It feels marvelous, Nathan. I'm honored you shaved for me."

Chapter Nine

"Where are you taking me?" Destiny half inquired, half protested, as she and James crossed a rickety foot bridge strung over the Old Pond.

"Not much farther," James replied, pulling her along.

She glanced at the murky, dank water just inches below her feet. When she was a child, she had been drawn, as all children were in Key West, to this wild, swampy place, this no-man's land of tangled underbrush and calla lilies skimming slimy water. Over the years, various owners had drained most of the swamp away, but there were still parts left untouched.

When she'd wanted to explore here as a child, Tilly had filled her head with stories of man-eating alligators and mosquitos big enough to carry her off. Being the cautious type, she'd steered clear of the Old Pond. Now, James Whitman, of all people, was leading her into its untamed depths. She wondered what could be so wonderful, hidden in this dismal place, that he felt the need to show her.

They crossed a long footbridge with many of the boards missing. Several times, James had to stop and swing her in his arms, lifting her across the empty spaces. She reveled in the strength of his arms around her, feeling the bunch and slide of his muscles beneath his proper frock coat, recognizing the powerful man beneath his gentlemanly exterior. After her talk with Angelina last night, she saw men in a different way. First Nathan and now James.

Each time he lifted her, before putting her down, he'd steal several kisses, quick, light kisses, promising, like an appetizer before dinner, a sumptuous banquet to come.

At the end of a footbridge, they entered a deep copse of trees, a rarity on the wind-swept key. The trees formed a kind of natural cathedral, arching overhead and blotting out the sky. Festooned with creepers and vines, they erected a barricade, closing around her like the walls of a building.

Following James to the heart of the copse, they discovered a small clearing of trampled and hard-packed earth. At the far end of the clearing was a break in the trees and, like looking through a telescope, she glimpsed the sea beyond. In the clearing were several rings of stones, embedded in the earth, interspersed with other, longer stones, laid out like benches.

There was also a great deal of garbage scattered about, Destiny noticed when she looked closer. The remnants of old fires held clumps of feathers and what looked like the bones of small animals, mingled indiscriminantly with brightly colored tatters of cloth and glass beads. And there was a distinct stench to the place, of death overlaid with the tangy scent of strange spices.

Wrinkling her nose, she demanded, "What is this place? Is this where you wanted to bring me?"

"Isn't it exciting, Destiny?"

"I don't know what you find exciting about this place. It looks like a garbage dump." She sniffed and tossed her head.

James faced her, his silver-gray eyes alight with a strange fire in their depths. "Voodoo," he whispered. "This is where the slaves come to do voodoo."

"James, there aren't any slaves, only freed Negroes."

He waved his hand in dismissal. "Semantics, my dear,

semantics. Since the first slaves were brought to Key West, this has been where they practice voodoo. The freed Negroes as you put it, still come here today. I have it on good authority.'' He glanced at her. ''I'm sure your Tilly knows about this place.''

What a ridiculous thought, Destiny grimaced. Tilly, hard-working, level-headed Tilly, dancing around a fire in some voodoo ritual? She shook her head and crossed her arms over her chest, replying, ''Tilly was never a slave. Gramps freed her as soon as he bought her. And she's a Christian woman. She faithfully attends the Baptist Colored Church every Sunday.''

''So maybe your Tilly is an exception,'' he acquiesced. ''But most Negroes come here at one time or another. They may attend church by day, but at night they revert to their primitive ways. I've heard stories that would curl your hair. Sacrificial offerings, feverish dancing, and . . .'' He lifted his eyebrows. ''Other unspeakable acts between men and women.''

Pulling her to his chest, he said, ''Just thinking about it fires my blood. Don't you feel it, Destiny? The raw magnetism of the place, the dark magic it weaves? Look around you. It's like a cathedral, but a cathedral for the worship of man's baser emotions.''

Gazing up at James's handsome face, she couldn't believe her ears. What was he trying to tell her? What was his point? She did feel something in this place, a strange force emanating from the silent stones. But what she felt wasn't excitement. Fear was closer to what she felt.

And if what he said were true, she understood why Tilly had been so adamant about her staying away from the Old Pond. But what did that have to do with her and James? And why had he brought her to this place?

Before she could formulate the questions, his mouth swooped down, covering hers. His tongue thrust against the seam of her mouth, demanding immediate entrance. His fingers roved down her throat, trailing feverish paths across her sensitive skin. She'd worn another of Angelina's dresses and it was cut low in the front, not as daring as the ball gown but provocative enough. Too provocative, she realized, as his fingertips skimmed the tops of her breasts, bringing heat to her cheeks.

Pressed so close to him, she could hear the wild throbbing of his heart. He groaned low in his throat and his hands trailed downward, cupping her breasts through the thin fabric of her gown. His mouth and tongue were insistent, too, dominating her with fierce demands. His tongue thrust in and out of her mouth, imitating that most intimate act between a man and a woman. In perfect counterpoint, he ground his hips against her, and she felt the rock-hard evidence of his desire.

She was awash in sensations, some pleasurable, some keenly embarrassing. A part of her mind told her they must stop, that he was getting out of control. But another part of her counseled surrender. After all, this was her beloved James. She'd given herself to him, in her dreams, many times, although not until last night had she understood what surrender might entail.

When his hands left her breasts and suddenly strayed to the back of her gown, she realized he was fumbling at the buttons to her bodice. Fear and a strange loathing penetrated her bemused mind, bringing her to her senses.

Reaching up between their bodies, she placed her hands on his chest and pushed. He didn't yield. His mouth merely ground into hers with renewed ferocity, and his hands continued their course down the back of her gown. She could feel the fabric parting and the cool, evening air on her back.

Glimpsing the setting sun through the break in the trees, she knew it would be night soon, and they would be marooned in the swamp. The thought gave her the shudders. Renewed fear streaked through her, lending her strength.

Wrenching her mouth from his, she pushed harder at his chest, thumping on it with all her might. Frantic now, her voice held a hysterical note. "James, stop. Stop now, I say! Let go of me! Night is falling and I won't stay here! Do you hear me?"

Her pleas must have finally reached him because he released

her and stepped back. His breath came in raspy pants, and his gray eyes glittered in the waning light. His features appeared contorted, harshened by lust. He looked at her, but it was as if he didn't see her. As if he looked through her and past her.

Seeing his look, she shuddered again and wrapped her arms around her torso. The chilly evening breeze whispered through the trees, making them bend and groan. Shivering, she realized the back of her bodice gaped open. Wanting to preserve her modesty, she turned her back and reached behind herself, trying to rebutton her bodice. But her fingers were shaking so, she knew she was making a mess of it.

"Here, allow me," he offered.

Half facing him again, she stole a glance and found that a semblance of sanity had returned to his features. This was the handsome, gentlemanly James she knew and loved. Relieved, she remembered Angelina's warning about how passion could transform men, rendering them unfamiliar creatures.

Uncertain of what to do, of how she felt, she ignored his offer and continued to button her bodice. But it was awkward from this position. Tilly usually helped her dress, or of late, Angelina. Suddenly, she wished she were home in her cozy and safe bedroom. She'd had enough of men and their passions for today. First Nathan and now James.

"Destiny, please, let me help you. I apologize for my . . . my unwanted advances . . . for my unseemly behavior. It's this place," he rationalized, "it does things to me. Makes me forget what I'm . . . that you're . . ." He ran his hand through his hair in agitation, repeating, "Please, forgive me. Accept my abject apologies."

Hearing his contrite words, she was touched by his sincerity. Relaxing a fraction, she yielded, "I accept your apology, James. And I do need your help."

With only the slightest trepidation, she turned her back again. "I've made a mess of the buttons. If you would straighten them out quickly, we can start for home. It's getting dark and I don't want to be stranded in the swamp. Please," she added for good

measure, softening toward him, trying to understand what had
driven him to bring her here in the first place.

His capable hands moved over her back swiftly, closing the
gaping fabric. She stood perfectly still, waiting for him to finish
and speak again, expecting him to speak. She couldn't help but
compare him to Nathan. Every time Nathan became passionate
with her, he apologized and then offered marriage. James had
already apologized; the next step would be to offer marriage.
She held her breath, hoping, urging him with her mind.

If he did offer for her hand, her every wish would be fulfilled,
her every dream realized.

The silence widened, a dark chasm opening between them,
filled only with the shrill calling of nightjars and the guttural
croaking of frogs. Shadows covered the trees, making their
shapes appear menacing, almost threatening. She released her
breath with a rush, disappointment flooding her.

When he'd finished with the task, he took her arm. "I know
another way back." Inclining his head toward the break in the
trees, he offered, "We can go through there to the seashore
and circle the southern end of the island by the beach. It's
longer but we won't have to cross the swamp."

She nodded, grateful for his solicitude but numbed by disillu-
sionment. He hadn't asked her to marry him after almost rav-
ishing her in this strange place. With Nathan, it was so different.
She knew he wanted her. He'd bluntly admitted his passion
this afternoon. But he wanted her in the right and proper way,
as his wife.

What did James want? What did he expect? Did he care for
her at all? She followed him blindly, her mind whirling, spinning out of control with questions and doubts.

Once they reached the beach, she breathed a sigh of relief.
They were in the open again, away from the forbidding swamp
and its dark secrets. Here, with the surf pounding the shore
and the sun slowly sinking into the horizon, she felt herself
again. Unfortunately, her internal relief didn't alleviate the
difficulty of their trek.

Key West was an ancient coral reef, ringed with boulders and sharp stones. There was precious little sand on the beach, mostly bits of coral, seashells, and rough rocks. With her thin slippers, she was at a distinct disadvantage. She wondered again at James's motive for taking her to such an inaccessible and hostile place.

When she stopped for the third time to shake stones and bits of coral from her shoes, James bent down and picked her up in his arms. She protested at first but he insisted, claiming she was as light as a feather and that it was the least he could do for having gotten her into this unpleasant situation.

Because she secretly agreed with him, she acquiesced and laced her arms behind his neck, relishing in the sensation of James Whitman carrying her in his arms.

When they rounded the tip of the island and the town came into sight, he asked, "Destiny, will you see me again? I haven't destroyed your regard for me, have I?"

Feeling in control once more, she tested him. "What did you have in mind, James? I might see you again if your offer is tantalizing enough."

His arms tightened around her and he hesitated, taking his time to answer. "I have a beautiful yacht—you've seen it in the harbor, the *Gulf Wind.* I'd like to take you sailing. We could have fresh oysters and champagne. You like champagne, don't you?"

It wasn't the answer she'd been hoping for. She'd hoped he would ask her to the church social. All of Key West would attend the social, she knew. Why hadn't he asked her?

Because he wants to be alone with you, not in a crowd of people, a voice in the back of her mind whispered. It was flattering but not what she wanted, especially after tonight. They'd been alone enough, now it was time to make their appearance together as a couple.

"What about the Methodist Church social next Sunday? I'd like to attend. Would you take me?" She surprised herself by boldly requesting.

He stiffened at her suggestion, and she could sense his discomfort. Grunting, he lowered her to the ground, observing, "There's mostly sand from here to the wharf. Do you think you'll be all right?"

"Yes, I'm fine," she murmured, keeping taut control over her voice.

But her frustration mounted with each passing moment as they ploughed through the deep sand. He'd ignored her request, acting as if she hadn't spoken a word about the social. Bitter disappointment gripped her, burning her stomach and making her eyes water. She dashed the unwanted moisture away and released his hand, plunging ahead, sloughing blindly through the sinking sand.

His touch on her arm stopped her. "Wait, Destiny. Don't be angry at me. I can't take you to the social. I'm sorry, but Father has some business for me to transact in Tampa at the end of the week. I'll be staying over Sunday with business associates."

"That's all right. I understand," she managed.

But she didn't really understand. If he wanted to see her so badly, he would honor her request and postpone his business. Doubts flooded her, too, rising from the depths of her despair. Doubts about his veracity and his feelings for her. Was he really going out of town or was it a convenient excuse because he didn't want to take her to a social gathering?

So far, all he'd offered were clandestine meetings at twilight, walks, and an outing on his yacht. Was she still a social pariah in his eyes? The thought made her cringe.

"I'll be back by the first of next week," he offered. "I'd be honored if you would join me on my yacht."

"I don't know, James." She surprised herself again when she responded courageously, gambling by putting him off. "Call on me at home and then we'll see."

* * *

Angelina sloughed through the mud, muttering curses under her breath that even Malvado didn't know. It was the rainy season in Key West. And each afternoon, the clouds opened up, showering the island with passing storms, making her research that much more difficult.

She'd spent the past few days touring the local cigar manufacturers, trying to get an idea of their operations. It had been an interesting few days, she had to admit. She'd been delighted to speak her native tongue, because the manufacturers were Cuban, like herself. Unfortunately, their reactions to her visits hadn't been promising. She'd met with every reaction from open contempt to patronizing dismissal.

She'd learned one thing, though, the most important lesson. The workers you employed were your gold mine. It was their nimble and skilled fingers that did the actual work, making the cigars perfect and whole. She wondered that she hadn't learned that bit of wisdom at her father's cigar factory but realized she'd taken his workers for granted. Most of them had been with her family for generations.

In Key West, it was different. Cubans emigrated here, looking for freedom and a better life for themselves and their families. In order to obtain decent jobs, they were willing to fabricate their past experience. A cigar manufacturer must be wary and screen workers accordingly. She wasn't worried about selecting the right blends for the fillers or the best wrappers. Those were skills she'd learned at her father's knee. But skilled workers were the key. Without them, her knowledge of cigar-making was useless.

Observing the factories, she'd come to another conclusion. Fifteen skilled workers would be perfect. With the right tobacco blends and careful quality control, she and fifteen workers could be successful. Fifteen workers, without a foreman to help, would be stretching the limits of her capabilities. But it would serve two purposes. First, it would keep quality control under her direct supervision. And second, it would be just enough workers, without a foreman to pay, to yield a tidy profit.

If she picked the most skilled workers, she reminded herself. That was the key.

She'd saved the Silva factory for the last. It was considered the most successful on the island, and she wanted to take her time, going over its operation, trying to divine what made it so successful.

Glancing over her shoulder, she tried to catch a glimpse of whoever was following her. Since she'd started touring the cigar factories at the first of the week, she couldn't shake the feeling that someone was shadowing her. And she knew better than to question her sixth sense. It was right more times than it was wrong.

There were only two possibilities, she knew, Cortez or Rafael. On the one hand, Cortez following her made sense. He would want to know if she was doing as he requested, researching cigar factories and coming up with a plan to protect his investment.

On the other hand, Rafael following her didn't make sense. There was no reason for him to do so, and she hadn't seen him since the ball. But she didn't discount her suspicion: It might be Rafael.

Whoever it was, she didn't like it. She'd left Cuba to be a free woman, not to be watched.

The Silva factory was situated on one of the few hillocks dotting the island, other than the high ridge where the town was located. A mule team and wagon moved ahead of her, straining up the only rutted path to the factory. She followed in its wake, planting her inadequate slippers in the slimy earth, straining to gain purchase.

Shouts assaulted her ears from the top of the hill. She heard, "Whoa, mule. Hey, mules! Hold up, whoa! Whoa, there! Dammit, stop!"

And then the earth shook beneath her feet and a terrible rumbling filled the air. Glancing up, she found the heavily laden wagon rushing at her.

Acting instinctively, she threw herself to the left side of the

track. But something hit her, bouncing off her shoulder and
then striking her head. Black dots swam before her eyes, and
she felt herself falling down a long, dark tunnel into oblivion.

Someone was beating on her, thumping her cheek with
uncommon zeal and shouting into her ear. Angelina cringed
and tried to crawl away. Anything, so they'd leave her alone.
Her head throbbed as if a sledgehammer were pounding her
brain into pulp. Why couldn't whoever it was have the decency
to leave her alone with her pain?

This must be a nightmare, she thought foggily. A nightmare
from hell. And her shoulder hurt, too, she realized groggily.
Burned like the very fires of perdition.

She breathed deeply, trying to assess the situation, but her
mind kept slipping away, going in and out, like some demented
dancer weaving across a ballroom.

The unmistakable stench of ammonia hit the back of her
throat with a rush, gagging her, clearing her mind with painful
acuity, bringing tears to her eyes. Reaching up, she flailed with
her arms, trying to push the awful stuff away. Her hand made
contact with something and the ammonia disappeared, leaving
only a lingering, astringent scent.

The deep timbre of Rafael's voice demanded, "Angelina,
open your eyes! I know you're awake. You just knocked the
smelling salts from my hand. You must be awake." His voice
lowered, taking on an almost pleading note. *"Por favor,* look
at me. Speak to me. You've been hurt. We've already sent for
the doctor."

In defiance of his commands, she kept both her eyes and her
mouth shut. Let him worry for a while. He was, most likely,
the cause of her accident anyway, she told herself. She'd known
someone was following her, and it had to have been Rafael,
as she had half suspected. If her attention hadn't been drawn
to wondering who was shadowing her, she wouldn't have been

hit by the wagon. She would have avoided the accident. Wouldn't she?

It was no good, she admitted to herself. Rafael wasn't the reason she'd been hit by the runaway wagon. It had just been one of those things. Fate or luck, if you would. Being in the wrong place at the wrong time. Since she'd come to Key West, her luck had been all bad, she thought grimly.

But that wasn't true, either. She'd met Destiny and gained a rare commodity, a true and loyal friend. And she'd found Cortez, who was willing to invest in her factory. All of her luck hadn't been bad, she silently amended. Only her luck in meeting Rafael. But she could ill afford the luxury of self-pity. She had a job to do, and accident or no accident, she wanted to see the Silva factory.

Opening her eyes, she saw Rafael's face above hers, hovering over her like a mother hen. His features held the unmistakable stamp of worry. He'd removed his wide Panama hat to assist her, something he rarely did during the daytime, she knew. Despite her conflicted feelings for him, his genuine solicitude touched her.

Gingerly, she pushed herself to a sitting position, in spite of the pain in her right shoulder. Unfortunately, her efforts were in vain because as soon as she rose, Rafael pushed her back down again.

"Don't try to move, Angelina. Not until the doctor gets here."

His domineering attitude infuriated her, making her head throb with more intensity than before. A moment ago she'd been touched by his solicitude. Now it irritated her. Who did he think he was, her keeper?

"Don't touch me, Rafael," she managed to grate out. "And don't tell me what to do, either. Why are you here? You've been following me for the past few days. Haven't you?"

"What if I have?" he countered. "As the Americaños are fond of saying: 'it's a free country.' "

"Sí, free for you men, but not for us women, especially not with you monitoring my every movement."

Her head was feeling a little better, and her back was up now. She felt suddenly good, upbraiding him, blaming him for her fears and doubts. The feeling was downright seductive, she decided. She sharpened her tongue mentally, thinking what she might say next to take him down another notch or two.

His voice was barely a whisper when he cautioned, "Angelina, couldn't we continue this discussion at another time. There are people . . ." He inclined his head.

She rose again to a sitting position. This time he didn't try to stop her. She glimpsed a crush of people behind him, and then the crowd seemed to dip and sway, going in and out of focus. She shook her head again, only to bite back a groan as pain lanced through her skull.

Finally, her vision cleared and she saw the ring of concerned faces. People from the Silva factory. She recognized a tall Cuban with a carefully trimmed goatee. That was Señor Silva, she realized. She'd interrupted his operations and caused a scene. And she had wanted to make a good impression on him. Had wanted him to explain his operations to her. She knew it was a lot to expect from a competitor, but she doubted he would take her seriously, either.

Some kind of impression she was making, lying in the mud, waiting for the doctor. She must look a mess. But Silva did owe her, she realized. After all, it was his wagon that had hit her. Maybe she hadn't been paying perfect attention, but he couldn't know that. By all rights, he should be more than willing to help her. Shouldn't he?

Having made her decision, she lurched to her feet and bent down to dust off her skirts. But when she did so, bile rose to her throat and a churning nausea gripped her stomach. The world spun on its axis. Blinding lights danced before her eyes, competing with an angry black swarm of mosquitos suddenly attacking her. Where had the insects come from? Panicking, she swatted at them with her hands.

Despite her efforts, they closed around her, engulfing her, blacking out her vision, invading her head with their angry buzzing. She shook her head again and again, trying to escape their invasion, their overwhelming presence.

Rafael was beside her, putting his arm around her waist and supporting her. She tried to push him away. She didn't want him holding her. His mere touch, despite slipping in and out of consciousness, gave her the shivers, raising gooseflesh on her arms. Now she could add those bumps to the mosquito bites, she thought groggily, realizing that the angry swarm had left as suddenly as it had come.

Her head cleared for a brief moment, and she wondered if the mosquitos had been only an illusion, a product of her feverish brain. Holding tight to Rafael, she felt herself relax. What was the use of fighting her attraction for him? She needed him. She was hurt, and a strong shoulder to lean on was distinctly preferable to wallowing in the mud or being left to the kindness of strangers.

Turning her face into his chest, she felt his strong arms enclose her, comforting her, lending her strength. Pressed against him, she heard the steady beat of his heart and smelled the familiar scent of him. Sandalwood and his own special musk. He smelled like home to her, like the safety and security she'd once known and forsaken in this strange land.

Chapter Ten

Angelina woke up, on and off, going in and out of consciousness as easily as a seal slips under the water, only to resurface. Each time she woke, there was a cacophony of voices at her bedside. She heard the rich, musical tones of Tilly's voice, fussing over her. Destiny's light soprano piped in, telling Tilly to fetch this or that. Briefly, there was the soft burr of Gramps's voice, checking on the patient and then withdrawing quickly. And then there was an unfamiliar voice, the baritone of someone named Doc Murdock.

Strain as she might, she didn't detect Rafael's deep bass voice in the chorus. Where was he? Her last recollection had been of him catching and holding her in his arms. Of his own particular scent, which for some reason reminded her of home and safety.

She woke fully when it was dark outside. For once, her room was quiet, too quiet. At first, she thought she was alone, but when she shifted in the bed and rustled the comforter, Destiny was suddenly beside her.

"How do you feel, Angelina?" she asked, worry lining her

face. "We were all concerned about you, although Doc Murdock said you should be fine with a few days' rest."

Pulling herself to a sitting position, Angelina felt the dull throbbing on the right side of her head. Destiny rushed to plump up the pillows behind her and settle her properly.

"Thank you, Destiny. I guess I feel like I've been run over by a wagon."

Reaching up, she gingerly touched the goose-egg lump on the back of her head. Looking down, she noticed that her right shoulder had been cleaned and dressed in a white bandage.

"Oh, Angelina, don't tease me," Destiny chided. "We're all so worried."

"I'm not teasing, that's what happened. A wagon rolled down a hill, and I didn't get out of the way fast enough. It hit my shoulder and head." She snagged her friend's gaze. "Didn't Rafael tell you? Didn't he bring me here?"

Destiny's hands flew to her face. "Oh, I forgot! Rafael did bring you home. As far as I know, he's still in Gramps's study waiting to hear how you are. If you hadn't mentioned him, I would have forgotten. I guess I should go and tell him you're finally awake." She reached out and squeezed Angelina's hand. "Do you want to see him if he asks? He's extremely worried, too. Gramps tried to get him to leave once Doc said you would be fine, but he wouldn't budge. Said he wanted to wait until you woke up."

Angelina shut her eyes, willing the throbbing to go away. Willing today to be a nightmare that would evaporate with the morning mist. But she knew that wasn't going to happen. To see Rafael or not? That seemed to be the question always plaguing her. Like poor relations, he seemed to turn up everywhere.

She should thank him, even though he'd been following her against her wishes. But he'd been there when she needed him.

Reaching out, she clasped Destiny's hand and gave it a little shake. *"Gracias, amiga mía,* for all your concern and for being here when I woke up. It's good to know that I have a friend

like you. Sometimes, I feel so alone in this new country. So
very alone . . .'' She turned her face into the pillow and willed
herself not to cry, knowing it would only further distress her
friend.

''You would have done the same for me,'' Destiny reassured
her. ''I've never had a friend like you. I can't tell you how
much—'' Her voice choked off and she sat on the bed, taking
Angelina in her arms.

The two friends hugged for a long time, and when they broke
their embrace, each surreptitiously dashed tears from her eyes.

''About Rafael?'' Destiny prompted.

''Yes, Rafael,'' she echoed. ''Go and tell him I'll be fine,
but I'm tired now. Could he come see me in several days? I'd
like to thank him personally for his help.''

Rising from her perch on the bed, Destiny said, ''I'll tell
him right away. While I'm there, should I send Tilly with some
food? Are you hungry? The doctor said you should eat to get
your strength back.''

''What else did the doctor say?''

''That you've got a lump on your head and a cut on your
shoulder. But you know that. The shoulder should heal completely in a few days; we just need to keep the dressings fresh.
As for your head, he mentioned that you have a pretty hard
head, especially for a woman.'' Destiny's eyes were alight with
mischief, and she stifled a giggle.

''Touché.'' Angelina couldn't help but smile at her friend's
quip. ''And my head—how long do I need to rest? Did the
doctor say?''

''Probably a few days until the swelling goes down. Doc
Murdock will be back tomorrow and you can ask him then.''

''I'll do that,'' she replied. ''I have things to do. I can't stay
in bed forever.'' She touched her friend's arm. ''And, yes,
please have Tilly bring me a tray. I haven't eaten since breakfast,
and I suddenly realize I'm ravenous.''

''That's a good sign, your being hungry.'' Destiny patted
her arm. ''I'll send Tilly with a tray and be right back.'' She

moved to the door. "Now I've got you all to myself. Don't you realize?" Destiny winked. "You'll be forced to gossip all night long."

Picking up a pillow from the bed, Angelina threw it at her friend's retreating back. "You slave driver, you, Destiny Favor. Remember, the doctor said I'm supposed to rest, not entertain you with gossip all night."

Nathan spread their blanket beneath the sheltering arms of a huge banyan tree a few yards from the beach. Some of the other couples had settled on the beach itself. Destiny glanced at the bright sun, grateful for Nathan's foresight. The couples on the beach, especially the women, were certain to be sunburned before they went home.

Like colorful mushrooms, every woman sported a parasol, ostensibly to keep the harsh sun from their complexions. But Destiny knew better. The thin material of the fashionable parasols didn't provide an adequate barrier. Being a redhead and living in a tropical climate, she'd learned quickly what the powerful rays of the sun could do.

Once the blanket was in place, she put their picnic basket in the middle, effectively staking their claim. Nathan smiled at her and offered his hand. She took it and stood by his side.

"What's first on the agenda?" he asked.

"The three-legged race," she replied. "You'll need to find a partner, though." She consulted the printed program from the church. "It's for men only. We females are supposed to cheer you on from the sidelines."

He laughed, a booming laugh. His laughter, deep and unabashed, caught her off guard. She couldn't remember him laughing before. And his laughter proved infectious, too. Without thinking, she found herself joining in and feeling happy to be with him.

After James's refusal to bring her to the social, her disappointment had been so great that she'd decided to stay home and avoid the outing altogether. But when Nathan came the next day, just as he'd promised, and asked her again, she couldn't find it in her heart to refuse him.

She liked Nathan a great deal, she realized. If it weren't for James . . .

"I saw Major Beale with one of the Murdock girls. I'll get him for a partner." He tugged at her hand. "Well, what are we waiting for? I expect you to be my personal and very loud cheering section."

"All right," she agreed, "I'm coming."

They strolled down the beach together, hand in hand, nodding at acquaintances. The crowd had gathered slowly, coming from all directions and converging on the sandy beach below the main wharf of the town. She'd been right, she realized. Everyone who was anyone was here.

If Angelina hadn't still been recovering from her accident, Destiny would have insisted that she come, too. As it was, her friend was missing . . .

She stopped in her tracks, her mouth hanging open. She would know that golden head anywhere. It was he! It was James! James, who had told her he'd be out of town on business.

Nathan turned and glanced at her, his eyebrows drawn together like two inverted question marks. Realizing how she must look and what he must think, she closed her mouth with a snap. But controlling her other reactions wasn't so easy.

She felt hot and then cold. Her stomach heaved and she gulped, not wanting to lose her breakfast. She was trembling from head to toe. Nathan must feel it. He had her hand clasped in his.

Withdrawing her hand, she managed, "I'm sorry, Nathan. I must have stepped on something sharp." To validate her hastily fabricated excuse, she reached for her left shoe.

"Here, let me help you." He offered his arm. "Hold my arm while you take off your slipper." Sliding his other arm around her waist, he said, "I've got you. You won't fall down."

She forced her lips into the semblance of a smile and placed her hand on his arm. Removing her left slipper, she made a great show of shaking it out and peering inside. But all she could think was, *He lied to me. James lied to me so he could bring Frances Brown.* Bony, spinsterish Frances Brown.

She'd glimpsed James and his party from the corner of her eye. While she made pains to shake out her shoe, she stared at them.

They made a great crowd, the two preeminent families of the island, the Browns and Whitmans, with several blankets spread together under the shade of three coconut palms. The older women huddled together on one end of the blankets, gossiping and caring for the infants. The older men strolled about, gesturing and puffing on cigars. Children darted between the groups, playing a form of tag. And then there were several couples, in various poses, holding hands and talking and emptying picnic baskets together.

James was there, helping Frances to unload one of the baskets. They had their heads close together and were obviously engaged in a lively conversation.

Destiny felt her heart constrict as if a giant hand had reached inside her chest and grabbed it. Tears of frustration and humiliation rose to the back of her throat and she swallowed several times, quickly.

How could he do this to me? The question repeated itself in her mind like a hideous litany. *Lie to me and then attend the social for all the world to see. Certain that I wouldn't be able to attend without him. Not me, not Destiny Favor, the social pariah,* she thought with disgust.

Nathan was gazing at her. She knew she'd drawn out the moment to empty her shoe beyond what it took, but she couldn't seem to drag her gaze from James and Frances.

Finally, Nathan reached over and took the slipper from her fingers. Shaking it and looking inside, he pronounced, "I think you've got the stone out, Destiny. Is something the matter?"

Forcing herself to look at him, she smiled and nodded. "Sorry, Nathan. I guess you caught me woolgathering."

"Well . . ." His voice sounded doubtful. She wondered how much longer she could go on like this, evading his questions, acting as if she wanted to be with him when her heart was tearing in two . . .

"Come on," he prompted. "I need to find Major Beale. They've already started to mark off the course for the race." He glanced at her, suspicion clouding his hazel eyes. "Unless you're not feeling up to it. If you're not, I don't have to participate. We can return to the blanket and just watch if that would make you feel better."

"No, no, I want you to race." She pasted a sickly smile on her face. "I want to cheer you on."

He brightened. Taking her hand, he brushed his lips across her skin and vowed, "In that case, I'll win. Just for you. And heaven help Beale if he's not ready to go all out!"

She giggled in spite of herself at his enthusiasm. Nathan was so sweet, so good, so attentive. Why couldn't she love him with all her heart the way she loved that no-good, lying, cheating James Whitman? Closing her eyes for a brief second, she willed herself to remain calm. To try and forget about James and enjoy Nathan's company.

But it was no good. The afternoon passed in a haze of misery for her. Nathan did win the three-legged race, despite stiff competition. Both he and Major Beale received a hand-embroidered Bible marker, which they both presented to their female companions with a flourish. Later, when Destiny happened to overhear that Frances Brown had embroidered the bookmarkers, she surreptitiously threw hers into the ocean, taking cheer as she watched the salt water ruin the colorful threads before it sank to the bottom of the sea.

Tilly had outdone herself with the picnic basket. It contained some of her finest cooking: golden fried chicken, tangy deviled eggs, honey-laced biscuits, and a frothy lemon meringue pie. Nathan ate with gusto, exclaiming and lauding each bite. It was all she could do to choke down a few morsels.

Several times, in the course of the afternoon, she and James

happened to exchange glances. Each time, he lifted his eyebrows, as if in silent salutation, and smiled at her. And each
time, she turned her face away, affronted by his frivolous attitude and humiliated that she'd begged him to bring her. She
wondered what he must think of her and how he could suppose
that she would want to have anything to do with him after he'd
lied and brought Frances.

When the festivities drew to a close with a long prayer from
the Methodist pastor, she felt a great sense of relief. No more
pretending. Now she could go home and cry and rant and rave.
And wonder what to do with the remainder of her life. Because
what James had done went far beyond the repercussions of a
single day.

She understood, only too well, why he'd refused to bring
her and had come with Frances instead. She wasn't acceptable
to his family or polite society in Key West. He could take her
walking and sneak around in the shadows with her because he
was attracted to her. But he'd never present her to his family.
And if he couldn't present her to his family, he'd never consider
marriage with her, either.

Her hopes of marrying James Whitman and being accepted
by Key West society were nothing more than dreams, she
realized bitterly.

It was a quiet Sunday afternoon. Angelina savored the lazy
day. Destiny had gone to a church picnic with Captain Rodgers.
Gramps and the servants were at home, but they seldom disturbed her, thinking she was resting. She had followed Doc
Murdock's orders and slept for long hours since the accident.

Once the headaches had receded, she'd began to put her
plans on paper, utilizing what she'd learned by visiting the
cigar factories. She'd sketched a picture of the structure and
made detailed lists of what she needed to start operations. She'd
even decided the two kinds of cigars she would manufacture:
coronas and perfectos. They were her father's specialties.

There was a knock on her door, and she looked up from a list of tobaccos and flavorings. "Enter, please."

The door opened and Rufus stuck his grizzled white head in, asking, "Is y'all decent, Miz Angelina? They's a gentleman caller to sees you'm. 'E's the one who brung you'm home."

Understanding that Rafael had finally come to pay his call, she sat up straighter in bed, plumping the pillows behind her. "Yes, Rufus, I'll see him. Do you think my appearance is acceptable?" She grinned. "I've never received a gentleman caller in bed before."

Rufus returned her grin, white teeth flashing in his dark face. "Don' worry 'bout bein' in bed, Miz Angelina. You'm jist call out iffen you's needs me. I'll come a'runnin'."

"Thank you, Rufus, that makes me feel much safer." She grinned again as the elderly manservant shut the door and went to fetch Rafael.

Realizing she didn't have much time, she grabbed a mirror from the stand beside the bed and checked her face and hair. Quickly, she drew a brush through her tousled hair, pinched her cheeks for color, and checked that the ribbons on her nightgown were tightly laced. Belatedly, she remembered the plans spread over the bedsheets. Not wanting Rafael to know more of her business than he already did, she scooped them up, hiding them beneath the bedclothes.

Ready to receive him, she didn't want to look too over-anxious, so she took up a Spanish novel Destiny had bought for her and pretended to be engrossed in the plot of the book.

Another knock sounded on her door, and before she could respond, the door opened and Rafael walked in. It had been a long time since she'd seen him—if she didn't count the afternoon of her accident, and she hadn't been particularly coherent then.

Watching him approach the bed, she couldn't help but admire the way he walked, his jaunty and almost feline grace of movement. In deference to being inside, he'd removed his hat, and his scarred countenance was bared to the light of day. But the other side of his face, the perfect side, revealed a man so handsome that he took her breath away.

Would she always feel like this about him? she wondered. As inexorably drawn to him as the moon drew the tides? What was it about him that made her feel as if she'd known him for a long time—as if, in some strange way, he was a part of her? Yet, he could make her more furious than any other human being on earth, including her domineering father.

It didn't make sense, she knew. None of it made sense. And her only defense was a constant, watchful wariness.

When he reached her bedside, he bowed low, murmuring, "I see you're feeling better."

"*Sí, gracias.* And thank you for being there and helping me."

"It was my pleasure."

Having done the polite thing, she wanted some answers. "Why *were* you there, Rafael? I don't remember much after the accident, but I distinctly remember asking if . . . No," she amended, "I *told* you that you'd been following me to the cigar factories. And I was right. You didn't answer then. Will you answer me now?"

"I was following you," he admitted simply.

"*¿Por qué?*"

"Because some of the places you went, you shouldn't have gone alone. You needed an escort."

"Because I'm a mere woman, you mean, and easy prey to nefarious types."

"*Sí.*"

"Are we going to start this again, Rafael? I've told you repeatedly that I refuse to be hampered by my . . . my sex. I intend to move as freely as a man would when conducting my business."

"You're borrowing trouble, Angelina. I'm well aware of your 'enlightened' view of the world. Unfortunately, the rest of the world doesn't necessarily agree with you. Just because you choose to ignore the danger doesn't mean it doesn't exist. If you want to move freely, employ yourself a bodyguard.''

"A bodyguard," she snorted. "You know I haven't the money for one. But I do have this." Picking up her derringer from the bedside table, she held it out to him in the palm of her hand. "This is my constant companion, or bodyguard, as you put it. And I know how to use it."

"That"—he dismissed it with a wave of his hand—"is a toy. It wouldn't stop a very large, very determined man."

"It will if I aim at the right place." She cocked one eyebrow at him and looked pointedly at a certain point below his waist.

"You're posturing, Angelina, and you know it. If trouble comes, it doesn't bow and offer salutations while you're fetching that toy from your reticule and aiming it just so."

His mockery infuriated her. Who did he think he was? It was useless to argue with him. He had an answer for everything.

"I refuse to argue with you." Her voice had pitched an octave higher. She crossed her arms over her chest. "The point is not what I do or don't do, Señor Estava, the point is that you have no right to follow me. That's harassment, pure and simple. I'll notify the authorities if you continue."

He shook his head and whistled low. "I've never known such a hardheaded, stubborn wench in all my—"

"Traits considered admirable in a man," she threw back at him. "And don't call me a 'wench.' "

"A thousand pardons." His voice was filled with bitter mockery. He bowed again. "Don't worry, Angelina, you needn't go to the authorities on account of me. If you want to risk your life and your . . . your . . .''

"Say it," she taunted. "Why can't you say it? Risk my feminine virtue." She snapped her fingers in his face. *"¡Mira!* I don't give that for my so-called feminine virtue. Most women don't, if truth be told. It's you men who are concerned about it, not us. Because you see us as a kind of property," she spat at him. "And no one wants damaged goods. Do they?"

It was his turn to cross his arms over his chest, to take a

defensive posture. His features stiffened to stone, and his sienna-colored eyes glittered with barely suppressed fury. He stared at her as if she were some odious insect that had just crawled out from beneath a rock.

"I wish to withdraw from this argument as well." His words were clipped and formal. "I've agreed to not follow you anymore. Can we put this aside and speak of other things?"

"*Claro que sí.* What do you wish to talk about?"

"About your purpose for visiting the cigar manufacturers."

"That's none of your business, either."

She could have reached out and slapped his face. Of all the meddling, bothersome males, he had to win the prize. Not only had he followed her, supposedly for her own safety, but he had the audacity to question why she'd gone to the cigar factories in the first place.

"I thought you knew what you wanted to do," he said. "That you had the plans for your factory already worked out."

She gazed at him. She knew she was shaking, shaking with rage. Taking several deep breaths, she tried to calm her racing heart. This encounter had certainly done her no good, she realized. Free of headaches for the last two days, her head throbbed mercilessly now.

He didn't deserve an answer. As she had pointed out, it was none of his business. "I think this interview is at an end," she declared. "I suddenly have a splitting headache. And the doctor won't let me out of bed until my headaches are gone."

At mention of her headache, his face fell. He dropped his eyes and modulated his voice. Where he'd been sharp and sarcastic before, now he was soft and almost pleading. "I don't want to distress you, Angelina. That's the last thing I want." He touched his scarred cheek, almost as if it were a talisman. "I'm sorry we got off on the wrong foot. It seems . . ." He stopped.

"It seems we can't have a civil conversation," she finished for him. "It's one of the reasons we should avoid contact in the future."

"You went to the factories to satisfy Cortez's demands," he blurted out. "Didn't you?"

She shrugged. "What if I did?"

He didn't care that he was distressing her, she realized, even though he paid lip service to it. All he cared about was his own agenda and wresting information from her about Cortez. He was like all men, accustomed to having his own way, no matter whom it might discomfort.

"Cortez made specific demands for your factory, didn't he? What were they?" he asked.

Suddenly, she felt very tired. Like sand in an hourglass, her fury over his cross-examination and meddling seemed to drain from her, leaving her empty and exhausted. She had her own doubts to deal with about Cortez. He had demanded certain things, such as a brick office and a storage area. And then there was the foreman he wanted her to hire. A friend of his, he'd said.

She'd chosen to put a positive face on Cortez's interest, telling herself that he had a right because it would be his money at risk. So, like the dutiful daughter her father had raised, she'd tried to fulfill his expectations by inspecting other cigar manufacturers and making a detailed plan on paper.

In the back of her mind she had doubts. What if he was just another domineering male, like her father or Rafael, who intended to run the factory to suit himself? Would she ever be free of men? All she wanted was a chance to show that she could take care of herself, that she could produce a quality cigar and make a living at it.

Unfortunately, she had no capital at her disposal. Men had all the money. They always had the money. It was one of the ways they kept women enslaved, she realized. Then she had a wild thought. Maybe Destiny had some jewelry worth hocking. Maybe she could get Destiny to . . .

But she knew the answer to that. Destiny possessed very little jewelry, costume or otherwise. As much as her grandfather seemed to love her, he, like all males, kept his beloved grand-daughter on a short leash.

Sighing, she didn't care anymore. If it would get rid of Rafael, she'd answer his questions. Capitulating, she admitted, "Cortez made several requests. He wanted a plan on paper, and for that I needed to do research. He asked that I build a secure office and storage space of brick. And he wants me to employ twenty workers as well as a friend of his as foreman."

Rafael listened carefully, his eyes narrowed. Then he grinned wolfishly. "Don't you see, Angelina, he plans on using your factory for his smuggling operations."

"No, I don't see. I've answered your questions." She lifted one hand to her throbbing head. "*Madre de Dios,* can't you see I don't feel well? Would you please see yourself out," she added pointedly.

"I'll go in just a minute. Try and concentrate because this is important. He wants a secure office and storage place to hide smuggled goods, and he wants to place one of his own men in your employ to get the goods in and out of their hiding place. If you go along with this, you're part of the crime. If he's caught, you'll be in trouble as well. Your factory could be forfeit. Then you'll have done it all for nothing."

"If, if, if!" She lurched up in bed. "Don't you see? I've no other choice. I have to take the chance that you're wrong or I won't have a factory to forfeit." She knew she was scream-ing but couldn't stop herself. "Don't you understand any-thing!"

"*Yo entiendo.*" His voice was soft when he answered, in blatant counterpoint to her own hysterical outburst. "And I'm willing to offer an alternative so you can have your factory. I've been saving money to go into business for myself. I'll lend it to you, no strings attached."

She gaped at him. Like waters eddying around a stone, her thoughts flowed and ebbed, some coherent, some not. What was that saying her father had taught her about knowing your enemies?

That the most dangerous ones are the ones you know . . . or was it the other way around?

It didn't matter. She knew this enemy. She knew Rafael. She might have her doubts about Cortez. But between the two of them, she'd take her chances with Cortez. At least with Cortez, she could talk to him without becoming furious.

And there wasn't that other thing between them, either. What she felt for Rafael. The way she was feeling now, although she was so angry at him, she could throw something. This raw animal magnetism that leapt between them with no effort on their parts.

Remembering her response to him at the Silva factory, she flushed. He was too seductive by far. If she gave free rein to her feelings, she'd shelter in his strong and comforting arms and forget about the factory. She knew he wanted her, just as she wanted him.

But then she'd be right back where she started, dependent on a man. And as seductive as that was, she certainly didn't need to complicate her life by giving in to her desires. Owing Rafael money and wanting him to touch her in the most intimate places and in the most intimate ways could prove to be an explosive combination.

If she took money from him, she'd never be free of him . . . or her desires. Not until she paid him back. Maybe not even then.

Lifting her chin, she stared straight at him. "I wouldn't accept a loan from you, not if you were the last man on earth."

"Of all the mule-headed, impossible, stubborn wenches," Rafael muttered while letting himself out the front door. Once outside, he turned and faced the house. "Wench, wench, wench, and *wench!*" he declared aloud with gusto. Frustrated and half angry, he stopped on the stoop and fished a match and cheroot from his pockets.

Lighting up, he puffed furiously until the tip glowed red.

Throwing the match away, he started down the sidewalk, only to come face to face with Captain Rodgers and Destiny.

They were a picture, strolling arm in arm, swinging an empty picnic basket between them. Destiny was looking at the Captain with adoration in her eyes, as if he were the last man on earth. Seeing them together like this, he paused, feeling as if a knife were slowly slicing open his guts. His hand strayed to his scarred cheek. He'd lost so much that tragic night. So much. If he were still as handsome as before, Angelina would welcome him as her business partner.

Now he was a mere shell of a man. Business and politics. Politics and business. Those were the two things he occupied himself with. And as luck would have it, he had some pressing business to discuss with Captain Rodgers.

Bowing low, he greeted them, wishing them a good evening. They returned his greeting and Destiny inquired if he'd been to see Angelina. He confirmed that he had and asked Rodgers if he could have a word with him. Rodgers agreed, asking him to wait while he escorted Destiny to the door.

Nodding, he strode to the edge of the lawn and leaned against a flowering magnolia tree to wait, drawing on his cheroot and enjoying the soft evening breezes. After a few moments, Rodgers approached. Rafael threw away the stub of his cheroot and straightened.

"You wanted to talk with me," Rodgers prompted.

"Yes." Rafael fell in step beside him. "Remember that day on the wharf, *Capitán,* when we spoke of a man called Cortez."

"I remember."

"Any luck with catching him? Any news?"

Rodgers stopped in his tracks and regarded him, his eyes narrowed. "If I did know something, sir, you would be the last person I would take into my confidence."

"And why is that? Capitán McEwen must have vouched for my character that day."

Rodgers nodded, admitting, "He did, sir."

Then he resumed walking, making Rafael catch up if he

wanted to continue their conversation. Rafael didn't like the fact that Rodgers was suspicious of him, but he realized there was no easy way to rectify the situation.

Captain Nathan Rodgers was known as an officer who did everything "by the book." To Rafael's way of thinking, that was the most dangerous kind of officer, one who saw things in black and white, ignoring all the grayish shades in between.

"I can only assume Capitán McEwen didn't convince you," Rafael remarked.

"McEwen is above reproach, sir. His character is solid gold. He only sees the good in other people."

"And men only come in two types, is that it, Rodgers? The bad and the good? No troubling mixtures for you, eh?" He couldn't help but bait him.

Rodgers took a long time to answer, as if considering. "I don't know if I hold with that line of thinking. Nobody is all bad or good, and I'm not setting myself up as a judge of moral character, either." Pausing, he cleared his throat. "What bothers me about you, Señor Estava, is that I don't understand what motivates you." He glanced at Rafael. "You're Cuban, and most of your countrymen are rabid patriots, filibustering and doing everything in their power to free Cuba from Spanish rule. You, on the other hand, seem to be opposed to freeing your country. You take great pains to stop armaments from reaching the freedom fighters. Why is that?"

"Would you believe me if I told you I abhor violence?" He touched his scarred cheek and considered how much he should confess to convince Rodgers of his sincerity. "I lost loved ones in the war in Cuba. I prefer to use other, non-violent means to free my country, such as propaganda and infiltration of the power structure. It's a slower process than armed rebellion, but no innocents get killed that way."

Rodgers halted again and looked him up and down, as if weighing the veracity of his statements. He stared at Rafael's scarred face for a long time and then, out of common decency, he averted his gaze.

"Besides, *Capitán,* Cortez is no patriot, no real friend of Cuba. He causes wrecks, sending men to their deaths, to plunder their ships and sell the arms to patriots at exorbitant prices. Even McEwen knows that."

A couple, also coming home from the picnic, approached. Rodgers bowed and greeted them. Rafael followed suit. After the couple passed, they resumed walking.

"What did you have in mind, Estava?" Rodgers inquired and then added, "But don't think you've convinced me. I'm still wary of you. I'll hear you out and reserve judgment. Is that agreeable?"

"It's more than I have the right to expect," he admitted.

Rodgers stared at him, open skepticism in his face. "Continue," he said.

"It's my belief that Cortez is behind the largest wrecking and smuggling ring that plagues these waters. I've been watching him for a long time, and he has his tentacles everywhere."

"I wouldn't disagree with you there, sir."

"I liked it better when you called me Estava."

"As you wish. And you can drop the captain, too. I'm just Rodgers to you."

"Fine, now that we have the amenities out of the way, we can—"

"What do you propose?" Rodgers interjected. "Spit it out." His voice held a note of impatience.

"All right, Rodgers, here goes. I think Cortez is in league with one of the powerful Key West shipping families. His knowledge of ships' courses and manifests is too perfect, even when the ships are supposedly operating under secret orders. I've seen it time and again. Cortez knows where the ships will sail and what they're carrying long before anyone else does." He shot a look at Rodgers. "Even you and the navy."

"That's quite an accusation. Why one of the shipping families? What about a clerk at the custom house? They'd be privy to—"

"Manifests," Rafael interrupted, "but not necessarily courses.

Cortez needs to know the specific course of a ship in order to plant false lights and drive it onto the reefs. A mere clerk wouldn't know that information, nor would he know about the ships operating under a cloak of secrecy. Don't you see, Rodgers? It has to be someone higher up than that. Someone with the big picture.''

Rodgers scratched his chin. Rafael noticed, belatedly, that he'd shaved his beard. An odd thing for a seafaring man to do, he mused.

"Maybe," Rodgers agreed halfheartedly. "It's possible, although I don't understand what the motive would be. The Key West shipping families have more money than they need. Why would they risk their reputations to join with Cortez in such a dangerous and illegal scheme?''

"I've often wondered that myself. It might be a younger son or a brother who doesn't think he's getting a fair share of the family profits. I don't know the why, but I'm convinced the information is coming from the highest level."

"Let's put that aside for a minute and concentrate on getting Cortez. If we get him, we should be able to get his associates. What do you propose, Estava?" he repeated.

"Set a trap for Cortez and his associates. Catch him red-handed, purposely wrecking a ship. If we can catch him, he'll hang. Which is what he richly deserves for killing innocent people. But I'll need your help. And this is no small favor to ask. I don't even know whether it's within your power to do. But I've thought about it for a long time, and I've decided it's the only way to trap him."

"What's the plan then? I'll tell you what is in my power."

"We'll need a naval supply ship, operating under secret orders, supposedly carrying a large shipment of armaments. Its secret course will take it past Alligator Reef. The route will be told to only the Whitmans and the Browns." He paused and regarded Rodgers, weighing his words carefully. "And we'll need a company of Marines to watch the reef."

Rodgers listened intently and was quiet for several moments.

Frowning, his eyebrows drew together. "I understand where you're headed, Estava. And it might work." Shaking his head, he observed, "But it's a tall order. And you were right, it isn't in my power to do. I'll need to inform my superior in Annapolis and see what he says."

Leaning close, Rafael counseled quietly, "Make certain you trust the man you contact, superior or not. And I hope you'll be using naval code for the transaction."

Before he could answer, Rafael stepped from the sidewalk into a copse of trees, fading into the dark night, leaving Captain Nathan Rodgers standing alone on Front Street.

Chapter Eleven

Angelina studied the papers laid out on the bed, trying to regain her earlier concentration. All she could think about was Rafael. How furious he made her and yet how he drew her. It would have been easy to accept his money and disassociate herself from Cortez. Unfortunately, she couldn't do that because it was tantamount to surrendering her freedom and goals.

The bedroom door flew open, banging loudly. She looked up to find Destiny, her face contorted and red. She ran headlong into the room and launched herself onto the foot of the bed. Covering her face with her hands, she began to cry in great big, gulping sobs.

Startled, Angelina threw back the covers and went to her. Placing her arm around Destiny's shoulders, she soothed, "What's this, *amiga mía?* It can't possibly be that bad. What has happened?" She patted her arm. "Capitán Rodgers didn't make unseemly advances, did he? He doesn't seem the kind of man who—"

"It's not that, not Captain Rodgers." Destiny raised her blotched and tear-stained face before burying it in Angelina's shoulder. Her words, muffled but distinct, poured out the story. "It's James. I saw him there. He was with that awful Frances Brown. And he . . . he . . ."

She gulped and lifted her head again. "He refused to take me, Angelina. I asked him to take me to the church picnic, but he said he would be out of town on business. He lied . . . lied to me."

Her face twisted again and a new wave of crying overtook her. Angelina, feeling her friend's hurt as her own, rocked her back and forth, as if she were a small child. Angelina wanted to know more of the details. It might just be a misunderstanding, and Destiny's tender heart was making more of it than she should. Then again, she bristled at the thought of James Whitman purposely hurting her best friend.

Men. They're all alike, she thought with heat. Men were lying, bullying, conniving cheats, willing to do anything to have their own way. It was a good thing she'd said no to Rafael earlier or he would have reduced her to this level of misery.

Holding Destiny in her arms until she'd cried herself out, she waited patiently, listening to the encroaching sounds of evening. The cicadas started their metallic whir and the evening breeze picked up, rattling the palm fronds and tree branches. Malvado called from the balcony, *"Mujer preciosa, mujer preciosa,"* as if to remind her it was time to cover him for the night.

Finally, Destiny pulled away and dabbed at her eyes. Her sobs had turned to hiccoughs and the tears had stopped. Angelina retrieved a handkerchief from the bedside table and handed it to her. Destiny took it and blew her nose noisily.

Then she gazed at Angelina with the saddest look, her eyes red-rimmed and watery, as if her world had ended. Angelina leaned forward and took her hands.

"Tell me everything from the beginning," she urged. "I know I've been busy with plans for the factory on top of my accident. We haven't had time to talk. I can't help you unless I know everything."

"There's no help for me, Angelina. I told you before, I'm a social pariah. It's plain to see that James didn't want to take me in public with his family. So, he made an excuse and lied . . ." She grimaced and Angelina was afraid she might start crying again.

"What made you ask him to the church social? That doesn't sound like you."

"I don't know. Nathan asked me first, but I wanted to go with James, so I put Nathan off." Destiny glanced at her and then averted her eyes. "I know it wasn't the nicest thing to do. I guess God is punishing me. And I deserve it."

"Enough of that, Destiny," she clucked. "Let's leave the Almighty out of this, shall we? So you put Nathan off and asked James to take you. I'm surprised by that. I didn't think you were so forward."

"I'm not, usually. It was that awful swamp and those voodoo stones."

"¿Qué? I mean, what do you mean?" she asked, unable to keep the incredulous note from her voice.

"James took me walking to the Old Pond. That's all he wants to do. Don't you see? Sneak around corners in the dark and hide and—"

"Stop. Stop, Destiny." She disengaged their hands and placed her hands on her friend's shoulders, giving her a gentle shake. "We'll talk of his motives later. First, I want to know what happened."

"Well . . ." Destiny colored, her face growing even redder. "James said he wanted to show me something in the Old Pond. That's a swampy area on the edge of town. Tilly wouldn't let me go there with the other children when I was little. Now I know why," she added, driving Angelina crazy with her roundabout explanation.

"And?" she prompted.

"He led me deep into the swamp to this place in the middle of some trees." She wrinkled her nose. "It smelled bad and there were rings of stones and lots of garbage. James said the slaves and then the freed Negroes went there to practice voodoo and engage in hideous rituals, like butchering chickens and things.'' Lowering her eyes, she whispered, ''Then he got all excited and said the place did funny things to him. He kissed me and started to unbutton my dress.''

''He *what?*''

Raising her head, she met Angelina's eyes and lifted her chin, declaring, ''But I stopped him, even though he frightened me. On the way home, I knew he was sorry and I knew about the picnic from . . . Nathan . . . so I asked James to take me.''

''But he refused.''

''Yes, he said he had to go to Tampa on business and stay over several days. I'd planned on refusing Nathan when he asked again, but for some reason, I couldn't bring myself to do it.'' Her shoulders drooped. ''I guess I'm an awful person and that's why God is punishing me.''

''Don't say that. It's not wise to invoke the Almighty's wrath. And don't judge yourself. As long as you didn't hurt Nathan by going with him today, there's been no harm done. Has there?''

Destiny screwed her eyes shut as if considering and then opened them slowly, avoiding looking at Angelina. ''I don't think I hurt Nathan, but I know he's starting to wonder why I act strangely at times. When I saw James at the picnic surrounded by his family and the Browns, I knew. He didn't take me because he's ashamed and his family won't accept me.''

''Let's not jump to conclusions.'' She patted Destiny's hand. ''You haven't spoken to James since he brought you home from the swamp?''

''No.'' She thrust her bottom lip out. ''He said he was going to Tampa. I didn't expect to see him until next week.''

''And you think he made up the excuse because he didn't want to take you. He only wants to see you alone, away from others. Am I correct?''

Destiny nodded.

''You could think of it as a compliment, you know. That he

wants you all to himself.'' She tried to put a positive spin on Whitman's behavior to comfort her friend. Privately, though, the more Destiny told her, the more she had to agree with her friend's negative assessment.

And just thinking about the brute's attack in the swamp made her blood boil. It reminded her of Rafael's assault on her at the ball. But she'd put an end to that. Unfortunately, Destiny thought she was in love with James Whitman.

''I wanted to think of it as a compliment. But if he doesn't present me to his parents, he'll never ask me to marry him. Will he?''

''Probably not,'' she had to agree.

''I don't know what to do. What would you do?''

''When he refused to take you to the picnic, did he offer to make it up to you? To take you to another social function?''

''He offered to take me on his yacht and have oysters and champagne,'' Destiny confessed, her voice sounding small and hurt.

''Ohhh,'' Angelina drew out the word, incensed.

What a mess, she thought to herself. Her friend had loved James Whitman for years. She'd wanted him to notice her and take her out. She'd gotten that wish. But the other thing, the dark secret of her past, the one that had driven Captain McEwen to become a hermit and placed her friend beyond the social pale, still seemed to hang over Destiny. Especially with someone as socially prominent as James Whitman.

It wasn't fair, she decided. Destiny's grandfather should at least explain what the scandal had been. Maybe it was something that, after all these years, could be rectified. But she knew she was grasping at straws, feeling sorry for her friend's plight. If James Whitman had decided Destiny wasn't acceptable to his family or society, she knew there was little hope of changing his mind.

In the meantime, Destiny would suffer. Thinking about it, she was grateful she wasn't in love. At least, she hoped she wasn't. Surely, the way she felt about Rafael couldn't be love. Could it? She shook off the thought.

She was merely attracted to Rafael. Nothing more. And she wasn't about to lose her head over him, either. Unfortunately, that wasn't the situation with Destiny. Her friend believed she was deeply in love with James Whitman. She remembered that first evening when Destiny had come home after being with James. Remembering, she wondered how long Destiny could go on like this, not knowing if he returned her love.

An idea took form in her mind. It was a gamble, and the outcome might not be what her friend wanted. But to her way of thinking, it was better to know exactly where you stood, rather than guessing. She didn't know if Destiny would agree, but she had to try.

"Destiny," she began, reaching for her hands again and giving them a reassuring squeeze. "Are you willing to try an experiment, even if it confirms your worst fears?"

"I . . . I don't know. What do you mean?"

"Are you going to spend the rest of your life pining for this James Whitman, even if he doesn't want you for his wife? If all he wants is . . . is . . ."

"To compromise me?" Destiny closed her eyes and sniffed, using the already sodden handkerchief to wipe her nose.

"Yes."

"I . . . I guess not. That's not what I'd dreamed about. Part of loving James was to be finally accepted by Key West society and to . . . to . . ." She covered her face with her hands again. Her voice was a harsh whisper. "I don't know anymore, Angelina. Parts of the ball were awful. I mean, the way so-called 'polite society' acted. If it hadn't been for Nathan . . ." She leaned forward and buried herself against Angelina's shoulder once more.

Angelina patted her back, trying to sound hopeful, "See, you've already found some answers. Reality rarely measures up to our dreams. And not being accepted by Key West society isn't the end of the world. There are other people, nice people, interesting people—like Nathan.''

Forgive her, she offered a silent prayer, for invoking a man to fill the void in her friend's life. But of all the men she knew, she had to admit she liked Captain Rodgers quite a lot. And it was plain to see he was devoted to Destiny. A little devotion might go a long way toward shoring up her friend's pain and insecurities.

''I know there are other people. It's just that . . .'' She pulled free from Angelina and threw up her hands. ''I guess I wanted to right old wrongs, something like that.''

''I don't want to meddle, but shouldn't you find out what happened in the past before you try to fix it.''

''I can't. Gramps won't tell me.''

She sighed, reaching up and stroking a lock of hair from Destiny's forehead. ''Maybe he will, when he thinks you're ready.''

''It doesn't matter.'' Her friend straightened and fisted her hands, rubbing her eyes. ''What did you have in mind? I'm ready to try anything. I want to know what James's intentions are. What should I do?''

''I believe you should give him an ultimatum. The next time he comes around, apologizing and making excuses for not taking you to the picnic, you should be gracious but firm. Tell him you won't see him again until he takes you to meet his family.'' She paused, regarding her friend, trying to gauge her reaction. ''It's the only way you'll know how he feels, what he's willing to do for you.''

Destiny expelled her breath in a long rush. ''I guess you're right. It does seem the right thing to do. Better to know now and try to . . .'' Her eyes got watery again.

''Don't think like that,'' she commanded. ''Try to think positive. Sometimes all men need is a gentle nudge. And he might have a very valid reason for going to the picnic without you. At least give him a chance. You've loved him for so long, what will a few more days matter?''

Her friend brightened instantly. "Do you think there's a chance, Angelina? Really?"

"Of course," she agreed, hoping she wasn't making a mistake by offering false hope.

Angelina leaned back in the rickety chair and fished a handkerchief from her reticule. Briskly, she mopped her brow and wiped her upper lip. It was like a furnace in the windowless, dank office, and she was exhausted. But she didn't want Cortez to guess her exhaustion or weakness. She needed to be on her toes around him. She hoped he hadn't heard about her accident.

Her hopes were dashed when he leaned across the desk and offered, "Can I get you a glass of water? You should conserve your strength, *señorita*. I was sorry to hear about your unfortunate accident."

She shrugged. "It was nothing, just a bump on the head. I'm fine now," she lied, forcing herself to sit straighter in the chair. "I would like a glass of water, though."

He nodded and rose. Going to a cabinet, he withdrew a pitcher and two glasses. Watching him, she felt her head start throbbing. She probably had pushed too hard, but after her exchange with Rafael yesterday, she'd decided that she had convalesced for long enough.

Today was Monday, the beginning of the business week. She'd risen early and gone to see the Silva factory. Señor Silva, obviously feeling guilty because his wagon hit her, had bent over backwards to be helpful, personally showing her around his operation. She hadn't learned anything new at his factory, but the efficiency of the place had impressed her. And she'd come away even more convinced that the key to a successful cigar factory was having a skilled labor force.

Cortez placed a glass of water in front of her, and she took it gratefully. Even though it proved to be tepid from sitting in the closed cabinet, she savored the liquid feel of it, sipping it slowly. He resumed his seat at the desk to look over her drawings and plans.

She tried not to be nervous, awaiting the outcome of his decision. Plucking at the folds in her skirt and twisting them into knots, she dreaded more arguments and wanted to get on with building the factory.

Trying to take her mind off his deliberations, she glanced around the tiny office. It was made of unfinished wood with one door and no windows. The walls were bare except for a calendar and a map of Florida and the Keys. The furnishings were sparse: a desk and padded chair, a cabinet, and two other chairs. If Cortez was as successful as he claimed to be, his office didn't reflect that success.

After what seemed like hours, he lifted his head and pursed his lips. "I can see you've done your research. You're to be commended on your thoroughness."

She relaxed a fraction, hoping they could come to a swift agreement.

Leaning forward, he stabbed at one of the papers with his index finger. "I have only one problem, Señorita Herrera. Your wanting to personally supervise fifteen workers. I don't think—"

"*Por favor,* Señor Cortez," she interrupted. "I've acquiesced to your other de—er, requests." She'd started to say demands but thought better of it, wanting to go softly and cajole him into letting her have her way.

"I've given the matter of the labor force a great deal of thought, and I believe it's the key to my success. I want to be personally responsible at first. That way I will be completely in control of the operation."

She leaned forward and spread her hands on the desk. "When I feel confident about the factory, I'll hire a foreman. I recognize that overseeing fifteen workers is stretching the limits of my capabilities, but by not paying a foreman and having fifteen workers, I think I can make a tidy profit." She pointed to one of the other papers lying on the desk. "As you can see, I've decided to limit my production to two types of cigars. That way, I can—"

"*Sí, sí, yo entiendo.*" It was his turn to interrupt, albeit impatiently. "But I still believe you should employ twenty workers and a foreman. You must consider the future, Señorita Herrera."

Taking a deep breath, she leaned back and gripped the arms of the flimsy chair. "You've said that before, Señor Cortez. Unfortunately, after careful consideration, I can't agree with you on that one point. I'm not comfortable with starting that way."

And after all, it will be me who's running the factory, not you, she wanted to add. But she forced herself to stop, not wanting to elaborate, to see how he would answer.

Their gazes met and held, silently battling each other for supremacy. After a few seconds, he dropped his eyes and took up the glass of water at his elbow, sipping slowly as if considering.

She held her breath, realizing this was the moment she'd been waiting for, the final decision. Would he agree and fund her factory or would they arrive at an impasse? Reaching up, she fingered the crucifix at her throat and said a silent prayer to the Blessed Virgin Mary.

There was a knock at the door to the office. The sound startled her, and she half jumped in her chair. Cortez put his empty glass aside and said, "*Entra.*"

A short, dark man with a pockmarked face entered, holding his straw hat in front of him like a shield. "Señor Cortez, you sent for me?" the stranger asked.

"*Sí,* I did," he said, rising from the desk. "I wanted you to meet Señorita Herrera. She might have a job for you in a few weeks, as foreman of her cigar factory. If I can convince her," he added pointedly.

Turning to her, Cortez declared, "Señorita Herrera, I'd like you to meet Rico López, the man I was telling you about."

Inclining her head, she murmured, *"Mucho gusto en cono-cerle*, Señor López."

She would have liked to say more to López, especially about the upcoming job, which she didn't plan on giving him. And she could have cheerfully scratched Cortez's eyes out for bringing it up in front of him and putting her in such an untenable position. As it was, she was still at Cortez's mercy, and she had a sinking sensation that he'd purposely sent for López to put additional pressure on her.

What Cortez didn't realize was that the more pressure he brought to bear, the more entrenched she became. Unfortunately, she remembered Rafael's warning, too. What if Cortez was adamant about having this man at her factory so he could use her storehouse for smuggled goods with López overseeing the clandestine operations?

That was the least of her worries. The factory wasn't even built yet. Besides, did Cortez and Rafael think she was so stupid as to not notice smuggled goods hidden at her own factory? She shut her eyes for a second, realizing they probably both thought that she, being a woman, was too idiotic to know the difference.

Men, men, she railed inwardly. They were so used to ruling women, they began to believe their own fantasies: women were pitiful creatures, ill equipped to take care of themselves. She would prove them wrong, prove them both wrong. *Bring on the smuggled goods,* she thought to herself, *and I'll throw them into the street.*

Thinking about beating Cortez at his own game if he was, as Rafael believed, trying to use her factory for smuggled goods, gave her an idea. Why not turn the tables on him now? She knew it was a gamble and might backfire, but she seemed to be in a gaming mood of late, willing to trust lady luck with her future as well as Destiny's.

Anything was better, even trusting to fate, then being the pawn of powerful men, she decided.

Focusing her attention on López, who stood awkwardly

beside the desk, she purposely directed all of her feminine charms at him. Smiling widely, she batted her eyelashes.

He blinked and stood up straighter.

Glancing at Cortez and then back to López, she used her most demure voice, "Señor López, *por favor,* Señor Cortez exaggerates. My cigar factory isn't even built." She spread her gloved hands in a gesture of supplication. "And it will be a humble concern. I don't have the money to hire a foreman. At least, not at first," she added quickly, shooting Cortez a meaningful look. "But I would welcome skilled workers, and I'm prepared to pay top wages. If you came to work for me, maybe later, as my factory grew, I could give you the position of foreman. As it is now"—she lifted her gloved hands and shrugged—"I'm not in a position to hire a foreman."

Cortez half rose from his seat and opened his mouth. But he must have thought better of it because he stopped himself and sat down again. His gaze swept her, and she sensed his barely controlled fury. She also glimpsed something else, too, a kind of grudging admiration.

He exchanged glances with López and finally said, "That seems a fair offer. Would you consider it, Señor López?"

López stared at Cortez as if expecting to find the answer written on his face. At that moment, she decided Rafael might be right. It was obvious López worked for Cortez, at least in some capacity. At the same time, she didn't care. Victory was within her grasp. She could feel it, taste it on her tongue . . , and the taste was sweet, very sweet.

As for the other, the smuggling, she'd trusted lady luck this far. She might as well go on rolling the dice, if it got her what she wanted. She'd deal with Cortez and López and their nefarious plans later.

"*Sí,* I would be more than willing to consider your generous offer, Señorita Herrera," López agreed.

* * *

Angelina stood at the edge of Frances Street, hands fisted, resting on her hips, admiring the construction of her factory. Everything was going according to the plans she'd drawn. Seeing her ideas take shape was imminently gratifying, she was learning.

The workmen Cortez had hired had made impressive progress in a week's time. The lot had been cleared and a cart track laid out that curved in front of where the factory structure would be. An outlying enclosure, a wood and wire fence, had already been erected. This barricade would serve as the factory's yard, useful for unloading crates and wagons. The structural posts that would support the factory's roof had already been driven deep into the marshy ground, anchored by several feet of gravel and crushed stone.

The next step would be to build the brick office and storage space. After that, the wooden slat floor would be framed in and the thatched roof raised. The last step would be to furnish the factory with tables for the workers, weights, gauges, and cutting boards. Using a portion of the funds Cortez had provided, she'd already begun to purchase the necessary items. Some things weren't readily available, so she'd ordered them from the mainland and was awaiting their arrival by ship.

Depending on how fast the masons laid the brick, she might, with a bit of luck, be ready to open in another two or three weeks. Before that, she needed to run an advertisement in the local newspaper to attract skilled workers. She planned to screen and interview each applicant, one by one, to assess their skill level. References from previous employers would be welcome, but she wanted each worker to demonstrate his ability before she hired him.

"It looks like your dream will soon be a reality. My congratulations to you."

Without turning around, she would have known that deep male voice anywhere. It belonged to Rafael. She hadn't seen him since the Sunday afternoon when he'd come to pay his respects and left her furious with his heavy-handed tactics.

She tried to tell herself that she hadn't missed him, either, him and his bossiness. That she'd been too busy to miss anyone, especially Rafael.

But that wouldn't be true.

Unfortunately, she had missed him. Why? She couldn't say.

Pivoting slowly, she greeted him, *"Buenas tardes,* Rafael. And thank you for your congratulations. Remember, you were the first one who believed I could do it." She paused, gazing at him. "Later, I don't know what happened. For some reason, you stopped believing in me. Or at least I thought you did." Tilting her head, she prodded, "What happened, Rafael? Why did you lose your faith?"

"I didn't lose my faith in you, Angelina," he replied. "What happened between us was Cortez," he remarked drily. "You know that."

"Ah, *sí,* the nefarious Cortez and his infamous henchman, Señor López." She tossed her head. "Don't worry, Rafael, if I find any smuggled goods in *my* factory, I'll throw them out in the street."

He grabbed her shoulders, commanding, "Don't make light of Cortez. And who did you say his henchman was? López? Rico López?"

She stared up at him, at his flashing sienna eyes, at his chocolate-brown hair curling from beneath his wide Panama hat. His scent surrounded her, sandalwood and musk. His broad shoulders blocked out the world, making a place just for the two of them. She should be angry that he was touching her, that he'd rudely grabbed her. How many times had she warned him to never touch her again?

And how she'd longed for his touch, yearned for it in her solitary bed during the long, lonely nights.

Shutting her eyes, she gave herself over to the sensation of his nearness. Moving closer, she placed her hands on the crisp linen of his shirt, hungry to feel his heart beat. Her own heart quickened with anticipation. Her breasts tightened pleasurably. Her tongue crept out and she wet her lips, preparing them.

Then her reason returned as suddenly as it had abandoned her. Her eyes snapped open, and she shook her head as if to clear it. She couldn't believe what she'd been thinking, what she'd been dreaming. She'd wanted him to kiss her, she realized. Wanted him to? She'd practically given him an engraved invitation.

He was watching her closely, his eyes narrowed, as if she'd gone mad in the broiling Florida sun. Releasing her, he retreated a pace. Disappointment, mingled with a strange kind of relief, swept through her.

Then he was demanding again, "Did you say Rico López?"

"Sí." She lifted one shoulder and turned to face her factory, wanting to hide the turmoil rioting through her. It would be a good thing when the factory was finished, she told herself. Then she'd be so busy, she wouldn't have time to think of Rafael. And at night . . . she hoped to be so exhausted that she would fall instantly asleep.

"I thought he might be one of Cortez's men, but I never could prove it," he murmured, half to himself. "Did Cortez introduce you to López?"

"Sí," she admitted again.

His constant harping on Cortez was beginning to wear thin. She almost wished for the impetuous man who had kissed her at the ball. Now everything was business with him, strictly business. He had a personal vendetta against Cortez and nothing deflected him from his goal. Not that she really cared, she assured herself. He could hang Cortez by his heels for all that it mattered to her, as long as the factory was finished.

"Why did he introduce López to you?"

She faced him again, impatience sharpening her tone, "He wanted López to be my foreman."

"So Cortez would control your factory through López. *Mira,* López would be responsible for getting the smuggled goods in and out." He laid his hand on her arm as if to emphasize his point. "Angelina, you can't—"

"Can't I?" she cut him off. "Who will stop me?" She gazed

pointedly at his hand. Taking the hint, he let it drop. Moving closer to him, she faced him down. "What do you take me for, Señor Estava, an idiot? I know Cortez wants to control my factory. He's a man, isn't he?" she spat. "Men want to control everything, particularly anything a woman owns. I accepted López, but on my own terms. And I know to watch López."

Rafael opened his mouth to speak, but she forestalled him, moving even closer, until she stood a mere breath away. Being this close to him unsettled her, but she hoped it unsettled him as well. And for some perverse reason, she wanted to make him forget, too, just for one brief moment, about the hideous game of cat and mouse he played with Cortez.

"If you didn't think I was such a witless female, you would stop to consider how helpful it would be for me to get Cortez out of the way." Her voice was deceptively soft, almost a whisper. "If you capture Cortez and imprison him, who will collect his debts? I would have my factory and a free hand, too. I can repay him when I'm ready." She waved her hand in dismissal. "Believe me, Rafael, you'll be the first to know if Cortez or López do anything illegal."

His gaze snagged hers, open admiration shining in the depths of his golden-brown eyes. *"Perdóneme,* Angelina. Once more, I've underestimated you. I won't make that mistake again," he promised. Tipping his hat and bowing, he said, "You know where to find me if you need me. *Buenas tardes."*

She watched him go, sauntering down Frances Street with that jaunty, sexy prowl of his. Suddenly, she wished he cared about something other than capturing Cortez. But that was ridiculous, she reminded herself. She didn't have the time to become involved with a man . . . any man.

Chapter Twelve

"It was nice of you to hire a buggy to take me for a ride."
Destiny made an outward show of enthusiasm.

Inside, she was dying by slow, painful inches. She'd agreed
to this outing for one reason: to tell Nathan that her heart
belonged to another.

The day after the picnic, James had called on her. He'd
humbly apologized and explained that his business trip to
Tampa had been postponed. His mother had already committed
their family to accompanying the Browns to the picnic. He
claimed there had been no way he could get out of it.

She had accepted his apology but on one condition; she
wanted to be presented to his family. He'd agreed to do so,
but unfortunately, his parents had just left for Tampa on the
delayed business trip and to visit friends. When they returned,
he promised to present her to them. In the meantime, he'd
invited her to a dinner party at the home of his married sister,
Jennifer Shaw.

Once James had committed himself to introducing her to his
family, she'd made up her mind. It wasn't right or fair to keep

Nathan dangling and hoping to win her affections. After all, the man wanted to marry her. The sooner she told him, the sooner he would forget her and get on with his life.

Unfortunately, when she thought about not seeing Nathan again, she experienced a sharp pain in the general region of her heart. She liked and admired him a great deal. He'd been a good friend and loyal champion. She would miss seeing him, miss talking with him. She blushed to think about it, but she would miss his kisses as well.

Nathan smiled down at her and snapped the reins, urging the matched bays forward. "I have another surprise for you. I'm taking you to see my ship, the *Columbia*. She's in port being refitted and the crew has shore leave. This is a perfect opportunity for you to look around," he explained and then cleared his throat. "Without having prying eyes watching."

"Oh, that sounds wonderful." She didn't know how long she could keep this charade up.

When would be the best time to tell him? Not yet. She knew how much his ship meant to him. The least she could do was to be polite and let him show her around. And she didn't want to tell him on the *Columbia*, either. It might jinx his ship with bad memories. Having been raised by a seafaring family, she knew how superstitious sailors could be.

When then? She couldn't put it off forever, although her cowardly inclinations urged her to do so. Sighing, she knew what she had to do. When he brought her home and the outing was over, she would have to tell him.

"I can't wait to show you my ship, but we'll have our buggy ride first. It would be a waste if we just drove to the wharf and back. Don't you think so?"

Destiny gritted her teeth, realizing he had the afternoon already planned. She hadn't wanted to drag this thing out, but she didn't see any other option.

Gifting him with a stiff smile, she nodded. He turned onto Duval Street and went east, heading away from the wharf, to the less populated area of the key. At least he wasn't taking her to that awful swamp, she thought grimly.

Once they'd cleared the town, he snapped the reins again and urged the bays into a fast trot. Destiny grabbed at her straw bonnet, holding it on her head so it wouldn't fly off. They skimmed along the beach on the Atlantic side at a fast clip. She struggled to tie the ribbons of her bonnet tighter. Once she had her hat secured, she dropped her hands and enjoyed the beach and sea speeding past her.

It was an exhilarating feeling, flying along behind the horses. The feeling took her breath away and made her heart pound harder—almost like being kissed, she thought wryly. It had been a long time since she'd ridden in a buggy. It was so easy to walk everywhere on the island, she'd forgotten what it felt like to go fast.

Nathan grinned down at her and took her hand. She grinned back, enjoying herself and savoring the feel of his strong, calloused hand enclosing hers. Hand in hand, it wasn't long before they'd rounded the island and pulled up to the wharf on the west side. The bays snorted and tossed their heads, their dark red coats covered with a light sheen of lather.

"Here we are, Destiny," he declared. "We'll let the horses rest a bit while we're on board. If you want to go fast again after we see the *Columbia,* I think these bays have the stamina."

She found herself nodding without thinking. She'd thoroughly enjoyed their madcap ride along the beach, managing to forget the painful task that lay ahead. With the buggy ride over and Nathan's ship looming before her, she remembered with a jolt. As soon as they were finished looking over the ship, she would insist that he take her home. She would tell him then. If she drew it out any longer, she knew she wouldn't go through with it.

The *Columbia,* a United States Navy revenue cutter, proved to be sleek and rigged for speed. Nathan explained that the sixty-foot, single-masted cutter had to be fast and maneuverable to catch smugglers on the high seas.

He led her up the gangplank and aboard the upper deck. They strolled the length of the cutter, and she realized how small it was compared to the schooners her grandfather and the other wreckers used. Nathan told her that his crew consisted of approximately twenty to twenty-five men.

The other thing she noticed were the guns. Gramps's schooner had one ancient cannon for emergencies. The *Columbia* carried ten nine-pounders, strategically located for maximum firepower. There were four guns on the starboard side and four on the port, with one gun at the bow and one aft.

Gazing at the ominous-looking guns, she shivered, realizing what a dangerous occupation Nathan had. But then, she knew he was a brave man. Thinking about how he'd championed her at the ball, her heart expanded. It was going to be difficult to give him up, she realized again.

After they'd toured topside, he took her below and showed her the cramped quarters, complete with hammocks and foot lockers, where his crew lived when they were at sea. The galley and storage rooms were little bigger than closets, but she was used to close quarters. Her grandfather's ship, although larger in bulk, had miniscule rooms below deck, too.

He saved his cabin for last. When he threw open the heavy brass door, he did so with a flourish. Glancing up at him, she saw the pride shining in his eyes. A lump rose to her throat, looking at him. He was honest and forthright, as well as brave and kind. If it hadn't been for James . . .

Bowing low, he ushered her inside. His cabin was as she expected, small but functional and as neat as a pin. One thing did stand out as unusual, though. He had fitted a long row of bookshelves around the perimeter of the room, and the shelves were crammed with books.

"I didn't know you liked to read," she said. "Are all these books yours?"

"Yes, they're mine. Next to the sea, I like nothing better than reading." He paused and tugged at his collar. "Except, of course, to be with you, Destiny."

When he leaned forward, she knew he wanted to kiss her, but she couldn't allow it. Not when she was going to tell him that she didn't want to see him again. It wouldn't be right.

Slipping past him, she made a slow circuit of the cabin, studying its contents intently, from his astrolabe to the official papers on his desk. At the opposite side of the room, she stopped to test the hardness of his bunk's mattress by bouncing on it. She'd grown up bouncing on her Gramps's bunk. It was fun, especially when the ship was moving, rolling from side to side.

But when she looked up and caught his gaze, she saw the bright flare of desire in his eyes. Realizing what she was doing and how it must look, she scrambled to her feet. "Out of the frying pan and into the fire," the old saying reverberated in her head. She'd avoided kissing him, only to crawl into his bed!

What must he think of her?

They stood at opposite sides of the cramped cabin. Their gazes snagged and held. The air in the close cabin crackled, vibrant with sexual tension, humming with unfulfilled desires.

It was Destiny who found her tongue, managing to keep her tone light, "You have a lovely cabin, Nathan. And so many books! They must be a great comfort to you when you're out at sea."

He closed his eyes and gulped. The cords of muscle in his neck stood out in stark relief. She knew then what an effort of will it took him to retain his gentlemanly manner. If she'd read the frank desire in his eyes correctly, he wanted nothing more than to grab her and throw her onto the narrow bed.

Remembering what Angelina had told her about how it was between men and women, she felt her body respond to him. Her skin flushed and her heart accelerated. Her breasts swelled, the nipples growing hard, and lower, she felt a pleasurable tightening between her thighs.

She craved his kisses, she realized. Yearned for his strong, muscular arms to embrace her, holding her close and safe.

Desire simmered in her veins, and she longed for his touch upon her skin, feather-light and gentle.

He cleared his throat again, offering, "I'm glad you like it. Any time you want to borrow a book, just let me know." His arm swept the narrow confines and he tried an awkward jest. "I've plenty to choose from."

His innocent words startled her, bringing her back to herself. What had she been thinking? What had she been feeling? She'd never felt this way about James, she realized. She welcomed his kisses and gloried in his affections, but her body had never craved his touch or longed for . . .

In fact, when he'd tried to touch her in the swamp, she'd been offended. Why was that? What was wrong with her? It was James she loved. She'd loved him since she was a child. But it was Nathan who inexorably drew her, filling her mind with erotic images, commanding her body's response as easily as he commanded this ship.

Was she making a mistake, giving up Nathan?

But that couldn't be. She'd dreamed and planned and plotted to have James, not Nathan. Maybe she felt this way because she'd never been in a man's bedroom before. That had to be the reason, she decided. If she'd been in James's bedroom with him, she would have felt the same way. As it was, that horrible swamp hadn't been conducive to . . .

Frightened of her turbulent feelings, she forgot her carefully laid plans to tell Nathan. Feeling guilty for desiring him when she loved James, she had to prove to herself where her true affections lay.

Without thinking, she blurted, "Nathan, I can't see you anymore. I love another."

Tilly grumbled to herself, "If'n I coulda found dat no-count Rufus, 'e shoulda been doin' dis. Not me."

She continued to mutter to herself as she plowed her way through the muddy streets, carrying a basket of food. It had rained earlier, and construction had stopped on Miss Angelina's factory, Destiny had taken pains to explain to her. That was why Miss Angelina had stayed late to oversee the building so the construction would stay on target. And Destiny couldn't take Angelina her dinner because she'd been all a flutter, getting ready to meet Mister Whitman's folks.

But that rascal Rufus had no excuse, Tilly knew, other than his customary disappearing act when there was work to be done.

"Foolish, foolish womens," Tilly mumbled, "stayin' out aftah dahk. Dat factoree, she be built all de same, daytime or night." She shook her head.

Rounding the corner to Frances Street, she found torches illuminating the construction area. Straining her old eyes, she looked for Miss Angelina but couldn't find her. If it weren't for the burning torches, she would have thought everyone had gone home. There weren't any workers in sight.

The sound of a wagon caught her attention, rattling down the street, coming from the opposite direction, from the cemetery. Tilly shivered and fingered the cross at her throat. It wasn't a good sign, a wagon coming from the cemetery at this time of night. And this wagon was covered, like an undertaker's hearse, she noticed.

At that moment, she glimpsed a figure about a hundred yards away, emerging from the shadows of the building site as if to intercept the covered wagon. She recognized the figure as Miss Angelina.

Then she saw Miss Angelina step into the street. The wagon stopped beside her. A short man leapt down and threw a burlap bag over her head. There was a shout, abruptly cut off, as the man lifted her into the wagon. Tilly watched her struggles with horror budding in her chest, glimpsed the white of her petticoats as she kicked her feet.

Frozen to the spot where she stood, Tilly couldn't quite believe her eyes. What had happened? She knew a young lady shouldn't be out after dark without an escort, but she hadn't expected her most dire prediction to come true. Her mind whirled and spun, like a child's top that was out of control.

The driver whipped up the team, hurtling past her. Cringing, she crouched in the shadows, suddenly fearful for herself. What if they were madmen? What if they saw her?

Miss Angelina's white face, half-covered by a bandana tied across her mouth, hove into view from the wagon. Then the burlap bag dropped over her head again. The wagon careened past, leaving Tilly choking on churned dust and mud.

The enormity of what had happened filled her mind, overflowing it, like a barrel left too long in a rainstorm. She closed her eyes, trying to form her thoughts.

Miss Angelina abducted!

She must get help. She first thought of Captain McEwen, but Miss Destiny was closer. She'd gone to a dinner party at the Shaws. Master Charles Shaw's house was just two streets over. Dropping the heavy basket, she lifted her skirts and began to run.

Destiny dabbed at her mouth with a snowy-white napkin and took a sip of wine. Lifting her spoon, she dipped it carefully into the tortoise soup and brought it to her mouth. She'd thought her table manners were impeccable, having learned them at Miss Prentiss's finishing school. But after watching Jennifer Shaw, James's sister, stare at her throughout the first two courses, she was beginning to wonder.

She sighed softly to herself. It had been a difficult evening. When she'd arrived with James, ready to charm his relatives, she'd found Jennifer's reception chilly and distant. Jennifer's husband, Charles, hadn't made the evening any easier. He'd been obviously drunk and much too solicitous of her, almost to the point of embarrassment. With Charles leering at her, was it any wonder that his wife hadn't taken to her?

Glancing up, she noticed the Shaws' English butler enter the dining room. He'd greeted them at the door but hadn't taken part in serving dinner. She hadn't been surprised by his absence. He'd looked down his long nose at them when they'd arrived, and she'd had the distinct feeling that he did little in the household besides open the door and greet visitors.

But now he appeared to be agitated and decidedly out of place, standing at attention to one side, as if waiting for someone to notice him.

Jennifer, who had been holding forth on the outrageousness of current Parisian fashions, stopped with her spoon midway to her mouth. Her eyebrows flew up and she frowned. Her soup spoon clattered to the plate beneath the bowl. Instinctively, Destiny cringed.

"Pickering, what is it?" she demanded, addressing the butler.

"There is a servant at the door," he intoned solemnly. "I believe she belongs to Miss Favor, and she's quite insistent—"

His words were eclipsed by the sliding wooden panel to the dining room being abruptly and vigorously thrown open. Tilly stood in the doorway, swaying, her dark face ashen, looking as if she'd seen a ghost.

"Miz Destiny, come quick! Miz Angelina, she's been taken by mens agin 'er will." Tilly thumped her chest. "Ah's seen it. They's grabbed 'er and throwed 'er in a wagon."

Destiny rose to her feet, scarcely able to believe what Tilly was saying. Tossing her napkin on the table, she started toward her servant. Before she could reach her servant's side, Pickering had taken hold of Tilly, shoving and declaring, "My good woman, you can't break in here and cause a disturbance."

Rounding on him, Destiny couldn't believe the butler's audacity. Furious at him and frightened for Angelina, she did her own shoving, pushing Pickering to one side and taking Tilly's arm.

From the corner of her eye, she glimpsed James. He'd risen also, demanding, "Destiny, return to this table at once! And let go of Pickering! I can't countenance this behavior. You're humiliating me in front of my sister and her husband. How can you allow this to happen? Your servant must be disciplined."

Shocked by his uncaring attitude, she hesitated for only a second. She didn't have time to argue with him. If he couldn't understand that Tilly's message took precedence over a dinner party, she didn't have time to convince him.

"I apologize for this interruption." Glancing briefly at Jennifer, she said, "Thank you for inviting me. But something has happened to my friend. I must get help." She didn't even bother to look at James; instead, she grabbed Tilly's arm and flew from the house, heading for the wharf.

Tilly, running alongside, huffed and puffed to keep up. Panting, she managed to ask, "Miz Destiny, whut 'bout yous granfader, Cap'n McEwen?"

"I want to find Captain Rodgers first. I know he can help. Then we'll get grandfather."

Breathing hard from her exertions, Tilly merely nodded. Several minutes later, they stood on the wharf. Destiny's gaze riveted upon one spot—where the *Columbia* had been moored, two days ago. But the space was empty; the ship was gone. She couldn't believe her eyes. Nathan had told her they'd be in dry dock for the rest of the week, finishing repairs.

Doubling her fists, she rubbed at her eyes, wondering if the wine she'd drunk at the Shaws had affected her vision. But when she looked again, she saw the same thing, an empty expanse of water, gently lapping at the wharf's pilings.

Groaning, she turned to Tilly. "We've got to get Gramps and ... and ..." Her mind somersaulted. Panic streaked through her, making her heart pound in her chest. She sucked in her breath. An idea formed.

"Señor Estava." She snapped her fingers. "That's it! He has an office here with quarters in the back. He'll help Angelina, and he'll know where to find Nathan."

Crossing the wharf, she headed for a row of offices. One of these offices was where Rafael's underwriting firm was housed. Ships' lanterns gave fitful illumination for the buildings. Moving along the row, she tried to make out the signs on the doors. Coming to one, she saw: "Medrano and Company, Ship

Underwriters.'' If her memory served her, this had to be his office.

Peering inside the small window, she saw the glow of a light from within. Hope sprang forth, bringing tears to her eyes.

Raising her hand, she curled it into a fist and pounded on the wooden door, calling, ''Señor Estava, Señor Estava, are you in there? Please, come out! Señor Estava, please. It's about Angelina—she's been taken!''

She heard movement from within and then a figure passed between her and the light. The door flew open and Rafael stepped out, demanding, ''What has happened? Señorita Destiny, why are you here?''

''It's Angelina—someone has taken her. Tilly saw it. I don't know the details. I rushed here to get Captain Rodgers, but his vessel is gone. He'd told me they'd be doing repairs. Do you know where he is?''

Rafael reached out, laying a steadying hand on her shoulder. ''Let's go slowly, Destiny. One thing at a time. You say someone took Angelina. Against her will?''

Destiny was breathing hard from her headlong run coupled with her own mounting panic. Gulping air, she tried to calm herself down as he'd instructed. She wanted to give him a coherent account. Facing Tilly, she urged, ''Tell him what happened. Exactly what you saw.''

Tilly recounted what she'd seen on Frances Street, including her own fears. Rafael listened attentively and then asked, ''The man you saw grab Angelina—was he stocky and short?''

''Yes'sah,'' she replied.

''The torches were burning when you got there, but no workers were around? And when the wagon came up, Angelina went to it?''

''Yes'sah, dat's whut huppened.''

''What does it mean?'' Destiny inquired, frantic to understand, desperate to help her friend. All she could think about were the seconds ticking away and Angelina being in danger.

Rafael faced Destiny. ''I have a pretty good idea who grabbed

Angelina. Now we've got to get her back. And for that, I'll need your Captain Rodgers."

"Where is Nathan? Do you know?"

"Yes, I spoke to him late this afternoon. I was surprised he was leaving port, too, but he said they'd completed the repairs ahead of schedule. He took his men to the other side of the key to do night maneuvers. I'll need a horse to get to him quickly."

"The stables. Mister Frick knows me—he'll open for an emergency. I came to get Nathan because I . . . I . . ." Destiny couldn't finish the sentence, couldn't put into words the conflicted feelings she possessed. "You say you need Nathan. Why?"

"Because he has access to a ship," Rafael explained. "There was a sailing vessel, bound for Cuba, left here about half an hour ago. I thought it strange to be sailing at this time of night. And if I had to place a bet, I'd wager Angelina is on that ship."

She placed her hand on his arm. "How do you know this? Are you sure? It's Angelina's life that is at stake."

Patting her hand, he tried to console her, but she saw the fear and desperation in the depths of his brown eyes. "I can't explain now. We've no time, but I'm certain she's on that ship." He gave her hand one last pat. "Quickly, take me to the stables. We've no time to waste."

Angelina tried to lie perfectly still because each time she moved or tried to turn brought on fresh agony. They'd doubled her arms and legs behind her back and bound them together, trussing her like a chicken ready for roasting. The scratchy burlap bag still covered her face, obscuring her vision. But it didn't matter. It was as dark as a tomb in the hold of the ship. And they'd gagged her with a bandana so she couldn't cry out. Her throat felt like a desert, parched and raw. It took an effort to swallow.

She could scarcely believe what had happened or divine the

reason why. She should have been suspicious when López said the crew wanted to continue working by torchlight, to make up for time lost during the rainstorm. But she hadn't questioned him because she'd been too eager to complete the factory.

And she hadn't even bothered to take her derringer to the work site with her, so intent was she on the construction. The last thing she'd expected was to be abducted by López. She knew Cortez must have given the orders. But why?

Voices from above stopped her feverish thoughts. She thought she heard the hold door slide open. Through the chinks in the burlap bag, she saw glimpses of light and heard footfalls on the ladder. Tensing, she realized someone was coming down. What would they do to her now?

The footsteps stopped above her head and Cortez's voice floated to her, "Good job, López. And you know where to take her for the reward?"

"*Sí, mi jefe*. Your suspicions were correct about the *señorita*. She isn't who she claims to be. Her father is rich and willing to pay handsomely for her return. When you sent me to Havana, I saw the handbills advertising for a Señorita Ximenes. The handbills had her likeness on them, and I knew it was she, although the name was different."

"*Muy bien, López*, you've done well. Half the reward is yours. And when you return, as I promised, the cigar factory is yours as well. This is much easier and more profitable than ruining her business and foreclosing. You're to be commended on your initiative."

"You're too kind, *jefe*."

"I like to reward a job well done." He paused before continuing, "You must take care of her, though. Once you're out to sea, loose her bonds and allow her to clean herself up. We want her father to be pleased with the merchandise and pay readily. Eh?"

"*Sí, sí, mi jefe*. I will handle her with care as soon as it's safe."

Then the sound of retreating footsteps reached her ears, along with more muttered conversation she couldn't quite make out. But it didn't matter. She slumped back, not realizing she'd been unconsciously straining forward to overhear their conversation. And of course, they'd meant for her to hear them, she was certain of that.

So, her father had offered a reward for her and even printed handbills with her likeness on them. She groaned behind the filthy bandana. She should have known her father would move heaven and earth to find her. When she'd fled to Key West, she hadn't gone far enough.

Cortez had had other nefarious plans for her as well. He hadn't even mentioned using her factory to hide smuggled goods. No, he'd had a much uglier purpose. He'd planned on ruining her business and foreclosing. He'd never really wanted to help her have a cigar factory, she realized bitterly.

Again, men had been her downfall. Between her father and Cortez, she hadn't stood a chance. Why had she thought she might succeed? she wondered despondently. Men controlled everything and they weren't above using force and committing crimes to get their way, either.

But not Rafael . . . the name rose unbidden to her lips. Rafael had tried to warn her about Cortez. He'd badgered and almost threatened her to not get involved with the man. He'd even offered to fund the building of her factory if it would keep her from going into business with him. Rafael, she knew, was a good man, honorable and decent. Why hadn't she listened to him? Why hadn't she allowed him to help her?

Because she'd been too proud and . . . too afraid. Because she hadn't wanted any man in her life, not even one as good and decent as Rafael. Because he exerted a strange power over her, commanding her body at will, transforming her strong-minded purpose into a welter of desire.

Thinking about her arrogance and shortsightedness, she gulped back the tears crowding her throat. With the bandana suffocating her, she knew it would be foolish to cry. Besides, her tears were prompted by self-pity, an emotion she could ill afford. Even if she cried an ocean of tears, her desperate attempt at freedom was over. She would soon be delivered to her father like a prize, and he would force her to marry that awful planter.

Her life was over, over, over ... The chant rounded in her head, keeping time with the slapping waves. Disjointedly, through the miasma of her personal misery, she realized the ship had set sail. She was on her way to Cuba. Even the thought of López loosing her bonds and allowing her to clean up didn't hearten her.

Turning her face into the musty wood of the hull, she closed her eyes.

Chapter Thirteen

She must have slept, Angelina realized, as voices sounded above her, waking her. She guessed they were far enough out that López was coming to free her. The hold door slid back. She rolled to one side, not caring whether López freed her or not. Freedom was a relative thing. Even if he untied her, she'd still be his prisoner . . . and then the prisoner of her father.

"Angelina, Angelina, are you down there?" The voice startled her. It sounded like Rafael's voice. She would have recognized it anywhere. But how could that be? López was her jailor, not Rafael. Had her capture and subsequent despondency deranged her mind? Was she hallucinating?

The voice came again and footsteps on the stairs. "Angelina, I know they've gagged you and you can't answer. I'm coming to free you."

It *was* Rafael!

She hadn't been hallucinating. A shaft of pure joy pierced her. Her heart thundered in her chest. Excited, she tried to scoot forward and rise to her knees, but the ropes were too tight and she fell heavily to one side.

He was suddenly beside her, moving quickly to loose her hands and then her feet. Snatching the bag from her head, he yanked the gag free, too. He'd brought a lantern with him and the dank hold was suddenly bathed in soft light. She looked up at him and tried to speak, but her mouth felt as if it were stuffed with cotton. And her jaw felt sore and bruised.

Seeing her discomfort, he offered her a water bottle, instructing, "Drink this, but do so slowly. Rinse some in your mouth first and spit it out. Then try to swallow."

She did as he directed, and after the first two tries her throat finally worked, accepting the liquid. Nothing had ever tasted so good, not the finest wine nor the sweetest punch, as the cooling water slid down her parched throat.

While she was drinking, Rafael chaffed her wrists and ankles. When the blood rushed to her hands and feet, it stung like the bites of fire ants. The pain was so swift and unexpected that it brought tears to her eyes.

Overwhelmed by emotion and relieved that Rafael had rescued her, she slumped against his chest. His strong arms came up, surrounding her, protecting her. She sighed and turned her face into his shirt, comforted by his own special smell, sandalwood and musk. The crisp, familiar feel of his linen shirt soothed her, too, and beneath the shirt, she heard the steady throb of his heartbeat.

She, who had prided herself on not needing a man, welcomed his protection with all her heart. It felt good and right to be held in his arms, to hear the beating of his heart, to feel the rise and fall of his chest with each breath he took. He felt like home, the best part of home, the warm, welcoming part.

"Angelina." He cupped her chin in his hand, raising her face to his. "Captain Rodgers is waiting with his ship. We must get you out of here. If you're too unsteady to walk, I can carry you."

"How . . . how . . . did you know where to find me?" she croaked.

"Tilly was taking you supper when she saw you abducted.

She ran and got Destiny and they found me. Together, we located Captain Rodgers, and his ship overtook yours. We're still in American waters, so the captain of this ship must obey."

"Then you know it was López and Cortez who—"

"*Sí,*" he interjected. "Captain Rodgers has López in custody topside. He'll talk to save his own hide and lead us to Cortez. In the United States, abducting a woman is a serious offense."

"Not so serious if the woman is a runaway." She sighed and dropped her head. "You might as well leave me on this ship bound for Cuba, Rafael. I can't go back. It won't do any good. My father will find me."

He gazed at her, waiting for the confession he knew was coming. López hadn't said much yet. When they had stopped and boarded the ship, everything had happened at once. He hadn't had time to dissect Cortez's motives for taking her. All he'd known was that Cortez had abducted her. All he'd cared about was getting her back.

"Would you explain why you can't come back with us?" he asked.

Taking a deep breath, she met his gaze. "I'm not Angelina Herrera, I'm Angelina Ximenes. My father is a prosperous Cuban cigar manufacturer, living in Havana." She hesitated before admitting, "I lied to you, Rafael, because you seemed familiar and I didn't want you to know who I was. I didn't want to go back to Cuba."

His heart lurched when she admitted she'd lied. He'd lied to her, too, by keeping his identity a secret. He wanted to tell her who he was and put all the deceit behind them. But something stopped him. This wasn't the time or the place to unburden his heart. First, they needed to deal with her situation and decide what to do. Later, he could tell her who he was.

"Why don't you want to return to Cuba? Why did you run away?" He had his suspicions, but he didn't know for certain.

"My father had social ambitions. He wanted me to marry above my class. He'd arranged a marriage with a very wealthy and socially prominent planter. A man who was old enough to be my grandfather,'' she added indignantly, burying her face in his shirt again.

Holding her trembling form close, pain and regret filled him, tearing at him with sharp-taloned claws. His heart, which he'd thought had died that fiery night, felt as if it were shattering into tiny pieces. The waste, the awful waste of two lives, he realized. All because her father had social ambitions.

He'd loved Angelina from the time they were children. When he'd been sent away to school in Spain, he'd written her faithfully for years. Upon his return, he'd gone to see her, innocently expecting to be allowed to court and marry her one day.

Her father had driven him away, telling him he was unwelcome at the Ximenes home. He'd tried to see Angelina, several times, despite her father's objections, but she was locked up in a convent. It had been years before he'd come to terms with losing her, but he'd reluctantly taken up the threads of his life. A dutiful son, he'd gone into business with his father and married the woman his family had chosen for him. He'd thought Angelina lost to him forever. But everything changed one fiery night, and he'd fled his own ghosts, escaping to Key West.

Then she'd come to Key West, a woman now, no longer the child of his dreams. And she'd been carrying secrets of her own.

Pulling apart from him, she dabbed at her eyes with the corner of her skirt. ''I couldn't submit to the marriage so I ran away to Key West, thinking I could support myself with a cigar factory. But I discovered my jewels were paste, and I needed money for the factory.''

She lifted her wide, violet eyes to his and shrugged. ''You know the rest.'' Folding her hands in her lap, she whispered, ''I know it's over. There is no escape. My father has offered a reward and had handbills printed with my likeness.'' She paused. ''I must thank you, Rafael, for trying to save me. I'm not ungrateful. I know you did what you thought was right. And you tried to warn me about Cortez, too. I was too proud and desperate to listen. Now you know why.''

"Why didn't you accept my offer of money?" He knew he shouldn't ask, but he wanted to know.

Her eyes met his for one brief second and then veered away. "I don't know why, Rafael. Pride, I guess. You were trying to tell me what to do, and you reminded me too much of my father." She shrugged again.

The earlier, aching pain and regret he'd felt at losing her and wasting their futures expanded, taking on a life of its own. It stopped his breath and surged through his brain, blinding him, searing him, hotter than the fire that had ruined his face.

Fighting back the dizzying agony, he tried to gain control of his emotions, struggled to refocus on Angelina and her needs. But it was difficult. She'd been polite enough to evade his question, to offer half-baked truths to assuage him. Unfortunately, he'd surmised the real truth. The real reason she kept sending him away. The reason she'd spurned him at the ball, turning on him in a frenzied rage.

He was ugly, scarred, and hideous to look at. Even Cortez with his bad teeth must have seemed handsome by comparison. She didn't want to be associated with him. She'd been kind at first, even forthcoming because she needed him, needed him to introduce her to people to further her plans. But as soon as she met Cortez, she'd changed. Wasn't the reason obvious? Having him around embarrassed her.

It was a good thing he hadn't followed his inclination and told her who he was. He could imagine how she would have reacted. In his mind's eyes, he could visualize the emotions on her face: amazement, followed by denial, replaced by scorn, and ending with pity. He couldn't have borne it. Better that she not know who he was. Better that she remember the boy who had departed for Spain, all those years ago.

With his thoughts occupying him, he hadn't noticed that she'd risen to her feet and stood, swaying slightly, holding on to a barrel for support.

With an effort of will, he brought his thoughts back to the

present. "Here, Angelina, let me help you." He prayed that she wouldn't push him away, offended by his touch.

"You said they were waiting. I think I can walk."

Anything so the hideous beast wouldn't carry her in his arms, he thought bitterly, self-pity almost swamping him.

"There's one thing I don't understand, Rafael." She faced him, still holding tight to the barrel.

"*Sí*. What is that?"

"I overheard Cortez and López talking before we left port. They wanted me to hear them, I think. Cortez didn't mention the smuggling, but he told López he meant to ruin me and then foreclose. Why bother to help me go into business, if he wanted the factory for himself? López knows how to make cigars."

"I can't say for sure what Cortez's motives were. I can guess, though. He conducts his business by furtive and circuitous means, never letting anyone know all of his plans. He probably wanted to use you as a diversion until it suited him to take over. That's why he made specific recommendations about the factory, to set you up. He might have used your factory to keep smuggled goods for a while and then foreclosed. Who knows? But I'm certain he had a plan."

"How could he keep smuggled goods under my very nose?"

"False walls or a cellar." He shook his head and grinned wryly. "Not a cellar, not on your property, probably a false wall. It was his men doing the construction, so it wouldn't have been too hard to 'add' to the storage space. Or López could have brought in the goods by night and gotten them out by morning. There are lots of ways. Having López was the key."

"I hadn't thought of all the ways. I guess I've been stupid all along."

"Don't call yourself stupid, Angelina. You're the most intelligent woman I've ever known."

"With *woman* being the defining word?" she taunted, and a slow smile tugged at the corners of her mouth. It was good to see her smiling again and recovering her stubborn pride. This was the Angelina he knew.

"Forget I said that. You're the most intelligent person I've ever known. Better?"

She smiled again and wet her lips with her tongue. "Could I have some more of that water, *por favor?* I can't seem to get rid of the awful taste in my mouth from being gagged."

He closed his eyes, blotting out the innocent darting of her tongue. She'd done the same thing that day at the factory, and it had taken every ounce of his self-control not to kiss her. But she didn't want him. Had never wanted him, so far as he knew.

When he was a youth away at school, she'd written back to him, but her letters had been childish and simple, filled with news of her family. It was he who had harbored a secret love for her. Not the other way around. He'd merely been a familiar playmate. And now he was a hideous monster in her eyes.

He handed her the water bottle and she drank thirstily, the muscles in her long, slender neck contracting. What would it feel like to run his tongue over her flesh there? To feel her pulse, beating softly against his lips? Groaning inwardly, he turned away.

"I feel better now." She passed the water bottle back. Her tone of voice was resigned when she said, "I guess I better face my fate. I hope Cortez paid for my passage to Cuba. Would you be so kind as to have Destiny ship my trunks to me? She'll find my address and some money in my jewelry box."

Facing her again, he gazed into the violet depths of her eyes. He would never see her again, he realized, if he let her go. But what else could he do? She was right—Key West was too close to Cuba. If her father wanted to find her badly enough, he would. There would be others who would recognize her from the handbills and want the reward. It was only a matter of time.

But how could he allow her to go, never to see her again, knowing he'd consigned her to a life of misery, married to an ancient planter? There was a way, he knew. Was he brave enough to offer it, knowing how she scorned him and his disfigured face? Could he accept it if she refused, or worse yet, laughed in his face?

He still loved her. More than anything in this world. More than his pride. More than his life. And because he loved her, he wanted her to be happy. He didn't want to send her to the bleak future that awaited her in Cuba. At least in Key West, she could make a life for herself. And later, she'd find someone to love. Could he face that possibility when the time came, if he kept her in Florida?

There was no other choice. He'd have to face it. Or he could move away once she was settled. Try his luck in Texas or California, in the Wild West he'd heard so many tall tales about from ships' captains. Before he left, though, he'd at least know she was happy and cared for.

"Angelina, there might be a way for you to stay in Key West. Will you hear me out before refusing?"

She nodded.

"It would be in name only," he explained, "done by a magistrate, not in the church." He couldn't bring himself to say the word marriage, not until he'd hedged his bet and explained the conditions, hoping she wouldn't refuse.

"But it would be legal and binding. And your father couldn't make you go back. After a time"—he shrugged, wanting to appear as if it didn't matter—"we could find a means to legally end it and free you."

"What . . . what are you talking about, Rafael? What do you mean?"

Drawing himself up, he prayed for the courage to say the words, to accept her rejection. Rushing into the fire to save his wife and child that night hadn't been as frightening as what he was about to do. If she refused him outright, preferring to return to Cuba, he would know how much she despised him. How distasteful he was to her.

"I want to marry you so you can stay in Key West."

Destiny paced the wharf, back and forth, back and forth. Her mind whirled, envisioning awful scenes of disaster. Desperate for Nathan's ship to bring news, she stopped and strained forward, peering out to sea in the dark night, hoping to see the running lights of his ship.

"They've not had time to return, lass." Her grandfather's soft burr broke the tense silence. "Come and sit beside me. It'll do no good to pace."

Once Rafael had left to find Nathan, she and Tilly had gone home and wakened her grandfather, explaining the situation. He'd wanted them to wait at home, but Destiny couldn't stand it. She'd convinced her grandfather to accompany her to the wharf. If Rafael had found Nathan and they were able to rescue Angelina, she knew they would return here.

She wanted to be here for Angelina when they brought her back, to comfort her friend as best she could. It was almost too fantastic, the events of tonight. Who could have wanted to abduct Angelina—and why?

If she were honest with herself, she knew it was her fault. She hadn't thought it wise for Angelina to go to the building site at night, but she'd voiced no objection. She'd been too busy getting ready to meet James's family. And what a disaster that had turned out to be.

His sister, Jennifer, had made it clear she thought Destiny beneath her. The brother-in-law had been a licentious drunk, pawing her at every opportunity. And James had proven to be an insufferable snob, more upset at her leaving his sister's dinner then at the news that her best friend had been abducted. If she'd thought he might show concern and want to help her, he'd effectively dashed her hopes.

Feeling miserable about everything, she stifled a sob. Needing someone to comfort her, she approached her grandfather, seating herself on the rough wooden bench and leaning against him.

"There, there, lass." He encircled her with his arm and patted her shoulder. "Everything will turn out right. Ye'll see."

She appreciated his reassurances, but she didn't know if she believed him. Right now, the world and her situation looked pretty dismal. James had disappointed her, his family had scorned her, and she might never see Angelina again. She brought herself up short. What was she thinking, feeling sorry for herself? It was Angelina who was in the real trouble. She voiced another silent prayer for her friend.

And then there was Nathan.

If all had gone according to Rafael's plan, she'd be seeing him soon when the *Columbia* docked. A part of her wanted to see him and another part didn't. When she'd confessed to loving another, he'd taken her immediately home.

Remembering the pain in his eyes, she cringed inwardly. She'd hurt him badly, she knew. On their trip home that day, he'd stayed silent. And when he led her to the front door, he'd bowed stiffly and left without a parting word.

Closing her eyes, she felt sick. The rich tortoise soup she'd eaten at the Shaws' rose in her throat, threatening to choke her. Her stomach churned. She'd made so many mistakes, like not warning Angelina. And leading Nathan on, using him to further her scheme to meet and attract James. And then callously hurting him, admitting she loved another man. She'd been so selfish and thoughtless, she deserved to be miserable.

"Destiny, lass, look there." Her grandfather leaned forward, pointing out to sea. Startled, she opened her eyes. "Yer young eyes are better than mine. Am I seeing lights to the starboard?"

Jumping to her feet, she rushed to the edge of the wharf. Far out and a little to the right, she saw a pinprick of light. Gazing at it, she watched as the light grew larger. It was coming toward them. It had to be the *Columbia,* she prayed. Few ships braved the coral reefs around Key West to dock at night.

With her heart in her throat, she waited, hoping and praying. Her grandfather joined her at the edge of the wharf, sliding his arm around her waist and pulling her close. She was thankful for his comforting presence.

Side by side, they waited, watching the light grow larger. Finally, after long moments, a sail came into view—one sail, white against the black night. Then she knew for sure. It had to be the single-rigged cutter, the *Columbia.*

Joy and hope filled her heart. Silently, she thanked God, over and over, hoping the news was good. Hoping Angelina had been rescued. More than hoping, realizing that if the news were bad, they wouldn't have returned so soon.

Within minutes, the distinct outline of the *Columbia* came into view. The ship maneuvered to a standstill beside the dock, throwing coils of rope to the wharf. Several sailors leapt down and secured the cutter.

Destiny hopped on one foot and then the next, barely able to contain her excitement. Her grandfather moved forward and helped to secure the gangplank. The next thing she knew, a sailor walked down the plank, leading a short, swarthy man in chains. Was he the man who had abducted her friend? she wondered. Probably so, and she had the overwhelming urge to slap his face, even though she knew her gesture wouldn't accomplish anything.

Holding her breath and keeping her gaze trained on the gangplank, she waited. This time, she didn't have long to wait. Rafael, with his arm around Angelina, appeared at the top of the plank. A cry of relief sprang from Destiny's lips and she ran forward, clambering up the gangway.

Reaching them, she practically shoved Rafael aside in her excitement. Grabbing Angelina, she hugged her tightly, murmuring, "I'm so glad they rescued you. It was all my fault, Angelina. I shouldn't have let you go there at night. Please, forgive me. I—I've been thoughtless and—"

"Hush, Destiny," Angelina interrupted. "Don't say such things. It was no one's fault." Patting her shoulder, she gently pulled free. "It was inevitable, *amiga mía.* I'll explain why later." She glanced at Rafael.

Then tears welled in her eyes, and she grasped Destiny again, hugging her with a fierce embrace. "You don't know how much your friendship means to me, Destiny. Rafael told me how you and Tilly found him and how he fetched Captain

Rodgers. If it hadn't been for your quick thinking, there wouldn't have been a rescue. I owe you an immense debt of gratitude. Don't you know that?''

Answering tears streamed down Destiny's face. They held each other for a long time, love swelling in Destiny's heart. Neither of them possessed sisters. Destiny didn't know how Angelina felt, but from this day forth, Angelina wasn't just a friend. They were sisters, sisters of the heart.

Finally, they both gulped back their tears and separated. Wiping at their eyes, they smiled at each other. But their smiles were wan and tentative, both realizing the danger that had been barely averted. Not wanting to relinquish Angelina for a moment, now that she was safe, Destiny encircled her waist with one arm.

Angelina lifted her head and gazed at Rafael again. He nodded. Destiny knew she should thank him for rescuing her friend, but there would be time enough for that later. Arm in arm, they descended the gangplank together. Gramps stood at the bottom, waiting to receive them, his face wreathed in smiles.

''I'm glad to see ye, Miss Angelina,'' he greeted her. ''It was a close thing. Aye?''

''Yes, Capitán McEwen, it was a close thing,'' she agreed.

''Ye look fit. They didna hurt ye, did they? I can send for the doc.''

''No, *capitán,* I'm fine. Thank you for your concern,'' she replied.

''Then it's off to bed, me lasses. Bed and rest is the thing to put ye to rights.''

They both nodded and Angelina glanced over her shoulder, obviously looking for Rafael. Destiny followed her gaze. Looking up, the breath left her body. Standing with his legs wide and his hands clasped behind his back, looking for all the world like the image of a watchful sea captain, Nathan stood at the top of the gangway.

Their gazes met and held for one brief instant. Then he lifted his eyes and barked an order at the sailors. Facing away, he disappeared from her line of vision. Her heart sank. How he must hate her. And she couldn't blame him. She'd used him abominably.

Her grandfather started for home, swinging the lantern he'd brought to light their way. Trailing after him with her arm around Angelina, Destiny thrust aside her conflicted feelings about Nathan. After all, it was her friend, Angelina, who had been through an ordeal. Angelina needed her. It was high time she stopped thinking about herself and thought of others. Tonight had been a kind of catharsis for her, a revelation of sorts.

Her dreams weren't so important, she realized, not in the overall scheme of things. She'd lived too long for her dreams, wanting to right old wrongs. Maybe they didn't matter anymore.

What had Angelina said? There were other people, interesting people, besides the society of Key West. What her friend had failed to say was that there were other people, people she loved with all her heart, such as her grandfather and Tilly and Angelina, who mattered more than fulfilling old dreams.

If Angelina hadn't been abducted tonight, would she have realized that fact? She didn't know. It was a sobering thought.

"Destiny." Her friend's voice brought her back to the present. "You've won the wedding wager. I'm going to marry Rafael."

The wedding was a hurried affair, thrown together in two days. For the occasion, Angelina had borrowed one of Destiny's dresses, a high-necked, ivory-satin gown. Tilly had rushed to let out the waist an inch and add a flounce of lace to the bottom. Angelina had purposely chosen to go bareheaded to the altar because Destiny had refused to honor the bet by giving her a lace veil, saying a marriage of convenience didn't count.

Angelina smiled to herself. Her friend had been scandalized when she learned she and Rafael were marrying so she could remain in Key West. Although Destiny had understood her dilemma, her romantic heart hadn't accepted it.

Standing in front of the magistrate, at the left side of Rafael, with his perfect profile to her, she wondered at her decision. He was so handsome. Too handsome by far. Living together as man and wife, even if the marriage was a ruse, would be her downfall, she knew. How could she resist him? Did she want to resist him?

Shaking her head, she tried not to think about the future. For the time being, she was safe. Her father couldn't reach her now. Capitán McEwen had been kind enough to act as surrogate father, escorting her down the short aisle, giving her away. And Destiny, despite her misgivings, stood beside her, acting as her bridesmaid.

Flanking Rafael on the other side was Capitán Rodgers, standing up as Rafael's best man. An unusual choice for her intended husband, but not so strange if she remembered how they'd acted together to save her. She couldn't thank Nathan enough for her rescue, and she liked him. Unfortunately, Destiny had parted from him, declaring her love for James Whitman. Their mutual discomfort at being thrown together for the wedding was obvious.

The magistrate cleared his throat loudly and intoned the opening words of the ceremony. Angelina tried to listen, but the words didn't register.

It was all so strange. Marrying Rafael to thwart her father. She'd acquiesced because it was better than returning to Cuba and facing what her father had in store for her. Rafael had promised she could live her life as she saw fit, running her factory without his interference. He'd even promised to end the marriage when her father was convinced to leave her alone.

Somehow, all his reassurances rang hollow. She was more than aware of their attraction for each other. How could they possibly withstand the temptation, living together as man and wife? If they succumbed, there would be no quick divorce papers, legally separating them. Even if they weren't married by the Church, if they shared a bed, they were married in the eyes of God. And what if a child came of their union?

There were no easy answers, she knew. And she doubted Rafael could keep his promises, allowing her to run the factory without his intervention. He was too bossy and domineering by far. Sighing to herself, she realized she was in the process of exchanging one prison for another.

The magistrate, attired in a worn frock coat and soiled linen, said something about taking this man and stared at her. Focusing on the matter at hand, she felt out of her element, as if she were hurtling headlong through a blinding fog.

Rafael squeezed her hand. She gazed expectantly at the magistrate. He met her look and frowned. Impatience colored his voice when he repeated, "Will you, Angelina Ximenes, take this man for your lawfully wedded husband? For richer or for poorer, in sickness and in health, to honor and obey?"

The word "obey" echoed in her mind, reverberating with a life of its own.

What had she gotten herself into?

There was no going back now. The die was cast. She'd gambled and lost . . . or won, depending upon how she construed the situation.

Gazing at Rafael, she shivered. He was good and kind, forthright and honest. He was young and a healthy physical specimen of a man. A far better "catch" then the ancient planter whom her father was determined she should marry.

She should be happy to have escaped her fate, to have been rescued from going to Cuba. It was the reason she'd accepted his proposal. Wasn't it? Or was it? There was that other thing between them. And she believed their physical desire would be her downfall, binding her to Rafael for life.

Would that be so awful? she asked herself.

Old memories rose in her mind, swamping her. When she was little, she'd been *Papi's* girl, following him everywhere with unswerving love, trust and devotion. And he'd reciprocated her love, doting on her, giving her everything her heart desired.

But when she'd grown into a young woman, her father had turned on her, changing before her very eyes. Gone was the easy affection, to be replaced by an aloof distance. Then he'd begun to plot her future and her marriage.

No longer was she his beloved *hija*. Suddenly, she was a thing to be bartered for and sold. Thinking about it, her throat closed and her eyes burned.

Was it any wonder she didn't trust men? That she cursed their controlling, domineering ways? As much as she respected Rafael and was grateful for him rescuing her, could she count on him to be any different?

The magistrate cleared his throat loudly. Rafael glanced at her. It was too late for regrets, she knew. She must speak.

"I do," she answered.

The magistrate moved on, addressing Rafael with a similar vow. Except his vow didn't include the obey part. It was society's convention, and she couldn't escape it, she knew. Her dreams of self-sufficiency faded, withering before her very eyes.

"With this ring, I thee wed," Rafael intoned solemnly, slipping something cold and hard on the third finger of her left hand.

Lost in her thoughts, his gesture drew her back to the ceremony. Glancing down, she found a gold band on her finger. But it wasn't the customary wedding ring. Opening her eyes wide, she stared hard at it. The ring was shaped like a cigar band, wide in the middle and tapering at the sides. Tiny, precious stones lined the edges, mimicking the colored lettering of a cigar label.

Understanding the thoughtfulness and caring that had gone into fashioning the special ring, especially in such a short time, her eyes misted. Lifting her head, she gazed at him, silently thanking him for the gesture.

"I now pronounce you man and wife," the magistrate thundered. "You may kiss the bride."

Closing her eyes, she felt cherished by Rafael's gift of the custom-made ring. He'd thought of what would please her, not what society dictated. It was a hopeful start, she decided. Maybe he really was different from other men, maybe they could live together as equals, respecting each other. Was it too much to expect?

Lifting her mouth to be kissed, she silently surrendered herself to him, heart, body, and soul. Expecting a searing kiss, she was startled when his lips barely brushed hers. Her eyes flew open, and she stared at him. He smiled but averted his eyes.

So that was the way of it, she thought. He planned to honor his promises, to make this a marriage in name only. She should have felt relieved, but instead, his aloofness drove an icy wedge into her heart.

Chapter Fourteen

Rafael brought her to the house he'd rented on Eaton Street. Standing at the edge of the street, Angelina gazed at her new home. It was what the locals called an "eyebrow" house because of its low, overhanging roof that obscured the upper-story windows.

She had noticed these unusual houses before when walking with Destiny. Her friend had explained that they were specially built for the Key West climate. The low roof eaves shaded the upper story and also caught the cool breezes to deliver them inside. Now this peculiar house would be her home, at least for a time.

Taking her elbow, Rafael urged her forward. "I know it's not much." He inclined his head toward the house. "It was all I could find on such short notice. We Cubanos have crowded into Key West so quickly, I was told we've caused a local housing shortage."

"You lived behind your office, didn't you?"

"*Sí,* it served my needs and was convenient." They climbed the front steps and crossed the deep, shaded porch. His voice was hesitant when he added, "I could still live there. You could have the house for yourself."

She gazed at him. He was doing everything in his power to make certain she understood their marriage was a sham. She'd thought he was attracted to her. That didn't seem to be the case any longer. He'd obviously offered his name to her for purely altruistic reasons, to keep her from being forced to return to Cuba. She was grateful to him, but perversely, his coldness piqued her feminine vanity.

"I don't think that would be wise," she observed, "your living behind the office and me living alone. It might make what we've done obvious, don't you think?"

Opening the front door, he replied, "You're probably right. I just wanted you to feel comfortable."

"I'll feel more comfortable with you in the house, Rafael." She hadn't meant to speak sharply, but even she recognized the edge to her voice. "Did you send the telegraph to my father?"

"*Sí,* I sent it. By now he should know that you're married. You should be safe."

"*Gracias,* Rafael, for all that you've done for me."

He shook his head as if he were embarrassed by her gratitude. Then he changed the subject. "This is the central hall. It cuts the house in two. On the left is a small parlor with a bedroom behind it."

Stepping into the parlor, she gazed at the monstrous, over-stuffed horsehair furniture and chipped tables. "Beggars can't be choosers," the old saying sounded in her head.

"*Muy bien,*" she remarked drily.

Moving ahead of her, he threw open a door at the rear of the sitting room. "This is the master suite. I think it should be your room."

She approached the door and peered inside. The room was furnished in the same manner as the parlor. Huge, ornate furniture stuffed into a tiny room. The oversized bed in the center of the room sported a filthy-looking canopy. Gazing at it, she decided to get rid of the canopy and refit it with plain mosquito netting.

Rafael followed her gaze. Shrugging, he offered, "I've some money. We can try to redecorate, if you wish."

For a sham marriage that might not last past the rainy season? That would be a waste of money, she thought bitterly.

"There are a few things I'd like to do, but nothing elaborate." She hesitated before asking, "Where will you sleep?"

"In the front bedroom off the other side of the hall."

That would put them at opposite ends of the tiny house. It wasn't much, but considering the size of their new home, he was doing his best to limit temptation. If there was temptation between them anymore.

"And the kitchen?"

"Véngase." He took her elbow again. "I'll show you. It's behind my bedroom."

They traversed the parlor again and entered the central hall. Passing the first door on the right, which she assumed would be his bedroom, they moved to the door at the end of the hallway. He opened it and led her inside. The kitchen held a wood-burning stove and a dry sink, along with an assortment of cupboards.

"Where do we dine?"

Crossing the room, he threw back a shabby curtain, revealing an alcove tucked into a large bow window. She followed him into the alcove. The bow window looked out upon an overgrown garden, but the sunlight streaming through windows on three sides at least made the area cheery. It was the first pleasant detail in the dreary little house, even if its appeal was somewhat offset by a ponderous table sporting claw feet, which didn't fit in the space.

"Do you cook?" he asked abruptly, breaking her reverie.

"No, I don't know how to cook. It wasn't something the sisters at the convent thought proper young ladies needed to know. Needlepoint and knitting, devotionals and languages, piano and singing, and some arithmetic. Those are my accomplishments, Rafael. At home we had servants to do the cooking.''

He nodded. "I'd expected that. I'll get a servant to cook and do the housework. Maybe Destiny's Tilly would know of someone.''

"Where would a servant sleep?''

"There's an upstairs.''

"Oh, I forgot.''

"It isn't furnished, though. There are two small bedrooms under the eaves and a storage space. We could buy some furniture to make a room for the servant.''

She lifted one shoulder in a half-shrug and allowed her gaze to fall upon the hideous dining table. "Anything we find might be an improvement,'' she noted sarcastically.

His face fell. "I'm sorry it's so ugly, Angelina. It was all I could—''

"Find on such short notice,'' she finished for him. *"Yo entiendo*. You said that. Don't apologize, Rafael. After all, if it weren't for my situation, you would be living behind your office. When my factory starts making money, I want to help with the rent and expenses. I realize this is a marriage in name only. I don't expect you to support me.''

He frowned and opened his mouth, but must have thought better of it because he shut it again before remarking, "If that will make you feel more comfortable.''

She gazed at him, trying to understand this new Rafael, her husband in name only. Before, they'd spoken their minds and often engaged in heated exchanges. Now, everything was different. No, that wasn't quite right, she decided. It was Rafael who was different, acquiescing to her every wish. She had liked the old Rafael better, she realized. At least his reactions had seemed more honest.

A steady diet of forced politeness, mingled with unspoken feelings, might prove more tedious than constant confrontation. She hadn't considered that part of their "marriage.'' The simple mechanics of day-to-day living. Fortunately, he would be busy with his work and she with hers. And Destiny lived only two streets over. If they were careful, they might not have to see each other for days at a time.

There was a loud knock at the front door and Rafael said, "That must be the men with your things. I'll move mine after we get you settled. If you'll excuse me, I'll go help."

"Esperate," she said. "I want to get Malvado myself. The move must be upsetting him, although I covered his cage."

"Quién es Malvado?"

"I forgot. You don't know that I have a pet." She laughed but her laughter was forced. "Malvado is my mynah bird."

The strangest expression came over his face, and he frowned again. "How long have you had this bird?"

"Almost ten years. A good friend of mine brought him back from Spain when I was a girl. Why do you ask?"

"I don't like birds."

His bald statement surprised her. It was so unlike the Rafael she thought she knew. But then, since they'd decided to marry, he'd been acting increasingly strange. She was beginning to believe she didn't know him at all.

Unconsciously, she straightened her back and squared her shoulders. "I'm sorry you don't like birds. But I won't give Malvado up. He's all I have from home."

She stared directly at him, challenging him. He gazed back at her, and then his eyes slid away. "I won't make you give your bird up, but I would prefer for you to keep him in your room. I don't want to see him."

"Bueno, I'll make certain I keep him out of sight."

"Gracias," he replied stiffly. "I'll go help the men." Turning, he left the kitchen.

Watching him leave, she realized she didn't know him at all. In the past, his presence had been comforting, and he'd reminded her strongly of home. Now she felt suddenly strange and very alone. Their conversation about her bird had possessed an almost unreal quality to it. Was this just the beginning?

What was the next thing he wouldn't like? The next thing he'd ban from this dismal place?

Wrapping her arms around her torso, Angelina hugged herself, wondering if their marriage had been such a good idea, after all. Maybe she should have gone home to Cuba and taken her chances.

"Your ship is a beauty, James," Destiny said, glancing around.

"Thank you. I'm proud of her, and she's very fast." He lifted his eyes. "She's single-masted with a cutter rig for speed." Taking her hand, he pulled her forward to the center of the ship where the cabin was located.

"But her hull design is the remarkable part," he went on, excitement tinging his voice. "She's modeled after the *America*, with a long, hollow bow and the maximum beam well aft. And she's light, so light she skims over the waves. I wish you would let me take you out for a quick sail."

"Now, James, that wasn't what we agreed upon."

After Angelina's rescue, James had called on her and apologized again for his behavior. She'd accepted his apology once more, but her forbearance was wearing thin. And nothing he could say would disguise the fact that his sister had taken a distinct disliking to her.

Destiny, wanting to be the perfect guest, had even written Jennifer a short note, explaining the situation and offering an apology for what had happened that night. Jennifer hadn't responded.

The elder Whitmans hadn't returned from Tampa, so Destiny hadn't met them yet. And she wasn't sure she wanted to. Not after her experience at his sister's house. Although she'd accepted his apology and resumed seeing him, things weren't the same between them, at least not for her. It wasn't as if they had quarreled—no, it was a subtle shift in her feelings. So subtle, in fact, she was having a hard time understanding how she felt about him.

Gazing at James as if she could discern the answer from his face, she wondered what had attracted her in the first place. He was handsome enough, but most of their conversations centered around him and his pursuits, such as this yacht. He never asked her what she liked or what her pursuits were. In fact, he didn't appear interested in anything she had to say. All he wanted to do was kiss her and make advances.

Having dealt with his roving hands for several weeks, she'd had the presence of mind to resist his request to go sailing. Alone on a yacht with James in the middle of the ocean was not her idea of a pleasant afternoon. She could just imagine what would happen.

"I know," he said, breaking her reverie. "We agreed you'd come aboard and see the ship in the harbor. But no sailing," he repeated emphatically.

"You know it wouldn't be proper to go out alone on the *Gulf Wind.* I would need to have a chaperone along and since you didn't like that idea—"

"I have another surprise, though," he interrupted. "Remember the oysters and champagne I mentioned before?"

"Yes."

"Well, there's no reason we can't indulge, sitting right here in the harbor." He winked and grinned mischievously.

Dropping her hand, he leaned down and threw open the double-door hatch, leading to the main cabin below. Bowing low, he murmured, "For the lady's pleasure." Taking her hand again, he helped her down the steps before following her.

She looked around, interested in her surroundings. She'd never been on a "pleasure" boat before. Her experience with seagoing vessels was limited to "working" ships such as her grandfather's wrecker, freighters, and naval ships, like Nathan's cutter.

She closed her eyes. What had made her think of Nathan? Probably because the situation was so similar. First, Nathan had given her a tour of his ship, and now James was showing off the *Gulf Wind*. The parallel wasn't easy to dismiss. She wondered if that had been the reason she'd hung back from seeing his yacht. Not wanting to be reminded of another ship, of another afternoon, and of another man.

Forcing her eyes open, she silently chided herself. What was done was done. She'd released Nathan because she cared for another. It had been the honorable thing to do, although she wished she had done it sooner. Having established that she'd done the right thing, why did she feel such regret?

James flung out his arm, urging, "Have a look around. I think you'll find the cabin very comfortable."

Pulling herself back to the present, she glanced around. The cabin was very different from those in other vessels. If she had to compare, she would say this was the height of luxury, especially in contrast to the plain, functional fittings of working ships.

The cabin was finished in a beautiful teakwood, polished to a fine sheen. All the fittings were of brass and they shone, too. The walls were lined with deep benches, holding plump, soft cushions covered in rainbow-hued cotton with braided tassels. Above the benches and paneling were portholes, large and glassed in, which allowed an inordinate amount of sunlight to stream through, making the cabin bright and inviting.

In the fore part of the cabin was a large inlaid table bolted to the floor. On the table stood a huge silver platter of oysters on the half-shell. Beside the platter was a silver bucket with the neck of a champagne bottle peeking over the rim. Two cut-crystal glasses, two china plates, silverware, and snowy white linen napkins completed the ensemble.

"It's lovely, James. The prettiest cabin I've ever seen," she said.

He seemed to swell up before her eyes. Smiling broadly, he replied, "I'd hoped you would like it. I had one of the maids come down from the house to clean and polish. Just for you," he added, sounding for all the world like a small boy showing off his prize agate-eye marble.

"That was very thoughtful of you." She started forward, making a short circuit of the room and gazing in the open doorway on the starboard side.

"That's the galley," he indicated. "It's small but functional. We don't do much cooking on board. Usually, we just pack our meals, like picnics."

"Sleeping quarters?"

She didn't know what had made her ask that. Maybe it was perverse upon her part, knowing it wasn't the proper thing for a well-bred young lady to inquire after—or maybe it was the poignant memory of bouncing on Nathan's bunk.

His eyes widened, and he grinned wickedly. "Not on a ship this size. When we're out overnight, we sleep here on the benches."

"I see." Purposely, she averted her face, acting as if she were looking around again. If she'd been wanting to incite his more lustful urges, she'd just done a marvelous job.

"Please, sit down, Destiny. Make yourself comfortable."

"Here by the table?"

"Yes, that would be the most convenient." Moving forward, he plumped the cushions for her. Then he drew forth the bottle of champagne.

She glimpsed glistening beads of moisture on the outside of the bucket. Could it be possible? Leaning forward, she was astonished to find masses of a white crystalline substance.

"It's ice!" she exclaimed.

"Yes." He smiled again. "I had a bit of luck this morning. There was a freighter in from Greenland, and they let me buy a small quantity." Peering into the bucket, he observed, "It's melting fast, though. We better drink up if we want our champagne to be cold."

"I don't think I've ever tasted cold champagne before," she responded dubiously.

"You'll love it," he declared. "It's all the rage in Paris, I'm told. Makes the bubbles fizz more."

Taking the bottle between his hands, he tore off the outer wrapping of foil. Revealing the mushroom-shaped cork, he placed both his thumbs under its lip and pressed upward. There was a resounding pop. The cork flew up and bounced off the teakwood wall behind the table. The wine spewed forth in a white froth.

Laughing, James grabbed one of the glasses and caught the effervescent liquid midstream. By the time he'd finished filling the glass, the champagne had tamed, fizzing quietly in the bottle.

Handing the first glass to Destiny, he advised, "Drink it quickly before the bubbles pop and it gets warm." He poured himself a glass and sat across from her.

Not being accustomed to drinking, she didn't know if she should heed his advice. After taking one sip, she changed her mind. She'd drunk the bubbly wine before, not very often, but on occasion. She'd never experienced cold champagne.

It was a revelation, a delicious revelation, she decided, sliding smoothly over her tongue and sensuously down her throat. The chill of the wine made the sensation even more piquant. If ever there was a liquid that deserved to be dubbed "nectar of the gods," this was it. Without even trying, she finished the entire glass.

"Good, isn't it?" he asked, refilling her glass immediately.

"It's marvelous. So light and delicious and bubbly. And you were right. I've tasted champagne before, but nothing like this. The ice makes it very refreshing."

"I'm glad you like it." Placing several oysters on one of the plates, he offered, "Here, have some oysters. They're plump and fresh. And they taste wonderful with champagne."

Accepting the plate and a tiny fork, she murmured, "Thank you."

Eager to taste the oysters with the chilled wine, she scooped one from its shell and popped it into her mouth. Following it with a sip of champagne, she was enchanted by the two tastes intermingling together.

"Wonderful," she managed. "I had no idea how delicious they would be together."

Beaming at her, he said, "I knew you'd approve." He leaned across the table, a speared oyster dangling casually from his fork. "You know, Destiny, you're wonderful too. You have very refined tastes. I find that very attractive in a woman."

Flushing at his compliment, she didn't know how to respond. It was the first time he'd complimented her taste, an integral part of herself. Always before, he'd only mentioned her outward attributes. It was a welcome change.

Finding herself warming to him, she was suddenly glad he'd talked her into coming. She'd had her doubts about the outing, and of late, the early excitement in their relationship had become tarnished.

"Thank you," she repeated and smiled.

He reacted quickly to her smile, reaching across the table and taking her hand in his. Lifting it, he turned it over and brushed his lips across her palm. She closed her eyes, willing herself to not think of someone else kissing her hand. It wasn't right or fair to think of Nathan at a time like this, she told herself. Not with this wonderful surprise James had prepared for her.

Holding hands and talking, they each consumed a plateful of oysters, followed by more champagne. When the contents of the bottle had dwindled, he apologized for releasing her hand and surprised her by producing a second bottle of the fizzy wine. Replacing the first bottle with the second in the bucket, he twirled it around and around until all the ice melted.

The second bottle wasn't as chilled as the first, but by that time, Destiny found she didn't care. The more she drank of the stuff, the easier it seemed to go down.

They talked and laughed, James providing her with interesting tidbits about the "aristocracy" of Key West and their private peccadillos. She found herself enchanted and allured, feeling for the first time as if she were a part of the island's society and privy to its secrets.

Shadows lengthened in the cabin, making their tryst even cozier. The cabin seemed to take on its own special glow. Destiny felt as if she existed in a dreamworld, suspended in a cloud of pleasure. She'd never known such pure bliss, such lighthearted happiness. He would say something, and she would giggle, finding everything he said funny or witty.

The ship rocked gently with the incoming evening tide. Reaching for her glass, she slid suddenly forward, losing her seat. Clutching the table, she tried to catch herself. In a heartbeat, he was beside her, keeping her from falling, taking her in his arms.

She clung to his shoulders, grateful for his steadying embrace. The cabin appeared to dip and sway, like a dancer executing a series of dizzying steps. Her head felt light and her limbs heavy. She tried to focus, but the cabin seemed filled with a fine-misted haze, making it difficult for her to see anything clearly, even her beloved James's face.

A feeling of panic overtook her. She'd never felt so strange in all of her life. As if her senses were failing her, and she had little or no control over her body.

James tightened his embrace and lowered his head. His lips found hers, crushing her mouth with the fierceness of his passion. At first she responded, but after only a few seconds, she felt smothered, as if she couldn't get enough air into her lungs. And with her eyes closed to kiss him, she felt as if she were moving, although they were standing perfectly still. The motion sickened her, making her feel nauseated, as if she were about to be sick.

With an effort of will, she raised her hands and placed her palms on his chest. Tearing her mouth away, she begged, "Please, James, I don't, I can't . . . That is, I feel—"

He snatched her words away, covering her mouth with his and bending her backwards, slowly forcing her to the cushions. They lay there for a moment, arms and legs entangled. Their prone position gave her a moment of relief and then the strange spinning motion started again.

His hands and mouth were everywhere. She couldn't fight him. If she moved suddenly, she knew she would humiliate herself and be sick. But if she stayed where she was, she might be sick anyway. Feeling dazed and as weak as a newly hatched chick, she barely registered what he was doing. All her thoughts centered on keeping the oysters and champagne down.

Cool air caressed her bare skin, bringing a brief respite. He'd abandoned her mouth. Gulping, she forced air into her lungs, feeling a little better. Gathering herself, she willed the spinning to stop. Closing her eyes, she counted to ten, trying to regain her composure, wanting to feel herself again.

A searing sensation in her right breast tore the fragile fabric of her composure. Glancing down, she found he'd loosed the buttons to her shirtwaist blouse, unlaced her corset, and freed her breasts! His head was bent over her, sucking her nipple into his mouth! Her other breast glowed obscenely white, looking like a pagan offering.

Lurching up, she knocked her head with his. He cursed and swore. But she was frantic. Pushing at him with her hands, thrashing her legs, and babbling incoherently, she struggled to get free. Caught off guard, he fell from the bench, landing with a loud thud on the floor. More oaths followed as he tried to regain his feet.

But she wasn't waiting. Forgetting her earlier discomfort, she leapt to her feet and started for the door, hastily lacing her corset and holding the edges of her blouse together.

Just when she reached the double doors, his hand closed over her arm. She tried to pull away, but he jerked her back, snarling, "Where do you think you're going?"

"Away from you—you—you lecher. Let go of me! Don't touch me!"

Ignoring her protest, he hauled her into his arms, lifting her as if she were no heavier than a feather. Swinging around, he deposited her on the cushions again and started to fumble with the buttons of his pants.

Scandalized by his behavior, she tried to get up again. But he was too quick for her. Pinning her down, he growled, "I'll have you now, Destiny. Enough of this cat-and-mouse game. I've been patient."

"No, you won't! I'll not sleep with you! If you want me so badly, why don't you offer me marriage?" As soon as the words left her mouth, she felt utterly humiliated and wished she could snatch them back.

Throwing his head back, he laughed. Obscene, nasty laughter poured from him.

Hearing his ugly response, she recoiled, stiffening, and feeling her face flame. Humiliation deepened into shame. Wriggling on the cushions, she tried to escape. But he was much bigger and stronger than she was. His hands held her arms down, his body bracketed hers, and his legs lay heavily entwined with her own.

His laughter died away, ending in a series of hiccoughs and a hearty belch. Gazing at his twisted and lust-filled face, she wondered that he'd ever seemed handsome to her. She turned her head away, suddenly nauseated again.

Drawing her arms together, he imprisoned her wrists in one hand while his other hand wandered over her throat, parting her still-open blouse. She shuddered at his touch. Not from passion but from distaste.

Plunging his hand down her corset, he pinched one breast hard, bringing stinging tears to her eyes. His voice was soft but harsh at the same time when he said, "Marriage? Do you think I would offer you marriage? What an imbecile you are. Don't you know you're a harlot?" His hand strayed to her other breast, fondling it.

Then, with a swiftness akin to lightning, he abandoned her breast and lifted her skirts. His hand snaked between her thighs. Desperate, she squeezed her legs tight.

He laughed again. "Know why you're a harlot? Your mother

was a harlot, dear Destiny. You're the bastard child of her illicit passions. Didn't you know? And all the finishing schools and all your grandfather's precautions won't change what you are. You're a whore like your mother, fashioned to give men pleasure. To give me pleasure,'' he added huskily. His gray eyes burned into hers, stone-cold, yet hot too, filled with a kind of lust-madness.

She closed her eyes, blocking him out, wanting to forget his hideous words. Her mother, her dear mother. How could he say such things? What right did he have to say such things?

"Oh, I'm prepared to be generous, Destiny,'' he continued in the same hideous vein. ''I'll buy a small house and set you up. If not here, under your grandfather's nose, then on one of the other keys.'' He brutally added, ''And your grandfather can't live forever. He can't protect you from what you are. No decent man would offer marriage for you. I'm willing to take care of you. Think of that. Think of your future.''

Behind her tightly shut eyes, tears burned, scalding her. He was wrong, so wrong, she told herself. A decent man *had* offered for her . . . Nathan. And she'd given him up for . . . this.

"But you'll offer marriage to Frances Brown, that bony stick of a woman,'' she blurted.

She knew it shouldn't matter. Didn't matter. He'd finally shown his true colors, admitting what he thought of her. She didn't care who he married.

But the unfairness rankled her. Condemned and categorized since birth, she'd suffered the snubs of Key West society. All because of something her mother had done. Ironically, she didn't even know what her mother had done, but she'd been made to pay . . . and pay.

"Of course I'll marry Frances,'' he sneered. ''She's suitable, possesses an immense dowry, and both our families agree.''

Then he changed again, trying to cajole her by kissing her throat and murmuring, ''But she's not who I want, Destiny. I want you. Can't you see that?'' His mouth strayed lower. ''I'll take good care of you. I promise.'' He nipped the tender flesh of her breast. ''You can have anything you want. Anything. We'll go on trips together. If you like, I'll take you to Europe.'' Lifting his head, he coaxed, ''You would like that, wouldn't you?''

Repulsed beyond belief, she reacted without thinking, spitting into his face. At the same time, she raised one leg hard, bringing it between his thighs with a resounding smack.

''You bitch, you . . .'' he managed, gasping for air.

His hands flew downward, grasping his genitals. Shoving his writhing form aside, she rolled from beneath him. He landed on the floor again, shock contorting his features. Crouched in a fetal position, he twisted left and then right, moaning and cursing in agony.

Knowing there was no time to lose, she bolted for the cabin door again. This time she managed to throw it open. Taking the three steps in one stride, she found herself on deck. Opening her mouth, she sucked air into her lungs and hastily buttoned her blouse over her gaping corset.

Hearing scuffling sounds and more curses behind her, she took flight. Running across the deck to the gangway, she hurtled down it. Without a backward glance, she flew down the wharf, turning onto Front Street.

Startled faces appeared and receded quickly. She didn't care what people thought. She was running wild, like a demented person. And then the sobs started, tearing up from inside, overwhelming her, consuming her.

Running and crying, all his terrible accusations, all his hideous words came back, playing themselves over and over in her mind. Her mother was a whore. She was a whore.

How could he say such things?

She had to know.

Chapter Fifteen

Angelina pushed the fried *plátanos* to one side and took a bite of black beans and rice. She toyed with a piece of *lechón,* cutting it into tiny pieces before nibbling at the fried pork. The food reminded her of home, although it was a trifle oily for her taste.

Glancing at Rafael, she found that he'd cleaned his plate. He appeared to find the cooking more than satisfactory and for that she was pleased. After all, she had been the one to find the cook, Alicia Ramírez. Alicia, like themselves, was Cuban.

One of the men she'd interviewed for her factory had been Alicia's husband. Newly arrived Juan Ramírez had been eager to secure employment with her. When he'd learned her factory wouldn't open for another two weeks, he'd been crushed, having only a few *centavos* to his name.

Angelina had empathized with his plight, remembering her arrival and subsequent impoverished state. They'd started talking, and she had suggested forms of interim employment, such as working on the docks. When Juan mentioned that his wife was looking for a position as a cook, she'd felt as if fortune were smiling on her.

She needed a cook, and the Ramirezes needed an income. And Juan was a wizard at assembling cigars, just the kind of employee she wanted to hire. She didn't want him to go to any of the other cigar factories, so she'd gladly agreed to give his wife a trial, hoping the money Alicia earned would keep him from starting elsewhere.

There had been an added benefit to hiring Alicia. She and Juan wanted their own place. For now, they were staying with other Cubans, and Alicia had no desire to live in one of the small dormer rooms above Angelina's bedroom. She came to work during the day and went home to her husband at night. There would be no need to furnish the upstairs, which freed Angelina to concentrate on the downstairs.

Already, she'd removed the immense claw-footed table from the dining nook, replacing it with a smaller table she'd found in the parlor. And she'd gotten rid of the shabby curtain, too, leaving the area open, allowing sunlight into the kitchen from the bow window. In the center of the table, she'd placed a vase filled with some day lilies she'd found in the overgrown garden outside.

Looking around, she was pleased with her results so far, and her efforts hadn't cost anything. She wished she could say the same for the remainder of the house, but that would take a great deal more effort and money than she wanted to spend.

"That was great," Rafael declared, breaking her reverie. "I can't remember the last time I had Cuban food." Glancing at her full plate, he asked, "Didn't you like it?"

"Sí, es muy bueno." She forced a thin smile to her lips. "I guess I'm just not very hungry tonight."

The food wasn't at fault, even if it was a little greasy. That wasn't what had taken away her appetite. It was eating across the table from Rafael. Dinner was one of the few times they were forced to be together. During the day, they went their separate ways, he to his office and she to her factory. After dinner, they retired to their separate bedrooms.

It was a strange way to live, almost as if they were tiptoeing around each other. She was often grateful for Alicia's ameliorating presence in their household and sorry to see her leave at night.

"How's the factory coming?" he inquired.

"Almost finished. We're setting up benches and gauges tomorrow."

It had been a struggle to finish the factory. After her rescue and López's capture, Cortez's workmen had melted away. She'd had to find other workers and use some of her dwindling resources to finish the structure.

"Will you have enough money to open?" he asked.

She bridled at the question. It really wasn't any of his business. She hadn't asked for his help. Already, she was deeply in his debt. He'd rescued and married her to keep her from being forced to return to Cuba.

At one time, she'd thought she knew why he wanted to marry her. That he'd actually desired and cared for her. But after living with him as man and wife, she wasn't certain of anything. He was so careful to hold himself aloof, to keep distance between them. She should probably be grateful for his gentlemanly demeanor, but perversely, she hated it. It was the source of the constant tension in their dreary, rented house.

Lifting his coffee cup to his lips, he took a sip. Watching him cradle the cup with his long, slender fingers, she shuddered. What would it feel like to have those same fingers stroke her in the most intimate places?

She'd known once, that night at the ball. He'd set her on fire that night, and it had frightened her. The intensity of his desire and her response had terrified her. And she'd pushed him away.

But she'd never forgotten his lips on hers, the way he tasted, his own special scent. And she'd misjudged him. He wasn't like other men, she'd finally come to realize. He'd been there

for her all along, protecting her, advising her, and helping her—
without wanting anything in return except her happiness and
comfort.

Thinking about it, her eyes filled with tears and she averted
her head, calling, "Alicia, could you fetch Señor Estava another
cup of coffee?"

Rafael's gaze met hers from above his coffee cup, and his
eyebrows arched in question. "You don't want to talk about
the factory?"

Alicia, a dark-haired, buxom woman, bustled in and refilled
both their cups. Rafael thanked her. Then she cleared the table,
softly clucking at Angelina for eating so little. Angelina reassured her, praising the dinner, claiming she was still full from
the lunch Alicia had packed for her.

After Alicia returned to the kitchen, Angelina fiddled with
her coffee, spooning sugar and taking a long time to stir it.
Rafael appeared to be waiting patiently, but she knew he wasn't
going to allow her to evade him this time.

"By cutting back to ten workers, I have enough funds to
open," she finally answered, telling him what he wanted to
know.

"I thought you said ten workers wouldn't be enough to make
a profit."

"Not if I have to repay Cortez." She lifted her shoulders.
"I don't know how to repay him, so I'll go ahead with ten
workers. I'll save as much as I can and when the time comes,
I'll have the money for him. But now it will be on my terms,
not his."

Pausing, she considered. There was a question she'd been
wanting to ask, but she'd purposely avoided the subject. And
Rafael hadn't offered any information, either.

"What happened to López?" she ventured.

"He's in jail, awaiting trial." He glanced at her. "You'll
have to testify, you know."

Releasing a long breath, she sighed. She'd been afraid of
something like that. "Is my testimony absolutely necessary?"

"If you want to put him permanently behind bars, it is."

"And Cortez? Have you seen him?"

"He's disappeared, and his office is abandoned. López tried to save himself by blaming Cortez, saying he was acting under orders. I'm certain Cortez knew López would blame him, so he made himself scarce."

She shivered, thinking about Cortez and what he might do. "Do you think Cortez will come back? Should I be concerned?"

He reached across the table and took her hand as if to reassure her. It was the first time he'd touched her, except for customary politeness, since they'd been married.

His strong fingers closed over hers. She savored the feel of his hand, the masculine contours, the calloused palm. And her body responded, too. Heat suffused her, igniting her blood. Her nerves strummed with a sudden awareness, an almost painful yearning. And her breasts swelled, pushing against the confinement of her corset.

"Don't worry, he won't come back. Pardon my bluntness, Angelina, but you weren't part of his big plan. He has other, more lucrative pursuits. He won't compromise himself by returning to Key West until López's trial is over."

Her lips felt parched. She wet them with her tongue. She noticed his gaze fixed on her mouth for one brief instant before sliding away. "And after the trial?" she forced herself to ask.

He smiled at her, a wolfish smile, filled with secrets. She didn't like him having secrets, but she doubted he would admit them even if she asked. He glanced toward the kitchen before lowering his voice. "I hope to have Cortez behind bars before López's trial is over."

"For smuggling?"

"That and wrecking ships."

"Oh. Wrecking is a serious offense, isn't it?"

"It's a hanging offense."

She shivered again and cast her eyes down. "I was a fool to get involved with him."

"Not a fool, Angelina, never a fool." He squeezed her hand.

"You just wanted to build your factory. And I want you to succeed, too. I know you only half believe me, but I do." He hesitated as if choosing his next words with care. "I wish you would let me help. I told you, I've saved some money. You're welcome to it. If you think fifteen workers rather than ten—"

"No." She cut him off. "I can't take money from you. I already owe Cortez, and I intend to repay him even if he's a convicted criminal."

He regarded her for a long moment. A strange look flickered in the depths of his sienna-colored eyes. Releasing her hand, he scraped back his chair and rose. "As you wish, Angelina."

Running through a red haze of tears streaming down her face, Destiny skirted the front of her home, bolting up the rear steps. Slamming the back door, she almost fell into the kitchen. Standing at the cookstove, Tilly jumped and dropped a frying pan, which fell to the floor with a loud clatter.

Arms akimbo, Tilly rounded on her, demanding, "Wha's dis, Missy? Comin' in 'ere slammin' de door. Skeerin' me outta mah wits." She shook her finger. Then her eyes grew huge in her face, and she started forward, holding out her arms. "Lam' chile, wha's wrong? Why you be a'cryin'?"

Destiny fell into her comforting arms, crying on her shoulder. Tilly patted her back and stroked her hair, murmuring low, soft words. It felt good to be held in Tilly's warm embrace, reminding her of the times when she was a child and had skinned her knee or cut her finger.

After a few minutes, the worst of her sobs subsided, becoming hiccoughs and then a runny nose. Tilly released her, standing back and offering a corner of her apron. She gratefully accepted, blowing her nose and wiping her eyes.

"Now, chile, wha's—"

"Oh, Tilly," Destiny cut her off. "Was my mother a harlot, a whore? How could that be possible?" She turned away, wringing her hands. Feeling more sobs crowding her throat, threatening to choke her, she fought them back.

"Laws, chile, wha's dat you say?" Her eyes were so wide now, they eclipsed her face.

"What happened with my mother and father? Were they married or not? Why did my mother die so young?" Her voice rose, taking on a hysterical note. "You have to tell me."

Tilly threw up her hands, palms out, as if to ward off the evil eye. "Miz Destiny, how you'm talk. Youse parents, dey was married. I done tole you everythin' I know 'bout dem. An' your mama, she took sick wit' a fever, dat's why she die. You know dat."

"But that's not all of it. I know it isn't! That's no reason for Key West society to snub me. That's no reason for James Whitman to call my mother a har . . . harlot." She gulped, fighting back the fresh tears stinging her eyes. "Where's Gramps? Is he home? He has to tell me what happened."

"Hummph." Tilly shook her head. "Ah don' tink dis is proper for a young'un to—"

"Where's Gramps?" she demanded again.

" 'E's on de wido' walk."

Destiny ran across the kitchen, but when she reached the swinging door leading to the dining room, she stopped. Turning back, she went to Tilly and wrapped her arms around her plump waist, murmuring, "Thank you, thank you for everything."

Tilly shook her head again and patted her back. "Ah hopes de cap'n can tell you wha' you'm wants to know. Jist 'member ole Tilly loves you, lam' chile."

Pulling away, Destiny said, "And I love you, too."

"Hummph," she repeated, her eyes suspiciously bright. Fluttering her hands, she urged, "G'wan now. Ah gots work to do."

Reluctant now, almost afraid of what she would finally learn about her parents, Destiny let herself out the swinging door. Climbing the three flights of stairs to the widow walk, she felt uncommonly out of breath when she reached the attic.

Gone was the frantic, desperate spurt of energy that had helped her to overcome James and sent her flying home. Exhaustion seeped into her, transforming her bones into jelly. Her throat was dry, her eyes gritty, and her head pounded like a bass drum. Crossing the cluttered attic, filled with trunks and rubbish and memories, her feet seemed to drag. It took all her strength to place one in front of the other.

A large, knee-high window, which provided the opening to the widow walk, stood open. Gramps must be outside, peering through his ship's glass. It was a favorite pastime of his at dusk each night. She'd always wondered what he searched for.

As she stepped onto the walk, the evening breeze caught her hair, blowing it back. Grateful for its cool comfort, she took deep gulps of air, trying to compose herself.

Gramps stood, as he always did, at the southwest corner of the narrow balcony surrounding the top gable of the roof. The southwest afforded the clearest view, unobstructed by buildings or tall palm trees. It looked out upon the main part of town, the wharfs, and the sea. He stood with his arm uplifted, and his spyglass affixed to his right eye. Again, she wished she knew what he searched for in the limitless expanse of ocean.

Remembering how she'd startled Tilly, she cleared her throat, hoping to draw his attention. Her ruse worked, because he lowered the spyglass and turned around.

His gaze rested upon her for a brief moment before his eyebrows knotted together. "Lass, what has happened? Ye've been crying," he observed.

Destiny scrubbed at her eyes with her fists, realizing she must look a fright, tearstained and red-eyed. But she must keep her wits about her, too, and not convulse into tears again. Her grandfather had evaded her questions long enough. Tonight, she wanted answers.

"Grandfather," she addressed him formally. "I want to know about my parents. I want to know how they were married. I want to know why it took my mother two years to find out my father died. Even more important, I want to know why you've kept me from Key West society. Why I've been snubbed and forgotten by my neighbors.''

''I've told ye what ye need to know about yer parents. As for society, I don't care about the hobnobbers. They're a pack of hypocrites, lass, not good enough to tie yer shoelaces.''

''Not good enough, Grandfather, not good enough,'' she repeated, shaking her head and twisting her hands together. ''It seems I'm the one who's not good enough. And I want to know why. I won't be put off this time. I'm old enough to know everything. More than old enough,'' she added softly.

Sucking in a deep breath, she admitted, ''This afternoon James Whitman made advances and called me a whore because my mother was a whore. He insinuated I was a bastard, too.'' Balling her hand into a fist, she struck the railing. ''What did he mean? I must know.''

Her grandfather's face flamed red and then deepened into a mottled purple. Swearing under his breath, he flung the spyglass against the wall of the house. Its lens shattered and the metal tube bounced to the walk with a resounding clatter.

Balling his fists, he raised them in the stance of a pugilist, declaring, ''I'll kill that young pup, Whitman. I may be old but I'm—''

''Stop it!'' she shouted, raising her voice in disrespect for the first time in her life to her grandfather. ''It's not important what Whitman did or said. I want to know *why*. Why did he say what he said? Why, Gramps?'' Her voice took on a note of pleading.

The color drained from his face, and his eyes teared. He looked away and leaned over the railing. She waited patiently, willing him to gather himself, to answer her with the truth.

''I dinna mean it to happen the way it did.'' His voice was so soft, she had to strain to hear it. ''Yer mother; God rest her soul, was the light of our life. Yer grandmother and I couldn't give her enough, do enough for her. She was our only child and she had the best of everything—clothes, schools, horses, and entertainments. And we wanted the best husband for her, too. Not for our sakes but for hers.''

Turning from the rail, he faced her again, but he didn't lift his eyes. ''We gave a ball and yer father, Dennis Favor, attended. A big, bold Irishman, he was. Charming and handsome as sin. All the ladies wanted him. He had the hint of danger about him, too.''

He paused before continuing, ''Yer father was a pirate. Not a real pirate in the true sense of the word,'' he hastened to add, ''but a privateer. He was of Irish nobility, but his family had lost their lands to the English. Because he had no inheritance, he took to the sea. Not wanting to serve under the British, he swore his allegiance to his holy ruler, the Pope. The Pope granted him monies for a ship and a license to raid non-Christian ships, primarily Moslem vessels from North Africa.''

''My father was a pirate,'' she gasped.

''In a sense, aye. But his plunder was for the Holy Roman Father, and he only plundered non-Christian ships.''

Remembering what her grandfather had said about Angelina when she arrived, about her being a Papist, Destiny finally understood.

''Did he carry my mother off and ravish her?''

''Nay, lass, he was a gentleman.'' He hesitated. ''Ye must try to understand. To yer grandmother and me, he was a Catholic and a privateer. Not a suitable match for yer mother. Not in our eyes. He asked, proper-like, for yer mother's hand, but we opposed the match, not understanding how much they loved each other.''

''What happened?''

''They ran off to Trinidad and eloped. Married by a magistrate, not by the Church, neither Protestant nor Catholic.''

''And then?''

''He kept her on his ship with him. Not a proper life, mind ye, but all he could offer. Until she conceived a child. That child was ye, Destiny. When she was along in her confinement, he brought her home to us, for safekeeping, until ye were brought into the world.'' He turned away again, moving to the opposite corner of the walk and staring across the island.

Gazing at him, she saw the tension in his body. His shoulders were hunched and his spine rigid. Guessing this was the part he had wanted to keep a secret, she urged, ''Tell me, Grandfather.''

''We were jubilant to have our daughter back. But we were dead set against the marriage, especially with a child coming. What life could yer father offer?'' He cleared his throat awkwardly. With his back to her, she couldn't be certain, but she thought he was quietly crying.

Her heart went out to him, loving him the way she did. She started forward to comfort him, but something stopped her. This was the secret she needed to know. The secret he'd been hiding from her all these years.

''Please, don't condemn us, Destiny. I know we were wrong. Yer grandmother and I dinna understand, couldna see it, at the time. But yer mother and father loved each other with all their hearts.'' He stopped and fished a handkerchief from his pocket, blowing his nose noisily.

''Yes,'' she prompted, prepared for the worst.

''Yer parents wrote to each other during the confinement. Yer mother wrote every day. And yer father wrote, too, not quite as often, but often enough.'' His voice dropped to a low, husky whisper. ''We intercepted the letters and kept them, wanting yer parents to break contact.'' He gulped, his Adam's apple bobbing. ''Wanting to break their marriage.''

''Oh, Gramps, how could you?''

''That's why I kept the truth from ye so long, lass. I knew it would hurt ye.'' He sighed, admitting, ''And I ... I ... thought ye might stop loving me, knowing what I did.''

''Oh, Gramps,'' she breathed, not certain how she felt.

One part of her wanted to go to him, to wrap her arms around his bulky frame, and reassure him of her love. Another part of her grieved over the injustice done to her parents, no matter how well-meaning her grandparents had been.

He faced her again. His features mirrored his misery. His

gaze implored her to understand, to love him still. But she averted her eyes, unable to absolve him completely. Unable to condemn him completely.

"When ye were a few months old, yer mother must have guessed what we were doing, stopping the letters. I don't know what yer father thought. Probably that his wife and child were safe and that was for the best. Yer mother managed to get a letter out without us knowing. Yer father was coming to fetch her when he was apprehended by the American Navy. They dinna care that he was working for the Pope, only that he was a privateer. They hanged him."

"Oh, no." She covered her face.

"When we heard about the hanging, we kept it from yer mother. She'd had a hard lying in with ye and was weak. We wanted her to regain her strength before we told her. Already, we were sorry for keeping yer parents apart. Yer grandmother felt especially sad, realizing how much they loved each other."

Uncovering her face, Destiny forced herself to ask, "How did my mother find out?"

"Some of her so-called friends told her. Her society friends," he added bitterly. "That summer, yer mother caught a fever. Mourning for yer father, she was too weak to fight. She died that summer. As soon as she was in the ground, the rumors started, saying yer parents weren't married and that ye were illegitimate." He raised his fists into the air and shook them. "I swore then, before the Almighty, that I would have nothing to do with their likes, nor allow ye to associate with them."

"And then grandmother died?"

He dropped his hands, as if admitting defeat. "Aye, the following summer. Poor woman, she never forgave herself. And I've never forgiven myself. It was wrong what we did. If only we'd known it."

They stared at each other across the few feet separating them, across the bitterness of past mistakes, of wrongs that could never be righted, of lost loves and lives that could never be recovered.

It was a mighty space, Destiny realized—a wide, yawning chasm. A veritable canyon that had stretched into every corner of her life, swallowing up her future and leaving her with an empty, echoing void.

"Why didn't you leave Key West and take me with you? Where we could have a fresh start?" she asked, mourning her loss, grieving over the injustices.

"I should have. I see that now," he responded, exhaustion and remorse deepening the wrinkles of his face. "I thought the scandal would blow over. That ye would find other friends here. I should have known better. The key is an island, after all, a small, gossipy place." He lifted his head and straightened his shoulders. "I had new hope when Captain Rodgers called on ye. He's a fine man and an upstanding officer. And he's not from here, so old rumors wouldna affect him. I thought he might ask ye to marry him and take ye away."

Yes, Captain Nathan Rodgers was a fine and upstanding man, a courageous and noble man, too, she agreed silently. But she'd been bent on loving James Whitman, on regaining her rightful place in Key West society. If only she'd known sooner what she knew now, she might have acted differently. If only her grandfather had told her the truth sooner.

She stopped herself. It wasn't fair to blame her grandfather for her own mistakes. Without being told the precise reason, she'd always known she was a social pariah. Despite knowing, she'd wanted to prove she could change the town's perception. And she'd planned to do that by marrying the most socially prominent bachelor on the island.

What a child she'd been! What a foolish, prideful child!

Key West had blackened her mother's name for no good reason except that they craved juicy gossip. And they'd never given her a chance, either. She, who had observed every social decorum, who had volunteered for every charity endeavor, and who had never set out to hurt another human being in her life. Despite everything, they had spat on her and her parents' memory. James, with his ugly lust, was the embodiment of their hypocrisy and hate.

Feeling as if she'd been forced to grow up in one day, she crossed the few feet to her grandfather and threw her arms around him, hugging him tightly. She still loved him. He'd done his best to raise and care for her. He'd made mistakes in the past, but he'd done what he thought was best for her mother.

The real villain was the community of Key West.

Nathan lifted the spyglass to his eye, squinting against the setting sun. Finally, the familiar outline of Key West appeared on the horizon. It was with a strange mixture of relief and melancholy that he realized he was almost home. Home, whatever that meant to a seafaring man.

He was relieved that the long, exhausting journey was behind him. But the minute the island hove into view, a deep depression settled over him. Key West was also home to Destiny Favor. And try as he might, he couldn't get her out of his mind. Nor could he stop loving her and wanting her.

Since the day he'd brought her to this ship, his life had been a living hell. He couldn't eat or sleep. Not usually a drinking man, he found himself taking refuge in the oldest form of escape, the bottom of a bottle. During the day, he drove himself with demonic fury, and he drove his men furiously as well. He'd bullied and pushed his men to complete the repairs to the *Columbia* in record time and then forced them to go out on night maneuvers. What had been a loyal, well-trained crew was fast becoming a churlish bunch of louts who couldn't stand the sight of him.

And who could blame them? He couldn't stand himself, either. And he couldn't seem to help himself. Was there no release in this world?

After helping Estava rescue Señorita Herrera, he'd stood beside Destiny while Rafael and Angelina were married. All he could think of was that it should have been he marrying

Destiny. Each mumbled word the magistrate had said in the hurried, arid ceremony had pounded into his head: love, honor, and cherish. He wanted to do all of those things for Destiny for the rest of his life. But she had spurned him for another. After the brief ceremony, he couldn't get away fast enough.

It had been that night, tossing and turning in his lonely bunk, that he'd conceived a bold idea. Instead of sending a coded message to Annapolis about Estava's plan, he'd decided to abandon his post and go to Maryland to present the idea in person.

He knew he was placing his commission on the line by leaving his post without permission, but he didn't care. After losing Destiny, nothing seemed to matter anymore, even his commission in the Navy. By going to Annapolis personally, he would gain two important advantages.

First, he would be getting away from the island for a time, hoping distance would help to erase her memory. Second, Estava's plan was controversial, and he'd already decided the only way to convince his superiors was to present the plan in person.

His gamble had paid off. He'd had to go all the way to the top to get the necessary authority to put the plan into action, but the admiral had finally agreed. The admiral had even excused him for leaving his post, given the circumstances and his past service record. He'd also warned Nathan to never countermand orders again.

If only the other part of his plan had worked. The part about Destiny. Distance hadn't helped; nothing had helped. He'd attended several social functions while in Annapolis and met several attractive and available females. But they all paled before Destiny's beauty. And while they were nice enough ladies, he missed Destiny's refreshing candor, her infectious laugh, and her sense of adventure. There could never be another woman like Destiny Favor, he realized. At least, not for him.

They sailed into Key West harbor at dusk. He barked the necessary orders to dock the boat and then gave all hands their liberty. They deserved it, he knew, especially after the way he'd driven them for the past month.

When the last sailor had departed, he glanced around the empty ship and decided he should find Estava and tell him the news. The question was: should he wait until tomorrow and catch him at his office or intrude upon his household at night?

Common sense told him to wait, but he didn't want to wait. Only by keeping himself in constant motion was he able to banish Destiny from his thoughts for a few brief moments at a time. And there was another compelling reason to go as well. Rafael's wife and Destiny were best friends. There was a slim chance he might find Destiny at the Estava household.

Seeing her again would be pure torture. Not seeing her again would be worse. It'd been a month since he'd gazed upon her lovely face. A month filled with anguish and emptiness, meaningless work and even more meaningless entertainments.

Striding down the gangplank, he crossed the wharf and took Front Street to Simonton, entering Eaton and going north. Estava's rented house wasn't far from the waterfront, only a few blocks' walk. When he reached it, he stopped at the front gate, hesitating. What if Destiny was here, visiting? What would he say to her? How would he act?

Throwing his shoulders back, he crossed the deep porch and knocked on the front door. Estava opened the door. Peering past the man, he saw that the small parlor was dark, lit only by one lamp. Regret and a black despondency descended, smothering him, making it difficult to breathe.

He tugged at his too-tight collar and stared at Estava, his mind a complete blank, unable to remember the errand that had brought him here. A door at the back of the parlor opened, and for one brief instant, his hopes soared again, but it was Estava's new wife who stood there, not Destiny.

"Rodgers, what brings you here at this time of night?" Estava glanced at his wife over his shoulder. "We were about to retire. I don't think—"

"Ask Capitán Rodgers in, Rafael," Angelina urged.

"No, no, ma'am, I don't want to be a bother." He met Estava's gaze. "If I could have a few words with you on the front porch. It shouldn't take long."

Rafael's wife had crossed the parlor and stood behind her husband. Peering at him, Angelina said, "Please, come in. You look tired, *capitán*. Let me offer you some refreshment."

Before he could decline again, Rafael reassured his wife, "It's all right, Angelina. We'll talk on the porch." Taking her elbow, he gently steered her into the parlor.

"Are you certain, Rafael?"

"I'm certain. Get ready for bed. You've an early start tomorrow." He patted her shoulder. "Don't forget, tomorrow is a big day."

She gazed up at her new husband, frank adoration in her wide eyes. Seeing her look pierced Nathan like an arrow. If only Destiny had looked at him like that, he thought.

"Well, all right then." Turning halfway back, she called out, "It was good to see you again, *capitán*. I'm still in your debt—and please, don't be a stranger. You're welcome in our home any time."

"Thank you, ma'am. I'll remember that."

The door closed behind her and Estava crossed the tiny parlor, joining him at the front door. Inclining his head toward the porch, he said, "Come outside and have a smoke. I've some excellent Cuban cigars." Fishing in his vest pocket, he withdrew two cigars and offered him one.

Taking it, he followed Estava outside. They lit up and puffed, working on getting their cigars going until the ends glowed red.

Exhaling, Estava remarked casually, "I don't know why you came to the house. Unless you needed me tonight. The less Angelina knows, the better. I don't want her involved if I can help it."

Nathan knew he didn't have a good reason for coming. And he couldn't tell Estava his real reason, that he'd hoped to find Destiny here. He shrugged, apologizing, "I'll bear that in mind and not come again. I understand your not wanting to involve your wife."

Estava nodded, accepting his apology and remarking, "You've been away for a long time, Rodgers. I had begun to think you weren't going to help me. That getting Cortez wasn't important to you."

He bridled at Estava's accusation. Sometimes, the Cuban could be downright cheeky. "Getting Cortez was important enough for me to put my commission on the line," he threw back. "That's where I've been. In Annapolis, visiting with the admiral."

The Cuban's eyebrows flew up, and he slapped him on the back. "You left without permission, without sending a coded message? To personally persuade the Navy?" He shook his head, removing his cigar and gesturing with it. "I've underestimated you, Rodgers. That was courageous, indeed."

Not comfortable with flattery of any kind, Nathan muttered, "It seemed the only thing to do. If we were going to do it right."

"And how right you are." Estava almost chortled with glee. Then he pinned him with a direct stare. "And what was the outcome?"

Nathan allowed himself a thin smile. "The admiral agreed, but it will take some time to put everything together."

"*¡Madre de Dios!* You did it, you son-of-a-seadog, you. I can't believe my ears, we're finally going to get *el bastardo*. After all these years," he whispered in awe. Then he grabbed Nathan by the shoulders and hugged him.

Unaccustomed to such a show of emotion, especially from another man, Nathan struggled to be released. Estava accommodated him, stepping back and smiling from ear to ear.

"I'll let you know the details when I find out," Nathan offered. "I set up a special code for the messages. No one knows it but myself and the admiral. The ship will be the first thing. The Admiralty will arrange for the Browns and Whitmans to receive the appropriate news. Last will be the marines. I'll let you know,'' he repeated.

"Sounds great." Estava lifted a finger. "One thing, I want to be in for the kill."

"No more than I."

"Then we understand each other. There won't be any problem about this being a Navy operation? And no civilians allowed?"

Nathan shook his head. "It's your plan, Estava. You should be there. I'll see that you are."

"You know, I like you better each time I see you, Rodgers."

Nathan couldn't quite suppress the grin tugging at the corners of his mouth. Estava was irrepressible. It had been a long time since he'd felt like grinning, but the Cuban's excitement was catching. At least, he had something to look forward to, something to plan for. It might take his mind off Destiny for a few hours.

They fell into a companionable silence, standing shoulder to shoulder, puffing their cigars and enjoying the quiet night. It had grown dark quickly, Nathan realized. The days were getting shorter. Autumn was upon them, but in this tropical climate, the progression of seasons was a subtle thing, the difference between a few degrees and a few hours of daylight.

When they'd finished their cigars, he observed, "I better be getting back to my ship. Someone has to stand watch. I gave my sailors liberty tonight."

"That was magnanimous of you, Rodgers. And you're right. It is getting late." Estava extended his hand. They shook and Nathan descended the steps, starting down the short path to the front gate.

Halfway there, something made him stop. Turning around, he found the Cuban still standing on the porch. "How's married life treating you, Estava?"

Estava shot him a look and then made an elaborate show of shrugging. "I can't complain." Touching his scarred cheek, he admitted, "It's no love match. You know that, Rodgers."

Nathan was surprised by the Cuban's remark. Having helped with the rescue, he knew why Angelina had been abducted and how Estava had offered marriage so she wouldn't be sent back to Cuba. But he'd thought he detected mutual attraction between the pair. And the look his new wife had given him tonight, before she returned to her room, had definitely told another story. Could the Cuban be that dense?

He shook his head. When it came to matters of the heart, maybe all men were dense.

"I wouldn't be so certain. I think your wife may surprise you," he replied obliquely. And then, as if the thought had just occurred to him, he added, "And Miss Favor? How is she? Are your wife and she still friends?"

Estava thrust his hands in his pockets and regarded him. In the half-light spilling across the porch, it was difficult to read the Cuban's expression, but he doubted he'd fooled Estava with his "impromptu" questions.

"Miss Favor is, as far as I know, in good health. And, yes, she and my wife are still friends, although they don't visit often. My wife is very busy with her new cigar factory. In fact, tomorrow will be the first day of operation."

"Give her my congratulations and best wishes."

"I'll do that." Estava's mouth quirked in a half-grin. "I'll give Miss Favor your regards, too, next time I see her." His grin widened into a broad smile. "Better yet, Rodgers, why don't you call on Miss Favor and personally give her your regards?"

Chapter Sixteen

Running down a long, dark tunnel deep in the bowels of the earth, she struggled and fought, twisting and turning, desperate to get away. But they followed her, filthy and bloated with sharp, yellow teeth. Their scurrying bodies made hideous scratching sounds. The rats swarmed and swelled, scratching and scratching, running over her feet, trying to climb her ankles. Scratching, scratching, scratching . . .

Angelina lurched up in bed, staring wide-eyed into the dark, realizing she'd been dreaming. She clutched the bedclothes as perspiration poured off her. Her heart pounded in her ears. But not loudly enough to blot out the hideous scratching noise. It rattled in her brain still.

Lightning bathed the room in a burst of silver-gray light, and she glimpsed a tree limb scraping at the window. It was making the scratching noise, she realized, and her nightmare must have incorporated the sound, making it seem sinister. Relaxing a fraction, she loosed her tight hold on the bedcovers.

Thunder rumbled, a deep throbbing bass that seemed to shake the tiny house. Rain thrummed on the tin roof overhead. She could hear the wind moaning. It must still be storming, she thought sleepily. It had rained all day, and there had been whitecaps on the ocean when she walked home from the factory.

Settling herself in bed again and pulling the comforter to her chin, she hoped the storm would abate by morning. Assembling and rolling cigars under humid conditions wasn't ideal.

The room flashed ghostly white again and the thunder boomed, sounding like a tidal wave. There was a crashing sound and glass flew from the window, raining down on her in a tinkling shower. Wind whipped through the room.

Bolting upright again, she lit the bedside lamp to find the tree limb had broken through the window. A piece of it lay incongruously on the braided throw rug, a wet, forsaken log.

Malvado shrieked and beat his wings against the bars of his covered cage.

Throwing back the covers, she ran to the window. Driving rain pelted her face, stinging her skin and obscuring her vision. The wind snatched at her hair, blowing it in frenzied ribbons about her head. Scraping her hands across her eyes, she looked out into the night. Illuminated by brief bursts of lightning, each tree and bush danced wildly. Tall palm trees, silhouetted against the stormy sky, appeared to bend double, ready to snap. Rubbish, twigs, and leaves whipped through the air.

A hurricane was coming!

It was autumn, and she'd been born and raised in the Caribbean. There could be no doubt about the force of the wind. This was no mere storm, she realized. But there had been no warning, she thought frantically. No reports of heavy weather from sailors.

Returning to bed, she pulled the comforter off and wadded it into a flat rectangle of cloth. Using a shoe, she broke out the remainder of the window, careful lest she cut herself. When she had the window free of glass, she stuffed the wadded comforter in the opening. It wasn't the best solution, but it kept most of the rain and wind out.

She didn't care what happened to the rented house. Her

factory was the important thing. She had to get there before the full force of the hurricane struck and save what she could. There was no time to dress properly, but she couldn't go out in her bedclothes, either, leaving herself completely vulnerable to the elements.

Pulling her loose hair back, she tied it tightly with a ribbon. Then she put on her heaviest boots and laced them up. Covering her nightgown with an oilskin slicker, she completed her ensemble with one of Rafael's discarded Panama hats. She had the presence of mind to tie the hat onto her head with another ribbon.

She ran to Malvado's cage and lifted the cover, peeking inside. Seeing her, he stopped shrieking and regarded her solemnly, his garnet eye glinting. She tried to reassure him in a low, calm voice, but he flapped his wings and hopped from perch to perch in obvious agitation. Knowing she couldn't do anything more to allay his fears, she covered his cage again and placed it on the floor behind the bed.

Crossing to the door, she jerked it open, wondering where Rafael was. Surely he couldn't be sleeping through this. She collided with him on the threshold. He was fully dressed with an oilskin slicker thrown over his arm. His face looked grim in the half-light.

"I was coming for you," he said.

"It's a hurricane, isn't it?"

"I'm afraid so."

"You were coming for me?" She glanced at the oilskin on his arm.

"I knew you would want to go to the factory."

She breathed a sigh of relief. She had hoped he would understand her need to go to the factory and be willing to help her. Most men would have told her to stay in the house while they took care of it. That he understood her feelings so well warmed her inside, making her feel as if they could face anything together, even a hurricane.

Grasping her elbow, he propelled her through the door. *"Véngase.* There's no time to waste."

The wind was blowing from the northeast and their front door faced north. When Rafael tried to open the door, it resisted, the force of the wind keeping it tightly shut. She watched helplessly as he struggled, leaning his shoulder against the wooden panel and straining. Finally, his efforts won out, and he managed to push it open a few centimeters. As soon as he'd done this, the wind snatched it from his hands, slamming the door against the front wall with a loud bang.

In a repeat of his earlier struggle, Rafael had to fight to close the door behind them. Grasping the doorframe with both hands, he tugged and pulled against the wind until the wind caught it again and pushed it shut.

Feeling as if they'd just waged a war, she was exhausted before they'd started. The deep porch had sheltered them from the worst of the storm's fury, but when they descended the front steps together, she felt the full force of the howling wind.

Bending at the waist, she looked around. Their small yard and street were already littered with debris. Everything that wasn't firmly rooted to the earth or nailed down hurtled through the air. And the very air boiled and foamed, like the sea during a storm. Glancing about, she saw their neighbors scurrying about their homes, preparing for the worst.

Rafael took hold of her arm and laced it through his. Starting forward, he directed, "Hold on to me tightly. No matter what, don't let go. *¿Entiendes?"*

It was difficult to hear him; the wind snatched the words from his lips and carried them away. Nodding her understanding, she clutched his arm tightly. But when they reached the front gate, she found herself floundering. The force of the wind was like a giant fist, pushing her backward, propelling her back toward the house.

By brute force, Rafael dragged her forward. Their painful progress reminded her of swimming in the ocean against a very strong current. She learned quickly to keep her head down and tucked into her chest, using the old Panama hat as a kind of shield against flying objects. Even though the factory was only a few blocks away, it seemed like hours before they reached it.

Several people yelled at them and gestured, obviously urging them to take cover. But Rafael doggedly plowed ahead and she followed.

When they finally reached the factory, she saw what the coming destruction would bring. Part of the thatched roof had already blown off. Work benches and tables, cutting boards and gauges lay overturned and scattered like so many fallen leaves.

Placing his mouth close to her ear, he asked, ''Where are the tobaccos and wrappers?''

''Locked in the brick storeroom.''

''We'll put everything else in there too.''

''And there's room in the office.'' She hadn't had the time or money to furnish her office. The brick portions of her factory were the most likely to withstand the hurricane. There were no cellars in Key West, since the water table was only a foot below the surface.

Nodding, he tugged her forward. Once under the thatched roof, they worked feverishly gathering the furniture and equipment and stowing it in the storeroom or office. Several times, the wind knocked her down, but with Rafael's help she regained her feet and they continued to empty the structure. Within half an hour, they had finished. The factory's planked floor stood bare.

Returning home wasn't as difficult. This time, the wind was at their backs, sweeping them along like an invisible broom. When they reached home, no one was outside. Their neighbors must have accomplished what they set out to do and gone inside to ride out the storm.

When they unlatched the front door, it blew outward again and they dashed inside, water streaming off their oilskins and puddling on the floor. Rafael grasped the edge of the door in both hands and leaned his shoulder into it again, fighting to close it. The muscles in his shoulders and neck corded with the effort.

Watching him, she was grateful for his strength and quiet competence. Without him, she knew she wouldn't have been able to reach the factory and save its contents.

Sometimes, she thought, it was comforting to rely upon a man. If he was reliable and respected you as a person, she silently amended. Only one man had respected her as an equal, and he was her lawful wedded husband.

When he finally got the door closed, he bolted it and turned to her, directing, "Get out of those wet clothes. I'm going to change and then close the window shutters from the inside. When you've changed, go to the pantry. If you get there first, empty it and stack the contents on the floor of the kitchen. Make sure the stove is completely out, too. And strip the mattress in your room. Bring any bedclothes and cushions or pillows you can find to the pantry." His gaze met hers. "Have you got all of that?"

"Sí, yo entiendo. We're going to take refuge in the pantry?"

"It's the most sheltered place in the house, surrounded by walls and no windows. We'll need a lamp, some extra oil, candles and matches, and a jug of water. I'm going to line the walls with our mattresses for extra protection. We'll use the bedclothes and cushions to cover the floor."

Nodding, she scurried off to her room. An angry gray dawn was breaking, and she noticed the broken window. She'd forgotten to tell him about it. The wadded comforter was still holding, but it was a sodden mass, dripping rivulets of water to the floor.

Quickly, she changed into her sturdiest clothes, some old riding breeches and a shirt she'd inherited from one of her brothers. Then she stripped the bed of the remaining covers, leaving the bare mattress for Rafael to fetch. Malvado must have heard her because he began screeching again. She'd have to bring him to the pantry. She knew Rafael wouldn't like it, but under the circumstances she had no choice.

With the bedclothes under one arm and Malvado's cage dangling from her right hand, she dashed for the kitchen. She could hear Rafael moving about in his room, securing the storm shutters on the windows. Placing Malvado's cage on the kitchen floor, she found the supplies Rafael had wanted, placing them in the pantry. Then she checked the stove. It appeared to be out, but she poured water over the ashes as a precaution.

Rafael came into the kitchen to fasten the storm shutters while she pulled staples from the pantry shelves and stacked them on the kitchen floor. Once he had the windows shuttered, he helped her finish. When the pantry was empty, he went to get the mattresses, dragging them in one by one. Then he told her to get in the pantry.

She pointed to Malvado's cage. "I know you don't like birds, but I—"

"Put him on the back shelf," he cut her off.

"I'll keep him covered. He's frightened enough as it is."

He smiled grimly. "That's a good idea."

Working together, side by side, as they'd done at the factory, they lined the walls of the small space with their mattresses. Then they covered the floor with a nest of bedclothes and cushions. She lit the lamp and placed it at the back of the pantry.

Standing on the threshold, he asked, "Are you ready for me to close the door? We can't come out until it's over. It might be hours, you realize."

Nodding, she moved to the back of the pantry and slid down onto a pile of cushions. He shut the door behind him. The only light came from the lamp. The pantry was a small, cramped space, barely large enough for the two of them to lie down. But it was the safest place in the house.

Rafael seated himself by the door, his legs stretched before him. If she stretched her legs out, too, they would touch. The only sound in the cramped space was their labored breathing.

Malvado had stopped squawking and cursing. It felt good to rest. She hadn't realized how exhausted she was until she stopped moving.

There was a resounding crash outside, the reverberation shaking the walls of the pantry. Malvado started shrieking and shouting obscene words again. And the wind picked up, too. Even inside the lined pantry they could hear it, almost feel it. It howled like a banshee and there were more loud crashes. What they'd experienced before had been merely the precursor. Now the hurricane was fully upon them.

Angelina wrapped her arms around her torso for comfort. She'd seen the aftereffects of hurricanes in Cuba. Whole houses had been leveled. Suddenly their secure hideout didn't seem so secure anymore.

Glancing at Rafael, she found he had his ear to the door, obviously trying to discern what was happening outside. His features were drawn with worry.

Realizing the danger they faced, her throat closed in fear and her heart raced. She wished for her rosary and gritted her teeth, silently mouthing prayers without her beads.

The house rattled and clattered around them, sounding like an old buggy coming apart at the seams. Another thunderous crash rent the air. She jumped and, to her ultimate mortification, started crying hysterically. Humiliated but unable to stop, she buried her face in her hands.

And then Rafael was beside her, pulling her into his strong embrace, holding her tightly and murmuring low, comforting words into her hair. She clung to him as if he were a lifeline, inhaling his special scent, burying her nose in the crisp linen of his shirt.

He cradled her in his arms as if she were a baby, pulling her halfway onto his lap. He reached up and stroked her hair gently, tenderly. Grateful for his comforting presence, she burrowed deeper into his arms. He responded by rubbing the base of her neck and shoulders. Arching into his caresses, she returned his gesture of solace by moving her hands over the muscled expanse of his back.

The fury of the hurricane receded. Malvado finally quieted again.

Rafael's fingers worked magic upon her, soothing her, gentling her, stroking away the terror and tension in her body. She gave herself over to the sensation, relaxing against him. She dried her tears on his shirt. Her eyelids drooped as if lead weights pulled at them. Exhaustion overwhelmed her and she slept.

Angelina woke with a start. The lamp had burned low, giving off a fitful light. She lay cuddled beside Rafael, his arms wrapped around her. They must have both fallen asleep. She wondered for how long—hours or only minutes? The lamp suggested they'd been asleep for a while. A thin gray line showed beneath the door. It must still be day.

Cocking her head, she listened for the storm. There was nothing. Not a sound. It was eerie, the complete silence. And then she remembered. The eye of the hurricane, the middle part of the storm, was calm. At least the house had stood this long.

Nestling her head against his shoulder, she gazed at his face. His beautiful and scarred face, like two sides of a coin, so different from each other. Yet, to her, both sides were beautiful, both suggested strength and caring. Most of the time she didn't even notice the scars. They were invisible to her, as much a part of him as his brown, wavy hair. She saw him through the eyes of love, perfect and whole and beautiful.

In her naivete and rage at what her beloved father had tried to do, she'd vowed to never love a man again. To never trust a man or allow herself to be vulnerable again. And she'd fought her attraction for Rafael. At first, she'd believed it was just a physical thing between them, a desire of the flesh.

But when she came to know him, she'd learned of his caring

and selflessness, of his quiet competence. Slowly, she'd come to rely upon his acceptance of her as an equal person, something no other man had given her. With these realizations, she knew she'd lost the fight.

She was in love with Rafael Estava.

And it felt right, so right. Almost as if preordained by the stars. Could that be the reason he'd seemed so familiar when she'd first met him? Because he was destined to be the love of her life, her soul mate? She didn't know because she had never felt this way about another human being before. All she knew was that her heart brimmed with so much love, it threatened to burst from her chest.

Acting on an impulse she'd often felt but had managed to resist, she reached up and gently stroked her fingers over the scarred side of his face, wanting to soothe away his suffering, needing to take his pain away. Slowly, tenderly, she traced the ridges of scars, taking his anguish inside her.

His eyelids fluttered open. They regarded each other for one long, breathless moment. Then the realization of her touch upon his disfigured face leapt in his eyes and he grabbed her wrist. Frowning, he sat up, pulling her with him. Her eyes implored him, brimming with the love she felt but couldn't declare, not certain of how he felt.

Gazing at her, only a whisper away, a new realization dawned in the cinnamon depths of his eyes. She held her breath, praying that he understood and reciprocated her love. As if in silent answer, he turned her captured hand over and nuzzled the palm, raining tiny kisses over it and her wrist.

She shuddered, closing her eyes, savoring the feel of his lips upon her skin. His mouth found hers, brushing her lips, feather-light, tentative but bold. Reaching up, she curled her arms around his neck, wantonly pressing her body against his, silently begging for more.

Responding, he crushed her to him and his mouth molded to hers. Like hand in glove, their lips fit together, warm and moist, giving and taking. She drank him in like the finest wine, and he devoured her with an equal ferocity.

The fine-nubbed flesh of his tongue teased the corners of her lips, and she opened herself to him. Their tongues met. Lightning streaked through her body. Heat suffused her, igniting her blood like a flame. Her pulse accelerated. She melted into him as their tongues dueled and danced. They explored the soft, hot contours of each other's mouths. She shuddered again, trembling with ecstasy.

His fingers moved to her throat, capturing for one brief instant the wings of her pulse. Stroking downward, he skimmed the tops of her breasts. She hadn't bothered with a corset, only a chemise beneath her shirt. The thin fabric melted away. His touch scalded her, leaving a scorched path of desire. Her breasts swelled and her nipples puckered, pleading for his touch.

Bolder now, he covered her breasts with his hands, caressing them, smoothing the fabric over her aching nipples, teasing them into hard buds. She arched into his hands, offering herself. Responding to her silent offering, his mouth left hers, trailing slowly down the column of her throat, his tongue sliding sensuously over her skin.

Her body thrummed with a pulsing awareness. The blood rushed through her veins, a hot torrent of need, of wanting. Between her thighs, she felt an unfamiliar tightening, an almost painful craving. Clinging to him, her hands moved feverishly over his torso, registering the raw, masculine feel of him, the coiled and bunched muscles beneath the fabric of his shirt.

She found the hollow of his throat and explored there, tasting the salty, masculine essence of him, reveling in the racing pulse of his heartbeat against her tongue. Reaching up, she combed her fingers through the thick, silky waves of his hair, savoring the texture.

He found the buttons on her shirt and parted them with ease. Bold in her desire, she helped him, shrugging out of her shirt and pulling her chemise over her head. Bared to the waist, she waited, silently offering herself. Inside, she trembled like a leaf blown in the storm.

His gaze drifted downward, followed by the sharp intake of his breath. "You're so beautiful," he murmured, his voice hushed, awestruck.

Lifting his head, he looked into her eyes, "I've never desired a woman as I desire you. I've never worshipped a woman as I worship you. And I've never loved a woman as I love you. Will you have me, Angelina?"

"Forever and ever," she gasped. Lacing her hands behind his neck, she confessed, "I love you, too, Rafael. I've loved you from the first day I saw you, standing on Frances Street. But I was afraid," she admitted. "Afraid to love and trust."

"I know. *Yo entiendo,*" he responded gently.

"Por favor, love me. I'm yours, and I want you so."

"You want me even with this . . ." He touched his scarred cheek. "It's not pity. Is it?"

"Oh, Rafael. I've never pitied you. I've wanted to erase your hurt and anguish, yes. But never pity. You're beautiful to me, both inside and out. Don't you understand? I feel as if I've known you always, loved you always."

And he did understand. He understood all too well. She *had* known him for most of her life, she just didn't realize it. Like the time he rescued her, it was on the tip of his tongue to admit who he was, but this time the feverish desire of his body intervened.

They were married, and she'd said she loved him. There would be time enough for confessions and the sharing of old secrets. But for now his body craved hers with a raging, unquenched need. He wanted to possess her, to drive deep inside of her, claiming her forever as his own. After today, there would be no going back. Their marriage would be real, not a sham.

Reaching out, he cupped her breasts in the palms of his hands, admiring their fullness, the delicious, ripe roundedness of them. Spreading his fingers, he explored the satiny texture of her skin, savoring the petal-soft feel of her, the warm silky flesh.

Groaning low in her throat, she bowed her back, thrusting her breasts forward, as if demanding more. Eager to please, he widened his exploration, gently rubbing her nipples in a circular motion, slowly teasing them to peaks. Her nipples puckered and tightened beneath his touch, pulling into taut points.

Leaving her breasts for a moment, he tore at the buttons of his shirt, wanting to bare his chest, wanting to crush her naked skin against his. Under his ruthless onslaught, the buttons popped. He threw off the confining cloth.

She gasped and then sucked in her breath. In the rush of passion, he'd forgotten. Now he wished he'd left his shirt on.

Her violet eyes widened. Closing his own eyes, he didn't want to see her pity or disgust. She'd said she didn't pity him, that his face didn't repel her. But she'd had time to grow accustomed to his disfigured features. Not so with his body. He hadn't prepared her for this.

Waiting, his body tensed, drawing as taut as a plucked mandolin string. When she touched him, her fingers felt as light as thistledown, whispering over his puckered flesh, gently exploring the ridges of his pain and suffering. Slowly, he relaxed, giving himself over to the novel experience of someone touching him with intimacy and tenderness.

Not since he'd been a young boy, and his mother had soothed away the inevitable scrapes and bruises of childhood, had anyone touched him. Really touched him. His first wife had been a shy and modest woman, not given to passion, carrying out her wifely duties in mortified stoicism. If there had been any touching, he'd been the one to do it, hoping to arouse her desires. But that had never happened. She'd gone to her grave a virgin to passion.

Holding his breath, his senses sharpened, centering on the feel of her fingers moving over his bare skin. She traced the contours of his disfigured flesh, from his right shoulder down, to a triangular patch that spread under his arm, tapering to a point at his waist. If he concentrated just so, and believed with all his heart, he could almost feel her smoothing away the blemished skin, restoring him, making him whole again. Erasing his anguish, as she'd said, with her love.

But as marvelous and reaffirming as her touch was, he had to know, to read the truth in her eyes. Like twin pools of twilight, her eyes always reflected her innermost feelings.

Slowly, he opened his eyes to slits, not wanting her to know that he watched her reactions. Her hands had moved away from his scars, and she was eagerly exploring the remainder of him, trailing her fingertips along the ridges of his muscles, scoring his skin lightly with her long nails, and combing her fingers through the mat of hair on his chest.

Carefully, he watched her expression. Like a stormy sky, it changed swiftly, from curiosity to wonder to passion kindled. But not one drop of pity or disgust that he could discern. Thanking God for this rare gift of love, he opened his arms and his eyes, pulling her against him, crushing her naked breasts against his bared chest.

The pebble-hard points of her breasts teased him, strafing his chest. Her eyes widened again and then drooped languorously. Newly awakened desire deepened their color to midnight velvet. Understanding the game they played, she purred and growled throatily, and like a cat, rubbed herself against him.

This time, it was he who sucked in his breath. His manhood rose, turgid and straining, threatening to burst from his pants. Pulling apart from her, he lowered his head and seized one coral-tinted breast, laving the nipple and aureola with the tip of his tongue before closing his mouth over her, drawing her deeply in, suckling her like a famished baby.

Her purrs became whimpers, and she grasped his head, clasping him tightly and silently urging him on. He complied eagerly, tasting and sucking both her breasts while his fingers searched for the buttons of her riding breeches. Feverishly, he worked to free the buttons and slide the breeches over the swell of her lush hips.

His fingers brushed silk. Glancing down, he found the barrier of her silken underdrawers. Beneath the lace and frills, he glimpsed the dark, secret triangle of her womanhood. The blood pounded in his ears. Tentatively, he touched her there, smoothing the silken fabric over her satiny flesh.

She moaned and tossed her head, arching her back and pushing her breast deeper into his mouth. Her fingernails raked his back, silently pleading. Reaching up, he cradled her in his arms and lowered her gently to the cushions. She offered no resistance when he removed her boots and slid her breeches down her legs, leaving her naked but for her undergarment.

¡Por Dios! She was lovely. Molded for a man's pleasure. Full, high-pointed breasts, a whisper of a waist rounding into voluptuous hips, and long, lean legs, it was a figure that could drive a man to the brink of madness. Even her feet were beautiful, exquisitely formed, high-arched with tiny toes.

Her hands drifted to the placket of his pants, and they shared a wicked grin. He didn't wear underdrawers. But of course, she couldn't know that.

Covering her questing fingers with his, he counseled, "Slow down, Angelita."

Lowering himself beside her, he trailed his fingers languorously over her bare skin, circling her breasts, dipping lower, exploring her navel, straying dangerously close to the juncture of her thighs, only to pull away at the last moment and retrace the path again.

Shuddering under his provocative onslaught, her passion-fogged mind registered the name of Angelita. No one had ever called her that, except the other Rafael, her childhood friend. She thought it curious but then, when his mouth found her breast again and his hands strayed lower, she didn't think at all.

Rational thought fled, replaced by only feelings, sensations of pure shivering pleasure, of uncompromising ecstasy. Her blood heated, and the fever ravaged her body. Pulsing waves rolled over her, carrying her on a floodtide of passion, transforming every nerve of her body into quivering yearning. Her hips lifted from the cushions, straining, wanting, needing.

He gentled her then, stroking her through the silk of her undergarment, finding the swollen nub of her desire. She bucked wildly against his hand, unable to stop herself. His fingers were like quicksilver, drawing the shuddering pleasure from her, bringing her to the very brink of release, promising heaven. Trembling, she swayed upon the precipice, suddenly fearful of the plunge, feeling strangely alone in her spiraling, almost tormented ecstasy.

His fingers abandoned her, and she moaned softly. She felt the whisper of satin against her legs and realized he'd removed her remaining garment. Her eyes drifted open. He'd shed his pants. He rose above her, gloriously male, superbly muscled, lightly dusted with black hair. His proud shaft jutted like a conquering lance from the crisp curls between his thighs.

One lone drop of moisture glistened on its proud head, beckoning her. Suffused with a kind of awe, she tentatively touched him, drawing a low moan from his throat. Their eyes met, exchanging a look as old as time itself and as primitive in its meaning. Her fingers trailed over his manhood. He felt like hot steel wrapped in softest velvet. The feel of him in her hands, of holding his most intimate self, afforded her a soaring pleasure.

Reaching out, he stroked between her thighs, rolling her budded desire between his fingers. She gasped and he covered her mouth with his, taking her breath into his body. His questing fingers stroked and caressed, bringing her to the edge again. But this time, she wasn't alone. Her hand moved up and down his shaft, bringing him to the same shuddering precipice.

Gently and slowly, he parted her thighs wider, lowering himself over her. She welcomed the weight of his body with an aching eagerness. His spicy scent filled her nostrils, mingled with the erotic musk of their lovemaking.

Raising his head, he murmured, "This first time might—"

"Hurt," she finished. "I know. My mother explained when I was—"

"Don't say it," he cut her off, growling, "don't even think it. You're mine now, forever. You're mine," he repeated, almost groaning.

"Forever," she agreed.

He plunged into her and she lifted her hips to meet his. The hurricane suddenly broke over them again, the wind howling and screaming. Their bodies crashed together, straining powerfully, mimicking the storm's fury outside. The tempest raged inside and out, carrying them along on a tide of molten, white-hot passion.

She felt her maidenhead shred and experienced a twinge of pain, but his fingers found her again, wedging between their bodies and absorbing the brief sting. Shuddering beneath him, she rose as if on the wings of angels, soaring high, no longer afraid of the precipice, bringing him with her, plunging headlong into ecstasy.

Clinging together, they drifted in the aftermath, absorbing the joy and savoring their oneness. Pulling her with him, he rolled to his side, his sex still deeply embedded in her. His hands tenderly caressed her back. He murmured words of love and promise for a bright and shining future.

The hurricane shrieked and keened around them. Loud crashes and shattering sounds reverberated, shaking the walls. Malvado, who had been so quiet during their lovemaking, awakened to squawk and batter himself against the cage bars. None of it mattered. She felt safe and secure, nestled in the arms of her beloved. Cuddled and cherished in the embrace of the one man she trusted with her life and soul.

Nothing could touch her now, she thought. Not her father nor Cortez nor even the forces of nature. She'd found love and happiness, fulfillment and a deep, abiding contentment. For the first time in her life, she felt gloriously whole and totally at peace with herself. She'd finally come home.

Chapter Seventeen

They stood together, their arms wrapped around each other, a silent island of misery. Rafael's comforting presence gave Angelina the courage to survey the hurricane damage to her factory.

The thatched roof had been torn off and scattered to the four winds; pieces of it lay strewn over the lot and Frances Street. The upright poles still stood, like naked trees, deeply embedded in crushed rock. The wooden floor remained, although warped and damaged by rain. The brick storehouse and office had survived, but their wooden roofs were half torn away, exposing gaping holes and a jumble of raw planks. And the fence had been uprooted, leaving a tangled skein of wire and posts.

"Come," he gently urged, pulling her forward. "Let's check the office and storehouse."

Numbly, she nodded, following him.

When they looked inside the storeroom, Angelina's heart plummeted. Bins of tobacco leaves, fillers, and wrappers had been overturned by the wind. Their contents lay strewn in haphazard piles or mixed with puddles of water, covering the floor in a slimy mass of greenish-brown vomit. The contents of the office had scarcely fared any better. Benches, gauges, and tools had been tossed about, as if by a giant's careless play. Gazing at the confused heap of implements, it was difficult to assess the damage.

Everything, or almost everything, was ruined, she realized. Everything that she'd worked so hard for, risked so much for. Her factory had been in operation for only one week. She'd gotten off one shipment, but the proceeds wouldn't even cover her workers' wages. All her money was gone. She had nothing left to rebuild with. Her dream had died.

She felt small inside, withered, like an almond that had dried in its skin and rattled forlornly in its shell. Sick at heart, she clung to Rafael, gripping his hand. In silent understanding, his arms came around her. Grateful for his solace, she buried her head against his broad chest. Sobs rose to her throat, burning for release. This time, she didn't hold back. Gasping in anguish, she poured her misery onto the crisp linen of his shirt, thoroughly wetting it.

When hiccoughs replaced tears, he gently cupped her chin and lifted her head. His sienna-colored eyes were warm and soft, filled with love and compassion. Looking into his expressive eyes and realizing he shared her misery, tears boiled again, threatening to spill.

Retrieving a crumpled handkerchief from his pocket, he tenderly dabbed at her swollen eyes. Then he offered it, and she accepted, taking the sodden cloth and blowing her nose. After she'd finished, he kissed the tip of her nose and enfolded her in his arms again.

"It's gone, Rafael, all gone," she whispered, laying her head against his shoulder.

"We'll rebuild it."

"But I haven't any money. You know that."

"Not you, Angelina, *us*. There is no more you and I, only us."

Lifting her head, she looked at him. "What do you mean?"

"I've offered before, but you were too stubborn to accept."
He smiled tenderly. "I've money saved. We'll use it to
rebuild."

"But that money was for the business *you* wanted to start."

He raised his index finger and pressed it against her lips.
Shaking his head, his gaze snagged hers, silently correcting
her.

She understood, repeating, "There's no more you or I. Just
us."

Nodding, he said, "I don't care about the business I wanted
to start. Not now. Not now that I have you. That business was
to keep the loneliness away," he confessed quietly. "To keep
me busy so I didn't have time to think."

"Oh, Rafael. How can I ever repay you? For all that you've
done?"

His eyes burned into hers. "With love, only with love."

Lowering his head, his mouth found hers. Clinging to him,
she savored the warm, moist feel of his lips. His kiss promised
so much, she realized—tenderness and caring, commitment
and passion. Two lives to be shared as one.

Destiny raced through the devastated streets, skirting crum-
pled heaps of rubbish, ignoring the destruction surrounding her.
Having survived the hurricane, cowering alongside Gramps,
Tilly, and Rufus in a brick alcove behind the cookstove, her
thoughts had turned to the other two people she cared about:
Nathan and Angelina.

Despite her grandfather's disapproval, she had set out as
soon as the storm abated to find them. She couldn't rest until
she knew they were safe.

Coming first to the house Angelina shared with her new
husband, she was surprised to find the damage to her friend's
home was minimal. Sections of the clapboard roof had been
blown away, window shutters were missing, and the front porch
had collapsed. Her home had suffered far worse. Most of the

roof and all of the widow walk had been blown away. She wouldn't miss the widow walk, she realized. It held too many painful memories.

After pounding on Angelina's door for several minutes and receiving no answer, she panicked. Then she thought about her friend's factory. Angelina would be there.

Racing the few blocks to the factory, she entered Frances Street. Seeing the ruin of her friend's business, her heart sank. Slowing to a walk, she saw two figures silhouetted against the sky. Locked in each other's arms, Angelina and Rafael stood among the wreckage, kissing. Her heart went out to them, grateful they'd survived the awful storm and found solace in each other's arms.

Not wanting to intrude upon their private moment, she retraced her steps to Eaton Street and headed toward the wharfs. If Nathan was in Key West, his cutter would be docked there. If his ship had been out when the storm hit . . . Her stomach clenched, considering the awful possibility.

Please, dear God, she prayed, *let Nathan be safe.*

It had taken a hurricane to bring her to her senses.

Wrapped in misery over what James had done and what her grandfather had revealed, she'd spent the last two weeks locked in her room, crying and feeling sorry for herself. It had been cowardly on her part, she knew, and Angelina would have heartily disapproved of her self-indulgence.

In a strange sense, though, it had been a necessary catharsis, a time to sort out her feelings. To clear away the past and consider the future.

Unfortunately, she had no future. All of her plans had centered on James Whitman, marrying him, and finding her rightful place in Key West society. But that had been a wishful, childish dream, she recognized now, a mirage without substance.

And she wanted her life to have substance. Having known Angelina and her friend's ambitions had changed her. Angelina had a purpose, a goal. She wanted the same thing for herself.

After much soul-searching, she'd decided to return to Miss

Prentiss's finishing school and complete her education. With a proper education, she could teach. There were never enough teachers in Key West. By becoming a teacher, she would *earn* her rightful place in the community that had shunned her. And her decision wasn't merely self-aggrandizing; she'd always loved children. Being an only child with no parents, she'd dreamed about having a dozen children.

If she could reach one child who needed her, as she'd needed someone when her parents died, she would consider herself a success. And she wanted that success, needed that success, as badly as Angelina wanted her factory to prosper.

Then there was Nathan.

In her soul-searching, she hadn't considered him as a solution. Not that he'd been far from her thoughts. Just that she wasn't worthy of him. He was mature and kind and thoughtful and brave. All the qualities she wanted to possess, but had yet to prove to herself.

When the hurricane swept Key West, all she could think about was Nathan and his safety. If something happened to him, she would somehow feel responsible. Rationally, she knew that was ridiculous. But the feeling stuck nonetheless.

She turned into Front Street, and the wharves loomed ahead. A scene of devastation greeted her. Crowded cheek-to-jowl, ships of all sizes had sought refuge in the harbor to weather the storm. The force of the wind had thrust some of them forward, tearing into the wharves and embedding them, like netted fish, in the splintered remains of the docks. Those were the worst.

The remaining ships had sustained varying degrees of damage. Most had lost their rigging, leaving a raw forest of broken masts and shredded sails. Anchors had been torn away, hatches stove in, railings split, and portholes shattered. Splintered boards and tangled ropes covered the ships' decks and the wharves. It would take weeks to sort out the wreckage.

Her grandfather had gone to check on his schooner, anchored in a cove off the southern tip of the island. She hoped his ship hadn't suffered too much damage. But right now, she was more concerned about Nathan.

Dodging debris and avoiding frenzied sailors and dock hands, who rushed to and fro trying to sort through the devastation, she searched among the ships for the *Columbia*. With each step she took, her heart sank lower. If the revenue cutter wasn't in port, she didn't know what she would do. Wringing her hands and muttering to herself, she kept going, running from ship to ship.

When she was almost at her wit's end, she spied the familiar outline of the cutter, anchored at the far end of the wharf. Its single mast was gone. And like the other ships, its decks were covered with a litter of debris. She expected to see its crew scurrying about, clearing away the wreckage, but the ship appeared strangely forlorn and lifeless.

What could have happened? she asked herself.

Her heart squeezed at the thought of any number of disastrous events. Where the sea was concerned, nothing was certain. Had the cutter survived but lost all hands to the storm? It wouldn't be the first time a ghost ship had been created. Stories of ghost ships were legion, she knew, when the ship survived but the crew was lost.

Then she saw him. A lone figure toiled at the stern, bent over, naked to the waist. The sun glinted on the raised blade of an axe. The axe swung down, striking wood, cracking like the shot of a revolver. It was Nathan, and he was clearing the ship himself.

Relieved to see him alive and well, her heart soared. The sun shone a little brighter. A huge weight lifted from her shoulders. He was alive and well, she repeated to herself, thanking God for his goodness.

Watching him labor over the broken mast, chopping it into manageable sections, she felt suddenly shy. Hanging back in the shadows, she debated whether to approach him or not. After all, as with Angelina, she'd accomplished her goal, to assure herself that he'd survived the storm. There was no need to interrupt his work, she told herself.

But she couldn't take her eyes from him. She'd never seen his naked chest before, she realized. Gazing at his broad shoulders, watching the bunch and coil of his muscles, did funny things to her insides. She longed to touch him, to explore the ridges of muscles, trace the lines of sinew and swelling veins. The feeling was so palpable, so real, she could almost taste it.

Closing her eyes, she remembered the smell of him, the masculine, salty essence intermingled with the bay rum he wore. She remembered the warm, moist feel of his lips upon hers, the touch of his strong fingers at her waist, and the way his eyes crinkled when he laughed. She almost wished he hadn't shaved his beard for her. It was an integral part of him. A symbol of his commitment to the sea and his vocation as a captain.

"Destiny? Is that you?" The deep baritone of his voice reached her.

Her eyes flew open. She'd hesitated too long, she realized with a start, feeling flustered at being discovered. He must have seen her, cowering in the shadows.

Opening her mouth, she tried to reply, but her throat closed. What would he think of her? Coming to the wharf to seek him out when she'd spurned his love before? She hadn't wanted him to know that she cared. After what had happened with James, if she sought Nathan out, it would seem as if he were her second choice. She didn't want him to think that.

Because it wasn't true. Leaning her cheek against the wooden bow of a freighter, she huddled there, wondering what to do.

If she hadn't been so wrapped up in childish dreams and selfish fantasies, she would have recognized the truth long before. She would have understood why Nathan's kisses thrilled her and James's repelled her. Instead, she'd clung fiercely to her old dreams, ignoring her growing feelings for Nathan— ignoring and discarding them, throwing her chance at happiness away with both hands.

If only she'd known about her parents, understood what had happened. Maybe she could have overcome the past and embraced the future with her eyes wide open. She wished her grandfather had told her the truth sooner, but she couldn't blame him, either. He'd done what he thought was best, protecting her from the gossip and pain. Holding on to her love the only way he knew, afraid to admit the part he'd played in her parents' tragedy for fear of losing her love.

She shook her head sadly. Gramps should have trusted her more, should have known she would forgive him, just as she had forgiven him that fateful night on the widow walk. But that wasn't fair, either. How could he know? How could she have known her own reaction until she'd faced life and suffered? Until she'd been forced to grow up.

Sighing, she realized she had no one to blame but herself. Sheltered and cosseted by her grandfather and Tilly, she'd grown into a singularly frivolous and self-centered young lady. Her association with Angelina had taught her that. But no more. Now she had a worthy mission in life, a blueprint for the future. Something she could call her own.

As much as she loved Nathan, she wouldn't use him, as she'd used James, to give her life purpose. And she couldn't let him know she cared. It would look as if she turned to him because James had let her down. She couldn't do that to Nathan, make him feel second-rate. He was too good a man. He deserved better.

It would be better that she go away to school and let him find another love. A woman who would recognize his goodness and put him first in her life. Because of her past mistakes, she could never offer Nathan that assurance.

The heavy tread of boots sounded on the wharf. Lifting her head, she realized she'd been woolgathering. Mourning her foolish actions, grieving for what she'd lost. Glancing up, she found Nathan looming over her.

His features were drawn. She glimpsed new lines etched into his handsome face. Now he looked his age. Before, he'd looked almost too young to command a Navy revenue cutter. He sported dark brown stubble on his chin, and she wondered if he was growing his beard again. He should, she thought. He should be his own man.

He halted a foot away and lifted his arms as if he were going to embrace her. Then a dark shadow flickered in his hazel eyes and he stopped himself, dropping his arms to his sides.

"Destiny, why didn't you answer? When I saw you, I called down. Didn't you hear me?"

She started to shake her head, to deny having heard his call. But she stopped herself. There would be no more lies between them, not even small evasions. She owed him that much.

"I . . . I didn't know what to say. I didn't know if you wanted to see me. I only came to see if you and your ship weathered the storm. I hadn't meant to stay."

"I see." He rocked back on his heels. Inclining his head toward the ship, he said, "The *Columbia* survived, as you can see. She's damaged but no more than most. We were fortunate."

"And yourself?" she asked politely, already knowing the answer.

He hadn't bothered to don a shirt. His naked chest gleaming with perspiration, he was the very picture of robust health. She tried to keep her eyes trained on his face, but it was difficult. Her gaze was drawn to the muscled expanse of his bare torso.

"Not a scratch." Shrugging, he stroked his stubbled chin, admitting, "Although I'm hardly presentable. Forgive me for appearing this way, but my shirt is in the cabin. I was afraid I wouldn't catch you if I went to fetch it."

It was her turn to shrug, making light of his admission. "I'm the one intruding, Nathan. You're working to clear your ship. I don't expect you to be attired to receive visitors."

He smiled then. A real smile that lit his eyes and crinkled the corners. Remembering his warm smile, she recalled all the fun they'd shared—at the ball and the picnic, even their madcap ride over the beach. Knowing how much she'd missed his smile and how much she would miss it in the days to come, she experienced the sharp-toothed fangs of regret, as if something was tearing her heart into tiny pieces.

Pushing away her self-pity, she inquired, "Where's your crew? Shouldn't they be helping you?"

"They will later. The ship can wait. I sent them ashore with the mayor's party to help in town. They're all strong and disciplined lads. I'm certain they'll find plenty to do. Someone had to stay with the ship. I'm doing what I can in the meantime."

Of course, he would do that, she thought. How kind and generous of him. But that was like Nathan. Tears stung the backs of her eyelids, and she lowered her head. She must stop this, she told herself. She was becoming downright maudlin.

"That was kind of you," she managed, trying to get a grip on herself. Swaying on her feet, she wanted to run and hide. To nurse her regrets in private. She'd had no idea the effect he would have on her.

"Here." He reached out and grasped her elbow, steadying her. "You've been through the storm, too. And you look a bit peaked. Come to my cabin and have a cup of tea."

"Oh, I shouldn't. I should . . ."

"Is your grandfather all right?"

"Yes, Gramps is fine. He went to check on his schooner. It's moored off the southern tip of the island."

He nodded. "Trust your grandfather to find the best place for his ship to ride out the storm. He's the finest seaman I've ever known."

"What do you mean?"

"The hurricane winds came from the northeast. I wish I had seen it coming and taken the *Columbia* south." Squeezing her elbow, he said, "If your grandfather is all right, then you've time for tea. How are your servants and your home?"

"Tilly and Rufus weren't hurt, either. We stayed in a brick alcove behind the cookstove where we store firewood. The house was damaged, but it's still standing."

"And your friend, Angelina?"

"Angelina and Rafael survived, but her factory is ruined. I saw them but didn't stop to talk." Lifting her head, she admitted, "I was in a hurry to get here."

Meeting her gaze, he cleared his throat and for the first time since they'd faced each other, he looked uncomfortable. "Then we've both been very fortunate."

"Yes," she agreed, realizing what he said was true. She hadn't personally lived through a hurricane before, but she'd heard enough of the old stories to know that when things were sorted out, there would be considerable loss of life as well as property damage in Key West.

"Come," he urged her. "Let's get that tea, and I'll get my shirt."

Nodding, she didn't protest this time. Heaven help her, but she wanted to spend time with him, even though she knew she shouldn't. Surrendering, she allowed him to guide her toward the gangplank.

Glancing at Destiny, demurely seated in his cabin with her hands folded in her lap, it was hard for Nathan to believe his eyes, to believe that she was really here, sharing his cabin. How many times had he dreamed this dream, only to awaken to the awful reality and the bone-chilling loneliness?

Closing his eyes for a moment, he opened them again. It wasn't a dream, he realized. She was really here. And it was she who had sought him out because she was concerned for his welfare. Knowing that she cared warmed him, making his heart pound and the palms of his hands perspire.

It had taken iron self-control to remain aboard ship and not seek her after the storm. He'd feared the worst but didn't know how she would receive him. He'd set himself to the hardest task he knew to stop his racing thoughts, breaking up the mainmast.

The setting sun slanted through the porthole, transforming her hair into a bright flame. Her milk-punch complexion shimmered in the light, tempting him, looking good enough to taste. He wanted nothing more than to take her in his arms and never let go.

She lifted her head and gave him a small, tight smile. Even that shy gesture couldn't mask the generous curve of her lips. And her blue-green eyes glowed with a brilliant luminosity, like the waters of his beloved Caribbean Sea.

Placing the tray on the table, he began to unload its contents—the steaming teakettle, a jar of tea leaves, cream and sugar, mugs and spoons. Before he could finish, she joined in, helping him. Their fingers brushed accidentally, striking sparks, sending a current of electricity leaping between them. Clenching his jaw, he held himself in check, hiding his reaction.

But Destiny didn't hide; she recoiled and looked flustered. Dropping her hands to her lap again, she allowed him to spoon the tea leaves into the mugs and add boiling water.

Had she felt it, too? he wondered. Was that why she'd retreated, to cover her reaction? Or did his touch repulse her so that she couldn't stand it?

Pushing his doubts aside, he concentrated on the moment at hand. She had come to him of her own volition and accepted his offer to have tea. That was all that mattered.

"Cream and sugar?" he asked.

"Both, please."

"One lump or two?"

"Two, please."

He poured a dollop of cream into her mug and added two lumps of sugar. Handing the mug to her with a spoon, he was careful to avoid touching her hand. Then he took his own mug and cradled it in his hand, waiting for it to cool.

Glancing at him, she inquired, "You don't take cream or sugar?"

"No, just plain tea."

She nodded and stirred her tea.

The silence stretched awkwardly between them, vibrating with unspoken words, teeming with unresolved feelings.

She smiled again. That tight grimace of a smile. He hated

it. This wasn't the Destiny he knew and loved. He'd never seen her so quiet and withdrawn. He missed her bubbling exuberance, her childlike enthusiasm. He wanted to hear her laugh out loud and chatter like a magpie.

"What's this, Nathan?" she asked innocently, breaking the painful silence. Her long, slender fingers traced the outlines of a map lying open on the table.

Sucking in his breath, he cursed his carelessness. It was a map detailing the covert operation he and Rafael planned. Destiny was very intelligent—too intelligent, and because of her seafaring grandfather, well-informed about Alligator Reef. It wouldn't do for her to ask questions.

Grasping the map, he rolled it up quickly, dissembling, "There's to be a new lighthouse at Alligator Reef."

She must have sensed his unease because she apologized, "Oh, I'm sorry I asked. I didn't mean to—"

"It's all right, Destiny," he interjected, wanting to assure her that she'd done nothing wrong.

It was obvious his words didn't reassure her. She sat stiffer than before, almost as if she were at attention. And she gulped her tea quickly before it had time to cool.

Rising, she said, "Thank you for the tea. I feel much better now. It's growing late. I should be getting home."

He rose, too. She was about to walk out of his life again, he realized, with nothing settled between the two of them. He couldn't allow that to happen. He loved her too much.

"What do you plan on doing?" he found himself asking.

She arched her eyebrows and widened her eyes. "What do you mean?"

"Now that you're unattached, I wondered . . ." he fumbled.

Her cheeks flamed crimson, and she averted her eyes. "So you know." Sighing, her shoulders drooped. "I'm not surprised. I guessed you would find out."

"Key West is a small town," he offered by way of explanation, hating himself for his bluntness and his inability to change his nature.

Inside, his soul twisted in torment for her. Embarrassed by her shame, he despised himself for reminding her of it. But how could they move forward, if they didn't put the past to rest? And he wanted to move forward. Wanted her to forget the past and learn to love him.

Lifting her chin, she faced him. "What are they saying?"

"That you've ended your alliance with Whitman."

"Only that?"

"Yes."

She appeared to breathe a sigh of relief, and he wondered what Whitman had done to her. Half of him wanted to call Whitman out and make him pay for hurting her. The other half abhorred the idea of a duel. Selfishly, he wanted to live so he could spend his days loving her.

"Nathan, the last thing I want is your pity." Her voice was a harsh whisper. "I must go." She gathered her skirts, brushing past him.

But he couldn't let her go. Not again. She'd sought him out. She must feel something for him. And he was crazy with wanting her, with needing her.

Acting on impulse, he grabbed her shoulders and crushed her mouth to his. At first, she stood perfectly still, feeling like a marble statue in his arms. Her rigidity didn't discourage him, though, but served as a spur to goad him.

With all the yearning bottled up in his soul, he worshipped her mouth. Fitting himself to the contours of her lips, he savored each touch of her flesh against his. Slowly, she melted into his embrace. Her arms came up and encircled his neck. And she responded to his kisses, opening herself to him.

Tentatively, he touched his tongue to hers, something he'd never initiated before. Fire leapt between them, hot and wild, scorching his soul. Their tongues circled, tasting and mating feverishly. Long-pent-up cravings poured through him in an unending stream. He'd dreamed of this, of kissing every inch of her satiny flesh, exploring every nuance of her curvaceous body, reveling in the hedonistic pleasure of their love.

Gathering her in his arms, he lowered her to the bunk. The same bunk she'd so innocently bounced upon, bringing him to the brink of insanity. And then she'd spurned him. But he wouldn't think of that. Not now. Not with her lying quiescent in his arms.

Taking himself in hand, he forced himself to go slowly, thinking that was what she would want. He wasn't very experienced at lovemaking. But if he went slowly enough, he hoped to enflame her desires. With infinite care, he kissed and laved her throat with his tongue tip, nuzzling her earlobes, tracing the blue veins of her neck with his lips and tongue.

But she had other ideas, he soon realized. Her passion was already at a fever pitch, like his own. Taking his hands in hers, she directed him to her simple blouse, closing his fingers over the first button. He understood her silent urging without having to be told.

His control slipped. Frantically, he parted the buttons of her shirtwaist, revealing the iron constriction of her corset. Her breasts rose and fell above the tight stays, their mounds alabaster white and luminous. Lost in wonder, he trailed his lips over their rich fullness.

She reached up and unlaced her corset. It parted and only a gossamer wisp of fabric remained. Gazing at her milky-white breasts, crested with pink nipples, he thought the world had ended, spinning out of control on its axis. Greedily, his mouth covered one nipple, suckling.

Lurching up, she buried her hands in his hair, urging, "Nathan. Oh, Nathan. How I want you."

Aching with desire, he responded. In a flurry of frantic need, they undid buttons and unlaced ribbons. Her clothing fell away, pushed into a crumpled heap at the bottom of the bunk.

The breath left his lungs. He'd often dreamed of how beautiful she would be, lying naked in his arms. But the dreams didn't do justice to the reality. Her milk white skin gleamed softly, dusted lightly with freckles. Her shell-pink-tipped breasts rose and fell, beckoning, rounded globes of delight. Her waist was a mere hand span, but her hips were generous, made for love, for bearing children. His children, he amended.

"You're perfect," he groaned. "Perfect and beautiful. My God, Destiny, I love you so much. More than life, more than the breath in my body. And I've missed you. You can't know." His voice choked off, filled with emotion.

Reaching up, she placed one finger on his lips, requesting, "No more words, Nathan. Just love me. Show me your love."

He didn't need further urging. His lips, tongue, and fingers feasted upon her, making her his irrevocably. If ever a mortal man had worshipped a goddess, he worshipped her. He couldn't get enough of her, couldn't taste enough of her silky skin, couldn't kiss her deeply enough. Like a starved man at a banquet, he reveled in each touch, cherished each kiss, savored each sigh from her lips.

And while he made love to her, her hands roamed over him, bringing him to the edge of madness. Her fingers were everywhere, questing and searching, easing the clothes from his body. He helped her, almost resentful of the need to get undressed, not wanting to stop touching her for an instant.

When they lay naked together, arms and legs entwined on his narrow bunk, he knew he'd touched heaven. If he died this instant, he would go to his death a happy man. Although he wanted her, desired her beyond the bounds of all reason, lying with her perfect body next to his was more than he'd ever expected, more than he had a right to expect.

Lifting her head, she circled his ear with her tongue. The wet, warm feel of her fine-nubbed tongue ignited his blood. Reaching down, he grazed one breast, reveling in her reaction, in feeling her nipple tighten into a hard bud. But now he wanted more. His hand discovered her woman's mound, that most intimate part of her. Tentatively, he stroked her, awestruck by the hot, moist folds of her body, the secret places of her.

Moaning, she arched up, pressing herself against his hand. His fingers caressed and explored, wanting to drive her to the brink of insanity as she'd driven him. Lowering his head, he captured one succulent breast in his mouth.

Like a flower, she opened beneath him. Her thighs parted and her hips lifted, pushing against his fingers with a pulsing need. Bowing her back and burying her hands in his hair, she forced her breast deeper into his mouth.

White-hot flames scorched him, burning a path through his body. Every nerve screamed for release. Every muscle trembled for completion. He felt his carefully nurtured control slipping. Rearing himself above her, he parted her thighs and plunged deep inside.

She was tight and hot. So tight and hot, he couldn't contain himself. His seed spilled forth in a rushing torrent. He died then, a little death, buried deep within her beloved body.

When he returned to himself, he burned with humiliation, silently lashed himself with castigation. He'd taken his pleasure and given her none. Wanting her so badly had been his undoing, had shredded his self-control. But she was too innocent to understand what had happened. She lay quiet in his arms, her head buried in his shoulder.

What must she think of him? What must she think of lovemaking? She was a virgin, he knew. He'd felt the barrier of her maidenhead just before he'd climaxed. She couldn't possibly understand or know. But he remembered her responsiveness. Knew she burned as he did. He just hadn't been equal to her need.

Rolling over, he brought her with him. Lying side by side, she regarded him. Lifting one hand, she stroked his cheek. Her turquoise eyes held a question. A question he didn't want to answer with words. A question only his touch could answer.

Slowly, carefully, reverently, he started over, kissing her with adoration and exploring every inch of her body, suckling her breasts, one by one, until she arched into him, whimpering with need. This time, his fingers were bold, parting her thighs, finding the bud of her desire, rolling it between his fingers until she gasped and panted.

With her rising desire, he found himself hardening again.

His manhood pushed against her soft belly, insistent with its own need. When she bucked and surged against him, raking her fingernails over his back, he knew she was ready. But this time, she would lead the way, he vowed to himself. Taking her pleasure at her own pace.

Moving under her, he seated her on his abdomen. Her eyes widened in surprise but she followed his lead. Gently, he grasped her by the arms and lifted her a fraction of an inch, positioning her over his shaft, directing, "Destiny, you lead the way. Do you understand what to do?"

She nodded, her eyes dark with passion. Tentatively, she lowered her hips. He helped her, guiding himself into her glove-tight passage. Shuddering, her eyes drifted shut. His fingers found the bursting swell of her female passion, caressing the swollen bud as she gingerly moved up and down his shaft.

The taut membrane of her maidenhood intervened and she panted, "Nathan, I don't know what to do."

Understanding what she needed, his fingers soothed and caressed as he bucked his hips upward, thrusting through her innocence, claiming her virginity. She whimpered once, a concession to the pain, and then went still.

But he wouldn't allow it to end like this. He would bring her pleasure if it was the last thing he did on earth. Capturing her breast in his mouth, he laved her nipple and continued to stroke between her thighs. She trembled and quaked and started to move slowly, taking him deeply inside of her.

The musk of her arousal filled his nostrils. Her movements were more frantic now, more feverish. He groaned with the earth-shaking pleasure of her riding him. Tossing her head back, her flame-colored hair flaring like wildfire, she keened deep in her throat.

He felt her release in the depths of his soul. The sweet vise of her tightening muscles, her soft whimpers, the hot gush of her female juices. Her release sent him over the edge again.

This time, they reached for the stars and found their fulfillment together.

Chapter Eighteen

Destiny rubbed her eyes, amazed that she'd fallen asleep. The cabin was completely dark. Night had fallen, and she had no idea what time it was. Gramps and Tilly would be frantic, she knew. Nathan lay beside her sleeping. Luckily, she was on the outside of the bunk and could get up without disturbing him.

Carefully, she swung her legs over the side. The sudden movement made her catch her breath as she realized that between her thighs she was sticky and sore. Remembering, she blushed, astonished at what had transpired between them.

Even Angelina's explanations hadn't prepared her for the reality of lovemaking. It was like nothing else on this earth, she decided. Like going a little crazy until you reached that final, earth-shattering release. A feeling both indescribable and incredible.

A feeling she would cherish for the rest of her life. And she would never forget tonight. She might go to her grave an old-maid schoolteacher, but at least Nathan had given her one taste of heaven, of how it was between a man and a woman.

Right now, though, she had to dress and go home. Fumbling at the bottom of the bunk for her clothes, she quickly realized they were hopelessly mixed with Nathan's. She couldn't get dressed without a light, and she should wash between her legs, too. She hadn't wanted to waken him, but it might be unavoidable, she realized.

Rising, she found the lamp on the table and the safety matches. Striking a match, she lit the lamp. Crossing to a corner of the cabin, she found his shaving things and a basin of water. Availing herself of soap and water, she sponged the insides of her thighs.

The towel came away smeared with traces of red. Gazing at the telltale blood, evidence of her lost virginity, gave her pause. What had she done?

She remembered how bitterly she'd fought James Whitman to save that same virginity. But she hadn't wanted to fight Nathan. She loved him with all her heart, and if she couldn't give him her love, she wanted him to have that most precious gift a woman could bestow upon a man.

After drying herself, she crossed to the bunk. Nathan slept on his side, facing the wall, his arms flung above his head. She watched him for several moments, memorizing the beloved features of his face. But she avoided looking at his nude body, knowing she would want to touch him, and if she touched him, he was sure to waken.

Moving carefully, she sorted through the pile of discarded clothes, finding her undergarments, shirtwaist, and skirt. Within a few moments she had pulled on her clothes. Then she bent down, looking for her shoes and stockings.

She felt a hand close over her arm, startling her. Nathan was sitting up in bed with one hand clasped around her wrist. He must have awakened while she was dressing. His hazel eyes glittered in the pale lamplight.

"Marry me, Destiny," he demanded.

"I can't." She shook her head as if for emphasis.

"You mean you won't. I know your grandfather would

approve.'' He cleared his throat and suddenly looked sheepish. ''Approve, hell. If he knew what we'd done today, he'd demand it, too.''

''Please, Nathan. Let go of my arm.''

He stared at her hard and then let go of her wrist. Swinging his legs over the side of the bunk, he reached for his pants and pulled them on. She tried not to look, not wanting to be reminded of what she was giving up. Instead, she continued her interrupted search, locating her shoes and stockings, tangled in the bedclothes.

Seating herself on a chair, she pulled on her stockings, lifting her skirts to fasten her garters. It was clear that Nathan possessed no compunction about watching her. His gaze greedily slid up her half-exposed leg, and for a moment she was afraid he'd take her back to bed. And heaven help her, she knew she couldn't resist him.

He rose, towering over her. ''Why won't you marry me?''

''I . . . I plan on returning to school and becoming a teacher.''

''That's not a reason. If you want to teach, you can. I'll wait until you finish your education. Then we can marry,'' he offered. ''There's always a need for teachers. Wherever the Navy posts me, I'm certain you'll find a position.''

''That's generous of you, but there are many reasons why we can't marry. Do I have to spell them out for you?''

''Yes. I want to know why you won't marry me.''

Sighing, she wet her lips with her tongue. He was making this so hard. Why couldn't he just let her go? She didn't want to discuss it, thinking about it was painful enough.

''There's my background for one reason. A Navy captain's wife must be above reproach. There are people in Key West who claim my parents never married. That I'm illegitimate.''

''That's nothing but old gossip.'' He snorted.

''You know about it?''

''Of course, I've known from the first. I always thought it a pile of rubbish. The locals didn't like your father because he was a privateer, a *Catholic* privateer,'' he emphasized. ''So they gossiped about your parents. But I won't be posted here forever. No one will know your background when we leave Key West. In fact, I would think you would welcome the chance to leave this place. It's brought you nothing but—''

''Don't say it,'' she interrupted. ''And I don't want to leave Gramps.''

Dropping on one knee before her, he took her hand in his. It reminded her of the time at the ball. The first time he'd proposed to her.

His voice was soft. ''I know how much you love your grandfather, but you must face the facts. He's an old man. He can't live forever. What will you do then?''

''I'll have my work. And by then, I'll have earned the town's respect.'' But she couldn't keep the tremor from her voice. Deep down, she harbored doubts about whether Key West would ever respect her.

He dropped her hand and rose, turning from her. ''Winning the respect of this town is more important than marrying the man who loves you with all his heart?'' Keeping his back to her, his voice sounded uncommonly harsh. ''I know you don't love me, but I've love enough for both of us. And in time, I hope you will come to have some affection for me. Other marriages have been built on less and prospered.'' Facing her, he beseeched, ''Please, think it over.''

Tears stung her eyelids, threatening to spill. He was so good and kind and selfless. And he loved her so much. How could she stand this? She wanted to throw her arms around him and confess her love.

But it was precisely because he was so good that she couldn't accept him, couldn't marry him. He wanted her now, but after they were married, the doubts would creep in. He would feel second rate, her second choice. Nothing she could ever do or say would erase the fact that she'd spurned him for another and hadn't realized the truth until James had . . .

Lifting her face, she whispered, ''Nathan, you deserve better. You deserve to find a woman who loves you with all her heart, too.'' Inwardly, she winced at the lie. Earlier, she'd told herself there would be no more lies between them. But she couldn't say what she really felt.

His eyes narrowed and he swung around again. Cursing under his breath, he smashed his fist against the wall. Startled by the vehemence of his reaction, she jumped.

Her Nathan, her gentle Nathan, had a temper! She'd never seen him angry before, she realized. But she knew he was passionate. Thinking about the wild love they'd just shared brought a warm flush to her cheeks.

He closed his eyes and brought his fist to his mouth, sucking on the shredded flesh of his knuckles. Rising, she started toward the washbasin to get some soap and water.

''Don't,'' his voice stopped her. ''I'm all right. It's just a scratch. And I apologize for my behavior.'' Crossing the cabin in one swift stride, he grasped her shoulders. ''Don't do this, Destiny. Don't martyr yourself for me.'' He gave her a shake. ''I understand what you're trying to do. You think I'll be sorry if I marry you. Don't you? That later I'll believe you came to me out of desperation because Whitman wouldn't marry you. That's it, isn't it?''

Raising her own fist to her mouth, she couldn't answer. The long-suppressed tears brimmed, streaking down her face. He'd guessed the truth and saying it out loud made it sound just as ugly as she knew it would.

Folding her into his arms, he held her tightly, promising, ''But it won't be like that. I'll not have second thoughts. Whitman did me the biggest favor in the world. When you left me that day, I was lost. I was miserable. I became a tyrant. My men used to respect me; now they fear me. I can't live without you, Destiny. Please, say you'll marry me.''

She stood trembling in his arms, tears rolling down her cheeks. It would be the easiest thing in the world to accept his proposal, to bury herself against his muscular chest for the rest of her life. But if it would be the easiest thing for her, it would also be the most unfair thing for him.

He deserved better, the mantra repeated itself in her head. She'd already hurt him enough. Right now, he thought he wouldn't have doubts later. But what man wouldn't? No, she couldn't marry him, knowing that some day she'd look into his blue-gray eyes and see mistrust and regret in them.

It took all of her strength of will, but she pushed against his chest, pleading, "Let me go, Nathan. Please, let me go," she cried, frantic to get away, to end it. "I can't, I won't marry you. It's for the best," she mumbled, as much to convince herself as to convince him.

With those words, she whirled around and fled from the cabin before she could change her mind and doom them to a life of regret.

Standing at precisely the same place they'd stood after the hurricane, Rafael and Angelina surveyed the rebuilt factory. Gazing at it, Rafael's heart swelled with pride and a sense of accomplishment. Despite a shortage of materials and manpower after the hurricane, they'd managed to rebuild quickly, in less than a month, what the storm had destroyed. And they'd done it together, working alongside the laborers until late each night by torchlight.

Putting his arm around her waist, he pulled her close, reveling in their joint sense of triumph. Their marriage was no longer a sham. They were building a partnership for the future. He shook his head, still amazed at the turn of events in his life.

Their dreams had come true. Angelina had her factory and her hard-won independence. And he had Angelina for his wife. But the really astonishing thing was that she loved him. Scarred and disfigured though he was, she loved him. Each night, she proved just how much she loved him. Just thinking about their nights together made him grow hard.

Dropping his head, he nuzzled her neck, sliding his tongue down the blue-veined column of satiny flesh. She squeaked and pushed at him, scolding, "Rafael, what are you doing? What if people are watching? And it's broad daylight!"

Smiling wickedly, he narrowed his eyes and recited from an old fairy tale, " 'The better to *see* you, my dear.' "

"Well, not here," she huffed, "not now." She crossed her arms over her chest. Lowering her voice, she whispered, "You *see* plenty of me at home at night."

Her pointed observation amused him. He laughed and drew her into his arms. At first, she was stiff and unyielding, but it wasn't long before she relaxed and grinned slyly up at him.

Brushing her mouth with his, he lifted her in his arms and swung her around, declaring, "Be happy, Angelina! We've done it! Rebuilt your factory and started a new life together and . . ."

He'd been about to say that he hoped they'd started a family together, but he stopped himself. He didn't know how she felt about having children. It was a strange thing not to know about your wife, he realized. But then, their marriage hadn't exactly followed the conventional path.

"Put me down, you big oaf," she demanded. When he did so, she bent and straightened her skirts before facing the factory again. Gazing at it, she breathed, "I am happy." Lifting her head, her wide violet eyes sparkled with joy when she admitted, "It's the happiest time of my life. All my dreams have come true."

Innocent of his thoughts, she'd repeated exactly the way he felt. His heart expanded in his chest, threatening to burst. *Por Dios,* how he loved her! How he wanted her! Right now, in front of everyone and in broad daylight.

Placing her hand in his, she confessed softly, "I'm so happy, I'm afraid. Afraid something will go wrong—"

"Don't," he cut her off, sealing her lips with the touch of his finger. "Don't conjure up bad thoughts, Angelina."

She sighed. "I know I shouldn't think those thoughts, but so much has happened in such a short time." She shook her head. "Sometimes, it all seems like a dream." Glancing at him, she said, "You know what I mean."

And he did know what she meant. It seemed like a dream to him, too. Then he remembered something. Something he'd been meaning to tell her but had dreaded, not knowing how she would react. This seemed the perfect time, he reasoned. They were on top of the world. Nothing could touch them.

"If it makes you feel any less superstitious, I have a bit of news. It's both bad and good."

"Tell me the bad part first."

"The constable decided to use prisoners to help repair the hurricane damage. While working on the repairs to the city hall, López managed to escape."

"Oh." She caught her breath. "They didn't find him?"

"No, they searched everywhere. And Key West isn't that big. Someone must have gotten him off the island in a boat."

"Cortez?"

He shook his head. "I doubt it. Cortez must know López implicated him. No, it probably was his family. Seems they're missing, too."

"Do you think he'll try to come back and . . ." She gulped. He felt her hand tremble in his.

Pulling her into his arms, he tried to reassure her. "He'd be a fool to come back. López was just a hired hand, doing a job for Cortez."

"But he wanted part of the reward," she pointed out. "What if he thinks there's still a reward for me?"

"He'd be a fool to come back," he repeated, wanting to soothe her fears. "And besides, his family is gone. That's a sure sign he won't come back." Pausing, he rested his chin on her head. "You haven't asked about the good part."

"There's a good part?"

"You won't have to testify in court."

"*Sí*, I didn't think. That *is* good news." Suddenly unmindful of broad daylight and any passersby that might be watching, she burrowed herself deeper into his arms.

With her body pressed tightly against his, he soon found he had reason to think, mostly unmentionable thoughts. And when she lifted her face to be kissed, he accepted her offering. Slanting his mouth across hers, he drank in the warm invitation of her lips.

Breaking their kiss, he placed his lips close to her ear, sharing some of his thoughts with her. Her twilight-hued eyes went wide in her face, and she blushed. When she disentangled herself from his embrace, he cursed himself for being so daring.

But she surprised him by winking and grabbing both his hands, pulling him forward. "I think we should go home, Rafael. The workmen said they'd have the new shutters up. Don't you want to *see* if they did a good job?"

"You want to go home in broad daylight?" he asked, his question fraught with double meaning.

It was her turn to grin wickedly. "The better to *see* you, my dear," she threw back at him.

Rafael sifted through the bills of lading on his desk, trying to sort out the most pressing matters first. Working alongside Angelina to rebuild the factory had been gratifying, but unfortunately, it had put him behind with his insurance business. Several cargos were due to be auctioned this week, and he hadn't had time to do his customary research.

The backlog of cargoes was a direct result of the hurricane. Based on the preliminary information at his disposal, he hadn't discovered any suspicious circumstances. If Cortez was still operating in these waters, he was covering his tracks well, utilizing the hurricane as a shield for his activities.

On the other hand, it was possible Cortez had feared López would reveal more than the scheme to abduct Angelina. If López knew about his clandestine wrecking operations, Cortez might have moved his operations farther up the coast. If López knew. That was the key.

And if Cortez had moved his operations, then his contact in

Key West would be worthless. Or there hadn't been any high-level contact in the first place.

Rafael shook his head. There had to have been a source. He'd bet his life on it. As if in answer to his circling thoughts, there was a knock on the door and Captain Nathan Rodgers appeared on his threshold.

Skirting the desk, he offered his hand, saying, "Welcome, Rodgers. You don't know how glad I am to see you."

Rodgers's eyebrows drew together, and he shot him a quizzical look. Pumping his hand, he asked, "To what do I owe your unexpected enthusiasm?"

"To my infernal second-guessing." Indicating a chair, he offered, "Please, have a seat."

The captain seated himself, repeating, "Second guessing? Is this some kind of game? I'm sorry if I interrupted you." His gaze swept the piles of paper on the desk. "But you didn't want me to come to your house and disturb your wife, remember?"

"Of course, I remember. And I know this isn't a game, except the most deadly sort." Rafael returned to the chair behind his desk. "It's just that I've been sorting through the wrecks, and they appear to be a direct result of the hurricane. In fact"—he paused, pulling a file from the bottom drawer of his desk and flipping through it—"I have no evidence of suspicious wrecks since Angelina was abducted."

"And?"

"That's where the second-guessing comes in. Might Cortez have moved his operations after being exposed by López? And if he did so, then he wouldn't need a contact in Key West. The contact would be worthless to him. Or—"

"Or there wasn't a highly placed contact to begin with," Rodgers finished for him, smiling tightly. "You're worried that you guessed wrong."

"But that's the problem, I don't see how I could have been wrong. I've watched Cortez for two years, and without a dependable source for information, it's impossible he could have been so successful."

Rodgers rose to his feet. "I can't stay. The wharf was deserted when I came, but I don't want anyone to see us together." Leaning on the desk, he said, "I hope to heaven you weren't wrong, Estava. My reputation and commission are riding on this. I came because I have news from my superiors."

Rafael noticed that the knuckles of his fists, supporting his weight, had turned white. Rodgers wasn't joking about the importance of the mission to him. Despite his anxiety, Rafael still believed Cortez was out there, waiting to ply his dangerous trade. The hurricane had provided the perfect hiatus, delivering plenty of wrecks without the need for resorting to criminal activities.

"What news?" he inquired.

"The Marines have already departed on a transport ship. They should arrive at a landing two miles above Alligator Reef in four or five days. The Navy ship bearing armaments is scheduled to depart from Charleston in three days. The ship's cargo and course will be wired to Key West under special code. Only the Browns and Whitmans will be privy to the information."

"Then the die is cast." Rafael expelled his breath and rose. "You'll come for me when you're ready to rendezvous?"

Even though Rafael was determined to see this thing through to the end, when he said the words, his heart skipped a beat. This was no picnic they were embarking upon. It was a dangerous operation. They might be wounded, or worse. Before, it hadn't mattered, but now it was different. His life was as perfect as any human being had a right to expect. And he loved Angelina so much. He wanted to spend decades sharing his life with her and raising a family.

But he couldn't back out on Rodgers now. This had been his idea, and as the captain had so bluntly pointed out, his commission and reputation were riding on the outcome. There was no going back. He had to see it through to the end. He owed Rodgers that much.

"Of course I'll come for you." Rodgers lifted his hands

from the desk, straightening. "I can't promise you much time. You might have to leave on short notice. I'll look here first, but if I can't find you—"

"You'll need to come to my house. I understand." Offering his hand again, he said, "You won't be sorry that you relied on me."

"I hope you're right. I'd like to catch the scoundrel, too." He shook Rafael's hand and turned to go.

The door to the office sprang open. Angelina swept in, demanding, "Rafael, I want you to talk to the Muñoz brothers about that last shipment of wrappers. I've already spoken to them, but . . ." Her words trailed off when she noticed Rodgers.

Backing up a step, she recovered quickly. "Capitán Rodgers, how pleasant to see you."

When she offered her hand, the captain took it, bowing low. "It's my pleasure," he murmured.

Her gaze darted to Rafael, and she wet her lips with her tongue. "I've intruded. Please, go on with your business. I'll wait."

"That won't be necessary, Angelina. He just came by to inquire how we were doing after the hurricane." Rafael shot a look at Rodgers. "He was just leaving."

"Yes." Rodgers took the hint. "I'm glad to hear all is well with you. If you'll excuse me, I must get back to my ship." Bowing again, he quit the office.

"Well," Angelina observed grumpily, watching him disappear down the wharf. "He never stays to talk when I'm around. Remember that time at the house? Doesn't he like me?"

"Angelina, don't be silly," Rafael remonstrated. "Of course he likes you. If you haven't noticed before, *el capitán* is decidedly shy around females." Rafael silently commended himself for his quick thinking, coming up with such a plausible excuse.

"He isn't shy where Destiny is concerned," she shot back.

He grinned. "You know that's different."

"I suppose so." She sank into the chair Rodgers had vacated. "Still, I feel as if you and he have some secret business you don't want me to know about. He appears and disappears but doesn't want to socialize. It's odd, to say the least.''

He caught his breath. Whoever had said women possessed intuition about certain things had been right. It was uncanny how Angelina had seen through the situation. How to deflect her? He hated lying to her, even if it was to protect her. He'd already lied about Rodgers's reason for being there, and he didn't want to make up more stories.

Deciding action was his best course, he rounded the desk and took her in his arms, whispering huskily, ''You didn't come to see me about the Muñoz brothers. Did you? I can slip away. We can go home and—''

''Oh, Rafael,'' she interrupted, giggling and blushing. ''You're incorrigible, you know.''

He reveled in her silliness, in her girlish response. It was so unlike the wary and guarded Angelina who had first come to Key West and so like the child he'd known in Cuba. At least their love had proven strong enough to overcome her fears and strip away her defensive attitude. He was happy to have given the innocent, trusting part of herself back to her.

Snuggling in his arms, she said, ''I know I'm being silly. I know you wouldn't deceive me. I trust you with my heart and soul.''

Holding her tightly, her words of love and trust should have been music to his ears, reaffirming how hard he'd struggled to win her, to reassure her of his abiding love and faithfulness. Unfortunately, with each day that passed, the shadow of his true identity cast a larger and larger pall over their relationship.

He'd toyed with keeping his identity a secret for the remainder of their lives, not wanting to reveal his deception. But he knew that was a pipe dream. One way or another, his identity would be revealed. And he wanted to be the one to tell her first.

But how and when? The two questions haunted his every waking hour and had begun to invade his sleep. He should have told her that first time during the hurricane, before they became intimate. Unfortunately, he hadn't wanted to spoil their perfect union. Now, looking back on it, he wondered if he'd been too big a coward to confess.

And the longer he waited, the worse it became. If he could kick himself, he would.

"About the Muñoz brothers," she murmured.

"Sí, mi esposa."

"You really must talk to them. The wrappers aren't what I ordered. They're thin and second-rate."

"I'll talk to them, I promise." And craven coward that he was, he ended their conversation by lifting her chin and lowering his lips to her luscious mouth.

Angelina bustled about the kitchen, humming to herself. The factory was doing well, and she'd treated herself to an afternoon off. With free time on her hands, she'd gone to visit Destiny.

They'd had a long talk, gossiping and laughing. When they went to the kitchen for a snack, Tilly had been cooking a gumbo. Fascinated by the spicy recipe, which included leftover vegetables and meat, she'd watched and learned how to make the hearty soup. Since today was Alicia's day off, she'd decided to prove her culinary talents in the kitchen.

It was amazing how love transformed a person, she thought. Before, she would have despised learning how to cook, wanting nothing to do with traditional female roles. Now she looked upon making dinner as a rare opportunity to please Rafael with her wifeliness.

The only shadow to an otherwise perfect day had come before she left for home. When she hugged Destiny in farewell, her friend had burst into tears and confessed her misery. They hadn't had time to visit in weeks, and it was the first she'd heard of Destiny's break with James Whitman.

Once her friend started talking, it all came pouring out: Whitman's disgusting behavior, Destiny's confrontation with her grandfather, the truth about her parents, her decision to become a teacher, and her love for Nathan and their brief liaison. She'd even tried to explain her refusal of Nathan's marriage proposal, although Angelina didn't know if she agreed with the decision.

Thinking of her friend's internal turmoil and juxtaposing it with her current happiness made her feel guilty. She wished there were something she could do to help Destiny. Some way she could advise her friend.

With her thoughts elsewhere, she reached for the lid to the rice pot, to see if the rice was steamed. The hot metal seared her hand. Dropping the lid, she jumped back and jammed her fingers into her mouth.

"¡Coño! ¡Maldita sea!"

The front door slammed and Rafael found her in the kitchen, seated at the table, holding her throbbing hand and bemoaning her stupidity.

"¿Qué pasa?" he asked, going to her side and pulling her into his arms.

Nestling in his comforting arms, she confessed, "I was trying to cook and burnt my hand. I feel so stupid. I know I'm not much of a cook, but I wanted to please you with—"

"Don't call yourself stupid, Angelina," he cut her off. "How many times do I have to tell you, you're the most intelligent person I know? And you do please me, *amorcita mía.* You please me very much. We have a cook, you don't need to—"

"It's Alicia's day off, and I learned a new recipe. I wanted to cook dinner for you."

"And I'm sure it will be delicious. You just need practice, that's all," he soothed. "Cooking is like anything else, an acquired skill." He reached for her right hand. "Here, let me see your fingers."

Slowly, she uncurled her fingers, revealing a deep red slash. He lowered his head and tenderly kissed the hurt away. She trembled. The touch of his lips on her flesh made her forget the burn. She wished he would continue kissing, up her arm, to her shoulder and beyond . . . .

But instead he lifted his head. "It's starting to blister. Do you have any lard?"

"Lard?" she repeated. "You mean the stuff you fry with? What do you want lard for?"

"You don't know?" He shook his head and grinned. "It's a remedy for burns."

Miffed because he'd stopped kissing her and was teasing her about her ignorance, she lifted her chin. "It's in that canister on the shelf by the stove."

He rose and fetched the canister. Then he dipped his fingers into the greasy gray mess. Angelina shuddered. It was all she could do to bring herself to cook with the animal fat. Before she had time to protest, he slathered the despicable stuff over her burn and wrapped her fingers with a soft dish towel.

Admiring his handiwork, he observed, "I don't think you'll be able to finish dinner. But it will be better by tomorrow, I promise."

She certainly hoped so. She'd taken the afternoon off because things were going well, but she'd left a pile of paperwork behind in the office. She needed her right hand to write with. Tentatively, she stretched her fingers. Despite her forebodings, the lard seemed to be working. It had already taken the sting away.

"Thank you. It already feels better. As for dinner, it's almost ready." Then she remembered what she'd been doing and leapt to her feet. "*El arroz,* Rafael! Get the rice. It must be burnt."

Crossing to the stove, he grabbed a towel and carefully removed the rice from the burner. Smoke curled from the open pot and the distinctive charred odor of burnt food assailed their nostrils.

"Oh, I knew it," she wailed. "It's ruined. You can't eat gumbo without rice. The dinner is ruined," she repeated.

"Don't worry. There's still plenty of rice left." He stirred the pot. "Only the rice on the bottom and sides is burnt." Lifting the lid to the other pot, he inhaled. "This smells wonderful. What did you say it was?"

"Gumbo. I went to visit Destiny this afternoon. Tilly was cooking gumbo, and she showed me how," she explained. "But I wanted it to be perfect for you. And I've made such a mess."

Pulling her into his arms, he murmured, "Nothing you ever do could be a mess. Don't you know that? To me, you're perfect."

"You're just saying that so I won't be upset," she sniffed.

"No, I'm not," he vowed, brushing kisses over her upturned face.

"You don't have to be nice. I would understand." His lips had found her earlobe, where he was nibbling expertly. She could feel her blood heating.

"I'm not being nice. I want to eat the dinner you made for me. Although," he growled in the back of his throat, "I seemed to have suddenly lost my appetite for food."

Understanding his meaning, she arched into his caresses. His tongue slid down her neck, leaving a trail of gooseflesh, making her heart accelerate.

"And I had something I wanted to talk to you about over dinner, too," she said, half taunting, knowing she didn't want him to stop. They could eat dinner anytime, whether it was burnt or not.

"About the factory?" His tongue had found the hollow of her throat. "Are the Muñoz brothers giving you trouble? I thought I set them straight." Circling her throat with the tip of his tongue, he laved her skin and then blew on it. She quaked, like a leaf tossed in a storm.

"Not about the factory," she managed. It was getting more and more difficult to concentrate. His hands came up and cupped her breasts. "It's about Destiny. She's fallen in love with Captain Rodgers. Oh!" She gasped as his thumbs rubbed the fabric of her gown over her nipples, setting up a delightful friction.

"*Díme,*" he prompted. His fingers had abandoned her aching, swollen breasts to part the buttons at her throat.

"She's fallen in love with Captain Rodgers," she repeated

with effort. He parted her gown and his tongue discovered the valley between her breasts. His lips and tongue, hot and wet, caressed her there, sending scintillating streamers of pleasure through her body.

"But that's good," he mumbled against her breasts. "Any fool can see how much he loves her."

"I know." Her simple statement became a groan as he found one nipple and suckled gently, bringing the filmy cloth of her chemise along with her heated flesh into the warm adhesion of his mouth. "But she refused his marriage proposal."

Using her good hand, she threaded her fingers through his thick, wavy hair, pulling his head down, silently begging for more, arching into the almost-painful ecstasy of his mouth at her breast.

Lifting his head from her breasts, he grinned wolfishly. "Why would she do that? Marriage is wonderful. I can vouch for that." As he spoke, one hand lifted her skirts, gliding up her thigh with feather-like strokes.

Shivering, she melted against him. Her bones felt liquefied, as if they couldn't support her weight. Clinging to him, she rained tiny kisses down his neck, lapping at the salty, spicy essence of him.

"Destiny thinks that . . . Oh, Rafael." His inquisitive fingers found the core of her being, insinuating themselves past her undergarment, touching her intimately. Moaning against his neck, she struggled to finish, "Destiny thinks Capitán Rodgers will feel second best because . . . because . . ."

He was using her own liquid heat to lave the center of her desire, rubbing and stroking. His mouth had found her breasts again. The burning ache flared, flaming higher, consuming her, stealing her reason.

Wanton and aflame, she bucked against his hand, pressing herself into the spiraling pleasure, giving herself over to the swollen, throbbing need. Her world shattered into a thousand tiny pieces, leaving only the shimmering bliss, the too-pure rapture.

They stood together, swaying, for several moments until she drifted back to earth. Astonished by their innovative lovemaking, she couldn't believe she'd just been transported to paradise in the middle of the kitchen.

Sweeping her into his arms, his voice was hoarse with passion. "I think we should retire to the bedroom. Don't you?"

Nodding, she curled herself against him, glowing in the aftermath but already looking forward to his expert efforts to arouse her desire again. With Rafael, it seemed she had an endless appetite for lovemaking.

Thinking about appetites made her remember. "Rafael, the gumbo! If we leave it, it will burn, too."

With a barely suppressed groan, he swung around. Lowering her to the floor, he found the towel he'd abandoned and grabbed the larger pot, pulling it off the stove. Turning to her, he demanded, "Satisfied?"

She arched one eyebrow and observed wryly, "More than satisfied. Although I could be enticed to—"

"Ven aca, mujer," he growled, taking her into his arms again.

Chapter Nineteen

Angelina approached slowly, cautiously, taking care not to make any sudden movements or to rush her pursuit. When she'd been cleaning Malvado's cage, the mynah bird had escaped. Now he was leading her on a merry chase around the tiny parlor. She prayed he wouldn't dart through the open window and fly away.

Edging sideways, she positioned herself between the bird and the window. He fluttered to the opposite side of the room and perched on a lamp. Flapping his wings, he settled and cocked his head. One garnet-red eye gleamed with interest, watching her every movement.

Whirling around, she grasped the window sash and pulled down hard. The old wood creaked and groaned, but finally slid into the casement with a dull thud. Triumphant, she pivoted quickly to find Malvado had advanced halfway across the room, landing on the back of the settee.

As if he understood she'd trapped him, he squawked and darted in a crazy zigzag path around the room, upsetting a hideous vase from the mantel. It fell to the floor with a loud crash, which only served to incite him to more frenzied flying and screeching.

He sailed past and she made a grab for him, netting several tail feathers. Further incensed by his loss of plumage, he soared to the ceiling, bumped his head, and ricocheted off the far wall, screaming imprecations at the top of his lungs.

Fast losing her patience, she cursed back, shaking her fist at him and trying to grab him as he flew around and around in a dizzying circle. After several minutes of their heated chase, Angelina leaned against the wall, dragging air into her lungs. Malvado perched on the mantel, his yellow bill wide open, as if he, too, were panting from their efforts.

They stared at each other, taking their opponent's measure, gathering themselves for the next round. She shook her head. It was always this way when he escaped; she had to chase him until he grew tired and allowed her to catch him.

Remembering that first day in Key West when he'd escaped at the harbor, she recalled how panicked she'd been. The thought of losing her bird had filled her with anguish. She'd felt so lost and alone, her only companion a foul-mouthed mynah bird. So much had happened since then. There had been pain and struggle in her new life, but from the pain had come a deep and abiding joy: her love for Rafael.

Thinking about it, her heart melted. Angry at Malvado a moment before, she found herself feeling fond affection for her pet. Maybe if she softened her approach and coaxed him . . .

The front door banged open, and the object of her new-found love, Rafael, strode into the foyer.

Wanting to throw herself into his arms but determined to catch her bird first, she called, "Rafael, *por favor,* close the door. Malvado is loose. I'm trying to catch him." Inclining her head toward the mantel, she indicated, "He's over there." Then she had an idea. "Maybe you could help. Could you move slowly from your side and drive him toward me?"

It was as if Rafael hadn't heard her suggestion. He stood stock still in the small foyer, his gaze trained on Malvado. The features of his face had tightened into a frown. And there was a strange expectancy there, too, as if he were waiting for something terrible to happen.

Then she remembered. He hated birds. If she hadn't seen it with her own eyes, she wouldn't have believed how intense his dislike was. She opened her mouth to withdraw the suggestion, but before she could say anything, Malvado shrieked and hopped from one foot to the other.

"Rafael Rivera, Rafael Rivera," the bird screeched across the taut silence. "Rafael Rivera *ama a* Angelita. *Te amo, te amo,* Angelita, *te amo.*" His yellow bill snapped shut and he preened, fluffing his feathers and appearing inordinately proud of himself.

Rafael reeled back a step, looking for all the world as if he'd been struck a blow. And then everything rushed through Angelina's mind at once. Bits and pieces fell into place, like a huge puzzle. Suddenly, everything made sense. Perfect but terrible sense. The feeling that she'd known Rafael from her prior life, the personal interest he'd taken in her, his willingness to marry her, the time he'd called her "Angelita," and his unnatural aversion to her bird—it all came together.

Rafael Rivera, her childhood friend, had brought the bird when he'd returned from school in Spain. On the voyage home, he'd taught the mynah bird to say that Rafael loved Angelita. She'd been away at a convent when he'd presented Malvado, but her father had kept the gift, obviously feeling the pet was harmless enough. When she came home from the convent, she'd been flattered by Malvado's recital of Rafael's love. Flattered but helpless to do anything, imprisoned in her father's house and his ambitious designs for her.

It had all been so long ago. She'd been little more than a child.

His treachery and deceit rushed over her, sucking her under a tidal wave of pain. Her throat contracted and her heart hammered. There was a roaring in her ears, and she felt very warm. Hot, in fact, red hot. Her face burned, thinking how he'd

deceived her, used her, and kept on lying to her despite their
intimacies. Hurt and hurting, her blood boiled, and her pain
became self-righteous fury.

Her vision narrowed to a pinpoint on his horrified face.
Raising her arms, she flew at him, fury spilling from her.
Reaching him in one gasp, she pounded his chest with her fists,
wanting to hurt him as he'd hurt her.

"You—you—you lying, conniving scoundrel! You misbe-
gotten pile of dung! I hate you! I hate you!" she screamed at
the top of her lungs.

Standing like a stone statue, he took her blows, never moving,
not even flinching. His face had turned to stone, too, she noticed
through the red cloud of her rage. When she tired of hitting
him and her fury had turned to a cold, hard lump of despair,
she sank slowly to the floor at his feet, crying uncontrollably.

He reached down to lift her up, but she shook his hands off,
sliding across the floor to keep him from touching her. She
didn't want him to touch her. She couldn't stand it. Not that,
not his touch. Thinking of all the times he'd touched her and
of all the places, rage blossomed again in her heart, growing
like a poisonous flower.

Laboriously, panting and heaving, with perspiration streaming from her body, she levered herself off the floor. Swaying
on her feet, she took several uncertain steps and dropped onto
the settee, weary and exhausted, drained and barren.

Malvado, the cause of all the commotion, chattered and
fluttered. As if realizing their attention had shifted from him,
he quit the mantel, darting like an arrow through the open
bedroom door and docilely entering his cage.

It took an effort of will to lift her head and look at Rafael.
Her eyes burned in their sockets, giving her a pounding headache. With morbid fascination, she studied his features, seeking
her childhood friend. He'd been but a half-grown youth when
he left for Spain, and because of her father she hadn't seen
him since. And half of his face was disfigured. It was strange,
but she'd come to ignore his disfigurement. Now it blotted out

all that was familiar to her, mirroring his twisted mind and soul.

Because only a twisted mind and soul could have whispered words of adoration and made glorious, passionate love to her without revealing his true identity.

"¿Por qué?" The mundane, everyday question escaped her lips.

How trite it sounded, given the circumstances, she thought. How trite and inadequate to encompass the situation.

He shuffled his feet, started forward, thought better of it, and stood his ground. His voice was so soft, she had to strain to hear it. "I don't think this is the time or the place, Angelina. You've had quite a shock, and you need to do some sorting out. I think we should—"

"And I think we should talk about it," she cut him off. "I think you've lied for long enough. More than long enough. You've had plenty of time to tell me who you were. But you didn't want to tell me. No, you clung to your deceit, didn't you? You even made up that silly lie about hating birds to avoid Malvado, didn't you?" The words rushed out of her. Taking a breath, she continued, "You were afraid Malvado would reveal your identity, just as he did today, weren't you?"

Sighing, he admitted, *"Sí,* Angelina, you're right about everything."

"Which brings us back to my original question. Why?"

This time, he moved forward. Stopping within centimeters of her, he asked, "May I sit down?"

"It's your house. Make yourself comfortable," she offered sarcastically.

Wincing at her tone, he didn't reply. Then he lowered himself into a chair across from her. "It's a long story," he remarked.

"I have all the time in the world." Try as she might, she couldn't keep the sarcasm from her voice.

He covered his face with his hands. She recognized it as a gesture of both despair and resignation. Thinking herself hardened to his manipulative ways, she was surprised to feel her heart squeeze in response. Pushing away her feeling of sympathy, she concentrated on his deception. On all the lies he'd told her since that first time they'd met on Frances Street.

She hated deceit. Hated all its forms and manifestations. She'd loved and trusted her father completely. She'd followed him around from the time she was old enough to toddle, like a pet dog, willing to do anything to win his admiration and love. Pitted against a houseful of brothers, it had been a formidable task.

Going against her natural instincts, she'd taken an interest in the things that interested him: cigar making and business. Even though her culture frowned on females who involved themselves in commerce, her father had seemed flattered and excited by her interest. When she was young, he'd encouraged her.

But with the onset of her puberty, he'd changed dramatically. He'd packed her off to a convent and guarded her like a rare jewel—but a jewel that was a possession, a thing, no longer a person. It had been as if the blossoming of her body had transformed her into a commodity to be bartered and sold.

At first, she'd been bewildered by her father's changed behavior. Over time, she'd painfully become aware that he'd deceived her. Lied and misled her, making her feel wanted for herself, for her quick intelligence and ambitions, only to relegate her to a shelf. Where she was displayed and viewed by wealthy men, to further her father's ambitions and dreams, not her own.

Until now, her father's deception had been the most hideous of crimes. The most heinous delusion of all, making her wary and distrustful of men. Until she'd opened her heart to Rafael.

And he'd crushed her. Crushed her and stomped her heart to dust with his deceit. But why? The question echoed in her soul, reverberating, keeping time with her pounding heart, repeating itself like a crazed mantra, pulsing through her veins.

To wed her and bed her, came the ugly answer. To bind her to him physically, using her as a thing, just as her father had wanted to use her. To use her as a concubine until he tired of her body. Recalling the scene on the terrace at the ball, she remembered his violent passion and the tearing of her bodice.

When she'd fought him and pushed him away, he'd changed his behavior, becoming gentle and caring. Deception and deceit, piled upon lies and untruths—those had been his tools and weapons. And to have belatedly admitted who he was, when he hadn't confessed in the first place, would have undermined the new credibility he'd cultivated with her.

And she'd fallen into his hands like a ripe mango. His rescue of her and their sham marriage had proven particularly fortuitous. After all, they weren't really married. Not by the church, only by an arid, meaningless ceremony, performed by a faceless cleric. If her parents knew the full circumstances, they wouldn't recognize the marriage.

Recalling that first morning in Key West and her naive boast to Destiny that she would take lovers to amuse herself, she shriveled inside. What a fool she'd been. What an innocent, stupid little fool.

Lifting her head, she thrust her chin out. At least she had her factory now. Nothing and nobody could take that from her. Let Rafael or Cortez try. She'd take them to court, fighting all the way, defaming them and revealing them for what they were.

The factory had cost her more than she had ever dreamed. Cost her pieces of her heart and soul. There would be no more stupid boasting on her part. She would quietly savor her financial independence and freedom from men. She'd learned her lesson the hard way, giving her trust, only to be deceived and used.

Never again.

Rafael uncovered his face and gazed at her, his eyes filled with pleading. She registered his gaze but wasn't affected by his silent plea.

"Are you ready to hear what I have to say?" he asked. "To try and understand why I didn't tell you who I was?"

She nodded, but her heart felt like a brick wedged inside her body. A cold, hard brick, unmoved by his words. She'd asked

for this. The reason he'd deceived her. But that had been another
Angelina. An Angelina in love, a trusting Angelina, who
believed in the joy of life and loving her husband. That Angelina
had just died, moments before.

Having demanded an explanation, she decided she must listen
to him. Shrugging to herself, she realized it didn't matter. She
understood now. Understood everything. Let him lie and twist
the facts. What did it matter? A few more minutes couldn't
hurt.

"I better start at the beginning." His voice wavered. "It
was a long time ago, the beginning."

Polite but distant, she repeated woodenly, *"Sí,* a long time
ago."

"We were only children when I went away, Angelita."

"Don't call me that."

Drawing his hand through his hair, he agreed, "As you wish.
I won't call you that."

"Bueno. ¿Y?" she prompted.

"I realize we were only children, but I loved you. I never
stopped loving you. That's why I brought the mynah bird back
with me. I didn't know if I would have the courage to tell you,
so I taught Malvado to say the words for me." He grimaced,
admitting, "It was foolish of me, I guess, but I was young and
shy and—"

"Basta," she interrupted.

"Lo siento," he apologized. "I brought the bird, and your
father sent me away, telling me not to come again," he continued. "You were at a convent. I still hoped, though. Dreamed
that one day I would see you again. I prayed Malvado would
give you my message and you would wait for me."

Pausing, he lowered his voice to a whisper, anguish reverberating in each word. "Years passed, and it became obvious your
father wouldn't relent. I tried several times to see you, only to
be turned away. I had to go on with my life."

His voice caught. "My parents had expectations, too. They
arranged a marriage for me. Being a dutiful son and having

lost hope . . .'' He took a deep breath. ''I followed my parents' wishes and married.'' As if in answer to her unspoken thoughts, he added, ''I'm a widower. My wife died three years ago.''

Recoiling before she could stop herself, she felt somehow betrayed. So he'd married, even though he'd pledged undying love for her. How could he think she would believe him? More lies, more deceit, to soften her. But she wouldn't be softened, she vowed to herself.

''Were you happy?'' she asked stiffly, hating herself for wanting to know. Shifting on the settee, she crossed her arms, willing herself not to care.

''After a fashion,'' he admitted. ''My wife was very young and naive. She didn't . . .'' He stopped himself, shaking his head. ''I can't talk about this, Angelina. It's not fair to her memory.''

Not fair, she thought to herself. What was fair? Had anyone been fair to her? But if he wanted to posture and appear to honor his dead wife's memory, let him. What did she care?

''Yo entiendo. Forget that I asked the question.''

He glanced at her, sideways, from beneath his eyelids. To gauge her reaction, no doubt. Hoping he'd struck a sympathetic chord. Her heart hardened at his maneuvering. Let him hope. He'd deceived her one time too many.

Never again, she repeated to herself.

''We had a child, a daughter. I became involved with the Cuban revolutionary movement against Spain,'' he explained as if the two things went together. ''The Spanish officials found me out. They burned my house down. My daughter and wife were inside.''

She gasped. She couldn't help herself. The old Angelina would have gone to him. Would have put her arms around him and held him, absorbing his pain as if it were her own. But the new Angelina couldn't afford such a luxury of feeling. Never again.

''I got there too late.'' His voice resonated with unresolved torment, vibrated with guilt and anguish. ''I tried to save them, but it was too late," he repeated, touching his scarred face. "The fire caught me, burning me. Friends pulled me from the fire. I hated them." His voice rose and caught. "Hated them," he repeated. "I wanted them to let me die, too."

"But you didn't die."

"Not physically, no. While I was recovering, I had a great deal of time on my hands. I thought about what had happened and my part in it. I still wanted freedom from Spain. It's the natural course for Cuba." He paused before continuing, "But I realized there are many ways to win freedom. Before, I had believed violence was the only way, outright rebellion and war. Having suffered the consequences of violence, I changed my mind. There had to be other ways, peaceful ways."

"So you left Cuba and came to Key West?"

"*Sí*. I needed to start a new life. I took my present position, knowing it would afford me the opportunity to stop illegal armaments from flowing into Cuba and fostering more violence. But I haven't stopped fighting for Cuba's freedom. There are other ways—peaceful demonstrations, pamphlets, speeches. I support them all."

"And you think those methods will work?"

"I don't know." He shrugged. "It's all I know to do without sacrificing more innocent lives . . ."

Rising, she interrupted, "It's been very interesting, Rafael. But it doesn't change what has happened between us. I wish you luck with your—"

"*Espérate, por favor,*" he tried to stop her, rising, too. "I haven't explained why I didn't tell you who I was."

She made a dismissive gesture with her hand. "It's not important."

"But it is important," he breathed. "At least, it's important to me." He touched his disfigured face again, confessing, "I didn't tell you who I was, Angelina, because I thought you would pity me." His cinnamon-colored eyes begged for understanding.

Avoiding his eyes, she folded her hands, waiting for him to finish.

"I didn't want you to pity me. When I recognized you, it was as if I were seeing a goddess, a beautiful and desirable goddess, far above me. If I had told you who I was, you would have felt obligated to care about me. I wanted you to desire me for myself, despite my . . . my . . ."

"Disfigurement?"

"*Sí.*" His shoulders slumped.

"You couldn't have trusted me?"

"I was a fool. A proud fool."

"You weren't the only fool, Rafael," she observed pointedly.

"Then you understand?"

"I think I understand only too well. Unfortunately, my understanding is very different from yours."

"I should have told you," he admitted, moving toward her, his hand outstretched. "I see that now. And I wanted to tell you, countless times. But I was a coward."

Ignoring his gesture, she drew herself up. "I want an annulment. I realize our marriage was only a clerical formality, but I want that erased."

He dropped his hand. *"Yo entiendo."*

"I think you should return to the quarters behind your office until the annulment is final. I'll be seeking new lodgings as well."

Lifting his head, he gazed at her, a painful yearning brimming in his eyes. "If that's what you want."

"That's what I want."

Rafael tossed and turned on his narrow bed. The night was waning, and he hadn't managed even a few moments of sleep. His thoughts had circled all night long, following tortuous paths, tormenting him with questions for which there were no answers. The more he thought about hiding his identity, the more he realized he couldn't have handled it any other way. But there was that nagging voice, telling him otherwise, insinuating that he would still possess Angelina's love if only he'd confessed who he was.

What would it have mattered if she had pitied me? Wouldn't love naturally follow with time? An abiding love, free of secrets and deceit, free to grow over the years together?

Rolling over, he punched the pillow and then flung it from the bed. Second-guessing what he should have done wouldn't change anything. He'd chosen the wrong path and lost her love. It was as simple as that. And as barren and desolate. How ironic that he'd lost the love of his life, not once, but twice.

Groaning, he threw his arm up to cover his eyes. The first light of dawn crept through the single dirty window. The thought of facing another lonely, meaningless day filled him with despair. If he thought his life had been empty before . . .

After his confession and Angelina's decision, they'd spent the night in their separate bedrooms. He hadn't slept that night, either. His eyes were gritty with fatigue, but his mind wouldn't stop spinning. Before yesterday's dawn, he'd gathered his meager belongings and moved to his office. Throwing himself into work, he'd managed to get through the day. But another day yawned before him. And then there would be another and another, a deadly procession of hopelessness to face.

And for what? For what reason?

He thought he heard something. Sitting up, he strained his ears. The noise might be coming from the docks. The loading and unloading of ships started with the dawn. Then he heard it again, and it wasn't coming from the wharf. Someone was knocking on his office door. But who would come so early?

His heart soared. Could it be Angelina? Had she changed her mind? Had she decided to forgive him? Frantic that she might change her mind again, he grabbed his pants and pulled them on. Shrugging into his shirt, he didn't take the time to button it before racing through his office.

With his heart in his throat, he threw open the outer door. Captain Nathan Rodgers stood on the threshold. Rafael's heart

plummeted, and his stomach clenched. He suddenly felt nauseated, as if he might be sick. When was the last time he'd eaten?
He couldn't remember.

Rodgers brushed past him, directing, "Close the door,
Estava. I came early to avoid being seen." His gaze swept
Rafael's disheveled state. "Sorry to have awakened you, but
it was urgent."

"How did you know where to find me?"

"I almost came last night. Saw your lantern burning late,
but I was waiting for a final dispatch. I had a hunch you'd be
here this morning." His words were nonchalant, but his hazel
eyes held a question. A question Rafael didn't want to answer.

The time had come to spring the trap, Rafael realized. That
was why Rodgers had come. And it couldn't have come at a
better moment. His life was worthless now. He no longer
dreaded facing an enemy and possible death. On the contrary,
the idea was oddly freeing. No more tortured thoughts, no more
second-guessing, and no more empty days and nights.

"When?" he asked.

"Tomorrow before dawn," Rodgers replied. "Can you
spend the night here again?"

Rafael laughed, an ugly bark of a laugh. "I'll be here."

The captain peered at him, started to say something, and
then shook his head. He wondered how much Rodgers surmised.
Rafael remembered Angelina trying to tell him something about
Rodgers and Destiny, something about their star-crossed love.
At the time, he hadn't paid any attention, being engrossed in
more compelling matters. Like the taste of Angelina's skin and
the feel of her arms wrapped around his neck . . .

Remembering, he bit back a groan. "What do I need to
bring?"

"Do you have a carbine?"

"Yes, but it's a single-shot."

"Then I'll supply you with one. Bring your sidearms if you
have them."

"I have a new Colt revolver and a military sword."

"Good. Bring those. The fighting may be hand-to-hand. There's no way to know for certain."

"I understand."

Rodgers clapped him on the shoulder. "Tomorrow before dawn."

"I'll be ready."

Nathan nodded. Cracking the door, he looked outside and then slipped through the opening.

Angelina twisted the cord to her reticule, knotting it around her fingers until it bit into her flesh. Releasing it, she found herself twisting it again. It was a nervous gesture, she realized. She hated facing Rafael. But she'd thought about it for two days and three nights, and this was the only way. The sooner she faced him and got it over with, the sooner she could resume her life.

She walked a little faster, rehearsing what she would say, wanting to put the confrontation behind her. Anticipating his reaction, her anxiety mounted. Forcing herself to take a deep breath, she glanced around, trying to relax. It was a fine day, bright and sunny. She should be at the factory, but first she had to see Rafael.

Staying up the past three nights, she'd gone over and over the income and expenses for the factory until her eyes burned. But in a way, her late nights had been a blessing. When she'd finally gone to bed, she'd been unable to sleep. And she'd given Alicia her notice, too. Food held no appeal for her, and it was frivolous to keep a cook for just herself. Besides, she planned on moving to a boardinghouse at the end of the month.

Her sleeplessness and lack of appetite had surprised her. She'd thought herself well rid of Rafael. At least that was what her mind told her. But not her heart. Her heart, silly and willful creature that it was, yearned for him, making her life a misery, turning her days and nights upside down. That was why she was desperate to make a complete break. After seeing Rafael, she would go to the magistrate's office and inquire about an annulment.

But she must rid her factory of the debt she owed him. Like the note she'd signed with Cortez, she would sign one with Rafael, promising to pay him with interest in a year's time. And if Cortez returned, she would pay him, too, she vowed. Anything to own her factory free and clear, to be independent and beholding to no man.

It was the dream that had brought her to Key West. It was the dream that would sustain her.

Once she repaid Rafael, obtained her annulment, and moved from the rented house that held so many memories, surely she would be free. Surely, her heart would heal and she could resume the life she'd envisioned for herself.

Clutching her reticule tightly, she wished it so. Wished to eradicate every trace of Rafael from her life. But Key West was a small place, a voice in the back of her mind warned. And with Destiny leaving for school, her life stretched empty and bleak before her.

Lifting her head, she thrust her chin forward. She could do it, though. She could overcome anything. After a year or so, Destiny would come home. And it would take a great deal of hard work to make her factory successful while repaying Rafael. Hard work was the key. She would work so hard, she wouldn't have time to think about anything else.

The wharf loomed into view, filled with the bustle of ships going and coming. Passengers stood in knots, waiting with their luggage. Porters and dock workers scurried about, dragging heavily laden carts across the wharf and up and down gangplanks. Turning the corner, she saw the sign hanging over Rafael's door: "Medrano and Company, Ship Underwriters."

A lump rose to her throat. A knot formed in her breast where her heart should be. Closing her eyes for a second, she gathered herself, willing herself to remain calm and detached, counseling herself that this was just a business transaction, nothing more.

Finding herself in front of his office, she took a deep breath and twisted the doorknob. But the brass knob resisted her pressure. It was obviously locked. Had she come too late? Had Rafael already gone to an auction? Auctions were held in the afternoon, she knew. And he usually did his paperwork in the mornings. She'd expected him to be in the office.

Deflated and feeling uncommonly betrayed, she went to the one grimy window and tried to peer inside. The accumulation of dirt on the windowpane defeated her. She couldn't see anything. Maybe he hadn't opened for the day. Maybe he was in the back. After all, he lived behind his office now.

Returning to the door, she pounded on its wooden surface, calling out, "Rafael, are you in there? It's Angelina. I must see you."

Stepping back, she waited, listening for sounds of movement from within. But she waited in vain. The office remained as quiet and still as a tomb.

Exasperated, she raised her fist to pound on the door again. Before she could deliver another blow, the door on the right opened and a man stepped from the next-door office. His face looked familiar, but she couldn't remember his name. She might have met him at the ball and danced with him, but she wasn't certain.

He held out his hand, presenting himself, "I'm Gerald O'Hara, merchant. I believe we've met before, Miss Herrera, at the Browns' ball."

Lowering her fisted hand, she accepted the handshake. It was obvious he didn't know about her marriage to Rafael. He'd called her by her maiden name. And she didn't care to rectify the situation. She would soon be Angelina Herrera again.

"Yes, I remember, Señor O'Hara. It's nice to see you again. I'm sorry if I disturbed you, but I was looking for Señor Estava. Have you seen him?"

"If I knew such a pretty lady was looking for me," he drawled, his gaze sweeping her, "I'd be waiting in my office with bells on."

Bridling at his effrontery and innuendo, she drew herself up.

Frost crept into her voice despite the polite words she offered, "That's very kind of you to say, Señor O'Hara. But my matter is urgent. Have you seen Señor Estava?" she asked again. "Or do you know where he's gone?"

"Well, if you put it that way . . ." He paused and stared pointedly at her bosom. Lifting his eyes, he smiled broadly. "I know it's early, but would you have lunch with me?"

Despising his lecherous intent and barely veiled blackmail, she wished for Rafael and his strong arms to shield her from . . . She shook her head, stopping herself. She couldn't look to Rafael for protection any longer. She was on her own. It was up to her to put this man in his place.

"I'm afraid I must go then, if you can't help me." She purposely ignored his offer of an early lunch. "I own a cigar factory on Frances Street, and I'm needed there."

Turning to go, she was surprised when he grabbed her elbow, saying, "Wait. I think I can help you. Although I wish you would reconsider about lunch."

"I think not." She shook off his grasp.

He exhaled his breath, capitulating, "I saw Estava leave before dawn with Captain Rodgers. I hope the information helps you, and you'll reconsider my offer for lunch. I'm available most days. Come and see me."

"Thank you," she replied stiffly, "for the information." Tossing her head, she threw over her shoulder, "But don't expect me for lunch, Señor O'Hara."

She walked away briskly, wanting to put distance between herself and his oily presence. Depressed at not finding Rafael and having to deflect O'Hara's advances, she realized this was what an unmarried woman in Key West faced: men making unwanted propositions. Her future was getting bleaker by the minute.

Sighing to herself, she hated Rafael for his deceit. Why couldn't he have told her who he was? She would have accepted him with open arms and not from pity. Not from pity at all. She'd loved him as a child, with a child's heart. And as a woman, she'd been attracted to him despite his scars. If he'd only been honest with her, they could have made a life together.

A sob caught in her throat, and she dashed the tears from her eyes. What a waste, what an awful, ugly waste.

And where was he? Gone off with Captain Rodgers before dawn. It didn't make sense. Why would he go off with the captain? She remembered the time Captain Rodgers had come to their house, before the hurricane, and Rafael had taken him outside to talk. And then there was the time, after the hurricane, when she'd found Rodgers in his office. She'd wondered what he was doing there, but Rafael had deflected her with his kisses.

What business could he possibly have with a captain of the United States Navy? Why all the secret meetings?

Then she remembered Rafael's vow to bring Cortez to justice, no matter what it took. She remembered how he'd warned her about Cortez's nefarious activities. How Rafael suspected Cortez of purposely wrecking ships and killing people for the cargo. It all came back to her.

Could he have joined forces with Captain Rodgers to bring Cortez to justice? The thought made sense. Too much sense. Her stomach knotted, thinking of the danger.

Her factory forgotten, she entered Duval Street. Panic gripped her, making her feet fly. Only her friend, Destiny, might be able to help. Destiny loved Captain Rodgers, although she'd refused his marriage proposal. But they'd been intimate. If anyone knew what Rafael and Rodgers were doing together, it would be Destiny.

Chapter Twenty

Angelina brushed past Rufus when he opened the door to Destiny's home. Without thinking, she ran for the stairs as if she still lived there and called out, "Destiny, are you up there? Destiny, it's Angelina. I need to talk to you."

Glimpsing Rufus's startled expression from the corner of her eye, she stopped and turned, explaining, "I must see Destiny. And it's urgent. Is she at home? Please forgive me for rushing in."

Rufus shook his grizzled head but gave her a sly grin. "Dat's all right, Miz Angelina. Ah unerstands. The missus, she be 'ere. And dis still be lahk your home. You g'wan up."

Tossing him a grateful smile, she gathered her skirts in one hand and raced up the stairs. Throwing Destiny's bedroom door open, she found her friend, oblivious to the commotion below, seated at her vanity, staring into the mirror.

Startled by the opening of the door, Destiny whirled around, facing her. Her eyes widened and Angelina saw how red they were. She'd been crying again, Angelina guessed.

But her friend's momentary joy was apparent when she rose

from the vanity bench and ran to her, hugging her. "Angelina, I'm so glad you've come. I didn't expect you. I know how busy you are at the factory."

Breaking their embrace, Destiny stepped back, admitting, "I dreaded another day alone." Taking Angelina's hands in her own, she smiled. "But now you've come. You don't know how much that means to me. Have breakfast with me? Tilly will bring a tray. It will be like old times."

Angelina shook her head. "I'm sorry, but this isn't a social call. And I've been up for hours. I've already eaten."

It was a lie. She had barely managed to choke down a cup of coffee. Why was she lying to her friend? She who hated deceit in all its forms. Because her pride had dictated that she do so?

Was that why Rafael had lied to her? Because of pride? He'd said he didn't want her pity. That had been pride, she realized. Had she judged him too harshly? People told small lies to cover their flaws and vulnerabilites. Why couldn't she accept it and understand?

Because his lie hadn't been a small one.

She recalled all the times she'd lied when she first came to Key West: first to Destiny, then to Rafael, and finally to Cortez. She'd hated lying then, as she did now, but she'd lied to save herself, to survive.

But Rafael hadn't lied to save himself. He'd deceived her without reasonable cause, and his deceit went to the heart of their relationship, tore at the very foundation of their love. If she couldn't trust him, there could be no love. Could there?

Shaking her head, she admitted, "No, that's not true. I haven't eaten breakfast, Destiny. But I couldn't choke down a morsel, even of Tilly's cooking."

Her friend's face fell. "What's wrong? Tell me." Taking her hands again, Destiny led her to the big four-poster bed where they'd spent many an hour gossiping and pouring their hearts out to each other. "Please, sit down. It must be something terrible to bring you this early.'' Destiny sat beside her, keeping one arm around her waist.

The tears that wouldn't come before spilled over, streaming down her face. Half-blinded, she groped in her reticule for a handkerchief. But Destiny forestalled her, retrieving one from the pocket of her dressing gown. With her friend's comforting arms around her, she finally let herself go. All the stone-cold misery that had lodged in her chest and the back of her throat broke loose, like a dam bursting, flooding her with grief and regrets.

And Destiny, good and true friend that she was, just held her in her arms, letting her sob like an orphaned child. When the tears slowed and her sobs turned into dry gulps, she lifted her head from Destiny's shoulder and blew her nose into the already-sodden handkerchief.

She remembered all the times Destiny had cried in her arms. But this was the first time she'd allowed herself that luxury. Before, she'd been too busy being strong, keeping her wits about her, and not allowing herself to be vulnerable. That was a form of pride, too, she recognized. Only with Rafael had she opened herself completely. And that was why it hurt so much now. To have opened herself, only to be betrayed again.

Sniffing and dabbing at her eyes, she confessed, ''Rafael and I have separated. I want to end our marriage because he lied to me.''

''Oh, Angelina, no. You were so happy together. What could he have lied about that would—?''

''He's the childhood sweetheart I told you about,'' she interjected. ''The one who gave me Malvado. I didn't recognize him because I was so young when he went away and because his face was scarred. He recognized me, but he didn't let on. He married me and we made love. And all the time, he kept his identity from me.'' Her chin trembled. She didn't want to break into fresh tears. Tearing at the soaked handkerchief, she twisted it in her hands.

Destiny took a deep breath, offering, ''But he must have had a good reason. I know he loves you. Did he tell you why he kept his identity a secret?''

''Yes, he told me he was afraid I would pity him because of his scars. That he wanted me to care for him as he was now, not because of our past relationship.''

''And you didn't believe him?''

''What does it matter if I believe him? He lied to me once, and he can lie again.'' Turning to her friend, she said, ''Don't you see, he betrayed me in the worst way possible. I can never trust him.''

''I see.'' Then, as if to herself, ''I wonder how Rafael is feeling, knowing he destroyed your love? It must be terrible for him.''

Angelina stared at Destiny, hurt that her friend would be feeling empathy for Rafael after what he'd done. But gazing into her friend's ravaged face, she understood. Destiny felt that she'd destroyed Captain Rodgers's love. And she was slowly destroying herself for it.

Did Rafael feel the same remorse, the same awful guilt? It hadn't occurred to her before. She'd been too busy licking her own wounds. Seeing her friend's anguish clearly for the first time, she realized what an awful burden it must be.

But Destiny loved Captain Rodgers and regretted losing him. Did Rafael feel the same way? Did he regret losing her? She remembered the misery etched in his features when she'd asked for an annulment. But he hadn't fought her decision. He'd accepted quietly and went away. She'd thought he didn't care. That he'd accomplished his objective of having her. Now she wasn't so certain.

Rising, she paced the room, twisting the handkerchief into a knot. ''I don't know if it's terrible for him, Destiny. And even if it is, I don't think I can forgive him.'' Stopping, she faced her friend. ''But I didn't come this morning to tell you about the end of my marriage. I came because of another matter. Something you might be able to help me with.''

"I should have known it wasn't about your personal life." Destiny folded her hands in her lap.

"What do you mean?"

"Just that you're so strong and capable, you don't need anyone, even when you're hurting. Or you pretend not to. You probably would have waited until you had the annulment before you told me."

Her friend's words cut her like a knife. Was that how she seemed? It wasn't very flattering, hearing it from Destiny. Although, if she were honest with herself, she knew that she'd purposely projected an aura of invulnerability to face the challenges of her new life. But she'd never meant to shut Destiny out. Had she seemed that way to Rafael, too? Had she appeared unapproachable to him? Was that why he'd been afraid to confess his identity?

"I'm sorry, Angelina." Destiny sighed. "Sometimes I envy your strength. Other times, I wish . . ." She shook her head.

"Don't." She crossed the room and took Destiny by the shoulders, kissing her cheek. "I know I've been . . . hard sometimes. But don't you see, I needed to be. I came to a new country, not knowing anyone. And I wanted to be free of men. A difficult thing to do when they hold all the power and money." Releasing her, she stepped back. "But I need you now, Destiny. And not just for what I'm about to ask." Pausing, she admitted, "I'm glad I came and told you about Rafael."

Seating herself beside Destiny again, she said, "You've helped me more than you know, *amiga mía*. I needed to cry but couldn't. Because you understood and offered your love, I was able to let go." Taking her friend's hands, she vowed, "I'll never shut you out again. I need you. The thought of your going away to school fills me with dread and . . ."

"Oh, Angelina." Destiny's arms went around her and they hugged again. "That's what I wanted to hear. You need people. You know it. And you need Rafael. Try to understand why he didn't tell you who he was. Don't throw your love away."

She pulled away and gazed directly into her friend's eyes,

asking softly, "Shouldn't you take your own advice, *amiga mía?* Accept Capitán Rodgers. Forget the past. He loves you."

It was Destiny's turn to rise and pace. Angelina watched her dear friend, understanding the soul-searching she was going through.

Understanding only too well.

Could she forget the past, as she advised her friend to do? Could she give Rafael a second chance, as she pled with Destiny to do? Seeing herself through Destiny's eyes was a revelation. A rude awakening. Had she appeared so unbending, so invulnerable, that Rafael had despaired of telling her who he was? Had she unknowingly played a pivotal part in the deception?

She closed her eyes. Thinking of Rafael, she knew how badly she wanted him and his love. Life without someone to love was arid and bleak. Success and financial security weren't enough, she realized. She needed to love and be loved in return. Rafael had shown her caring and affection. He'd always been there for her. And he'd always loved her. Except for not telling her who he was, she couldn't fault him.

And she shouldn't compare him to her father. That wasn't fair. Her father had betrayed her to further his own ambitions, not caring what she wanted or needed. Rafael wasn't like that. He'd made her needs a priority, wanting her to be happy.

Then she remembered what had brought her to Destiny. Her stomach clenched. Her heart beat double-time, and she began to perspire.

What if Rafael and Captain Rodgers were in mortal danger? Had she thrown away her only chance for happiness? Had Destiny done the same? Was it too late?

Rising, she said, "Destiny, look at me."

Her friend obeyed, stopping her pacing.

"Listen, this is important. Whether you want to accept Capitán Rodgers or not, I came because I'm afraid he and Rafael are in danger."

Destiny's expressive eyes went wide in her face. "Wha—what do you mean, in danger?"

"I don't know for certain. I thought you might help me. I hoped that Capitán Rodgers might have said or done something to provide you a clue."

Rushing on, she explained, "I went to Rafael's office early this morning, and his next-door neighbor told me that he left with your Nathan before dawn. I wondered why. And then I remembered the two times Capitán Rodgers came to Rafael, once at our house and once at his office. Both times, Rafael was secretive about their meetings, but looking back, I wonder if they could have been plotting together.

"The reason for their plotting would be Cortez," she continued. "I know Rafael wanted to stop him. He claimed Cortez was causing wrecks and killing people to take their cargo. But he couldn't stop Cortez by himself. He would need the authorities to do so. Could he have come to your Nathan for help? Would your grandfather know?"

Destiny opened her mouth to speak and then closed it. Her brow furrowed as if she were trying to remember something. Then her hands flew to her face and she grimaced. "The map. The map. I saw it in Nathan's cabin and asked about it. But he rolled it up and put me off."

Sinking into a chair, she said, "It was a map of Alligator Reef. That's where a lot of wrecks happen. The currents are especially treacherous there." Lifting her head, she gazed at Angelina. "They must have set a trap there for Cortez. Now I understand the lines and curious notations on the map. Nathan was setting a trap."

Angelina's stomach knotted tighter, squeezing like a vise. She couldn't seem to gulp enough air into her starving lungs. Her suspicions were confirmed. Rafael and Captain Rodgers had gone to confront Cortez. And they might die.

Memories rushed at her, pummeling her. Memories of her childhood with Rafael. Memories of their married life. Sweet memories, beguiling memories. She couldn't face life without Rafael, she realized. To have loved him and lost him twice was too horrible to contemplate.

Destiny rose, gasping, "I won't let him die. I can't let him die. I love him. Please, dear Lord, let him be safe." She locked her gaze with Angelina's. "We can't let them die. It will be too late."

"I know," she breathed.

"I'll get Gramps. He'll know what to do." Destiny ran from the room, leaving Angelina trembling with fear.

Rising on tiptoe, Destiny fitted her grandfather's spyglass to one eye and scanned the horizon. Angelina, standing beside her, tugged at her elbow, impatient.

Lowering the telescope with a sigh, Destiny said, "Nothing in sight." Holding out the glass, she offered, "Here, you take a look."

Stepping back from the attic window, Destiny shut her eyes. The waiting was horrible. She hated waiting, having nothing to do but worry and fret. Each moment dragged by as if shackled to the weight of the world. She remembered the other time she'd stood waiting, consumed with fear. The time Angelina had been abducted and Nathan had gone to rescue her friend. This time, she stood beside Angelina, waiting for Nathan, worried for his safety.

If you'll return him to me safely, dear Lord, she prayed, *I'll never let him go again,* she vowed. *I'll love him and take care of him and stand by his side forever. Only let him come home safely, dear Lord. And watch over Gramps, too, and make him keep his promise,* she added.

When she'd told her grandfather about their suspicions, he'd swung into action, alerting his wrecking crew and having the schooner readied. He'd agreed with her that Nathan and Rafael had probably set a trap for Cortez at Alligator Reef. Spoiling for action, he wanted to see the trap sprung.

It had taken copious tears and frantic pleas to convince him to stay clear of the fighting. As worried as she was about Nathan, she'd never forgive herself if she sent her grandfather into danger. Finally, he'd yielded, promising not to take part in the fighting, only to see if their suspicions were correct and bring news.

He'd been gone three hours, just long enough, by her reckoning, to have reached Alligator Reef and come home. If he'd been blown off course or had stopped to help survivors, it might be hours before he'd be back. She didn't know how much longer she could wait without tearing her hair out by the roots and screaming.

She and Angelina had paced downstairs and then in her bedroom, fortified only by Tilly's rich coffee. Then she'd had an idea and brought Angelina to the attic. After the hurricane, her grandfather had repaired the roof and wanted to replace the widow walk. She'd convinced him not to rebuild the walk because it held so many bitter memories for her. Instead, he used this attic window, which had opened onto the walk, as his private observation post.

Angelina lowered the spyglass. Handing Destiny the glass, she fisted her hands and rubbed at her eyes, commenting, "The glare from the sea is so bright, it hurts my eyes."

Destiny looked out the window, agreeing, "Yes, this time of day is the worst."

With a seasoned mariner's eye, she calculated the position of the sun. If they'd left before dawn and now it was late afternoon, they should have returned by now. Unless something had gone very wrong.

Panic rose in her. Like a live thing, it twisted and flailed, tearing at her with razor-sharp talons, closing up her throat and urging her heart to a gallop. Without Nathan, her life was over before it had started. She finally understood how her mother must have felt, loving her father so much that it hurt. Waiting for him when he never came.

With understanding came her final forgiveness . . . both for her mother and for herself. She was free finally, free to take up her life and go forward, without looking back. Free to love and accept love, unconditionally.

But what if it was too late?

Feeling at one with her mother and all women who waited for their men to return from the sea, she wondered how Angelina was feeling. Was she tormenting herself with the same regrets? Glancing at Angelina, she tried to gauge her feelings. At first glance, her friend appeared outwardly calm, but Destiny understood the agitated dance of her fingers.

Angelina plucked at her skirts, knotting and twisting them. Seconds later, she released the crumpled folds and smoothed them before starting again. Watching her friend's unconscious turmoil, Destiny bit the inside of her mouth, forcing back the scream threatening to erupt. Feeling desperate and helpless, she wanted to scream and slap at her friend's hands.

Covering her face, she wondered what was happening to her. She'd never felt like this before in her life. As if she were spinning out of control, coming apart at the joints, like some demented Humpty-Dumpty, never to be put back together again. Gulping air, she prayed for strength, realizing she was going slowly mad.

She felt a tugging at her elbow again, bringing her back from the abyss, compelling her to return from some dark and terrible place. As if from down a long tunnel, she heard Angelina's voice, "¡*Mira!* Look! You've the spyglass. I think I see sails. Could it be . . ?"

With trembling hands, Destiny forced her arm up, bringing the glass to her eye. The telescope felt as if it weighed a thousand pounds, and she could almost trace the arc of its movement through the still air. Her senses felt dead, numbed, unable to bear hope.

Far out on the horizon, she found the sails. Adjusting the glass, she brought the pinpoints of white into stark relief. There was a one-masted cutter, followed by the distinctive rigging of her grandfather's schooner.

Her heart leapt in her throat. Feelings, blessed sensations, flowed back into her body, bringing hope, bringing life.

Dropping the glass, she grabbed Angelina and whooped,

"It's them! It's their ships, Nathan's cutter and Gramps's schooner."

James Whitman, restrained in chains about his ankles and wrists, was the first person to descend from the cutter. Destiny gasped, unable to believe her eyes, wondering what part he had in this. A Navy seaman walked behind James, pushing him forward.

But the questions flew from her mind when she saw Nathan. He followed close upon James's heels, striding down the gang-plank, his left arm in a sling. Rushing forward, she brushed past James without a second glance and flung herself onto Nathan's broad chest.

Relief and joy bubbled in her veins. Rejoicing that he was alive, she clung to his neck while avoiding bumping his injured arm. She opened her mouth to speak but no sound came forth, only sobs, great gulping sobs.

Nathan pulled away, holding her at arm's length while patting her back awkwardly with one hand, demanding, "What's this, Destiny?" Inclining his head toward Whitman, he asked, "Your tears are for him?" Dropping his hand, he expelled a breath. "I think I understand." Removing her arm from around his neck, he grasped her elbow, directing, "Here, let's move aside and let the others pass."

Following Nathan down the gangplank, she managed, "It's not that . . . It's not about James."

"He was caught red-handed," Nathan remarked. "You have a right to know."

"Nathan, please, don't," she breathed. "That's over. I don't care about James Whitman. Please, believe me." Clutching the lapels of his uniform, she pled, "That's why I refused you before. Don't you see? I didn't want you to think that—"

"That I was your second choice," he finished for her. "I guessed as much."

"Then you understand?"

"Yes, I understand." He expelled a long breath. "Does it change anything between us?"

"Oh, Nathan, yes, I've changed my mind. But it doesn't have to do with James. You must believe me."

"Tell me."

"I was so worried. So afraid you wouldn't come back . . ." She wanted to blurt out her love for him but felt awkward, knowing he would doubt her motives.

He took up the thread. "Your grandfather told us that you and Angelina guessed where Estava and I had gone, to trap Cortez. You're to be commended for your insight. No one else guessed." He paused. "We expected to catch Cortez, but Estava suspected Cortez had a silent partner. He believed Cortez's knowledge of the shipping schedules and cargoes was too accurate for an outsider. He thought someone highly placed in Key West shipping was supplying Cortez crucial information. And he was right. It was Whitman."

Destiny stared up at him, surprised and incredulous. "But why? He has everything. His family has everything. What could he have possibly gained?"

Nathan shrugged. "Adventure and risk, a chance to thumb his nose at his powerful family. Wealth that he didn't inherit but made on his own." His gaze snagged hers. "I'm just guessing, but I've known men like him before. They want to make their own mark on the world, however misguided their actions."

She considered the startling information about James. What would Key West think about one of their precious own, being a part of such a hideous plot? The island would be abuzz for weeks with gossip, she knew. But it no longer touched her. She didn't care. All she cared about was Nathan and their future together. Thinking about what Nathan had said, though, she had to admit his supposition fit with James's personality.

James had always chafed at his family's overweening power and control. He'd always been eager to prove himself. She just hadn't realized the depths to which he would lower himself to realize his ambitions. But remembering that awful day on his sailboat, she wasn't surprised by his complete lack of morals and regard for other people.

She was over James. She'd been over him for weeks. She'd always loved Nathan. But how to convince him of that?

Standing beside him, she watched as the other men, chained like James, were led from the cutter. At the last, two seamen brought down a stretcher. Rafael lay on it, one pant leg stained with blood.

Gasping, she looked for Angelina on the crowded wharf. But her friend was already running to Rafael's side. Tugging on Nathan's good arm, she asked, "Rafael? Is he badly hurt?"

"No, he'll be fine. He's a tough one, Estava is. Got a bullet through the fleshy part of his thigh so he can't put any weight on the leg." Nathan cocked his head, murmuring, "Come to think of it, I'm jealous." He plucked at the sling on his arm. "My wound isn't half as dramatic. But the stretcher is a nice touch, very moving." Inclining his head, he said, "Just look at your friend's reaction."

Destiny followed the direction of his gaze. The two seamen had set down the stretcher on the wharf. Angelina sank to her knees beside it, half covering Rafael with her body and kissing him thoroughly.

"What about Cortez?" she asked.

"He was killed in the fighting. And good riddance. We didn't lose any men, only a few wounded. Cortez's ship was sunk, some of his men killed, and the others we brought back to justice. They'll probably hang."

Hearing his bald statement, she searched her heart for any sign of pity for James's fate. But she felt only a disembodied sense of emptiness, of regret for a life wasted and pity for his family's grief.

"It's too bad," she said quietly. "Such an awful thing. Wrecking ships purposely for profit. Gramps has always said it was the dark side of Key West's prosperity."

"Your grandfather is right about that." His voice was

thoughtful when he added, "Where there is easy money, men will be tempted to step over the line."

How she loved him, she thought, a shiver running up her back. He was so good and perfect and true. So brave and self-sacrificing. She'd never known anyone so perfect as her Nathan.

"I love you, Nathan Rodgers, with all my heart and soul," she announced.

"What do you mean, Destiny?" he asked. "Do you know what you're saying?"

Flushing at his pointed question but filled with rejoicing, she responded with all her heart. "That I love you, Nathan. That I've always loved you but was too blind and caught up in the past to see it. That the past is dead and only the future matters. Our future together."

He sighed, a deep rumbling from his chest. "Does this mean you'll marry me?"

Snuggling into his arms, she replied, "Tomorrow, if you like."

Grabbing her with one arm, he spun her around, whooping at the top of his lungs. Returning her feet to the ground, his hazel eyes glittered with unshed tears. "Tomorrow isn't soon enough."

"I know." She buried her head against his good shoulder, feeling uncommonly shy.

"Aren't you going to ask?"

"About what?" She lifted her head and gazed at him. "About your arm? I don't care as long as you're alive and we're together. I'll take care of you, Nathan. Today, tomorrow, and forever."

His good arm encircled her tighter, and his voice was gruff. "You don't know what that means to me, Destiny, hearing you say you love me. I've waited a lifetime to hear those words."

"I know, forgive me for my—"

"Don't apologize for the past," he interrupted. "All I care is how you feel *now.*"

Pulling back, she repeated, "I love you, Captain Nathan Rodgers, with all my heart."

Then she ducked her head, realizing she didn't even know how bad his wound was. But she didn't care. If he lost the arm, she couldn't love him less.

"And your arm?" She inquired, wanting to please him. "Is the wound bad? I don't care, Nathan, if it is," she rushed on, wanting him to understand the depth of her love.

"It's nothing but a bullet graze." He shrugged. "Should be fine in a few days."

"Oh, Nathan, I'm so glad."

"But you've promised to take care of me today and forever." He grinned.

"And I shall." She tossed her head, grinning, too. "The very best of care, whether you're wounded or not."

He kissed her then, long and hard, hinting at just the kind of care he might favor. Lifting his head, he said, "You can be a schoolteacher if you want. I won't stop you. So long as you're my wife and you love me."

Unable to answer, she stood there quivering in his arms, her head lowered, searching for the right words to say. Wanting him to know that the most important thing, the only thing, was that they would spend their lives together.

He cupped her chin in his hand and raised her head. Their gazes met, slow and tender, filled with understanding and longing. His voice was soft and filled with wonder. "You do love me. Whitman is the past."

"Yes." She put all her heart and soul in that one simple word.

Nodding, he accepted her reassurance. She could feel his body relax against hers, as if the tension had miraculously drained away. Then he lifted his head and smiled. "What's this?"

Destiny glanced up to see Rafael's stretcher moved closer to them, two seamen bearing it aloft. Angelina stood beside Rafael, holding his hand.

"Well, Rodgers, have you finally convinced her to marry you?" Rafael asked without preamble.

Angelina glanced at Destiny, snagging her gaze and giving her a secret smile.

"What about you, Estava?" Nathan countered. "Is your wife going to let you back into the house?"

Rafael laughed, a short bark. And then he looked at Angelina, his gaze brimming with love. He squeezed her hand. "Better than that. We're going to have a proper wedding. This time with a priest."

"Oh, Angelina," Destiny cried, going to her friend and kissing her cheek. "I'm so happy for you. And Nathan and I are to be married as soon as possible, too." She glanced back at Nathan. "Isn't it wonderful?"

"And high time, lass," her grandfather's Scottish burr interjected.

Destiny hadn't seen him approaching. Whirling around, she threw her arms around his neck, realizing belatedly that she'd been so worried about Nathan, she'd forgotten about Gramps. She'd assumed he'd kept his promise and returned home unharmed.

Returning the hug, he patted her back. "I thought ye'd never come to yer senses and marry this fine captain."

"Oh, Gramps."

"I'll be happy to give away the blushing bride," her grandfather declared.

Thinking about the wedding, a thought formed in her mind, a happy wish. She turned to Angelina and opened her mouth. Then another thought occurred, and she felt strangely deflated, closing her mouth.

Angelina, attuned to her shifting moods, asked, "Destiny, what is it?"

"I wanted us to have a double wedding," she admitted. "But I realize that isn't possible. You'll be married in the Catholic Church by a priest, and we'll be married by a Protestant minister."

"But that won't keep me from fixing up the house, opening the ballroom, and giving ye lasses a proper wedding party," her grandfather surprised her by offering.

"Gramps!" Destiny squealed, hugging him again. "Will you?"

"It'll be my pleasure, granddaughter. It'll be my pleasure."

Epilogue

Angelina leaned over Rafael, plumping up the pillows on the settee. With a satisfied grin, he settled back. He really didn't need so much tending anymore; his wound was almost healed. She suspected he liked being pampered, even though he could walk on the leg with the help of a cane. Since it was only a few days to the wedding, it was a good thing his leg was better.

Catching her wrist, he pulled her down beside him. His mouth slanted across hers, tasting and teasing, sampling and savoring. Her body responded to his kisses. The blood thrummed through her veins, heating her body and making her heart race. Her nipples peaked, begging to be touched and suckled. And lower, she felt the now-familiar tightening, the craving pressure beginning to build between her thighs.

His leg wound hadn't hampered their lovemaking. In fact, with Rafael confined to the bed and settee, his convalescence had afforded them the time to honeymoon in their rented cottage. Wanting to take care of her husband, she'd turned over the day-to-day running of the factory to Juan Ramírez.

Rafael's hands were busy now, parting the buttons of her

shirtwaist, skimming the tops of her breasts. Arching into his touch, she gave herself over to the sensation. He was insatiable, making love to her several times a day. And, to her surprise, she couldn't get enough of him, either.

A pounding on the door brought them up short. Startled, she raised her head and Rafael stopped his titillating exploration, cursing under his breath and urging her to ignore the summons.

Flushed and fumbling with her buttons, she explained she couldn't ignore the knock. She was expecting a delivery for the wedding. Exasperated, he yielded, helping her with the buttons he'd so eagerly parted a moment before.

Patting her hair into place, she went to the door and opened it.

But it wasn't a delivery boy standing on the porch. To her astonishment, it was her mother and father!

They looked the same, although time had altered her perception of them. She hadn't remembered that her mother was so short, or that the hair at her father's temples had turned completely white. But finding them standing on her doorstep was like a gift, the best wedding present of all. Forgetting all the old acrimony, she flung her arms around her mother's neck.

"Mami y Papi, I'm so glad you're here! You came to see me! I can't believe it. It's too wonderful to be true."

Her mother returned her embrace, and then she went to her father. His arms went around her, but she sensed the stiffness of his gesture. He patted her back awkwardly and kissed her cheek, saying, "It's a pleasure to see you again, *mi hija.* You're looking well."

His stiff welcome gave her pause. She sighed to herself, wondering if her father would ever completely unbend. But right now she didn't care. What was important was that they'd come.

Her mother took her hands. "We came because of that terrible hurricane. When we heard about it, I was distraught for days." She glanced at her husband. "It took me some time to convince him to come and see how you were."

"You could have sent a cable. I would have answered," Angelina offered.

"We wanted to come and see you, Angelita. See you for ourselves so we would know you were happy and cared for."

So her mother did love her after all, she realized, feeling warm inside. And her mother had finally stood up to her father for her sake, too, forcing him to come to Key West.

"Where's this husband of yours? I want to meet him," her father declared.

"You've already met him," Angelina confessed, wanting to get the difficult part over with. *"Mi esposo es Rafael Rivera.* After his wife and child were killed in the revolution, he came to Key West and changed his name."

"Why the need for subterfuge?" her father asked sharply.

Taking a deep breath, she admitted, "It's a long story. But if you'll stay a few days, we can explain." Glancing at her mother, she smiled. "And I have another surprise. We're to be married again. By the priest this time. Before, it was a civil ceremony. I want you both to stay for the wedding."

Her gaze went to her father. *"Por favor,* stay for my wedding."

"Claro que sí, we'll stay," her mother agreed.

But her father harrumphed, saying, "A civil ceremony and a false name. Seems you're not really married. Seems you're—"

"Now, *Papi,"* her mother interjected, patting his arm. "I'm certain there's a good explanation if we're willing to listen."

"Vénganse," Angelina urged. "Rafael is just inside on the settee. He's been wounded in the thigh, capturing shipwreckers." She glanced at her father again, admitting with a wry smile. "It's also a long story."

Rafael had, of course, heard everything. And he'd managed to lever himself into a sitting position, in order to properly receive her parents. Greetings and handshakes were exchanged. Angelina settled her parents in chairs across from him. Then she winked at Rafael and offered to fetch refreshments from the kitchen. But when she turned to go, another knock sounded on the front door.

Wondering if this could be the long-awaited delivery, she opened the door. But she was surprised again, finding Destiny and Nathan on her doorstep. Embracing her friend, she welcomed them in, explaining that her parents had just arrived from Cuba and wanting Destiny and Nathan to meet them.

They agreed willingly, but Destiny laid a hand on her arm, saying, "Wait, Angelina. First, I have something for you." She offered a brown-wrapped package.

Angelina took the package, guessing what was inside. *Where was that delivery boy?* she wondered again.

As if in answer to her thoughts, a third knock thudded on the door. Throwing it open, she finally found the long-awaited delivery boy standing there, holding a brown-paper package. Thanking him, she accepted it and turned to Destiny with, "And this is for you."

Her friend's eyes lit up, and they giggled. "You go first, Angelina."

"No, you."

"We'll do this together then," Angelina compromised, ripping into her package. Destiny followed suit. Inside both packages lay delicate lengths of the finest Brussels lace, perfect for wedding veils. Their wedding wager had been satisfied. They had both won.

Hugging Destiny, Angelina's eyes filled with tears. Murmuring their thanks to each other, Angelina felt as if she had finally come home at last. Such a long and arduous journey to arrive at this happiness. But it had been worth every sacrifice.

Escorting her friends into the sitting room and introducing them to her parents, her heart swelled with joy. All the people she loved most were in this room together. And her father had accepted a cigar from Rafael, appearing to warm to him and his story of adventure about capturing the shipwreckers.

Her father would come around. She knew he would. After

all, he'd journeyed to Key West to make certain she was happy and well. He loved her, too, she realized, in his own way.

Moving to her husband's side, she took his hand and squeezed it.

She had won the wedding wager, truly won the most precious prize of all: the shining promise of a lifetime of love.